BROKEN
MACHINES

. . .

BROKEN MACHINES

. . .

Michael I. Leahey

THOMAS DUNNE BOOKS
ST. MARTIN'S MINOTAUR
NEW YORK

This novel is a work of fiction. The characters, names, incidents, dialogue, and plot are the products of the author's imagination or are used fictitiously. Any resemblance to actual persons or events is purely coincidental.

THOMAS DUNNE BOOKS.
An imprint of St. Martin's Press.

www.minotaurbooks.com

Library of Congress Cataloging-in-Publication Data
Leahey, Michael.
    Broken machines / Michael Leahey.—1st ed.
      p. cm.
    ISBN 0-312-26130-6
      1. Private investigators—New York (State)—New York—Fiction. 2. Corporations—Corrupt practices—Fiction. 3. Brooklyn (New York, N.Y.)—Fiction. 4. Serial murders—Fiction. I. Title.

PS3562.E215 B76 2000
813'.6—dc21   00-031742

First Edition: October 2000

10 9 8 7 6 5 4 3 2 1

FOR LYNN

Man seems to be a rickety poor sort of thing, any way you take him; a kind of British Museum of infirmities and inferiorities. He is always undergoing repairs. A machine that is as unreliable as he is would have no market.

—*Mark Twain*

Justice is a machine that, when someone has once given it the starting push, rolls on of itself.

—*John Galsworthy*

PROLOGUE

■ ■ ■

Clifford Brice lay against the slope of the roof, his hands folded behind his head. He was very small for a ten-year-old and looked even smaller wrapped in the big green blanket he'd gotten from Ms. Fein, the social worker. It was a cold, clear night, with a sky full of stars that sparkled in the reflection of his thick wire-rimmed glasses.

"Cliff, what you doing, baby? You gonna catch your death."

He didn't answer and his mother, Ruby, went back into the bathroom. She was getting ready for a night on the street and Clifford didn't want to watch. Besides, he knew the routine. Right now she was sticking a needle into her thigh, or maybe an ankle. Before long she'd be numb and then it was like talking to a zombie. Instead, he tried to focus on the stars overhead.

There was something magical about the night sky. He'd read about the stars in books and studied the constellations till he could name them all. But nothing he'd ever read compared to the real thing. He let out a long sigh.

"Clifford, I gotta go now, honey," Ruby said softly, her words beginning to slur.

The child looked over at his mother. She was leaning against the window sash, looking sad and tired. When he didn't speak, Ruby smiled nervously, showing all her teeth.

"I love you, Momma," he said without blinking.

Ruby could feel the tears coming. She leaned way out, picked up her precious bundle, and held him close.

"Don't you stay out here all night, little man," she said seriously. "I don't want nothing happening to you. I got a big score coming down and then we be outta here."

He just nodded his head.

"No, baby, don't be shaking your head. This time is for real."

They stared at each other a moment longer, and then Ruby Brice turned and headed for the door.

"Good-bye, Momma," he whispered.

From his perch on the little roof over the front stoop, Clifford could watch his mother as she walked down the block, stopping under the lone streetlight before crossing the avenue and disappearing into the shadows on the other side. His gaze lingered for a moment and then he retraced her steps, studying the abandoned houses, crippled cars, and week-old piles of garbage that lined the path. Somewhere nearby a dog started barking, and then another. Pretty soon the whole street was awake as garbage cans tipped over. Cats screamed and people started yelling for quiet. When the clouds moved in and rain began to fall, Clifford gave up and crawled back into the bedroom.

Ruby made her way to Berriman Street, where the factories had men working nights. She was just trying to make a few bucks and then get home to her baby. She had fixed herself up and painted a big smile on her face, but it hadn't done much good— the night was too quiet. Before long it started to rain. She didn't worry about Clifford catching cold up on the roof; the child had more sense than any grown-up she'd ever met. But thinking about him made her sad.

She'd been walking the block for about an hour when she noticed the headlights. A real cool ride, like a new Chevy or maybe a Lincoln, jet-black with a touch of chrome. It slid up to the curb; a big cat on the prowl. The windows were tinted charcoal and she could see her reflection in the glass.

The interior of the car came to life as the driver lit a thin cigar and motioned her to the door. Ruby could just make out the figure of a bearded man in a flashy suit, diamond ring on his pinky as he held the lighter. Then the flame went out. There was a low hissing sound as the passenger door shut behind her, like the seal on a vault. Then the car edged slowly down the street, heading for Flatlands Avenue.

A burst of thunder startled Clifford, spilling his book onto the floor. The room was cold and dark except for his reading light. He pushed his glasses back up on the bridge of his nose and crawled down to the end of the bed to look out the window. It was raining harder and the wind was howling. He thought about his mother, standing in some doorway trying to keep warm, and his lips began to tremble. He opened the window and stuck his head outside, but the stars were all gone and there was nothing to be found in their place.

ONE

...

It was Tuesday, September 17. My birthday. I don't usually like birthdays, but I was trying. My nose was pressed up against the big window in the kitchen and I was hoping to spot something out there to cheer me up. When the rain started coming down in sheets, I gave up and switched on the lights.

My name is James Joseph Donovan, but most people just call me Donovan. I'm six feet, two inches tall, weigh about 195 pounds—some of which is still cut into muscles—and have light brown hair and green eyes. Women have told me I'm not bad to look at, which is a polite way of describing the wear and tear on my weathered profile. My home and office are near the top of an old high-rise building between 101st and 102nd Streets on Amsterdam Avenue in New York City. I have a plain white business card that reads J. J. DONOVAN—CONSULTANT. I don't have a cute logo.

I do have a partner, however. His name is Boris Mikail Koulomzin, and he lives in the apartment next door. This is a necessary convenience, since Boris rarely leaves the building during daylight hours. Because of the way our building tapers as it rises, there are only two apartments on the seventeenth floor, and we own them both. They were gifts to us from Harry Noble, the landlord. He was once a client, and the apartments were Harry's way of showing his gratitude for our help.

Our consulting business offers services to people who think

they've run out of options. In most cases, they have problems that the legal system has either created, made worse, or is incapable of addressing. We're not licensed detectives, lawyers, paralegals, or anything like that. We're just two private citizens attempting to help people who've been screwed by the system.

Lest you think that a modern-day Robin Hood and his faithful Slavic Little John have taken up residence in the Big Apple, I should point out that we generally expect and receive payment for our services. The amount and form of the payment depends on the circumstances, but I think it's fair to say that we do pretty well for ourselves. I like to think we also do some good.

I was in the kitchen fixing lunch. A man needs fuel to sulk. The menu included a cold vinaigrette salad of artichoke hearts, feta cheese, and whole black olives; grilled chicken cutlets on a bed of Spanish rice; fresh bread from the local bakery; and several well-chilled bottles of Peter Michael Chardonnay. A pleasant little distraction to temper the aches and pains one begins to notice at the age of thirty-nine.

The telephone rang.

"Hey, Donovan," a voice bellowed, "happy birthday! How's my baby feeling today?"

It was my friend Janet Fein.

"Good, Janet. Good, but older," I said with the resignation of an Irish martyr climbing the steps to the gallows.

"Cut the shit, Donovan!" she roared. "You're nearly ten years younger than me and I'm fresh out of pity today. Besides, life doesn't even start till you hit forty."

My friends are all very understanding. I continued my work at the stove.

"What's all that racket? I hear pots and pans banging."

"Oh, nothing," I said innocently.

"Wait a minute, you're cooking, aren't you?" She didn't wait for an answer. "Set another place at the table, I'm on my way over."

"You know, Janet, it's customary to wait for an invitation," I deadpanned.

I was speaking to a dial tone.

Janet Fein is a case worker for one of New York City's Child Welfare Services. She's forty-eight years old and lives alone; no husband, no children. The families she meets at the office keep her too busy. Day or night, she's available to settle arguments, post bail, locate doctors, or just provide words of comfort. It's a hard job, but she keeps at it because she cares.

I don't mean to create the impression that Janet is the saintly all-suffering type. Mother Teresa she is not. Ms. Fein stands five foot, eleven inches in flat shoes and is a solid 175 pounds of kinetic energy, heralded by a booming, gravelly voice nurtured on Brooklyn's Flatbush Avenue. She's a walking encyclopedia where the rights of the family are concerned, and with twenty-three years of the system filed away, she can move mountains when the need arises. When the mountains refuse to budge, she sometimes calls on me. I have never refused her.

So I threw another cutlet into the pan and took out a second plate. I also wondered why Janet was free for lunch on a Tuesday afternoon. It was hard enough to drag her out on a Saturday night, and even then she brought a beeper. About ten minutes later the house phone rang.

"Yo, Donovan, happy bertday, gringo!"

This time it was Manny Santos, the building's superintendent and my personal screening service.

"Listen up, bro, Ms. Janet, she's on huh way up and she bringin' you a nice leetle cake."

Manny chuckled. He thinks he's a comedian.

It takes a while for the elevator to groan its way up to my floor, and the grating sigh of relief when it finally stops is louder than any doorbell. I opened the front door and a soggy Janet Fein swept in, leaving little puddles in her wake. She was cradling a small package and dragging the suitcase she uses as a pocketbook.

"Nice weather—for a freakin' duck!" she said, handing over a freshly baked cheesecake and planting a big red-lipstick kiss on my cheek. "Happy birthday and what's for lunch?"

6

I've known Janet a long time, long enough to know this was not a social call. I also knew she'd take her time before getting to the point. There was no rush. I opened a bottle of wine and served lunch. We talked about her job and laughed a lot as she jumped from one crazy story to the next. I was even required to blow out some candles stuck in a piece of cheesecake while she sang me a chorus of the birthday song. If you can imagine a serenade from Ethel Merman, you've got the picture.

Finally, when the birthday party and small talk were out of the way, Janet was ready to get serious. I cleared the table and poured mugs of fresh-brewed coffee.

"J. J., I'm here because I need your help," she began, her voice softer now. "I tried to handle this myself, but no one would listen to me. So now I'm knocking at your door."

"Hey, you name it, kid," I said, putting one of my big feet into my even bigger mouth.

"This isn't a simple problem, dear. In fact, by the time I'm through you'll probably think I've gone soft. Everybody else does." She shook her head slowly. "The mother of one of my kids was killed last week. We don't know who his father is, or was, and there's no other family. That leaves me and the state. It's not a good situation."

She didn't have to explain. New York City isn't Never-Never Land. Orphans don't rate a very high priority.

"The mother's name was Ruby Brice," Janet continued. "She was a twenty-five-year-old prostitute with a heroin addiction. Not exactly a debutante, right? Well, I won't bore you with the details of Ruby's short time on this earth. You can take it from me, she never had a chance. From birth to death, her life was a long series of crushing disappointments."

She stopped for a moment to collect herself.

"Look, I'm not trying to drum up sympathy for Ruby Brice. God knows she doesn't need it now. But it's important that you understand where this is coming from."

"You don't have to justify yourself to me," I said.

"I can't help it, J. J., it's becoming second nature. I spend too much time dealing with hard-nosed assholes who don't understand and bureaucrats who just don't care. Do you realize that there are fifty thousand people living on the streets of this city? Fifty thousand. And the average person looks at a homeless man like he's a bag of garbage the sanitation truck forgot to pick up. That way of thinking trickles down to me and it's a big problem. I'm trying to help the children. You'd think children would catch a break, right? I mean, after all, these kids aren't responsible for the lives they're leading, and they don't have any control over their circumstances. Doesn't seem to matter. They keep right on paying for the sins of their parents. Why do you think I had to come to you? No one else considers people like Ruby Brice and her son worth the trouble."

There was another pause.

"I better just get this over with," she said after a few moments. "When Ruby Brice was fifteen years old, she had a baby boy. His name is Clifford. Don't ask me to explain it, because it's something that comes from God or nature, but that boy changed her. He didn't stop the abuse she put herself through, but he gave her a reason to care about the future. If she could have given him a chance for a decent life, it would have made up for a lot.

"J. J., this woman was different. She came to me for help. It usually doesn't work that way. In most cases it takes me months to win the smallest confidences. Not with Ruby. She wanted to help Clifford and was willing to do whatever it took. That made her special to me."

I could see now why this conversation was so difficult. Janet had believed they were going to make it. She'd allowed herself to look forward to their success.

"We began about two years ago. I got Ruby into an out-patient drug program and even managed to get her a small increase in child-support money. It may not sound like much, but it was a start. We met once or twice a month, and we made a lot of plans. I knew she was still working the street part-time, but I ignored it. What can I say? Miracles don't happen overnight, baby."

She set her jaw as if she expected me to judge or challenge

her methods. When I didn't say anything, she relaxed a little, lowering her guard.

"What I needed most was time," she said sadly, "but I guess it just ran out. About two weeks before the murder, Ruby ditched a meeting and I began to worry that she'd gone back on the needle. I called a few times, but she wasn't home. I even stopped by her apartment. We never did connect. By the time I tracked Ruby down she was just a piece of wax taking up space in the morgue."

Janet's eyes grew cold.

"Well, Ruby's gone now and I've got a ten-year-old boy to worry about. His mother was right—he deserves a chance. I plan to see that he gets it."

She paused again. I used the time to refill our mugs and to turn on some lights. The afternoon had come and gone and the room was full of shadows.

"Thanks, honey," Janet sighed as she tasted the coffee, though I think she was mostly grateful for the change in the atmosphere. The light seemed to slice through the gloom. She took another sip and continued.

"The thing is, J. J., Ruby's death was no accident. She didn't overdose or disappear. The woman was butchered!"

It finally clicked. The story had been page-three news in New York's picture papers. Janet dug into her bag and pulled out a thick manila folder. Inside, I found copies of the police report and the autopsy. There was also a stack of eight-by-ten color photos. As I leafed through them, my lunch began to turn in my stomach.

The body was found on Logan Street between Atlantic and Liberty Avenues in East New York, Brooklyn. The address belonged to a business that manufactures cardboard boxes. When the killer finished playing with her, he dropped Ruby Brice into a Dumpster in an empty lot behind the factory. I found a picture of the scene. It was taken from above, looking down into the Dumpster.

The dead woman was lying awkwardly on a twisted bed of

cold gray steel parts, her wrists and ankles bound with strapping or baling wire. At first glance, the metal parts around her seemed to glow as if they were white-hot. But it was just reflected light from the flash bulb on the evidence camera. It had been raining and the body glistened, which helped explain why there wasn't more blood. There should have been a lot of blood. Ruby's body looked as if it had been run through a shredder, with strips of her flesh hanging loosely like rags. I put the photos down and turned to the autopsy report.

The coroner noted a total of thirty-eight lacerations on the corpse. None of those wounds had been life-threatening, but they'd all been painful. The killer had toyed with Ruby, playing a sadistic cat-and-mouse game as his excitement grew. I pictured him cutting and slicing his way toward a climax. The report noted physical evidence of both anal and vaginal penetration, yet they didn't find any seminal fluid. The rain had probably washed that away too, or maybe the creep was firing blanks. In the end, he got off by placing a large butcher knife under Ruby's chin and thrusting it straight up into her brain.

A note had been attached to Ruby's left cheek with a large, stainless-steel safety pin. I found an enlarged photograph of the note. The neatly printed lettering read: YO SOY DE LA TIERRA DE LOS ALACRANES! I COME FROM THE LAND OF THE SCORPIONS!

I took a deep breath.

As I flipped through the papers, I came across a statement from a homeless man who called himself Doc. On the night of the murder, Doc was making the rounds with his shopping cart, looking for redeemable cans and bottles. He'd seen a shiny black car parked down the street on Flatlands Avenue, near the landfill site. The car had been rocking and bouncing on its springs like a cheap mattress, he said. There was a lot of noise too, which he figured was one of the girls putting on a show for her tip.

Unfortunately, Doc was a little too crazy to be much help in a courtroom. He'd gone on to describe himself as a wizard and proudly confided to the detective taking the report that he was four hundred and sixteen years old. The *New York Post* had used his picture, and there was a copy of it in the folder. I had to admit, if nothing else, the guy knew how to dress the part.

It didn't matter who Doc thought he was. No one would be calling on him to testify. The police already had a suspect in custody and he didn't own a car of any description. He was a twenty-two-year-old crack addict from the Dominican Republic who owned an extensive rap sheet and had a history of mental illness. His name was Oscar Mendosa.

On the morning of the murder, Mr. Mendosa was arrested by police officers on a routine patrol. They found him wandering naked in the chilling rain, not more than ten blocks from the site of the body. He had the victim's blood-soaked stockings tied around his neck and was ranting incoherently in Spanish. The man was so hyped up that a backup team had been needed to subdue him. Mendosa was currently under observation at Kings County Hospital, where he was keeping the shrinks busy.

"This is an incredible story," I said, looking up from the report.

"What it is is a load of bullshit!" Janet cried, startling me. "I knew this woman. Ruby was street-smart and tough. There's no way she would have let a nut job like Mendosa anywhere near her. Besides, this guy was so whacked he couldn't even sign his name at the arraignment. How did he manage to write a note and pin it to his victim if he couldn't hold a pen? Better still, where do you think he got a pen and dry paper in the middle of the night? It was raining, and the guy was stark naked!"

She started rooting around in her purse again. Finally, she pulled out a crumpled piece of sheet music. It was a song called "The Ballad of Durango." The words were in English and Spanish:

Yo soy de la tierra de los alacranes, yo soy de Durango, palabra de honor, en donde los hombres son hombres formales y son sus mujeres puro corazon . . . ;

11

I come from the land of the scorpions, I'm from Durango, I give you my word of honor, where men are
men and women have big hearts . . .

"Last I heard, Durango was in Mexico," she added sarcastically. "Mendosa's from the D.R.!"

I was going to mention that sometimes the facts don't connect
in ways that make sense, especially in crimes of madness or
passion. But the look I got made me think twice about arguing
with her.

"Where did you find this?" I asked, holding up the sheet music. "I mean, come on, *The Land of Scorpions* theme song isn't
exactly Top-Twenty material."

"I surfed the Net," she snapped. "Look, J. J., this isn't a joke.
Clifford Brice told me that Ruby saw something down at one of
the factories, something she could cash in on. She was gonna
get them some money. I don't know what Ruby was up to, but
she told him it would be enough so that they could move away."

Janet paused one last time as the thought of a future for Ruby
and her boy came and went. She finally sighed, clearing the slate.

"A couple of days before the murder, Ruby gave the kid a
little plastic key ring with the astrological sign Scorpio stamped
on it. She told him it would bring them luck."

She dropped the evidence on the table in front of me, as if it
resolved all doubt. I picked up the small glow-in-the-dark key
ring and examined the crude picture of a scorpion stamped on
its face. I had to admit there was something eerie about the
recurring scorpion image. And she did have a good point about
the Mendosa note. The copy I saw was carefully printed. It
wasn't written in the rain and I doubted it was written by someone agitated or excited. But that didn't mean very much—he
could have written it earlier, in a less manic state of mind. Besides, the cops are right more than they're wrong. Mendosa
sounded like a pretty good suspect to me.

"Okay, Donovan, so this is wild and far-fetched," Janet said, reading my face. "But Clifford is convinced that Ruby stumbled into the middle of something big. I need to know the truth. Either way, it'll give me a place to start rebuilding. Besides, I'm not asking you to turn into Sam Spade. What I want is enough evidence to convince the police to reopen the investigation. That's not such a big deal."

"Has Clifford spoken to the police?" I asked, trying to dodge the inevitable. "Has he told them his suspicions? I mean, this sort of thing is way outside our normal line of work."

"You know as well as I do that the police want only one thing in a case like this, and that's to close it," she said emphatically. "Besides, kids from Clifford's neighborhood don't talk to cops, there's no percentage in it. Hey, they dismissed my opinions out of hand. What chance would the kid have had?"

She was pretty worked up.

"Let me ask you this, Donovan, and this is the bottom line: If Ruby Brice was killed by somebody else, not Oscar Mendosa, should her killer get away with it because a nigger whore with a habit isn't worth the time it takes to answer a few simple questions?"

She was aiming for my sense of fair play and had just scored a direct hit. I tried to avoid the question by pretending to study the wood grain in the dining table.

"Janet, what makes this particular child so special?" I asked finally. "God knows he's not the only one of your kids getting a raw deal. Why the extra effort for him?"

"You're gonna have to take my word on that, J. J.," she said. "When you meet him, I think you'll understand."

We sat in silence for a while, listening to the wall clock ticking. The quiet was eventually broken by the sound of Janet's beeper calling her to some new human tragedy. She went into my study to use the phone.

A few moments later she rushed back into the room. "Gotta go, hon."

I didn't bother asking about the latest emergency—she'd already given me enough to worry about. I walked her to the elevator and she gave me another big hug.

"Happy birthday, J. J., and thanks for lunch."

Janet was smiling and looking up at me with those big, tired eyes, the edge long gone from her voice.

"About this other thing." She paused. "Well, you'll let me know, okay?"

The elevator doors hesitated, then groaned shut, and she was gone.

I went back into the kitchen and reached for the Chardonnay, feeling like all the energy had been drained out of me. The rain had stopped and I could see the night lights of the city, but the view didn't bring me any inspiration. Raising my glass, I saluted my reflection in the window, then started cleaning up the dishes. But my thoughts kept drifting back to Ruby Brice and the boy she'd left behind. I had just decided to be mad at Janet Fein when the telephone started ringing.

"Hello, honey. Happy birthday!"

It was my mother.

Thirty-nine years old and the sound of her voice still brightened my day. I managed to say "hello" and "how are you" before she took over, bringing me up to date on the local news. From baptisms to funeral masses, she covered it all, moving seamlessly from grandchildren to car alarms without pausing for breath. Eventually, my father grew impatient and grabbed the phone, bringing me back to earth. I took a big gulp of wine.

"By the way, what's the news from Kate?" he asked, forgetting to wish me a happy birthday.

There was a telegram open on the counter. I picked it up and read it again. It was from Tokyo.

HAPPY BIRTHDAY. DO NOT SULK. THIRTY-NINE IS NICE.
WILL SEE YOU IN TWO WEEKS. HAVE SPECIAL PRES-
ENT. MUCH LOVE. YOUR EX-WIFE. KATE.

14

"She's just fine, Dad," I said patiently, flicking the telegram across the counter with my index finger. "I saw her last week and she asked me to send you her love."

"Did she?" He sounded pleased. "Well, you tell that girl your mother and I both love her and pray every day that you'll come to your senses."

"Look, Dad, let's not get into that right now. I'll tell her that you were asking for her, okay?"

"Fine, you do that," he said, as if he'd just solved a major problem. "What's that? Oh. Your mother wants to say something else."

I took a deep breath and refilled my glass.

"J. J.," she began, speaking softly, "I just wanted to tell you that I remember the day you were born as if it was yesterday. All these years later and it's still one of the happiest days of my life."

The warm feeling came back.

"Thanks, Mom," I stammered.

My father volunteered an uncomfortable cough from the extension.

"Anna, our program is coming on the television, say good night to your son."

Dad likes to take charge, especially if he thinks things might be heading for dangerous emotional territory. We all said good night.

After the phone call, I gave up on the dishes, poured myself a large brandy, and sauntered into the living room. With the patio doors open and a cool, damp September breeze refreshing my senses, I lit a pudgy robusto cigar and pulled my grandfather's old leather club chair up to the window. I let the brandy melt me a little, then settled back to think about mothers and their sons.

TWO

∎ ∎ ∎

"Amazing," he muttered. "Simply amazing!"

My body was too stiff to risk movement, but I opened an eyelid. Staring back at me happily through bloodshot eyes was Angus, the mixed-breed Irish wolfhound who looks after my partner. I took my feet off the coffee table and forced myself to sit up.

Dr. Boris Mikail Koulomzin was sitting across the room on my sofa, all two hundred and eighty pounds of him, comfortably wrapped in a maroon quilt. His thinning blond hair was combed straight back, exposing a round, pale face with a high forehead and large blue eyes. The eyes were magnified by thick wire-framed glasses. Underneath the quilt, the good doctor wore over-sized brightly striped pajamas. He's been known to stay in these pajamas for days at a time, so I barely took notice. A gold-tipped Balkan Sobranie cigarette dangled from the first two fingers of his right hand, while its predecessor burned away in the ashtray. In his left hand, Boris held my brandy snifter critically. It contained several fingers of cognac and the remains of my cigar.

"Whoa, I guess I dozed off," I said sleepily, scratching Angus behind the ears.

"As I was saying," Boris snorted, "*this* is remarkable."

He held out the offending crystal and raised an eyebrow.

"This is the cognac I gave you, is it not?" he asked.

16

I nodded my head.

"Darroz La Brisse armagnac, vintage 1929. A magical potion. And you have used it to extinguish a cigar?"

"Look, Boris, I was really tired."

"Ah, that explains it. And because you were in such an extravagant mood, did you also light this"—he peered at the label and winced—"this *cigar* with a one-hundred-dollar bill?"

Once he got started, there was no predicting where the diatribe would lead. I glanced at my watch. It was two o'clock in the morning. My back was stiff and my neck had one of those kinks that really hurt. With difficulty, I managed to stand up and close the patio doors. By morning, I was going to feel a lot older than thirty-nine.

"Yesterday was my birthday," I began, hoping for a little slack.

"I am well aware of the anniversary," he shot back. "It is hardly an excuse for this kind of savage abuse."

Savage abuse? I raised my hand, palm out.

"Drop it, Boris. You're right. I admit that I am a savage and a wastrel, which leaves no room for discussion. Besides, I'm tired, I've got a stiff neck and probably a hangover. So, let's just have some of my birthday cake and let it go."

Boris grunted but held his peace. I took the brandy snifter from his outstretched hand and hobbled into the kitchen. While the coffee brewed, I put big slices of cheesecake on plates and carried them into the living room. Boris hadn't moved.

"Janet Fein came by for lunch today," I said, handing him a napkin.

"I heard the singing," he admitted, shaking his head.

"Yeah. Well, her visit wasn't entirely social."

Boris patted the Ruby Brice folder next to him on the couch. "Is this what she came to discuss?"

I nodded and waited, but Boris was more interested in the cake.

"So?"

17

"So, what?" he asked, maneuvering his plate.

"So, did you read through the file or were you just sitting over there making a study of my sleeping habits?"

Boris paused, an enormous piece of cheesecake balanced on his fork.

"As a matter of fact," he said carefully, focusing on the cake, "I did."

Using the thumb and index finger of his right hand, he managed to squeeze the entire piece into his mouth, making further conversation difficult. I gave up and headed for the bathroom. After washing my face and neck with cold water and brushing my teeth, the fog began to lift. There's even a chance I was smiling as my nose led me back toward the kitchen and the promise of fresh coffee. I put milk, sugar, coffee mugs, and a full pot of the dark brew onto a tray, balanced it on my left hand, and then scooped up the rest of the cheesecake and tiptoed carefully back to the living room.

Boris made absolutely no effort to help me, though he did rouse himself enough to eat three more pieces of my cake and drink most of the coffee. He likes his coffee light and very sweet. The sight of him dumping teaspoon after teaspoon of sugar into his mug made my teeth ache so badly I had to drink my coffee black. Apparently not satisfied by four pieces of cheesecake, Boris's eyes kept drifting back to the piece I'd set aside for myself.

"So, you read through the file," I said, picking up my plate and eating the distraction. "What do you think of the case?"

"I guess that depends on what I'm being asked to think about it." He snorted unhappily.

"Okay, that part's simple." I put my empty plate back on the tray. "Janet Fein wants us to get a murder investigation reopened. The victim, Ruby Brice, had a little boy. The boy is now in foster care and Janet is trying to help him. According to Janet, the kid believes his mother was killed because she knew something, or stumbled into something, valuable enough to have gotten them out of the ghetto. The poor kid's clinging to the notion that his mother was trying to do something good for him. I don't know

18

if this is right or not, but Janet says getting closure on the murder is a good place to start rebuilding the kid's life."

Boris dropped his cigarette butt into the ashtray and immediately lit another. He took a deep drag, leaned way back, and blew the smoke toward the ceiling. His eyes were almost completely shut, leaving dark slits incapable of betraying his thoughts.

"Why," he began at last, "why does Janet always bring us these problems for which we are so clearly ill-suited? I am a scientist, a mathematician, for God's sake. Why does she want to drag me into this violent world? I have seen the pictures." He touched the folder again. "The person who did this deed is obviously demented."

I pointed out that Janet had nowhere else to turn.

"Ach, that isn't true!" he huffed. "The woman simply cannot find anyone else foolish enough to listen to her."

"You're probably right about that part," I agreed. "But just because there's nobody willing to listen doesn't mean she's wrong."

"Please." He raised a hand. "Don't insult me with such a simple ploy. People have been listening to her; they just don't agree with her conclusions."

He sat up and reached for the coffee.

"What are our current obligations?" he asked, spooning more sugar into his mug.

"At the moment, all we've got is the insurance-company project. The interviews are finished and the report is drafted. As soon as you deliver the statistical analysis, we're done."

Boris shifted his bulk. The idea of actually working made him uncomfortable.

"Nothing new, nothing interesting?" he wondered hopefully.

"We're fresh out of new, let alone interesting, business," I reported. "Don't forget, it was your idea to turn down that lawyer from the Rutherford Institute. That would have been a big job and a fat fee."

"Please, don't remind me. That dreadful little man should be horse-whipped."

Boris let the cigarette dangle from the corner of his mouth

19

and played with the stubble on his chin, weighing this new project against his balance of unfinished work.

"I suppose we have a responsibility to our friends," he sighed at last, choosing to avoid the work. "Besides, there is enough of a point squirreled away in this Ruby Brice material to warrant a conversation with the little boy. It's the least we can do for Janet, though I doubt it will lead to much beyond that. What do you think?"

I shrugged. At three in the morning it didn't matter to me either way.

"It's settled, then. You and I will visit the child tomorrow evening," he announced, rising awkwardly from the sofa.

"You're coming with me?"

The probability of Boris volunteering to leave the building fell into the hell-freezes-over category.

"As a matter of fact, I am," he said calmly. "I would like to meet this special young man. Rest assured, I am not encouraged by the thought of traveling in your hot rod."

"Uh-huh. I'll believe it when I see it." I yawned.

"Have Janet make the arrangements," he commanded, shuffling off, his big smelly doggie in tow. At the end of the hallway they turned into my kitchen, where they ducked into an old broom closet that has been modified to serve as a connecting passage into the Koulomzin domicile. At times like this, the easy access seemed like a big mistake.

It was too late for anything but sleep. I got up slowly and stretched, checking my watch. It wasn't my birthday anymore. I was three hundred and sixty-four days away from turning forty. Great. I wandered down the hallway, picked up the house phone, and dialed the lobby.

"Yo!" It was a voice I didn't recognize.

"Who is this?" I asked.

"Who da fuck's this?"

In the background I could hear laughter. Obviously the dominoes game was still in full swing. Most nights, Manny Santos and his neighborhood pals sit in the lobby drinking Colt 45 and playing dominoes until dawn.

"This is Donovan," I began. "Put Santos on the phone before I decide to come down there and kick your butt."

There was silence on the other end, so I tried the command in Spanish. I could hear the listener repeating my threat for the benefit of the group, after which I heard raucous laughter.

"Yo, gringo, what's the matta, you havin' a bad bertday?"

It was Santos.

"Can it, Manny," I growled. "I'm not in the mood. I called to let you know that Dr. Koulomzin and I are taking a ride out to Brooklyn tomorrow afternoon. I want you to bring the car around at three o'clock. You got that?"

Silence.

"Manny, I said have you *got* that?"

"I hear you, Don-O-van," he said slowly, slurring his words a bit. "I just don' bee-leaf you. The doc ain't goin' no place inna daytime and he ain't ridin' wit you!"

Manny immediately began to translate his disbelief into Spanish, which caused a great deal of excitement. Among other things, Santos runs the local numbers game, but his group will bet on anything. I've seen them trade odds on the length of time it would take a cockroach to climb a can of soda. The news that Boris might leave the building before sundown had created a market.

"Manny? Manny, are you there?" I asked.

He didn't come back on the line.

"Manny!" I yelled, getting frustrated.

It was no use, he was too busy making book. Just before I hung up the phone, I heard him offer odds of fifteen to one.

THREE

...

I guess you could say that the group in the entrance foyer had nothing better to do, and technically that was true. But it was also true, thanks to Manny, that the Polhemus sisters had been broadcasting the news since early morning: Our own Dr. Koulomzin was planning to leave the building while the sun was still brightly shining.

The lobby was charged with a festive air. Manny Santos and his entourage were assembled around the dominoes board. Old Will Manners, who rents two small apartments for himself and his fourteen dogs, was pacing up and down the sidewalk out front with six or seven of his favorite puppies. The Polhemus "girls" (octogenarian twins dressed in matching Shirley Temple outfits) were hurrying to repot one of the ficus trees guarding the front doors. And there was a sizable group milling about over near the mailboxes, even though the mailman had come and gone.

At precisely three o'clock, the elevator groaned to a halt. I emerged first and tried to ignore the gathering. After I had passed, a general hush fell over the group. Boris didn't let them down. Like a true showman, he allowed the tension to build a few seconds longer, then stepped into the lobby.

His entrance was greeted with applause, some loud whistling from the Santos contingent, and at least two *bravos*. Boris had draped himself in several layers of fabric. He wore a black shirt, black tie, black suit, and black topcoat. His hands were covered in black gloves, and there was a white scarf wrapped around his neck and chin to a point just below his nose. He also wore a very large pair of dark glasses and an enormous fedora hat, which was pulled down even with his eyebrows. He bowed slightly, acknowledging his audience, then walked directly to my car, which was waiting for us at the curb.

Boris has a problem with sunlight; what began as a minor phobia slowly matured into a full-fledged obsession. I believe it started with a touch of sunburn when he was a college student. The origin no longer matters; Boris has long since built a mighty list of complaints against the sun. The more he reads about our mother star's harmful rays, the more convinced he becomes that direct exposure to her nurturing light is deadly for humans, and especially so for a Koulomzin. In my opinion, this aversion to sunlight provides a rather convenient excuse for an aging bachelor to keep roughly the same hours as Count Dracula.

"Nice show, Boris," I said, sliding behind the wheel of my old Chevy Nova. "I have a birthday and nobody notices, but you dress up like Claude Rains in *The Invisible Man* and the building turns out as if it were opening night at the Belasco!"

I didn't need to see his face to know that Boris was pleased with the performance. To exact some satisfaction of my own, I put the accelerator to the floor and took the left at 101st Street on two wheels. That wiped the smirk off his clock.

Forty-five minutes later, I turned onto Baylor Street and instinctively slowed down. It was a bleak scene. There were charred, rusting car bodies abandoned in parking spaces on either side of the lane; just empty shells, picked clean and then burned. I counted only five houses that showed signs they supported habitation. There were clothes hanging out to dry at one or two, and at the others you could see people in the yard or through the windows. The rest of the block had disintegrated into vacant lots and abandoned buildings. It had an unhealthy look, like a gap-toothed smile.

We pulled up to the curb at 4210, then sat and stared at Clifford Brice's foster home. It had once been a quaint, middle-class, single-family dwelling, but now the faded wooden structure looked unsafe and seemed to be sagging on its foundation. There was a porch, but the roof had caved in on one end and all the screens were gone or shredded. The shingles covering the sides of the building had fallen off in spots, exposing irregular patches of tar paper, and the last coat of paint had worn off completely, giving it the weather-beaten look of an old farmhouse.

Checking the map, I noted that 4210 Baylor Street was less than a mile from the Logan Street address where they'd found Ruby Brice. It couldn't have been far enough away for the little boy whose mother had been killed there.

Janet Fein was sitting on the front porch steps, waiting patiently for us. When I opened the car door, it startled a large brown rat who'd been browsing through a pile of garbage in the yard. The creature took off in Janet's direction like a Pony Express rider. It veered left and right before darting between her legs and down a hole in the bottom step. I doubt Janet's feet touched the ground more than once as she cut a path to the sidewalk.

Meanwhile, Boris was moaning and complaining as he struggled to unfasten the seatbelt and extricate himself from the cockpit. It was a tight fit, though not nearly as difficult as he made it sound. He'd been whining and complaining for the entire trip. I felt like smacking him in the side of the head.

"Boris, is that you?" Janet exclaimed happily.

He ignored the question and, elbowing me out of the way, pointed at the house.

"I would very much like to know how this hovel qualifies as a foster home," he demanded.

"Well, hello to you, too, honey. Now, would you mind keeping your voice down?" Janet pleaded. "We need Mrs. Washington's cooperation or we don't get inside the house."

She glanced over her shoulder to make sure Mrs. Washington, the foster parent, wasn't standing right behind her.

"All right, but what gives?" I asked, jumping on the bandwagon. "This can't be right."

"Look, you two, this is not the time to debate the ills of the child welfare system. Mrs. Washington completed an approved training program and she is recognized by the city and state of New York as a foster parent. Her home is registered with a foster-care agency, and the courts recognize her as a temporary adoptive resource. If you want to start a crusade against the system, that's fine with me, but for now those are the facts."

Boris's expression indicated he wasn't mollified.

"I know the outside isn't pretty," she continued, gesturing toward the house, "but it's clean inside, and each kid has his own bed and plenty to eat. That's more than they would get if it weren't available. Okay?"

I said nothing. Boris turned back to the house, memorizing the details.

"There's one more thing," Janet said nervously. "You guys aren't exactly supposed to be here. I mean, technically I should have gotten an official blessing. But when I told Cliff that you were trying to find out what really happened to his mother, he insisted on meeting you."

"Whoa, time out. I hope you didn't make him promises we can't keep," I said, getting angry again. "Because if you did that, Janet, you were way out of line. We'll probably never know what happened to Ruby Brice. You're gonna end up breaking the boy's heart a second time, and that's not fair."

"Oh, for goodness sake, why don't you relax, Donovan? We're not talking about some preppie tart. Cliff knows the score. He doesn't think that you're going to resurrect his mother. The fact that some effort is being made on her behalf is what counts to him. Besides, don't tell me you're not going to make a difference. I have faith in you guys."

The blind leading the blind.

"Okay, we accept the compliment," I said. "But it's very premature. All we're planning for today is a simple conversation with Clifford Brice. This could be the beginning and the end of our involvement."

She gave me a knowing smile.

"Excuse me, please," Boris interrupted gracefully. "I think it would be best to proceed with our current objective. We came here to meet with Clifford Brice."

That stopped us long enough for everyone to take a deep breath. I decided to try a different tactic.

"Look, if we're not supposed to be here, how are we going to get past the professional parent?" I asked.

"Oh, that's already taken care of." She smiled. "Mrs. Washington thinks that you guys work for Child Welfare."

"Is that right?" I asked cynically. "And how are we supposed to live up to that billing? For instance, what if the woman asks to see our credentials?"

"Don't worry about credentials," Janet said, shaking her head. "I told Mrs. Washington that I was bringing a doctor and an investigator to interview Clifford. That happens to be true."

Sure it was.

"Anyway, she'll be very cooperative as long as you don't put her on the defensive." She turned to Boris. "Remember that. At the first hint of trouble, she'll toss all three of us."

It didn't sound very promising to me.

"I think it might be a good idea for you to talk with Mrs. Washington," Janet said, taking my hand gently. "While you're confusing the poor woman, Boris can meet with Cliff."

I tried to speak, but she cut me off.

"Stop worrying, Donovan, I'll be there in case something unexpected comes up."

Janet smiled and patted my shoulder.

"How come I get Mrs. Washington?" I complained.

"Call it women's intuition," she said evasively. "Once you've seen Boris and Clifford together, you'll understand."

I couldn't imagine it. The way Boris was dressed, he'd probably scare the poor kid out of his wits. But there wasn't time to argue—I had to start thinking of snappy questions to ask the foster-parent lady.

"By the way, Janet, thanks for the advance warning," I sulked as we climbed the porch steps.

"What are you talking about?" she fired back. "Boris called this morning and I laid the whole thing out for him. Didn't he tell you?"

We both turned back to the Invisible Man bringing up the rear. He shrugged his shoulders, deflecting the questions before we had a chance to ask them.

Janet marched up to the front door and knocked. By the time we were all crowded together on the porch, the door had opened and a very short, very fat woman filled the doorway like a cork.

"Why, Ms. Fein, how nice to see you all."

The cork spoke softly and had a pretty Southern accent.

"Thank you, Mrs. Washington. I would like to introduce my associates. This is Mr. Donovan . . ."

"Mrs. Washington." I shook her hand warmly.

". . . and Dr. Koulomzin," Janet continued.

Boris didn't offer his hand. He nodded his head slightly and looked annoyed. Mrs. Washington took this snub in stride. It probably wasn't the first time a public-health official had given her the cold shoulder.

"May we come in?" Janet asked.

"Why yes, please do."

"Thank you," Janet said again.

We were all being very polite. Everyone, that is, except Boris. He was rudely inspecting the interior of the house. It was actually better than I'd expected. For one thing, it was warm. And it smelled good, like home cooking. Boris piled his coat on a chair in the hall and we moved into the living room. Without his outer layers, Boris looked more like the psychologist he was portraying.

27

Janet started explaining our agenda to Mrs. Washington. Either Boris wasn't listening or he didn't care.

"I've come here to talk with Clifford Brice," he interrupted rudely. "Please produce the child and show us to a private room."

Mrs. Washington looked a bit taken aback.

"Why certainly, Doctor," she said after a pause.

The lady was cooperating, but it was obvious she hadn't liked his tone of voice. Rising slowly, she went to the foot of the stairs and called up into the shadows.

"Cliff-*ford?* You come on down here now, they's people to see you."

Suddenly there was lots of activity over our heads. I could hear footsteps and furniture being dragged into place. At one point, there was a loud crash and then more footsteps scurrying about. It was a wonder the ceiling didn't collapse.

"How many kids have you got up there?" I asked, trying to lighten the mood. "It sounds like an entire football team."

"I have six boys at present," she answered, "but two of them is down playing basketball. So they's only four up stairs now. You should hear the racket when they all at home."

Her expression wavered between pride and exhaustion. I was starting to like Mrs. Washington.

"How come we didn't hear them before?"

"You from the city, Mista Donovan. You people usually don't bring much good news wit you. They was just waitin' to see who you was after."

She gave me a sideways look, as if I must be some kind of fool. I started worrying about the interview I was supposed to conduct. This lady was gonna see through me like I was a pane of glass.

"Please, call me J. J.," I said, relying on charm.

"That's just fine, Jay," she murmured softly, nodding her head. "My name's Anne, but most folks call me Annie."

Before we could get any further, a little boy came into the room. He was small for a ten-year-old, and so thin he seemed

28

lost in his baggy clothes. Ruby Brice had been a dark, ebony-skinned woman and I had expected to meet a very black child. But Clifford's skin was much lighter than his mother's, more of a caramel color, and there were freckles on both of his cheeks. His hair was light brown and closely cropped.

The child wore very thick wire-rimmed spectacles, not unlike the ones Boris was wearing. In fact, his face and the eyes behind those thick lenses had a familiar intensity. It was as if the child was absorbing and analyzing everything he saw. I recognized the look. Janet was right; Clifford and Boris were going to get along just fine.

At first glance, I didn't notice anything unusual about the boy, though I would have sworn he was wearing a pair of white athletic socks. As he moved farther into the room and came closer, the socks grew shiny and translucent, like alabaster, and I could distinctly make out his toes. Suddenly, I realized that the rough white patches I'd mistaken for tube socks weren't made of cotton. That white stuff was his skin, or what was left of it. It was hard not to stare.

Janet scooped Cliff up and gave him a big hug. For a minute the boy disappeared, lost in her ample bosom. When he resurfaced, I saw him smile broadly as she whispered something in his ear. Janet put him down, and they came over to us. Clifford nodded his head politely and said hello to me, but that was it. I was a little disappointed—I'm usually a big hit with kids. Then he walked directly up to the Boris and stuck out a tiny hand.

"Dr. Koulomzin, I am very glad to meet you," he said, pronouncing the difficult last name correctly.

Boris took the child's hand and knelt so that he was closer to the boy's level. His tone, in fact his whole demeanor, softened.

"From the looks of those dirty glasses, young Clifford, I doubt you can see very much of anything," Boris pointed out, smiling. "Would you believe, I have exactly the same problem?"

The boy nodded his head enthusiastically. Boris took a clean linen handkerchief from his pocket and carefully unfolded it.

29

Then he took his own glasses and breathed on them, fogging the lenses before wiping them clean. Clifford watched every move intently, and when the cloth was offered, copied Boris exactly.

"You need your own handkerchief," Boris said, when Clifford tried to return the monogrammed linen. "Why don't you keep that one. I've got another at home."

"Aw right! Thanks, Doctor."

Clifford's voice, like his frame, was small, but clear and confident. Boris stood up and turned to the rest of us, smiling.

"I wonder, Mrs. Washington, is there someplace—a private room perhaps—where we could sit and chat for a bit?"

The polite change in his tone worked wonders on our hostess, who got up and led the way to the kitchen.

"What's wrong with his feet?" I whispered to Janet.

"You mean, why are they white?"

"Yeah."

"That's scar tissue. When Cliff was a baby he had colic and he cried a lot. His father didn't like all the crying, so he stuck Clifford's feet into a pot of boiling water to teach him a lesson. The old man hasn't been seen or heard from since."

We sat in silence, looking at the threadbare furniture, and I tried to guess the original color of the wallpaper. Pretty soon Annie Washington came back into the room. She was carrying a tray with glasses of soda and a plate of homemade cookies.

"Annie, you're a mind-reader," I said, grabbing a cookie. She accepted the flattery with a smile.

"Now, what was it you wanted to talk to me about?" she asked, settling into her chair.

"Well, in the first place, let me assure you that our investigation has nothing to do with the care Cliff's been receiving in your home."

I smiled and reached for another one of her delicious oatmeal cookies. It was important to stay in character, and my character really liked her cookies. "As you know, we have a mandate to locate any surviving family members before a decision can be made about the child's future," I said, improvising.

Annie nodded her head, familiar with procedure.

"In this case, the mother's death was particularly violent and shocking. We're anxious to resolve the question of family, so that Clifford can be placed in a permanent family setting as quickly as possible."

I took a drink of soda, hoping I didn't sound too phony. You couldn't tell from Annie's expression. Her face was a blank.

"You're an experienced professional," I continued, spreading the goodwill. "I was hoping that you might have learned something in the time Cliff's been with you that would help us. What's it been now, a month?"

"It's exactly six weeks today," she said, correcting me.

"Right, six weeks," I repeated. "Is there anything you can think of that would help?"

I tried to look as sincere as possible, and even reached for another one of her cookies. Annie wasn't taking this interview lightly. Her face clouded over as she gave the question serious consideration.

"I'm sorry, Mr. Donovan—I mean, Jay," she began, finally, "but I cain't think of anything that would help find that child's family. I can tell you this, however. They must be some pretty smart folks, because that boy is about the smartest little fella I've seen."

"Can you tell me what he likes to talk about?" I asked, groping.

"Ha! Everything! My Lord, the boy never shuts up!" She laughed loud and deep. "Do you know that child balances my checkbook?" she asked, leaning forward in the chair. "Come his second week, Cliffy had me on a budget. Lately, he's been helping them other boys to read and write. Even James."

Janet raised her eyebrows and made a funny face. I couldn't resist the temptation.

"Who is James?" I asked.

"Honey, James is a big, sweet boy, but the good Lord has seen fit to test him. James come into this world without a brain in his head."

For the next twenty minutes Annie and Janet treated me to James stories. There was something appealing about this over-grown, clumsy kid who acted first and thought later, and didn't seem to understand his own size or strength.

"Excuse me please, Ms. Fein, but with all this talkin', I think I do remember something," Annie said, interrupting Janet, who was in the middle of a story. "Cliffy and James were talking a while back and Cliff said something about an uncle."

Janet and I kept quiet. Six rowdy young boys can say a lot of meaningless things. Annie closed her eyes and searched for details.

"Cliff got mad," she said slowly, feeling her way, "and he said something like: 'Yeah, well my Uncle Tito has got one, only he doesn't let me near it.' James didn't believe him and he started makin' fun of Cliff and calling him a liar. I thought Clifford was gonna cry. He got real quiet, but then I heard him say: 'I am not lying, Tito is Mama's friend. She's the one who said I got to call him Uncle.' "

Annie Washington sighed and let the memory fade away. "I can't say why I remember that particular little bit. Maybe I'm just getting old and losing the beginning and the end of everything." She chuckled and rubbed her face with an open palm. "Anyways," she continued, "they was inside at the kitchen table, and I remember feelin' sorry for the boy. He don't have an uncle and one of his momma's friends didn't seem like much of a bargain."

"What do you think about this uncle?" I asked.

"I don't know, just some man his momma was using or, more likely, being used by." Annie grimaced. It was obvious she didn't have much respect for people like Ruby Brice.

"Do you know what Cliff and James were arguing about?"

"No sir, I honestly don't. I'm sorry."

It wasn't much, but it was a nibble. I was just starting to wonder if Boris was making any headway when he and Clifford came back into the room. Boris was walking with his head down and his hands clasped behind his back, and Clifford was mim-icking him.

"I see, yes, that's very observant of you, Clifford," Boris was saying as they entered.

We all stood up, dwarfing the little boy.

"Is everything all right, Dr. Koulomzin?" Janet asked, staying in character.

"Yes, Ms. Fein, for the time being, we're through. It was a very pleasant, enlightening chat. I look forward to many more of them in the future."

Boris leaned down and shook hands with Clifford Brice and I saw him wink. He straightened back up, collected his belongings, bowed from the waist, and strode out the door. Apparently we were supposed to follow, like faithful minions.

"Would you mind answering a question for me?" I asked, squatting down in front of Clifford.

He looked at me for a moment, trying to decide.

"I guess I don't mind," he said at last.

He spoke very softly, and I sensed some apprehension.

"What does Uncle Tito have that he won't let you use?"

Clifford looked at me and his eyes grew very wide.

"Don't be afraid," I continued, misreading the silence. "You can tell me anything."

Next thing I knew he was laughing so hard he had to hold his stomach.

"I'm sorry, Mr. Donovan," he squeaked, catching his breath, "but you musta been talkin' to James, because, I mean, you got it all wrong. I told James that Tito wouldn't let me *near* his car. I never said I wanted to use it. I'm only ten years old, I can't drive!"

He looked at the others and they all started to laugh, like I was the second dumbest guy on the block.

"Was it a nice car?" I asked, getting back to Uncle Tito.

He hesitated before answering.

"I guess so," he said softly.

"What was wrong with it, Cliff?" I urged.

"I don't know exactly," he said, the diffidence returning to his voice. "The car was new and shiny, so I mean, it was nice like

33

that. But it was all black and the windows were black like sunglasses. I don't know, there just wasn't anything nice about that
car. It looked mean, just like Tito."

He spit the name out and backed up defensively. This wasn't
a laughing matter.

"Did you and Dr. Koulomzin talk about Tito?" I asked.

He looked away, trying to avoid the question. The poor kid
had been through a lot; I didn't blame him for being reticent.
But I couldn't leave it alone. It was too important.

"Cliff," I asked again, "did you and Dr. Koulomzin talk about
this guy Tito?"

He hesitated a second longer, then nodded his head.

FOUR

...

Boris was already sitting in the car, his seatbelt in place, blowing smoke through the open window. When we tried to ask him questions, he put a finger to his lips and told us to get in the car. Janet hadn't planned on leaving with us, but she had no choice if she wanted information, so she slipped into the backseat.

"I would like a tour of the neighborhood," Boris said without turning around.

"Are you talking to me, Pops?" Janet quipped from the back.

"Please, if you would be so kind," he said, softening his tone. "It would help if I could see the neighborhood in which Ms. Brice worked and died."

"I guess we could take a quick ride," Janet began, "but remember, it's getting dark out, and that creates a potential health hazard. We'll have to keep moving; no stopping to admire the local color. Got it?"

Boris said he did. I didn't say anything. I was sure we weren't going to be making any unnecessary stops, not while I was driving. We pulled away from Annie Washington's house and the relative safety of the streetlight out front, heading for Logan Street between Atlantic and Liberty Avenues. It was a good thing Janet was there to give me directions; most of the streetlights were out, and many of the signs were missing.

East New York is an ugly part of New York City. Empty lots and burned-out buildings could be seen on most blocks, along with piles of garbage, abandoned cars, and stray dogs. It was a wasteland in the growing darkness, surreal against the backdrop of the New York City skyline twinkling in the distance. As we approached Atlantic Avenue, there were more obvious signs of life. One- or two-story brick factories were plentiful, their windows painted black and covered with steel bars, remnants of a once-thriving light industrial center. They weren't pretty buildings, but they were obviously in use. Cars were parked in the street and on the sidewalks, next to tractor trailers and flatbed trucks. Forklift drivers were busy taking material to and from the big trucks, their forms silhouetted by the bright lights on the loading docks. After so many streets of near-total desolation, the sudden activity seemed like an exaggeration.

We drove up and down the little side streets, slowly weaving our way in and around the crime scene, while Janet reinvented the local history. Because she was born in Flatbush, she claims the right to blame all of the borough's problems on the misguided decision to merge the City of Brooklyn with the City of New York. The history lesson continued until we reached the house where Ruby and Clifford Brice had kept a small apartment. After that, she launched into a diatribe about urban subcultures as she pointed out the local street corners where Ruby had advertised her goods. It was a Friday night and the weather was mild, but we didn't see any working girls. By the time we reached the third empty corner, the lecture had stopped.

"What gives?" I asked, looking at Janet in the rearview mirror. "I thought these streets were busy. Are we too early?"

It was six-thirty.

"I don't know," Janet murmured, wrinkling her brow. "As far as I know, it's never too early; out here, nobody worries about being seen with a hooker. Besides, darkness just increases the chances of something bad happening. I don't know what's going on, but it's awful quiet. Let's get the hell out of here. Turn left at the next corner and I'll show you a shortcut to the highway."

I turned left onto Berriman Street as instructed and drove right

36

smack into the middle of a major police action. The lane was barricaded by a couple of squad cars parked at angles, and official-looking vehicles crowded the narrow street. We couldn't go forward, and when I tried to back up an EMS wagon and a couple of fire engines pulled up behind us, forcing me onto the sidewalk. We were stuck.

After a very few minutes, Boris started complaining and giving me advice on how to "extricate ourselves" from the scene. I was trying to reason with him the way an adult negotiates with a obnoxious child, when Janet Fein suddenly hopped out of the car and started running down the street.

"Now what?" Boris demanded, squirming in his seat.

I watched Janet run up to a burly cop who smiled when he saw her coming. They had several minutes of animated conversation, during which the patrolman pointed down an alley on one side of the street and then away from us, toward Flatlands Avenue. She nodded several times, then motioned toward my car. The cop looked over at us and shrugged. A few minutes later, Janet was back in the Nova.

"There's been another murder," she announced breathlessly.

"What do you mean by *another murder?*" Boris asked. "There are many hundreds of murders each year in this city."

"No, no, I mean another murder like Ruby's murder," she shouted, so excited she was bouncing up and down in her seat. "A friend of mine from the seventy-fifth precinct is on the job tonight and he tells me that another woman is dead. She was cut to ribbons, just like Ruby, only this time the creep tied her to a stake and set the body on fire."

Boris and I looked at each other. The expression on his face told me we were thinking the same thing—the little favor for Ms. Fein was beginning to take on a life of its own. It was like getting knocked down in the first round of a prize fight.

"Come on, boys, let's go take a look." Janet started to get out of the car.

"Whoa, hold on there," I protested. "We won't get close enough to see anything."

"Sure we will," Janet assured me. "I'm a credentialed officer of the court and I'm bringing a doctor onto the scene."

"You don't mean Boris?" I asked.

"Why not?" she said. "He's a doctor, isn't he?"

"He's a mathematician."

"So what? Annie Washington just bought it!"

"That's right, but what you don't know is that the guy gets weak if he picks up a splinter. How's he going to inspect a charred cadaver?"

"I beg your pardon, James," Boris put in, "but I think you exaggerate my delicate sensibilities. No person likes to be confronted by such a horrible sight, but I can assure you that I will play whatever role is necessary."

I gave him a hard look, but he was resolute. Five minutes later the three of us were turning down a side alley across the street from a business called the National Manufacturing Corporation. I noticed they had a big HELP WANTED sign out front. Something told me that a hooker getting barbecued in their backyard wasn't going to improve the pool of applicants.

The alley was a dark, narrow lane between two buildings that led into a small court yard. There was smoke in the air, and it smelled putrid. Boris lit a cigarette and proceeded bravely, though I could tell that his conviction was starting to waver. There was enough official confusion, with the cops, medics, and firemen all moving at once, for us to get close enough to see the body.

I was standing about fifteen feet from the victim. It was too close. Janet said the victim had been badly cut and repeatedly stabbed, but the fire had erased the visible evidence of those wounds. The poor woman had been crudely nailed to a makeshift two-by-four crucifix with eight or ten penny nails—lots of them. Just in case the nail holes ripped loose, her arms and legs had also been secured to the boards with metal baling wire—the same stuff used to bind Ruby Brice. Once the crucifixion was complete, the cross had been lowered into a metal sleeve buried in the ground so that it stood upright. Then it had been set on fire. I could smell gasoline or kerosene, so I guessed that she'd been doused with fuel, like a torch. Her hair, eyelids, eyes, lips, and ears had all burned away. The rest of the body was charred black, and smoldered like dying coals in a fireplace. I stared much longer than necessary, but I was unable to turn away.

Janet had her credentials out and was interviewing a young detective in a jogging suit, who'd probably been off-duty when his beeper sounded. I forced myself to let go of the ghoulish scene and tried to listen to the conversation, but there was just too much noise competing in that confined space. Janet was taking copious notes, so I stopped worrying. I was just standing there, taking up space, when I felt a tap on the shoulder. I turned and found myself looking down at a skinny little detective in a wrinkled suit.

"Who the fuck are you?" he asked without blinking.

I began to stammer a response, but Janet quickly intervened.

"Lieutenant Negro, I'm so glad to see you," she bellowed, rocking the poor man back on his heels.

"Right," he said, collecting himself "who the fuck is this?" He pointed a finger at me. Janet told him I was with her.

"Is that so? Then maybe you should start by telling me what the fuck *you're* doing here," he said without smiling. "As far as I know, this ain't a juvenile case."

"Oh, well, that's simple enough. I was visiting Clifford Brice. You remember him. His mother's brutal murder remains unsolved."

"Now don't start that shit with me again, Janet," Negro said with an exasperated sigh. "You know as well as I do that we got the guy who did her."

"And this killing doesn't raise any doubts in your mind, Chris?" She was taller than the detective, and used the height to her advantage.

"I'm not tellin' you nothin', lady," he said, getting angry. "This is *my* crime scene, and as far as I'm concerned you are trespassing. Now, I'll ask you again, what are you doing here— and I don't mean in the vicinity, I mean *here!*"

"As I tried to tell you, Lieutenant, we were visiting Clifford Brice, and these gentlemen asked to see the neighborhood. We were merely driving by when we stumbled into this mess."

"Gentle*men*? What gentlemen?" he shouted, looking around. "You mean there's more than this guy?" He pointed an angry thumb in my direction again.

"Well, yes. In addition to Mr. Donovan, I have Dr. Koulomzin with me this evening," she said seriously, grabbing Boris by the arm and pulling him forward.

"You got a doctor with you? Well, that's different," Negro said, warming up a bit. "Nice to meet you, Doctor. I've got a little problem here and maybe you could help me out. I'm just standing here holdin' my dick waitin' for someone from the coroner's office. If you could pronounce this broad dead we could turn the hoses on her. You may have noticed she's still smoldering."

Boris was like a man in a trance. He looked at the detective, turned slowly to look at Janet, who nodded encouragement, and then turned back to me. His normally pale complexion was like alabaster, but he'd given his word. He took a deep breath, filling his lungs with the foul-smelling air, then raised his right foot and started moving toward the burning corpse. He took two, maybe three small steps, then fainted dead away.

FIVE

...

I suppose things could have been worse. In the rush to attend to the *doctor* and get him out of the smoke-filled alleyway, Lieutenant Negro got pushed into the background. There were a couple of emergency services crews on the scene who'd been standing around waiting, unable to treat the corpse. When Boris Koulomzin hit the deck, they had six feet, five inches and nearly three hundred pounds of patient to work with, and they went about their business enthusiastically. By the time Boris had revived enough to stand and walk to the car, an official from the coroner's office was on the scene, and he kept Negro too busy to bother with us. Janet's cop friend got some vehicles moved, and I quickly backed the Nova down the sidewalk and away from that nightmare scene.

We reached the relative safety of the highway in about five minutes. Boris sighed loudly and reached for his cigarettes. There had been an uncomfortable silence in the car, but when he torched that coffin nail the kid gloves came off.

"Nice going, Tinker Bell," I whispered.

Janet burst out laughing.

"What did you say?" Boris thundered.

"Yeah, good show, Doc," Janet chipped in from the back.

Boris started to sputter defensively, but there was really nothing he could say.

"Take it easy, Boris," Janet said kindly, "we're only kidding.

That was a bad, bad scene. I don't blame you for doing a belly flop."

Boris puffed on his cigarette and stared out the window, but held his tongue. I wasn't too worried; in a couple of hours he'd have a revised version of the fainting incident filed away, and his ego would prosper again. Pictures of the dead woman wouldn't be so easy to erase.

For the next twenty minutes we drove along in silence. About the time we reached Brooklyn Heights, I decided there had been enough private contemplation. Besides, what's a wake without a good stiff drink? I veered onto the exit ramp before anyone could object, then got lucky and found a parking spot directly across the street from Henry's End.

The sun was long gone, so Boris didn't bother wearing his costume to the restaurant. The sunglasses, overcoat, scarf, and fedora were neatly stacked in the trunk of my car, ready for his next performance. By the time our second round of drinks arrived he was smoking thoughtfully, but he still hadn't broken his silence. When the waiter stopped to ask if we were finally ready to eat, he seemed to perk up. Two or three martinis and the warm smells of the restaurant had reminded us we were hungry, so we decided to order.

"Come on, Boris, forget about the fainting spell, okay?" Janet said when the waiter was gone. "I want to talk about Clifford Brice. Did he tell you anything helpful or not?"

"Fainting spell?" he asked, blinking. "There was no fainting spell. I was overcome by the stench in the confined space and the loss of oxygen caused me to become disoriented. Nothing more." He reached for his drink, bracing for a challenge.

"Yeah, fine, whatever," Janet smirked. "What about Clifford?"

He made us wait a bit longer as he stubbed out his cigarette.

"Well, my dear," Boris said finally, leaning back in his chair, "I admit that he is a truly remarkable child. He is mature beyond his years and intelligent with insight, which is a rare combina-

42

tion. He should be in an environment where his abilities are developed and nurtured."

"I know that, and so did his mother," she said, smiling sadly. "He's our diamond in the rough. I thought you'd understand if you met him."

They were both getting kind of starry-eyed.

"That's all fine and dandy, Boris," I interrupted, "but what did you learn from Clifford Brice that might prove useful to this investigation?"

Boris was trying to stab an onion with a toothpick. "Well," he began, eating the onion before clearing his throat dramatically, "we spoke about his mother's murder. It was a very frank discussion for a child of his age."

We sat and waited as Boris drained his Gibson. "The boy was able to clear up several points with respect to possible motives for the murder of Ruby Brice," he continued. "According to young Clifford, his mother had a passion for money-making schemes. She wanted to get some fast cash and get them out of Brooklyn. Like many people who are trapped by their circumstances, she kept looking for a big score that would make possible their escape. I don't blame her. Her circumstances were dire, and the thought of this gifted child being dragged into her world would have made Ms. Brice desperate. However, we have been operating under a misconception. Although it is true that Ms. Brice claimed to have a secret knowledge from which she planned to profit, Clifford does not believe that had anything to do with her murder."

"But what about the key ring and her plan to get away?" Janet asked.

"Apparently one of her customers became rather enamored and made her promises of both a personal and a financial nature. This man was born under the sign of Scorpio; hence the symbolism of the key chain. It was given to her as a token."

"Was the boyfriend's name Tito?" I asked.

Boris turned to me, impressed.

43

"Why didn't he tell me the truth?" Janet muttered, obviously wounded.

"Dear lady, unless I am very much mistaken, your office does not condone or promote prostitution."

Janet was speechless for once.

"That is correct, is it not?" Boris asked.

She nodded.

"Clifford's deception was meant to protect you. He was afraid there would be trouble if your superiors learned that his mother was soliciting men, like Señor Tito, while also receiving benefits from the city. I understand these were benefits you fought long and hard to get them."

"Well, I'll be damned," she whispered.

"Besides, it wasn't really a lie. His mother told him that she had witnessed some sort of illegal transaction at a local business called the National Manufacturing Corporation. She told Clifford she was working on a plan to turn her secret knowledge into a profit. The boy has no doubt that his mother witnessed a horrible crime, but he doesn't think she would have been able to capitalize on the information. A more realistic target was this Uncle Tito. Clifford says that she built up this other scheme as a distraction, so it wouldn't be too obvious how much her plans were dependent on Mr. Tito."

"Ruby named the National Manufacturing Corporation?" I asked.

"Yes, apparently she did," Boris said carefully, as if he'd missed something. "Why, what do you make of that?"

"Nothing really, it's just that I noticed the building tonight. It's on Berriman Street, right across from the alley you made famous. There was a big help-wanted sign out front."

Boris and Janet both looked at me, waiting for a punch line. But there wasn't anything to add; it was just something I had noticed. I was thankful when our dinners arrived. The food looked and smelled so good, we lunged for our forks.

"Okay, so what about this Uncle Tito guy?" I sighed, finally pushing my plate away.

Boris, who was contemplating a final bite of his roasted duckling, raised an eyebrow.

"Well, what do you already know about him?" he asked.

"I know that he's a mean guy who drives a shiny black car," I said.

"So I understand," he muttered, reaching for a glass of wine.

"And?! Come on, Boris, what else did Clifford say?"

He took a sip, clearing his throat.

"He remembers a tall, heavy-set white man with a salt-and-pepper beard. The man is a natty dresser who smokes pencil-thin cigars and drinks from a silver flask. As you mentioned, this Tito drives a glossy black car with tinted windows. According to Clifford, Mr. Tito is a rich man, though given the boy's frame of reference, I think a man of modest circumstances would seem rich to him."

"Cliff told me that Uncle Tito was mean," I volunteered. "He said you talked about it, so I didn't push him, but I could tell the kid was scared. What's that about?"

"Suffice it to say that this Uncle Tito character has something of a Jekyll-and-Hyde personality. At his worst he could be very cruel."

"Did he hurt the boy's mother?" I asked.

"Yes. Repeatedly." Boris paused to take another sip of Merlot. "Apparently she was willing to endure this abuse to achieve her goal. As you know, Ms. Brice was hoping to extort some money from this person, this Uncle Tito. If successful, she and Clifford would have simply disappeared."

"How was she going to do that?" I asked.

"According to the boy, Ms. Brice concocted a story whose central figure was a nonexistent manager named Lamar. She was going to tell Mr. Tito that Lamar didn't want her spending so much time with just one man. The gist was that time was money, and Tito was hurting Lamar's business."

"Ruby wasn't the kind of talent who needed a manager," I said sarcastically.

"What?"

45

Boris hates to be interrupted.

"A whore doesn't have a manager, she has a pimp," Janet explained.

"I know what a pimp is," Boris snorted. "I was trying keep this on a higher plane."

"I wouldn't bother on our account, honey." Janet chuckled.

"Oh, very well then." He sighed irritably. "She was going to tell Señor Tito that her *pimp* wanted ten thousand dollars to release her from her obligations to him. If said *pimp* didn't get his money, the consequence would be that Ms. Brice would no longer be available to Uncle Tito, or maybe something even worse. I can imagine that a resourceful woman like Ruby Brice had her own methods of persuading this man that she was worth the investment." Boris looked away, avoiding the flash of anger in Janet's eyes. "In any event, with Mister Tito's cash in hand, I take it the disappearing part would have been fairly simple," he concluded.

"She actually thought that was going to work?" I asked.

"Apparently. It seems she felt this Tito was naive enough to believe anything she told him."

Or crazy enough, I thought. "The plan didn't work too well, did it?" I asked.

Boris shook his head.

"It's not much to go on," I said, thinking out loud.

Janet had been watching us, trying to follow the conversation. She kept looking from one to the other as she listened. Suddenly she got it. "You mean that old wizard was right?" she asked. "He really did see the killer's car?"

"It's a possibility," Boris said. "A distinct possibility."

46

SIX

. . .

After dinner, we dropped Janet Fein at the subway entrance near Borough Hall, then drove across the Brooklyn Bridge into lower Manhattan. Between Fulton Street and our crumbling old building up on Columbus Avenue, Boris smoked and brooded, and I worried about the traffic. It had been an exhausting day.

Sleep is usually good medicine for me. But with sleep comes dreams, and the stuff we'd seen in that alley in Brooklyn was the stuff of nightmares. Alone in the darkness of my bedroom, it all came back to me—the smoldering body, the smell, the noisy confusion. And no amount of tossing and turning would make it go away. When I finally dozed off, it was merely the beginning of a long night without rest.

I was in the car with Janet Fein, and we were searching for someone. As we drove up and down unfamiliar streets, the sound of my heart beating filled the car, accelerating the already-excited pace. Then, suddenly, it stopped, and we could hear a new sound, far off in the distance. It was so faint at first that I couldn't distinguish it, but the sound grew louder and louder as we approached, until suddenly it was the voice of a woman crying out in pain. The next thing I knew, we were out of the car and racing through an alleyway with brick walls that twisted and turned like a maze. The screaming had stopped, but ahead of us, seemingly around the next bend, I could hear anguished sobbing. It was a pitiful sound, and it infuriated me.

Finally the walls disappeared, and we were in a clearing full of smoke. A young woman with amber skin lay naked on the grass, her arms and legs spread wide and tied to stakes in the ground. Her face was hidden from me under a tangle of sweat-soaked hair. There was a fire burning by her side, and a metal poker lay in the coals. In the glow of the fire, I could see welts and blisters on her thighs, stomach, and breasts. As we approached, the woman began to moan and shake her head from side to side. Reaching down, I gently brushed the hair from her face, whispering that she would be all right. But when I pulled the hair aside, her face was crawling with tiny scorpions, their twisted tails arched and ready to sting. She opened her eyes, looked straight into mine, and shrieked.

I bolted upright in bed, a cold sweat on my forehead. The dream was gone and the room was full of sunlight, but my head was heavy and I felt queasy, as if I'd spent the night inside a bottle of scotch. The telephone was ringing. I reached for it slowly, suddenly afraid.

"J. J., he's gone!" Janet Fein shouted.

"Who's gone?" I asked numbly.

"Clifford Brice! J. J., he's gone. What the hell are we gonna do?"

"Okay, wait a minute," I said, getting out of bed.

I put the receiver down, stumbled into the bathroom, and put my head under the shower for a minute. The cold water hurt, but it cleared away the fog and brought me back to life. Grabbing a towel, I ran back to the telephone.

"Now, start over," I said, trying to sound calm. "And this time, tell me exactly what happened."

"Well, I'm not sure what all happened," she began, "but about the time we were reviving Boris in that alley over on Berriman Street, a big, dolled-up Hispanic dude claiming to be Uncle Tito showed up at the foster home and asked to see Clifford Brice."

I sat back down on the bed. My head was starting to hurt again.

"Annie Washington is no fool. She saw the look on Clifford's face when you asked him about Uncle Tito," Janet continued breathlessly. "She told this Tito character to get lost, and shut the door in his face. Next thing she knew he was kicking it in. Instead of looking for a place to hide, Annie ran into the kitchen and grabbed a big cast-iron frying pan and started swinging. Tito was still in the front hall trying to get past Mrs. Washington when James came home from playing basketball.

"When James saw what was going on, he grabbed Tito by the shirt collar and threw him back out the door and down the front steps. Apparently, big bad Tito only fights with women, because he picked himself up and ran away before James could get to him."

"So, what happened to Clifford?" I asked impatiently.

"I'm coming to that," Janet said, catching her breath. "With all the excitement and the police coming and going, it wasn't until sometime later that they realized that Clifford was actually missing. At first, Mrs. Washington figured Cliff was hiding, but they searched the house and couldn't find him anywhere."

"So what happened, he got scared and ran away?" I asked.

"I guess so." Janet sighed. "This really sucks! When I finally got home last night, I was so tired I decided to turn my phone and beeper off and went to bed. You got any idea how many times I've done that in twenty-three years on the job? So, naturally, all hell breaks loose. The poor kid was wandering around alone all night while I was home sleeping."

I started to say something comforting, but she interrupted. "Wait, Donovan, this gets worse. Following up on this incident with Uncle Tito, my boss learned all about our little visit with Cliff yesterday. He is not a happy person and neither is Annie Washington. I've been summoned to headquarters to explain why I brought two strange men impersonating child-welfare personnel to meet with Clifford Brice. This is not a good thing."

"Would it hurt to tell the truth?" I asked, wondering what she had to lose.

"I have no idea," she moaned.

The alarm clock read 7:30.

"Okay, listen to me," I said, getting up and going to the bureau for clothes. "You go to work and deal with your boss. Don't worry about Clifford. I'll head out to Brooklyn and nose around."

"J. J., this job thing, it could get pretty ugly," Janet whispered.

"I'm sure it'll be fine," I lied. "You're one of the good guys, they'll take that into consideration. And don't worry about Clifford, we'll find him."

"Really?" She sounded dubious.

"Really," I lied again.

The truth was that I hardly knew Clifford Brice and had no idea where to look for him. But I had to try: Uncle Tito was looking for Clifford, too.

I got dressed and made myself a thermos of tea. While the tea was steeping, I sent Boris an e-mail. The man's a creature of the night; I wouldn't have been able to rouse him if I'd tried. The e-mail gave him an abbreviated version of the latest turn of events and told him I was headed to Brooklyn. Before I left the apartment, I clipped my .32-caliber Beretta to the back of my jeans.

It wasn't a coincidence that I owned a pistol. As I drove out to Brooklyn, I remember thinking that this favor for Janet Fein was beginning to follow a familiar pattern. The first time Boris and I worked together had started out innocently, too. When we met, I'd just given up on a ten-year career doing leveraged buyouts for a big Wall Street firm. It had been ten years of looking at grand old family businesses that the children didn't want and figuring out how to turn them into cash. My firm rarely tried to save the companies; usually it paid the greedy kids with money they didn't know they already had. In most cases, the fathers or grandfathers had sweated blood to build a future, and the current generation, having enjoyed the spoils, didn't want any part of it. The bricks and mortar alone often bought enough credit to satisfy junior. Then we'd take over and liquidate or turn the assets into some more profitable use before bailing out. I had made some money, but I also lost my wife and my moral compass along the way.

Boris had his own sad story. In his case, greed and ambition had destroyed old friendships and nearly ruined his academic career. We met over a crisis involving martini olives, and became friends because misery loves company. When Harry Noble, our landlord, got himself into trouble by getting too big for his britches and trying to pull a fast one on some very slippery people, we decided to help him out. It was really just a lark, which we both agreed would provide a much needed distraction. The distraction took on a life of its own and almost consumed us both.

Fortunately, Boris and I complimented each other very well. The doctor turned out to be equal parts analytical genius and technological snake charmer. I played the straight man. After looking at hundreds of business operations, I could walk into most situations and figure out what was wrong in a couple of days; sometimes it only took a few hours. In the end, we solved the problem and managed to turn a nice profit, which made Harry Noble so giddy he actually gave us our apartments. That first experience had launched our partnership, but it also set an unfortunate precedent—when you're dealing with hard-luck cases, it is never as easy as it looks.

It took less than an hour to get to Clifford's old neighborhood. Using the road map, I started cruising the local streets, hoping I'd get lucky. You never know, the poor kid could have been walking around in a daze, not sure where to go or what to do. On a hunch, I parked near the house Clifford had lived in with his mother and started poking around in the yard. I didn't find the little boy, but after I'd been there a few minutes an ugly little man with colorful tattoos popped out of the basement. He started yelling at me in Spanish and waved a tire iron under my nose. I decided to move on.

Not long after that I turned onto Berriman Street, scene of all the excitement the night before. The cops, firemen, and paramedics where gone, but the yellow crime-scene tape was still blocking the entrance to the alley. I parked the car again and got out. Across the way, at the National Manufacturing Corporation, the HELP WANTED sign was still posted, and it looked like business as usual. I decided to see for myself.

The factory took up about a third of a city block. You couldn't walk completely around it, but if you started from the Berriman Street side it was possible to make a big U and cover the perimeter. As I rounded the first corner at the bottom of the block, I walked smack into a shopping cart brimming with redeemable cans and bottles.

"What's your damn hurry, son?"

It was the old street wizard. He turned his body sideways, crossed his arms, and closed one eye. With the open eye, he gave me a thorough inspection. That done, the old coot straightened up and stood staring at me, scratching his long gray beard. His fingers were coal-black with grime, and my scalp started to itch as I watched him. The wizard was a very tall, thin old man who wore a cockeyed, dented hat made from aluminum foil and adorned with ribbons. His coat looked like a heavy quilted robe. You could see that there were many layers of clothing underneath it.

"I was ... ah ... just going ... well ... for a walk," I babbled.

"Where'd you learn to speak English like that?" he snorted.

"I beg your pardon, sir," I said, bowing politely, as my composure returned, "it's just that you startled me."

"Is that so? How do you think I feel? Strange people dashing out of the shadows, barreling into me like runaway freight trains?" He turned sideways again and closed one eye, his face screwed up like a prune.

"Well, again, I'm very sorry," I said contritely. "Allow me to introduce myself. The name is James Joseph Donovan. I am at your service."

"Don-o-van," he repeated, trying the name out on his tongue. "I once knew a man name of Donovan. Patrick Donovan. The fellow was a philosopher. He worked behind the stick in a fine old pub up in the Woodlawn area. That's a territory to our north, known as the Bronx."

As soon as he finished speaking, the wizard snapped back into his sideways pose, one eye closed tight as a walnut. He was sizing me up.

"I can't say that I know your friend," I told him, "but, if he likes to drink beer and plays darts, he's probably a relative."

That seemed to settle the matter. My new acquaintance opened both of his eyes and relaxed, leaning an arm on the handle of his shopping cart. "To the local folk, I'm the wizard, an E-nig-ma," he said profoundly. "But, to you Don-o-van, to you I am Doc."

He managed a low theatrical bow, then extended a filthy hand which I shook freely. "Remember this," he warned, spreading his arms. "I am a sorcerer of tremendous power. I walk these streets in humble rags because it is best to conceal the true nature of my mission."

He spoke with a soft Southern accent. The trip from Dixieland to Flatlands Avenue probably made quite a story.

"What's your mission, Doctor?" I asked.

"I am Doc to you and to all those who earn my respect," he insisted, correcting me.

"Okay then, Doc." I waited for an answer. It didn't come.

"What's your mission, Doc?" I asked, again.

"Why, to serve and protect!"

Naturally.

"Would you mind if I asked you a few questions?" I began carefully. "I'm new to the area and I'd be obliged if you could help to set me straight."

Without warning, he dropped into a crouch and put a finger to his lips. I watched as he reached into the shopping cart and slowly removed a stout walking stick. The old boy backed up against the wall of the factory and stood ready, as if he expected

53

a frontal assault. He remained like that for a few minutes, slowly scanning up and down the street. When he was satisfied that the coast was clear, he lowered his stick and turned back to me as if nothing had happened.

"The very first thing to remember, boy, is the dogs. Don't forget about the dogs!"

"Which dogs are those, Doc?" I asked, a little confused.

"I think," he said, straightening up, "that the time has come for a small donation to the cause. Don't you agree?"

Crazy like a fox, I thought. "Would ten dollars be a respectable contribution?"

"Not nearly as respectable as twenty," he said quickly.

"Twenty dollars?!" I sounded shocked. "That's a small fortune, Doc."

He looked uncomfortable, as if he'd just blown a good thing. I let him dangle a little longer, then reluctantly produced two tens.

"The cause is a worthy one," I said graciously. "Now, please, tell me more."

"Ah, finally a man who understands the value of wisdom," Doc said with satisfaction. He carefully folded the bills and slipped one into each of his shoes before continuing. "Well, son, as I was saying, there's a pack a wild dogs living over yonder on the landfill. They can be fighting mean when they're hungry. More than once, now, I've had to rescue the Negro ladies from them. Yes, sir."

Wild dogs? In New York City? I didn't believe him.

"Speaking of the ladies," I began, "one of them was a friend of mine. Her name was Ruby, Ruby Brice. I don't suppose you remember her?"

He stepped back and turned sideways. "You a cop?" he demanded, closing an eye.

"No, Doc, I'm just trying to help her kid. Did you know Ruby had a little boy?"

He relaxed a bit.

"Surely. I knew Miss Ruby well, though I never met the boy.

54

Didn't I share my wealth with her?" He indicated the basket full of bottles and cans. "And, of course, I protected her from those pesky mongrels."

He took a quick look around, to make sure the dogs weren't trying to sneak up behind him.

"Then you know that Ruby was killed?" I asked.

He hesitated, then nodded his head.

"The night she was killed, you didn't happen to see anything? I mean, anything that would help me find the person who killed her?" I was taking a chance.

"What I saw that night was a shiny black motor car. It was parked over by the landfill. There was exhaust smoke coming out of its pipe and it was bouncing up and down. I already told the policemen." His voice became mechanical as he grew tense. "They put my picture in the newspaper," he admitted after a pause. "Made me out to be a fool. Worse still, they directed the bad one to me. Set me up. It was enough with them dogs, now I got this. Pretty soon, I'll have to take my magic elsewhere."

"Who's the bad one?" I asked as casually as possible.

"Why the killer, of course," he replied in earnest.

"What do you mean, Doc? The cops are saying they know the man that killed Ruby. They have him in jail."

His face showed contempt. "Sure, just like they caught the heathen who stole my shoes back in June," he spat. "I'm talking about the man driving that black car. I have ears, haven't I? Didn't I hear Miss Ruby calling out and moanin'? To my eternal regret, I mistook those sounds for the requirements of her profession." The old guy was genuinely upset.

"You said the papers directed the bad one to you. What does that mean, Doc? Have you seen the driver of the black car?"

His whole body grew rigid, defensive.

"Hey, Doc, it's okay, really."

I'd asked one too many questions. He started shifting his weight back and forth.

"I haven't seen the man," he whispered finally, "but I've seen that big black car. He's been cruisin' the streets searching for

55

me from behind those dark windows. They tell me he's gone and killed another woman; burned her at the stake. Forced me into hiding, he has. This is the first I've been out in days."

He was describing the same car Clifford Brice remembered. It was Tito's car.

"Doc, is there anything strange or unusual about the black car? Something that would help me find it?"

He screwed his face up and concentrated on the question.

"Anything at all?" I asked again after a long interval.

Old Doc started fingering his walking stick nervously.

"I better be going," he said at last.

The guy was spooked.

"About the car, Doc, can't you tell me anything?"

He was tinkering with the contents of his shopping cart, preparing for departure, pretending not to hear me. I repeated the question, only this time I held a twenty in my hand. Doc's eyes focused on the money. He wet his lips.

"*Kitty,*" he said, snatching the bill.

"What's *kitty?*" I asked hopefully.

"Don't know," he said, carefully folding the bill.

"But what am I supposed to do with *kitty?*" I sighed helplessly. "I don't have the foggiest idea what that means."

"Didn't I just tell you, Don-o-van? Neither do I." He turned his cart around. "Now, I'll say good day to you!"

With those parting words, Doc, the old wizard of Flatlands Avenue, rattled off down the street.

As I walked back to my car, my eye caught the HELP WANTED sign outside the National Manufacturing Corporation again. For some reason, the sign seemed to be calling out to me. I decided to see where it led me.

"Morning," I said, flashing my biggest smile.

"We don't want any, honey," the receptionist said.

She was sitting behind a thick sheet of bullet-proof glass, typing into a computer. She used a pencil to hunt and peck because her three-inch paste-on fingernails made anything else impractical. The woman was at least forty, but she was working hard to hide the evidence; her hair was dyed platinum and she apparently applied her make-up with a pallet knife.

"Hey, I'm not selling anything," I told her, still smiling. "I saw the sign out front and thought maybe there was an opening. Now that I've seen you, I'm *really* hoping there is."

I dropped the smile and gave her a look that meant business.

"Go-wan," she sputtered, obviously pleased. "That stuff won't dazzle me, honey. Besides, a big, good-lookin' man like you don't need or wanna a job here." She leaned forward confidentially. "This place is a rat's hole. Try somewheres else."

Strike two.

"Look, Alice," I guessed, reading a nameplate on the counter, "give me a break."

"My name ain't Alice, sweetie. She's gettin' coffee. I'm Patsy."

"Okay, Patsy. Look, I really need some work right now."

"What'd you do?" she asked in a little-girl voice. "You been a bad boy?"

"I been to Atlantic City and stayed too long," I sighed, trying to look broke.

"Oh, honey, do I know about that," Patsy cried sympathetically. "Last month, I shoulda just mailed my paycheck to Donald Trump care of that goddamn Taj Mahal casino. I cried all the way home on the bus."

The telephone rang and Patsy held up an index finger for me to wait. I stood in front of her bullet-proof window, trying my best to look rugged and forlorn, while she dealt with the call. Given the fingernail situation, it took her a while to write down the message. Finally she stood up, straightened her skirt, and holding the message between her index finger and thumb, she sashayed into the back office, out of sight. I thought I'd lost her, but a couple of minutes later, the inside door opened and there she was in her skin-tight leather mini and push-up bra, holding a clipboard with a job application form on it.

57

"Here you go, baby," she cooed, holding the clipboard and a pen out for me.

When I went over to take the application, she slipped her arm around my waist and grabbed a handful.

"Now, don't forget me, sugar," she whispered, squeezing playfully.

It was her turn to wink.

I took the application over to a folding chair against the wall and started filling in the blanks. While I was busy scratching away with the ballpoint pen, the street door opened and an old man in a gaudy, full-length mink coat burst into the room.

"Yo, babe," he shouted, pointing at the door.

On the other side of the plexiglass, Patsy looked worried. "Sorry, Mr. Greenberg," she said, buzzing him into the inner office.

"Yeah, right, whatever," he snarled.

Mr. Greenberg had the door open and was about to step across the threshold when he noticed me.

"Who the fuck are you?" he demanded.

"Donovan, J. J. Donovan," I said, standing up. "I'm looking for work."

"What makes you think we got jobs here?" he snapped.

"There's a sign out front," I reminded him.

"Oh, yeah, well, don't get your hopes up, bubba." Greenberg started into the office, then stopped suddenly and turned back to me. "Where you from, Donovan?" he asked, sizing me up more carefully.

"Here and there," I said evasively. "I've done a lot of different things—welding, roll forming, production management. It's all here on the application."

Greenberg was eyeing me suspiciously.

"Does it say why you picked *this* factory?" He smirked.

"I told you, there's a sign outside," I said, smiling brightly.

"So you did, Donovan." He nodded his head. "So you did."

I stood there waiting while Greenberg drilled me with his beady eyes. "Okay, you gimme the application," he ordered. "I'll take

58

a look and if anything comes up, we'll call you." He snatched the clipboard and stepped into the inner office. That was it—no good-bye, just the door slamming shut in my face.

I'd had enough of East New York for one day. Blowing Patsy a kiss, I left the National Manufacturing Corporation. My car was still parked where I'd left it and had all its tires, which was probably lucky. I stood next to the Nova for a minute and took another look at the neighborhood. It was a desolate place, so inhospitable that wild dogs hunted its streets in packs. This was not a place for Clifford Brice or any other child, and Boris and I were going to have to do something about it.

SEVEN

. . .

My trip home started out just fine. I managed to locate the highway and was making pretty good time until I reached the Mill Basin Bridge. After that, the traffic started to back up, and before long the road was a parking lot. Fortunately I had my cell phone.

The first person I called was Janet Fein. Her number rang four times before the machine picked up. I left a message and my cell phone number, then paged her beeper. I must have had the wrong beeper number because somebody named Zipper called back and tried to sell me a gram of cocaine. I took a deep breath, then punched in our work number. Boris answered the telephone on the first ring.

"Hi, it's me," I said, pleasantly enough.

"Where have you been?" he growled.

"Well, the short answer is Brooklyn," I cracked. "And, no, I didn't find Clifford Brice."

"No one has," he muttered, sounding worried." The child has been missing for twenty-four hours."

"Have you heard from Janet?" I asked.

"Unfortunately, I have heard from Janet Fein." Boris sighed. "The meeting with her superiors did not go well. She has been suspended indefinitely, pending a full investigation."

"You're kidding," I stammered. "She's given them her entire life. How can they do this to her?"

60

"It is shameless and idiotic, of course," he said seriously. "But, the best solution for her, for everyone concerned, would be to find the child."

"Hey, I found the old wizard," I cried, remembering the good news. "Actually, I kind of bumped into him. He is quite a character."

"One would expect as much," Boris mumbled.

"Well yeah, but there's more to the guy than a funny suit of clothes. In between the wacky stuff, he has lucid flashes. The old man fancies himself the neighborhood defender of virtue, says he looks after all the ladies. The night Ruby Brice was killed he saw a black car like the one Clifford remembers Uncle Tito driving, and he's positive he heard Ruby's voice crying out from inside the car. He didn't do anything because he thought she was putting on a show for her trick, but he's sure about Ruby and about the car, and I believe him."

"Would anyone else?" Boris asked cynically.

"No, probably not," I said honestly. "But, check this out, he claims the black car has been cruising the neighborhood looking for him. Blames the newspapers for putting the murderer onto him."

"He might just have a point," Boris mused. "After all, we know that this Uncle Tito character has been in the area." He started making a little humming noise, a sure sign he was about to drift off.

"Oh, yeah, before I forget," I cried, interrupting his train of thought, "I stopped at that factory on Berriman. The National Manufacturing Corporation. You know, across the street from *the alley*."

"And what would have been the purpose of such a visit?" he snorted.

"Well, aside from the fact that Ruby Brice specifically mentioned the place to Clifford, they had a help-wanted sign out front. I decided to see what kind of jobs they had open. Look, there's no longer any question in my mind about this Brice murder. Something is rotten and we're gonna find out what it is and fix it. At some point, I thought we might need a presence in the neighborhood. You know, a base of operations."

"Ah, you've got this business all figured out, have you?" he asked sarcastically.

"Nothing's been figured out," I snapped. "On the other hand, it doesn't take a genius to see that Janet was right to question the official version of the murder. And frankly, there's just something about the whole stinking affair—the murders, the attitude of the cops, that horrible neighborhood. If we don't do something about it, I'll never get a decent night's sleep again."

"And so you volunteered to work in a factory?" Boris sounded amused.

"Okay, smart guy, let it go. Besides, I don't think they'll be calling me back."

"For now, perhaps the best thing would be to focus on finding the boy," Boris suggested diplomatically. "When you get back here, we'll contact Janet and try to piece together a map of places Clifford would consider safe havens."

Before I could agree with him, the phone went dead. *Beep*—disconnect—dead battery! I threw the cellphone into the backseat, turned off the air conditioning, and rolled the windows down. The way my day was going, it seemed wise not to let the engine overheat.

I doubt there's any good place to get stuck in a traffic jam, but there can't be any worse than New York City. The highways are ugly and dirty, and the frustration brings out the worst in the natives. Every few minutes, the cars would all move a few hundred feet and the horns would start blaring as drivers jockeyed for position. There was no shoulder to pull onto because that was jammed with cars who'd tried to use it as a fast lane around the delay. As a result, any car with a problem, like overheating, had to stay where it was, complicating the snarl even further. The traffic mess was quickly going from bad to worse.

To avoid the madness around me, I put the Yankees game on the radio and pretended I was in a field box next to first base. It worked for an inning or two. The bombers were piling up runs against a weak Detroit team, and the crack of Yankee bats was a good substitute for the honking horns. I could have sat there pleasantly enjoying the game for a long time, but it wasn't the kind of day when things worked out pleasantly.

The cars on my right started to move, causing a mad rush to switch lanes. Unfortunately, it was only a temporary opening and traffic ground to a halt again. When I looked over, the car next to mine had moved up several car lengths. The elderly couple in the new Lincoln Continental had been replaced by three big, fresh-faced kids in a shiny new convertible. They were drinking beer and acting stupid. I tried to ignore them, but they were leaning on the horn and had their stereo turned way up. To compensate, I turned my radio up a bit, then sat back and closed my eyes, listening to the play-by-play.

"Hey, man!"

The kid screamed so loudly I flinched. He was leaning in through the passenger-side window, and his beer breath filled the car.

"What's your problem?" I snapped, turning my body to face him.

"What's my problem?" he sneered. "You're my fucking problem, asshole. This is Mets country, dickhead, and we didn't give you permission to listen to no fuckin' Yankees."

He looked back over his shoulder at his buddies who cheered him on with hoots and whistles. I took a deep breath. I had just turned thirty-nine years old—my days of fighting young bullies were supposed to be over.

"Tell you what," I said, evenly. "You get your face out of my car like a good boy, and I'll pretend this never happened."

There was probably a better way to put that, but it didn't come out when I opened my mouth. I expected him to either walk away or challenge me. I didn't expect him to spray a can of beer in my face. He must have shaken it pretty good, because the spray blinded me and pretty much coated the inside of the car.

I used my sleeve to get the suds out of my eyes, then stepped out of the Nova and walked slowly around it. The kid with the beer can backed away from the car and then threw the empty can at me as I approached him. The blood started to pulse in my temple. The fact that this boy thought he could assault people for his own amusement made me very angry. He just stood in the road, arms folded across his big chest, grinning at me. His two buddies jumped down to stand by his side.

I'll never know what the big dope expected, but he sure looked surprised when I veered to the right and kicked the guy next to him in the kneecap. His friend hit the ground with a howl as I dropped into a crouch. The beer man took a mighty swing, caught a fistful of air, and lost his balance. His crew cut was sculpted into a funky design that included a ponytail growing out of the back of his head. I grabbed the ponytail and rammed the big kid's head into the driver's door of the convertible, where it left a nice dent. The third guy ran around to the other side of the vehicle, so I couldn't get to him, and started yelling something about his father's car and how I was gonna pay for the damages.

I stepped back, thinking the fight was over. It was a mistake; I should have known better. While I was standing there staring at the wimp who'd run away, the first guy, the one I kicked in the knee, snuck up behind me and jumped on my back. That gave the beer man a chance to get back into it. I struggled, but once they both got a hold on me there wasn't much I could do. When it looked like his friends had me under control, the daddy's boy came back and took a couple of cheap shots. There was nothing behind his punches, but he was wearing a ring that cut me above the left eye.

"Whaddya say now, tough guy?" he hissed.

"How's about we hear him say the Yankees suck," the beer man suggested.

64

"Yeah, yeah, and the Mets rule," chimed in the guy with the sore knee.

It was unbelievable. They had me pinned on the hood of my own car in the middle of the Brooklyn-Queens Expressway, and were beating me because I'd been listening to a Yankee game. This is the kind of stuff you cannot make up.

"Okay, enough," I gasped. "This has gotten way out of hand."

"You bet your ass it has, Yankee man," Daddy's boy shouted. "Look at my fuckin' car! This shit is what you get from hangin' in the Bronx with all them spic Yankees fans." He cocked his arm, ready for another swing.

"Who you callin' spic, white boy?"

We all turned. Standing no more than ten feet away was a young Hispanic man in sunglasses and a red bandana. He was of medium height, with a weight lifter's build, and sported a thin black goatee. He wore a sleeveless T-shirt with DOMINICA in bold letters across the chest, and had a large tattoo running down his muscular right forearam. The tattoo spelled out YANKEES. Behind him, a group of about five or six more teenagers, some wearing Yankees hats or uniform shirts, stood with their arms folded, looking very serious. The guy with the tattoo had a toothpick in his mouth and he rolled it back and forth as he waited for an answer. Nobody said or did anything for about a minute.

"Yo, I asked you a question, faggot," the guy with the tooth-pick growled.

The beer man, the big guy who'd started the whole thing, let go of me and stepped out front to face the Dominican delegation. The bump on his head hadn't taught him a thing.

"He said *spic,* like in a general way," Beer man smiled. "But, I guess that pretty much covers alla you scumbags."

There was some shuffling of feet and murmuring, but nothing happened.

"Oh, I see." Toothpick nodded.

"Why you beatin' this man?" he asked, pointing at me.

"*These* man?" the big guy replied, mocking him. "*These* man

65

is a fucking Yankees fan and we been teachin' him some manners. 'Cause it's like this, my bro, we don' like no stinkin' Yankees fans 'round here."

The beer man stepped up to the guy with the toothpick and poked him in the chest to punctuate his answer. That was all it took. Fists started flying and connecting, guys were yelling and shouting, and other people jumped out of their cars to come watch or join the fight. The guy with the bad knee let go of me and ran to help his friend. I got up and wiped the blood out of my eye. I was sitting in the middle of a brawl and nobody was paying any attention to me. It was like being inside a tornado. A bottle whizzed past my head, reminding me to get out while I had the chance. I thought about giving Daddy's boy a parting shot, but he was busy trying to duck and cover as a guy in a Don Mattingly shirt cleaned his clock. There was nothing I could add to that picture.

In the midst of this melee, the cars in front of mine finally started moving again. I took my shirt off and wiped my face again. Then I walked around the car and slid behind the wheel. I used my shirt to clean the beer off the inside of the windshield and started the engine. Nobody paid any attention; they were all too busy burning up testosterone. I put the car into gear and eased her forward. As the lane opened up in front of me and we started to pick up speed, I turned the Yankees game up as loud as it would go and left the Mets fans behind me.

By the time I got to the Upper West Side, it was dark. Instead of going to the parking garage, I pulled the Nova up in front of my building and asked Manny Santos to have it cleaned. When he saw my face and heard the story, I thought he was going to load his boys into the Nova and drive right back out to Brooklyn. It was too late for that, but he changed into a blue Yankees T-shirt with Derek Jeter's name and number on the back and ordered all the other dominoes players to change into team colors, too. He was so busy making a statement, he forgot to extort beer money out of me.

As the elevator groaned its way to the seventeenth floor, I decided to explore the knots and bumps on my face. After all, one look had fired Manny up pretty good. The family profile was sore and bruised, but that didn't bother me nearly as much as the cut over my left eye. The stupid thing was going to keep on bleeding until I got stitches or a butterfly bandage on it, and then it would probably leave a scar.

Once inside my apartment, I found a light on in the kitchen and a note on the counter from Boris. He was upstairs in Madame Karina's apartment and suggested that I come up as soon as possible. Before I went anywhere, I needed to put a bag of ice on my face, take a hot shower, and fix myself a martini, maybe two. While the water heated up in the shower, I chilled a dirty vodka martini and added a couple of colossal Spanish olives. Holding a Baggie full of ice cubes over my left eye, I started rummaging for food. The refrigerator yielded a day-old baguette, sliced turkey breast, and Swiss cheese. I constructed an impressive sandwich and took it to the bedroom. The light was blinking on the message machine, but I decided to ignore it.

After a long, hot shower, a second martini, and the foot-long sandwich, I felt strong enough to face Madame Karina and her entourage. As always, I tucked a bottle of Rémy Martin under my arm before heading to the stairs.

Madame Karina Mariya Petrovsky-Simenon-Van Buren-Kostopolis lives above me in the penthouse apartment. It takes up the entire eighteenth floor. Madame Karina has been a resident since the building opened in 1952. That was the year her third husband, Victor Kostopolis, passed away.

"And so, when Victor left me, it was time to explore the next phase of my life, darling!"

There have been many phases.

Karina Mariya is a small, delicate nonagenarian who dyes her hair red and dresses like a peacock. She was born in Moscow at least ninety years ago. Since she steadfastly refuses to admit her age, I've been forced to try other means to date her. Using information gleaned from her stories, I have concluded that Karina was born no later than 1910, though it is probable she appeared much earlier.

In any event, Madame Karina has lived a long and remarkable life. For starters, how many people have forty-six letters in their name? The woman grew up during the twilight years of the Russian aristocracy, was a witness to the Bolshevik revolution, and later survived nearly a year as a fugitive while escaping to Paris with her family. When she got to be a little older, Karina started collecting husbands.

The first was Jacques Simenon, an artist. They were married when she was seventeen.

"Darling boy, he was the most romantic love of my life!"

Unfortunately, Jacques suffered a ruptured appendix and died after three short years of marriage. He left Karina a small collection of paintings and barely enough money to pay for his funeral. Next came Perry Van Buren. Perry was the shy, sensitive type. He was from New York City, where his family owned a bank or two. Over his father's objections, Perry married Karina in 1931 and brought her to America. This second marriage didn't last nearly as long as the first. Young Perry made an embarrassing error at one of the family banks and decided to shoot himself instead of facing up to the disgrace.

"My banker was incredibly vain, don't you see, darling? After all, he was guilty of no crime, and they don't banish men for stupidity. He preferred to be a dead gentleman rather than a live fool. Pride! Perry, my banker, was a sweet man, but a complete boob!"

In Madame Karina's case, the third time was the charm. Her next and last husband was a large, powerfully built Greek named Victor Kostopolis. He was old enough to be her father and rich enough not to give it a second thought. In the pictures I've seen,

Victor has a strong, carved chin, a bright smile, and sad, intelligent eyes. He was her savior.

"I was prisoner at a horrible dinner party. Do you believe, they were serving cocktails? Not a glass of champagne to be found anywhere. It was primitive, my dear. But then Victor arrived, and I was rescued."

They were married in June of 1935 and charged through the next seventeen years, hopping from one continent to the next. When Victor died, Karina felt it was finally time to settle down. She chose our building.

"It whispered to me, darling. I was able to build my nest in the sky."

She also decided that it would be a widow's nest. A trio of husbands was plenty for one lifetime.

"Dear boy, I have had three of them! And now, all of their memories vying for my attention! It is more than enough."

Instead of complicating her spiritual life with a fourth husband, Karina began a serious study of mysticism and the occult. During the next forty years, she dabbled in all sorts of religions and sects, while also studying related sciences like psychology and anthropology. Using her maiden name, Ms. Katrina Petrovsky has published more than twenty books and hundreds of articles on subjects ranging from the *Kama Sutra* to the Salem witch trials. On matters related to spiritual or supernatural events, she is recognized as an authority.

To balance an otherwise respectable academic reputation, Karina also does astrological charts and readings for a very select group of clients.

"*Pfuit,* they come to me like timid babies, seeking guidance. It is ridiculous! I tell them to attack life . . . à toute force, à tout hasard, à tout prix!"

Madame Karina has a few screws loose. In our building that makes her one of the gang. By New York City standards, she's basically unremarkable, just another eccentric. But in Ohmygosh, Arkansas, they'd probably have her committed.

Naturally, she and Boris became close friends. This kinship didn't evolve solely on the basis of their shared Russian heritage, though I have to put up with plenty of that stuff, too. I think on some cosmic level their idiosyncrasies complement each other. Back here on earth, the explanation for this mutual affection society is more obvious: Boris never had a mother figure, and Karina never had a child. I could be wrong, but I doubt it.

The door to Madame Karina's apartment was unlocked. As I entered the foyer, the sounds of a piano and a cello greeted me. The sonata was coming from deep inside the apartment, but I could hear it clearly. The music was appropriate for the milieu. Looking up at the chipped facade of our slightly shabby, unimaginative building from the street outside, you would never guess that it contained an apartment like Karina's.

The penthouse has seven rooms including the kitchen, and all of them are large and comfortable. There are picture windows in the perimeter walls that fill the rooms with light during the day and frame the bright silhouettes of the city at night. The terraces, which surround the apartment, are tiled with glazed terra cotta, and open up behind the elevator shaft to form a nice-sized patio. All of the rooms, including the kitchen, have French doors leading onto these balconies.

The upper floors of the building are stepped, so they grow progressively smaller as the building rises. Karina can look down from her perch and see the urban answer to the terraced effect as patios fan out for seven floors below her. It's a mixed blessing. If she fell off the penthouse balcony she'd only travel about ten feet, and chances are good that she'd land in one of my plantings. On the other hand, Karina once had a lap dog named Pierre who liked to relieve himself while strolling along the upper deck. Few tears were shed when Pierre moved on to accept his next incarnation.

Once inside the front hall, I followed the custom of the house and removed my shoes. Madame Karina's floors are covered

70

with handwoven Chinese and Persian carpets that must be treated gently. I added my loafers to the odd collection of shoes by the door, and tried to avoid knocking anything over as I moved down the hall. The place is cluttered with souvenirs from all over the world. Carved jade and porcelain from China, incense burners from India, a balalaika from Russia, watercolors from Japan. But the most curious pieces are the angels. There are hundreds of them, and they seem to be everywhere you look. Carved angels. Sculpted angels. Angels in wood, marble, and glass. Bronze castings of angels. Prints and paintings of angels. Angels!

The angelic images, in all their many forms and poses, accompany you down the passageway. They're in the kitchen, which you leave on the left, and the dining room, which opens up on the right. In fact, they continue on down the hall and beyond. But if you walk east from the dining room across the hall and through an archway, you will find yourself in the living room. There are no angels in the living room.

This space is reserved for the small art collection Karina inherited from her first husband, Jacques Simenon. Turns out the paintings had some value after all. There are four canvases—a Kandinsky, a Matisse, and two Chagalls. It doesn't matter what they're worth, because they aren't for sale. The paintings will end up in a museum someday or, more likely, she'll take them with her.

If you leave by the door at the southern end of the living room you wind up back in the hallway, directly in front of the study. To your left and farther down the hallway are the bedrooms. The first door you come to is Madame Karina's room. It occupies the southeast corner of the floor. Next comes the guest room, with a private bath and terrace. There is a third bed-and-bath combination located down a little side corridor. This room is for Karina's personal secretary.

Karina's secretaries usually come from Barnard College, which is about a mile and a half north of us and across the street from the main campus of Columbia University. In addition to English, they are required to speak French, Italian, or Russian, and must be able to assist in the preparation of her manuscripts. In exchange for these talents and their companionship, Madame Karina provides room, board, and her own personal brand of instruction. In some cases she has also subsidized the cost of tuition. It's a good deal, especially since there are no domestic chores to worry about.

The cooking, cleaning, and marketing are the responsibility of Mrs. Martha McCabe. Martha's a tough old girl whose official title is housekeeper. If you know what's good for you, you stay on Martha McCabe's good side. She lives in her own little apartment on the twelfth floor. Every day, from seven in the morning till six forty-five in the evening, Martha is busy in the penthouse. But when the clock nears seven, she rushes downstairs to watch that day's videotape recording of *Days of Our Lives*.

The final room is the study. It's a large, messy, comfortable place that strongly suggests a late-nineteenth-century Parisian salon. The walls are lined with overstuffed bookcases and there are a couple of antique chairs I'm not afraid to sit on. In the corner, across from the entrance, is a baby grand piano. At the other end of the room, to the right of the fireplace, two desks have been pushed together. This is where Madame Karina and her secretary work.

I made my way slowly down the hall and stood in front of the study's big double doors. The music was coming from inside. It was a Beethoven sonata; Opus 69 in A major. After all the years I'd spent around Boris, I knew that much. And since there was cello music, it meant Boris was probably inside sawing away at his oversize fiddle. I turned the doorknob gently and slipped into the room, trying not to disturb the performance. As I suspected, Boris was seated on a sturdy wooden chair with his cello wedged between his knees. He'd wrapped himself around the instrument and was busily coating his black trousers with rosin dust as he fiddled away with his bow. Next to him, Clara Reland, Karina's sweet, young secretary, was tickling the keys on the baby grand.

72

The musicians were concentrating on their duet. Madame Karina was comfortably seated in her usual chair by the fireplace. Janet Fein sat next to her and looked as if she was about to fall asleep. It was a very warm and peaceful scene; the fire crackling in the background, the music a little sad, but rich. I let my gaze travel around the room, looking for a good seat upon which to rest my weary bones. There was a Victorian loveseat in the corner with an old blanket piled on it. I tiptoed over and lifted the blanket, then stopped short. Underneath the blanket, curled up in a little ball, was Clifford Brice.

"What's going on here?" I blurted out, bringing everything to a stop.

"Hush up, you silly man," Madame Karina ordered. "Do you want to awaken him?"

"What I want is an explanation," I said, lowering my voice. "I've just spent the better part of twelve hours searching for this kid."

They just sat and stared at me.

"What's the matter now?" I demanded.

"My question exactly," Boris stammered. "Have you, by any chance, taken a look at yourself in the mirror?"

Actually, I'd purposely avoided glancing in the bathroom mirror during and after my shower. Seeing the damage just made it hurt worse.

"I had a little trouble," I mumbled self-consciously. "It's no big deal."

"With all due respect, old man, you look like a badly dimpled squash," Boris added seriously.

"James, dear boy, come and sit next to Karina," she coaxed. "Tell me your whole, sordid tale."

Madame Karina made it sound like an invitation for some tender loving care, but I knew the old girl better than that—she just wanted the cognac I had tucked under my arm. There was no use arguing with her. She had all the powers of the occult on her side.

EIGHT

...

Six-thirty the next morning my telephone started ringing. Second day in a row. I hate waking up to the telephone. To make matters worse, it had taken two full snifters of Karina's medicine to calm me down the night before, and now the inside of my head hurt almost as much as the outside. The only good news was that I'd snored right through the nightmares.

"What is it?" I snarled into the receiver.

"Mr. Donovan?" The voice had the stiff formality of a legal eagle.

I admitted to being myself.

"This is Jonathon Powers, Mr. Donovan. A mutual friend suggested that I contact you."

I doubted that we had any mutual friends.

"I am an attorney representing Mr. Stanley Greenberg," he continued. "Mr. Greenberg has asked me to discuss retaining your services in connection with a rather delicate matter."

I didn't say anything. Powers was annoying.

"Mr. Donovan, are you still there?"

"Yes, Mr. Powers, I'm still here," I said. "Perhaps you could give me some more information. For instance, what exactly are you talking about?"

"Well." He coughed, lawyerlike, smoothing his ruffled feathers and searching for the right words. "My client is concerned about possible misconduct on the part of his business partner, and wishes to have the matter discreetly investigated."

"And just who is your client?" I asked, proving I hadn't been listening.

"Mr. Greenberg is co-owner of the National Manufacturing Corporation, a custom display-and-fixture business located in the East New York section of Brooklyn."

Small world. His client was the nasty old man in the mink coat.

"Mr. Donovan?" The lawyer was getting jittery.

"Perhaps I should meet your Mr. Greenberg," I said finally.

"Okay, great!" Powers sounded relieved. "I'm sure that can be arranged."

"Good, arrange it," I said, and hung up on him.

He called back about fifteen minutes later, waking me again. This time we agreed upon a time and place for the meeting. I used the opportunity to tell Powers that he wouldn't be welcome to join us. He didn't like that too much, but it didn't matter. I put the receiver in the cradle, swallowed three aspirin and a big glass of water, then rolled over and went back to sleep.

Four hours later, I opened my eyes again. Sunshine was streaming through the bedroom windows and the noise inside my head had gone away. In fact, as I lay in bed adjusting to the new day, I decided that things were actually looking up. Clifford Brice was safely stashed in Karina's apartment, and the call from Greenberg's lawyer had opened up a whole new line of investigation. After all, Powers wasn't calling me about an opening for a spot welder. Mr. Greenberg had gone to a lot of trouble looking me up, and he wasn't the kind of guy who wasted his time.

I took a shower, got dressed, and went back up to Madame Karina's apartment. By the end of the previous evening, we had all agreed that Clifford Brice should stay in the penthouse. It

75

made the most sense. He had no prior connection to Karina, making it virtually impossible for Uncle Tito or anybody else to trace him to her, and a penthouse is pretty easy real estate to defend. Besides, Madame Karina had full-time help, a well-stocked refrigerator, and a guest room with clean sheets on the bed. As a bonus, there was the innocent Clara to read him bedtime stories. All in all, it was not a bad deal for young Clifford. My biggest concern was hiding him from the authorities. Janet Fein was already on suspension; if they discovered that we'd been hiding the Brice kid, there's no telling what would happen. On the other hand, the child had been left in their care once before, and it hadn't worked out too well.

When I got to the eighteenth floor, I was pleased to discover that the front door was closed and locked for a change. I rang the bell and waited for Martha McCabe to let me in. On her best days Martha can be difficult, so I hesitated before ringing the bell a second time. But she kept me standing out there for a pretty long time.

"And just what do you think you're doing, James Joseph Donovan?" she thundered, swinging the door wide, catching me with my finger still on the buzzer. "Do ya think I'm deaf, ringing and ringing that bell?"

"What do you think I'm doing?" I yelled back. "I've been standing out here so long I'll need a second shave."

"Is that so? Well, then you can just go back where you came from, you awful man, and stop bothering the working class."

She tried to shut the door on me, but I slipped inside before she could.

"Ah!" she cried, startling me. "And now you're standin' on the carpets with them dirty shoes. Get off this minute. Get off or I'll get me stick!"

I slipped out of my shoes and she stormed off to the kitchen.

"Hey, Martha, what's for breakfast?" I called after her.

A moment later, she stepped back into the hall.

"Do you mean ta tell me that you've come up here expectin' breakfast and here it is almost noon?" she asked, putting one fist on each of her ample hips. "Oh, you are a lazy thing. And good for nuttin', I'm sure."

She went back into the kitchen. But as I slinked past, I noticed her taking out the big frying pan.

"Good morning all," I said cheerfully, stepping into the study.

Janet Fein, Madame Karina, and young Clara Reland were huddled around Karina's desk. Boris and Clifford were not in the room. The ladies looked up and nodded when I came in, then immediately put their heads together again.

"Hi ho," I said, undaunted. "How are my conspirators this morning?"

They ignored me.

"Look, I think this is a bit rude," I pointed out, hoping for a reaction.

"James, you are trying my patience," Karina growled. "Your Ms. Fein is giving us a history of poor Clifford's life. I find it so fascinating, I'm considering writing a book about the child."

"A book? Well now, that should help solve his mother's murder," I snorted.

Karina took her spectacles off and glared at me.

"How are those stitches feeling, big guy?" Janet Fein asked none too kindly.

That explained the cold shoulder treatment. It seems I'd been rather difficult the night before. When I got through telling the little group about the riot I'd started on the Brooklyn-Queens Expressway, they had insisted on waking Richard Steinman. Dr. Steinman is an internist who lives on the eighth floor of our building. In addition to playing his violin with Boris and drinking his way through my wine collection, Richard happens to be my personal physician. They'd gotten him out of bed to put a couple of stitches in my eyebrow. By the time he arrived, I had decided not to cooperate, which led to a bit of a scene. But with the dawning of a new day, I'd assumed that all was forgiven and forgotten.

"Stitches are fine, eyebrow is fine, everything is fine," I answered stiffly.

"Richard will be so pleased to hear that," Janet continued. "In fact, in his joy he may change his mind and decide to speak to you again someday."

"Okay, I get the point," I sighed. "But look, this is no big deal. A decent bottle of vino and we'll be square. The guy's a real sucker for cabernets."

"James, did you want something?" Karina asked, with saccharine sweetness. "You see, dear, as I have already said, we were involved in something both important and interesting. Unlike this present conversation."

Talk about your cold winds.

"Well, actually, I was looking for the boy," I said defensively.

"Clifford slept through the night, ate a good breakfast, and went downstairs to visit with Boris," she said evenly.

There followed an uncomfortable interlude as I racked my brain searching for some other good reason for the interruption. Fortunately, I was rescued by Martha McCabe, who barged into the room and took over.

"So, here you are, Mr. James Donovan," she grumbled. "And did you think I'd be bringing the food in here on a tray like you was lord and master?"

With the doors open, the smell of bacon wafted into the room. Without another word I arose and followed Martha into the kitchen like an obedient child.

"Poached eggs on rye toast, your lordship," Martha said, dropping the plate on the table. "And bacon, too, though why I go to the trouble is anybody's guess."

"I'm the son you never had, Martha," I ventured, shoveling a forkful of eggs into my mouth.

"In that case, I thank the Lord ya weren't born twins," she sighed, settling down at the table with a mug of strong tea. "Now, James, you tell me what is goin' on around here. The old girl has her flights, but she usually keeps pretty close to the ground.

I've got a feelin' that takin' this boy into the house could mean real trouble for her."

Martha listened carefully as I told her the story, or least the parts I knew.

"Well, I met him this mornin' and I must say he's an impressive lad," she said seriously. "I mean, he carries himself like a much older person. Made me a bit edgy he did, explainin' the formation of an egg to me while I was tryin' ta cook."

"Did he remind you of Boris?" I asked.

"Well, now that you mention it, I guess he did." She nodded.

"Me too," I said, sopping up the last of the egg yolk with my toast. "Kind of scary, isn't it?"

"Now, don't you be talkin' about the doctor like that," she snapped. "He is a brilliant man who's putting his talents to good use, unlike some people we could talk about. Speakin' of which, have you looked in the mirror lately? Ya look like a beat up old tomcat."

"Now Martha, let's not resort to flattery," I teased.

"Flattery?! Why ya fool, I meant nuttin' of the kind," she sputtered.

"Okay, okay," I chuckled, getting up. "Boy, everybody's so touchy this morning."

I leaned down and gave her a big kiss on the cheek, then got out of the way before she could land any punches.

"Thanks for breakfast, kid, you're a marvel," I said sincerely, backing into the hall.

"That guff might charm the other ladies, bucko," she barked, trying not to smile, "but it will do ya no good with Martha McCabe. And, I might ask how is the missus Donovan that you've abandoned?"

Mrs. McCabe loves my ex-wife, Kate Byrne, and long ago decided that our divorce was all my fault. Martha believes I'm just another scoundrel who refused to let himself be tamed by a sensible woman. When Kate and I started dating again, after the divorce became final, the old girl misinterpreted this positive development as a ploy. She thinks it's my way of satiating my carnal desires without taking responsibility.

"Let's not get into that again, Martha," I said firmly. "Kate is fine. She's in Japan, where I'm sure everybody loves her."

"Everybody except the one what counts," Martha muttered.

This was one of Mrs. McCabe's favorite topics. I grabbed my shoes and headed downstairs before she could really get started.

Safely back in my apartment, I checked the answering machine for messages, then used the opening we'd cut through the back of my old broom closet and stepped into Boris's front hall. As always, the hallway was cluttered with piles of books and magazines, but I could hear voices coming from the big workroom he'd made by combining the living and dining rooms.

As I navigated down the long dark passage, I tried to imagine my crusty old bachelor partner spending quality time with a ten-year-old boy, but it just didn't compute. When I got within a few feet of the living room, Angus, who was guarding the entrance, lifted his head, opened one eye, then yawned and rolled over. It wasn't his fault. Boris keeps the poor guy up all night prowling around the city.

The Koulomzin apartment was originally laid out just like mine, only reversed, like a matching glove. Then Boris started making changes. In fact, the only room he hasn't altered is kitchen, but that's because he rarely uses it. The big, open work space has floor-to-ceiling bookcases along the walls and an enormous desk at one end. Both of our apartments are centrally air-conditioned thanks to units we had installed on the terrace, but that wasn't good enough for Boris. To make sure that the sun could not intrude, he had a special blue gelatin material glued onto all the windows. The blue tint gives the place a weird look and makes it feel even colder than it is. In the back, where I have my bedroom and an office, Boris again combined rooms. This is the bedroom where he sleeps the day away under many layers of bedding on a massive, antique four-poster bed.

I stepped over Angus, maneuvered around a couple of piles of books, and found an empty chair. Boris and Clifford Brice were each hard at work. Dr. Koulomzin was behind the big, open table he uses as a desk, comfortably seated in a large upholstered chair, staring at his computer terminal. As usual, he was dressed in black, although the purple ascot did give the ensemble a touch of color. Clifford Brice was across the room on a stepladder. He was wearing jeans and a T-shirt and he had a towel draped over his shoulder. Clifford was sorting books.

"Hey, Mr. Donovan," he chirped, stepping down. "How're you doin' today?"

"I'm fine, Clifford," I said, happy to finally meet someone in a good mood. "What's going on?"

"Oh, I'm helping Dr. Koulomzin organize his library," he answered cheerfully. He held up two books and Boris peered at them over the rims of his glasses.

"More of the Harvard Classics," Boris said.

"Right, I got it, Doctor."

Clifford took the towel off his shoulder and carefully wiped the bindings before placing the books in order on the bookshelf.

"And how are *we* feeling today?" Boris asked without looking up.

"If you're asking about my health, then the answer is I feel fine," I said, slowly. "If, on the other hand, you are implying that I should feel guilty about my behavior last night, then the answer is yes, I do. But I plan to make amends to Richard with a special bottle of cabernet sauvignon."

"Better make it two," Boris suggested.

"All right, I'll make it two," I promised, anxious to change the subject. "By the way, I got a call this morning from a lawyer named Powers. Turns out, he works for that mean old guy I met at the National Manufacturing Corporation."

Boris stopped what he was doing and turned to me. "They have an attorney hiring laborers for the factory? How odd," he mused. "I would guess that could prove rather expensive."

"No, no, he wasn't calling me about a job in the factory," I said quickly. "The owner, a Mr. Greenberg, wants to talk to me about a problem he has within the company."

I looked over at Clifford. He seemed pleasantly preoccupied sorting through stacks of books.

"You know what I mean," I hinted. "More in our usual line of work."

"You don't need to worry about Clifford," Boris said, waving a hand in the air. "We keep no secrets from young Mr. Brice. Isn't that right, Clifford?"

The boy nodded his head enthusiastically. "Don't worry, Mr. Donovan, I can handle the truth. My problem is that I just don't hear it too often."

I paused for a moment and looked over at him. The kid was even smaller and more fragile-looking than I remembered.

"Well then," I said finally, "if we're going to have that kind of a relationship, you'd better start calling me J. J., don't you think?"

I stuck my hand out for a shake. He ran over and shook it very seriously. His grip was strong and there was a bright, confident sparkle in his eyes.

"Boris tells me you know something about the National Manufacturing Corporation," I said, trading on our new relationship. "Is there anything you wanna share with me? The guy who owns the place has asked me to meet him for lunch."

"Well, now, let me think," Clifford said, twisting his mouth with the effort. "Momma said she was gonna make a pile of money outta that place."

"Any idea how?" I asked.

"No, not really. She and her friends used to—" He paused and squinted up at me. "—you know, they worked nearby that factory. She was always talking about how bad the people in that place were, but she never got very specific. To be honest, I just thought she was making up stories to tell her little boy. You know, so I wouldn't think she was wicked for working the street."

Pretty straight talk from a kid.

"What did this lawyer, Powers, want from you?" Boris asked, shifting his chair out from behind the big computer monitor.

"He said they'd checked up on me and they know what we do for business. Apparently Mr. Greenberg needs some help with a problem. Powers made it sound like the guy's partner is cheating him. That was it. When I heard the name of the business, I decided it was worth a meeting."

Boris closed his eyes and started tugging on his chin. "This is an unexpected turn of events," he said finally. "Logically, I find myself repelled by it. The idea that some sort of a coincidence has brought us together is more than I'm willing to believe. You should proceed with caution."

"Look, Boris, we don't have much of anything to go on right now. I figured we've got nothing to lose by hearing this guy out. You never know; if I get my wish, it could turn into something big."

Boris didn't say anything for another minute or two. Clifford and I just watched him and waited. There was nothing else to do. Finally, he snapped out of it like a person coming out of a trance.

"You said something about a lunch meeting," he muttered, looking at his watch. "It's approaching noon. Hadn't you better be on your way?"

"Yeah, I suppose so," I said, knocking over a large pile of books as I stood up.

"Never mind the books, J. J.," Clifford said, hurrying over. "I was planning to put these away next anyway."

The little guy smiled up at me.

"Thanks, Cliff, you're a good kid," I said, patting him on the back.

As Clifford Brice started organizing the books, I turned to go back down the hall.

"James, you will be careful, won't you?" Boris asked from behind the computer terminal.

I assured him that I would.

"And remember," he continued, "we must also be careful what we wish for."

That was a bit deep for me, so I didn't bother asking for a clarification. Besides, there was no time. I had a lunch date with Stanley Greenberg out in Brooklyn.

NINE

■ ■ ■

The meeting took place at a kosher deli off Linden Boulevard in Brooklyn. The place was called Gold's, and it was a dump. The front window was practically opaque with grease and the interior wasn't much better. A sign on the front door advertised the special of the day: a chopped-liver appetizer followed by matzo-ball soup and grilled white fish with beans. Delicious. The big clock on the wall behind the hot counter indicated 2:30 P.M. as I headed toward the back.

I couldn't have missed Greenberg if I'd wanted to. He was wearing his full-length mink coat, under which I could just make out a bright pink tie. His left wrist sported a gold Cartier watch with diamonds surrounding the face. On his right wrist he wore a solid gold chain bracelet. There were pinky rings on both hands with stones the size of small marbles, and a plain gold wedding band on the appropriate finger. He rose as I approached, extending his hand. I ignored it and took my seat in the booth.

Before I left Manhattan, I'd made a few calls of my own. Stanley Chasin Greenberg hadn't come out smelling too good. He'd made money over the years, lots of it, but his methods wouldn't win him any humanitarian awards. The way I heard it, he was lucky to have a partner, and it was the other guy who should be worried. Greenberg owned two or three businesses in the New York City area and a good deal of valuable real estate in Florida. Over the years, he'd left behind a trail of disgruntled employees, bankrupt partners, and broken promises. Curiously, he always seemed to profit, even when others lost big.

Mr. Stanley Greenberg, man of fashion, was in his late sixties. A big pile of curly silver hair sat atop his head, and he sported a deep, permanent tan. He flashed me the kind of smile you get from the dentist right before he turns on the drill. His small, dark eyes gave away nothing, and even seemed to absorb the light around them. The hand I'd ignored was old and gnarled with arthritis.

"So, Powers was right about you," he began, still smiling. "You're a tough guy, right?"

I didn't bother to answer.

"Hey, babe, let's not make a whole story outta this. We'll eat, we'll talk. Okay? By the way, my friends call me Stan."

I nodded and handed him a business card.

"So, what do I call you? I mean, J. J. doesn't sound tough enough," he chuckled, looking at my card.

"You can call me Donovan, Mr. Greenberg," I said.

"Hey, come on, Donovan, it's Stan," he urged.

The waitress came to attention at our table.

"Gloria, honey, bring me the usual, okay, babe?" he asked sadly.

Greenberg explained that he was on a special diet prescribed by a doctor at some health spa. He claimed that rich food had ruined his stomach. Judging from the size of his gut, the only thing wrong with his stomach was that he put too much food into it.

I ordered a cup of soup and a hot pastrami sandwich.

"So anyway," he began, getting back to business, "you checked me out, right?"

I told him I'd made some calls.

"Look, Donovan, there's no need to be cute. Big, strong white guys who can talk in full sentences don't just walk in off the street lookin' for work. So, after our little chat yesterday, I decided to do a little checkin'. You see, I got serious problems, and I gotta watch my back all the fuckin' time. Who knows, you coulda been workin' for my scumbag partner, Morty Katz. How the fuck would I know?

"Anyway, like I said, I checked, and now I know all about you and your Russian pal. They tell me you guys can get pretty self-righteous and everything, and that somebody like me is beneath your standards."

I started to speak, but he stopped me.

"Don't bother with the bullshit, I don't give a fuck what you think of me. Besides, from what I heard so far, there's no way you guys would ever do business with a crook like Morty. So, before we even get started, I've eliminated one of my worries. Now, I still haven't figured out what you're doin' in my neighborhood, though I'm willing to bet it's some goody-goody project. But hey, I don't give a fuck about that either. What I have is a business proposition, and it could be heavy dollars. I was told you guys don't mind getting a little dirty for the right price. Am I wrong?"

The answer was no, not exactly. For some jobs we've had to wade pretty deep into the mire. And sometimes, when we're done, a lot of cash changes hands, which doesn't bother us at all. In fact, we really enjoy separating people like Stanley Greenberg from the money they love so much. But old Stan was dead wrong to mistake our primary motivation for anything more than an arrogant desire to even up the odds a little.

"Good. That's good," he grinned, misreading my expression. "I'll give it to you short and sweet. I bought into this metal-working business called National Manufacturing about five years ago. I'd just sold another company out on the island and I had a couple of loose dollars floatin' around. My partner, Morty Katz, was on his balls at the time and he was lookin' for help. You see, Morty's a good salesman, but he's not much of a businessman."

At this point the food arrived. He dug right in, but continued talking.

"When I came along, the company was stuck at about five million dollars in annual sales, and most of that money went right back out to the trade because the operation was a mess. The equipment was old, the plant was a disaster, and the men were worthless. I'd be embarrassed to tell you the operating margins. For Morty, as long as he got to shmooze like a big shot, it was a good living, but it wasn't a business."

Greenberg's lunch included a large bowl of finely chopped salad, poached white fish, and a lot of boiled vegetables. He was shoveling food into his mouth faster than he could chew or swallow, and was spraying the excess all over the table as he talked. I ignored my soup, which now had bits of partially chewed salad floating on the surface, and tried to eat my sandwich by cupping it between my hands. He went right on eating and talking.

"Anyway, Morty managed to land a couple of nice, fat contracts for store fixtures from the big retail chains. It was the kind of stuff you can make some real dough on. Unfortunately, he couldn't bankroll the production side. And even if he could of come up with the money for materials, it was outta his league. That's where I came in. I arranged a line of credit, dropped a quarter million of my own dough into machinery, and we were off. To make things fair, I took fifty-one percent of the stock."

Real fair. He'd arranged a line of credit, which cost him nothing, dropped a couple hundred thousand into machinery, and now he owned the business. If my guess was right, old Morty had probably been forced to personally guarantee the new debt in addition to handing over his business.

"Anyway," he continued, taking enough of a break from his lunch to fill his lungs with air, "everything was fine in the beginning. I took over manufacturing operations and got the place organized. That happens to be a specialty of mine."

There was no false modesty in his voice. This was a matter of fact.

"Don't get me wrong, it was a big job. I had to set up the new equipment and get a crew in to repair all the junk Morty had on the floor. The company had no system for manufacturing, so I came up with something simple to get the product moving out the door. Then I put the purchasing guys on notice to get the costs down or find new jobs. I also hired some experienced welders and brake-press men who answered to me, and fired the deadbeats Morty called supervisors. Finally, I picked out a computer and some accounting software and hired a guy to plug in the numbers so we could produce operating statements.

"It wasn't perfect, but it was a good beginning, and the place started running like a real business. We did six and a half million in sales the first full year, and better than nine million the second. I'm happy to say I more than tripled my money."

His eyes sparkled. Stanley Greenberg got a charge out of making money. He reached over, grabbed a piece of meat out of the sandwich on my plate, and popped it into his already-full mouth.

"Hey, that's nice and tender," he pointed out between bites, as if I'd invited him to paw my food. I finished what was in my hand and left the rest.

"In year three," he continued, "we get up to around two hundred and fifty employees and the operation starts falling apart again. There wasn't strong enough management in the plant to handle the volume we were doing, and they started fucking up orders. This you cannot do to a big retail chain. If they lose confidence, they dump you quick. Besides, this shit was costing me in labor and materials. If I was twenty years younger I'd have gone back into that plant myself and kicked ass till the lazy cocksuckers got it right."

His face was drawn and tense and he was drilling me with those black eyes. I could see that he meant business. He really did wish he could take out the whip and do the job himself.

"But I already paid my dues," he shrugged, his face relaxing back into a smile. "Besides, I spend the winter down in Florida."

That explained the tan. Greenberg kept smiling and let twenty or thirty seconds pass before he continued.

"Well, then Morty introduced me to his son, Alvin," he said, getting serious. "I was lookin' for a no-nonsense guy, somebody who could put a stop to the bullshit, and he seemed like a good choice. Alvin has this small trucking company in Jersey, and he had some time on his hands 'cause the trucking gig basically runs itself. I mean, he has his people on such a short leash that they'd rather work all night than deal with him over a mistake. That was the best recommendation I could've heard. The fact that he was family didn't hurt, either. I don't need any loose lips, if you know what I mean. Not the way I operate."

I had a pretty good idea how Stanley Greenberg operated. He took a deep drink of water to wash down the last of his meal, then grabbed the other half of my sandwich. I couldn't wait for lunch to be over. He went right on chewing and talking.

"At first I thought Alvin was the perfect solution to all our problems. The guy's a real ball-breaker, and that's just what those bastards in the plant needed. I can tell you this, things started moving when he showed up.

"One of the major problems was space. The plant is only fifty thousand square feet, and when you get an order for a couple thousand glass display cases, you can be up to your ass in parts before you blink an eye. We cut a deal with Alvin to rent space at his building in Hoboken, which enabled us to really improve the layout of the factory. Now we warehouse raw materials and some of the work in progress over there in Jersey. In the first month, I think we sent him more than twenty truckloads of parts.

"Since he was trucking all this stuff back and forth, it seemed natural to let Alvin handle the shipping too. Besides, the shipping clerk we had was this drunk mick who couldn't count past twenty without taking off his pants. He'd been with Morty about forever, so dumping him was a little delicate. Instead of canning the schmuck, I made him the porter and figured after a few weeks of cleaning the bathrooms he'd quit and save me the severance pay.

"Believe it or not, the guy's still with us. Those fuckin' Irish may be dumb, but they're stubborn. You should have seen old Gagan's face when he first checked out the bathroom detail. I mean the characters we got in the plant aren't exactly into personal hygiene. The prick's face got so red I thought he was gonna explode."

Greenberg started laughing and slapping the table, but the expression on my face slowed him down.

"Whoa, Donovan, don't take yourself so serious. I know lots of nice Irish people. It's just a way of speakin.' Besides, if you get into the plant you're gonna meet the worst human garbage you ever saw. You name it, we got it."

When I didn't respond, he forged ahead.

"In the beginning, Alvin was only going to work two days a week, but that changed pretty fast. I mean, he was overseeing plant operations *and* shipping, which is a lot. After a couple of months he started coming in every day, and it's been that way ever since. Maybe one morning a week he's in Jersey, but the rest of his time is spent here in Brooklyn. We let things ride like that, on a trial basis, and I paid him a grand a week plus the trucking business. The output went back up and the plant seemed to be running pretty smooth. After about three months, I decided to make the arrangement permanent.

"The deal we cut included a base salary of seventy-five thousand, plus an exclusive on the trucking, which I figured would double the base. Hey, the trucking piece I was already paying to independents, so it didn't cost me nothin'. To sweeten the deal, we leased him a new car, and I threw in five percent of the stock. I should say Morty threw in the stock, since it didn't come out of my piece.

"I stayed around for a couple more months to keep an eye on things. It didn't matter, I don't usually go south till after Thanksgiving anyway. What I saw, I liked. We did ten and a half million that year, and even though the margins were down a little, I felt confident that we were back on track."

He paused for another quick gulp of water. When he was ready to continue, his expression clouded over.

"I usually come north for the summer, but when I saw the ten and a half million, I decided to stay in Florida and look after some of my other investments. Well, not long after I made my plans known things started going haywire. At first, the reports

Alvin gave me on the phone were all rosy. You know, like, 'Everything's fine here, don't worry about a thing,' or 'We came up with a new spot-welding system and we've doubled the output on wire shelves!' That kinda stuff. But pretty soon the story changed to a lot of complaining.

"Get this. Alvin Katz calls me up and tells me the supervisors I hired, *my* guys, were no fuckin' good and that they were screwing up *his* production! Then he starts going on and on about how the machinery was constantly breaking down and he couldn't find anybody to do repairs. Hey, a fuckin' moron could find a repairman. It got me thinkin', because it sounded like he was makin' excuses and I couldn't figure out what for. If things were so good, why all the flak? But when I ask Morty, he says sales are up and everything is just great. Morty tells me Alvin's going through a bad time, you know, personally, and that's all there is to it.

"Then in April, they send me the year-end statement and I almost had a fuckin' coronary. There was no growth in sales and the margins were way down. I'm talkin' six percent against more than ten million in sales. That's over six hundred thousand dollars in new expenses! We were still makin' money, but it just didn't make good sense. Something wasn't right and I don't think it was an accident. After all the bullshit I'd gotten from Morty and Alvin, we should have had a real good year, not this crap they were handing me. The warning bells were goin' off in my head.

"As if that wasn't bad enough, Alvin starts to lose it. I mean nutso, outta control. Okay, maybe he's having problems. For all I know, his girlfriend's fuckin' the mailman. But it don't give him the right to try and push me around. If he needs to unwind, let him take it out on the men. I wouldn't give a shit. Hey, they might even do a little work for a change. But now he was comin' after me. I mean, I have some serious questions that need answers, but if I ask Alvin a question he starts screamin' and rantin' like a freakin' nut job. According to him, he's surrounded by stupid people, myself included, whose mistakes are makin' him look bad. And he's got everybody else so fuckin' nervous they're afraid to talk."

Greenberg was growing more and more agitated—the situation was wearing him down. As he struggled to collect himself, I remember thinking that what goes around comes around.

"I should never have let it get this far," he continued after an embarrassed pause. "While I was gone Alvin replaced a lot of my people. He even hired a new computer operator. I sent my accountant in, but he doesn't know what's goin' on either. He's got access to the computer, but that doesn't mean shit. He can't tell what's up 'cause Alvin's plugging the numbers in. He could be makin' them up, for all I know. I wanted a strong manager, but this has gotten completely out of hand. My mistake was going with the son. I should have picked my own man."

It was obvious he wasn't accustomed to admitting his mistakes. Watching him squirm a little made me feel better, even though it didn't last long. The fire returned pretty quickly.

"I'm convinced that smart fuck and his old man are ripping me off," he snarled. "The problem is, I can't afford a big disruption right now. Alvin has too much of the business under his control, and if I start making accusations, I think he could cause a lot of trouble. I don't want that to happen. Not right now.

"What I want is for you to get something on these two fucks. I want you to hang them. I want to know what they're doing and how they're doing it. When I have them cold, I'm pretty sure Alvin will leave quietly. Morty can stay because I need him to sell, but he'll go on commission and he'll have to turn over the rest of the stock. That's it. You get me what I want and I'll make it worth your while."

So Stanley was looking for an excuse to screw his partner and get the rest of the business in the process. The fact that he didn't want any disruptions probably meant that he was planning to sell the company.

"What does 'worth your while' mean?" I asked, playing out the hand.

"How does a hundred grand sound?" He was smiling again.

"It sounds like enough for one person," I said, "but I've got a partner." I was toying with him. A hundred thousand dollars was already too much for the kind of information he wanted. There was something else behind it.

"I tell you what, tough guy," he countered without hesitating, "I'll give you a check for twenty-five thousand right now. Call it your retainer. No matter what, you keep it. I'll put another one hundred and twenty-five thousand, in escrow with the lawyer, Powers. If you can get rid of Alvin Katz and get me the rest of the stock, it's yours."

This guy was good. You can convince people to do almost anything for money, and he knew it. He was ready to spend $150,000 to squeeze his partner out, which meant he stood to make a real killing in the process, though getting even with the Katz family had probably upped the ante a bit. And Stanley Greenberg was confident that he could get me to help him. All he needed to do was make the pile of money big enough.

Normally I'd have walked away from this kind of mess. All three of the principals sounded like real sweethearts and they probably deserved each other. Since Greenberg had come to Boris and me, it was obvious he didn't want auditors or lawyers sticking their noses into the books, which was another reason to leave it alone. I was willing to bet that the National Manufacturing Corporation had been operating under a set of rules you wouldn't find in any accounting text.

"Assuming we take the job," I began, fishing for details, "how do you propose we go about this thing? I would need to really dig into things, and it doesn't sound like Alvin Katz is going to appreciate a stranger walking in off the street to check up on him."

"For one hundred and fifty thousand you want me to tell you your business?" he asked, mocking me. He was sure I'd been sold on the idea.

I just stared at him in silence.

"Okay, okay, Donovan, deflate the muscle-man suit. I was

94

only kiddin'." There was nothing left to eat, so Stanley began to play with the flatware. "As I understand it, you were pretty successful before you got into your Friend of the People act."

He was right. I have a master's degree in business and more than ten years of hands-on management experience, which is what I'd brought to the partnership. That and a willingness to go toe-to-toe with the Stanley Greenbergs of this world. I nodded.

"My idea is to bring you on as plant manager. Alvin's always complainin' he's got nobody with any brains to help him. So I'll give him you. That way you're inside, and you can get a good look. It's a cinch. I'll provide you with references and maybe while you're checkin' things out you could do a little management consulting. After all, I'm gonna have to make some changes when this is over."

He was really happy with the plan, and I could tell it tickled him to think of me working in his factory. Amusing Stanley Greenberg didn't appeal to me. On the other hand, the job would put me in a position to check out the neighborhood, and take a closer look at the Ruby Brice killing and the fiery crucifixion I'd witnesses across the street.

"By the way, I understand they found a stiff on your street," I began carefully. "What was that about, you got a psycho killer on the payroll?" I smiled casually.

"How'd you hear about that?" he asked, bearing in with those beady eyes of his.

"I read the newspapers," I said, as if it was a really stupid question. "Why, is there a problem?"

"No, not at all, it's just that I don't like trouble, it's bad for business," he said seriously.

I didn't say anything.

"Okay, look, some whore got cut up and burned across the street. It was nothing. We got loads of these doped-up broads in the neighborhood. A couple of weeks back, another one got herself filleted over on Logan Street. One or two less hookers makes no difference."

I had to take a deep breath to stop myself from taking a shot at him across the table.

"Hey, Donovan, there's people dying every day in East New York. Don't tell me a big boy like you can't handle it."

"I was just curious," I said, trying to let it go.

All of a sudden, he slapped the table.

"I got it," he shouted beaming, "you're lookin' after the hookers! That's what you're doin' in the neighborhood."

He was so pleased with himself, it made me feel sick.

"Hey, don't sweat it, Donovan," he said, misreading my expression yet again. "I don't give a fuck what brought you to me, as long as you help me get my problems solved."

He pulled out his checkbook and started writing.

"Whoa, Stan-lee," I said sarcastically, "I don't remember saying yes to anything. I've got a partner to think about."

"Yeah, right, but you didn't say no, either. I tell you what, Donovan, I'm gonna write two checks: One for five thousand and one for twenty thousand. You take them both home to the Russian and see what he thinks. If it's no-go, you send back the bigger one and keep the five grand. That way this conversation becomes privileged information between you and a client, and you've gotten a little something for your time. Otherwise, keep them both and show up Monday morning to start your new job."

The waitress came over and Greenberg ordered rice pudding. There was no way I was going to watch him eat anything else. I picked up the checks he'd written and said we'd let him know. He flashed me that crooked smile of his one more time and stuck out his hand.

I didn't shake it that time, either.

TEN

...

An hour with Stanley Greenberg made the ride back to Manhattan seem like a vacation. I used my recharged cell phone to call Boris and report on the lunch. He listened patiently and refrained from his usual commentary. In fact, except for the occasional grunting sound, he took the whole story pretty much in stride, which meant he wasn't paying attention. There was no point trying to compete with a cunning algorithm, so I offered to cook dinner; a medium-rare porterhouse steak would get his undivided attention.

I called Leonard's and ordered the steaks and a pile of cooked shrimp for an appetizer. It's probably the most expensive butcher shop in the country, but the meat is indescribable. Since I was going to be on the Upper East Side, I stopped on Sixty-seventh Street and picked up a case of the 1994 Ridge Zinfandel at Garnet's. The big red wine was a good complement for the meat and the perfect way to apologize to my good friend Dr. Steinman. My next stop was a produce market and then the bakery. By the time I finished shopping, there was a sizable dent in the retainer check I had in my pocket. But I figured since Stanley Greenberg had ruined my lunch, it was only fitting that he should foot the dinner bill.

Once the goodies were all loaded in my car, I drove up Madison Avenue to Ninety-seventh Street and crossed the park. In less than ten minutes, I pulled up in front of our building on

Columbus Avenue. Santos came running out of the lobby with a dolly and actually offered to help me unload the car. I was touched until I found out he just wanted to borrow it. He and his boys were low on beer and needed to drive up to University Avenue in the Bronx to stock up at the discount store. I was touched again when he borrowed forty dollars.

It was nearly six o'clock, so I didn't bother putting the food away. I seasoned the meat and whipped up a little marinade, then washed and prepped the potatoes for the grill. I made a big green salad and put it in the refrigerator, opened two bottles of the wine and left them on the counter to breathe, then put two more bottles in a brown bag and took them down to Rich Steinman's place on the eighth floor. The doctor wasn't home, so I left the bag in the hall with a little note: *Thanks for stitches. Sorry for hard time.—Donovan. (P.S. Get over it!)*

As usual, the elevator was acting up, which made the trip to the eighth floor a journey. When I finally got back to my apartment, it was time to go out on the terrace and start the coals. I scrubbed the grill with a wire brush, then loaded the metal funnel I use to start the fire with briquettes and set a match to the crumpled newspapers in its base. When the charcoal was smoldering nicely, I decided to look for Boris and Clifford. It was cocktail hour, and I didn't feel like drinking alone.

I took the usual route through the old broom closet and made my way down the cluttered hallway, but I was in for a shock. The big workroom had been transformed. All the books and journals were back on the shelves where they belonged, creating so much space you could actually make out the pattern in the oriental carpet. A little desk with an old computer had been set up against the wall next to Boris's big worktable on which several large computer screens competed for his attention. Clifford Brice had his face pressed up against the screen of his new toy and was busily clicking away with the mouse. Angus was asleep at his feet.

"Hiya, J. J.," he said, looking up brightly when I entered the room.

98

"Did you do all this by yourself?" I motioned with both hands.

"Yup, I fixed the books," he announced proudly.

"And Boris didn't mind?" I wondered how the big guy was handling the change.

"No way. We found all kinds of stuff he's been looking for, like his wallet and the keys to his office down at Columbia. You shoulda seen how happy he was when I found this paper he thought he already sent to his publisher. That coulda been some trouble."

"I'll bet," I agreed, smiling. "Where'd the computer come from?"

"Oh, well now, Dr. Koulomzin set that up for me to use. Got me my own password and hooked me up to the Internet." Clifford was beaming.

"That's cool. Maybe you could help me too," I suggested. "I'm supposed to handle all the accounts, but I get a bit behind sometimes."

"Could I? Man, that would be great!" He jumped up. "Ya know, I was taking care of Mrs. Washington's bills and her checkbook and stuff. I'm really good with numbers."

"I know. She told me you're a whiz," I said seriously. "Hey, before I forget, where's Boris? I'm making dinner tonight and he better not stand me up."

"He's out on the terrace smoking, and he's a little grouchy," Clifford said, looking guilty. "All I did was tell him how bad smoking is for your health and now he won't smoke in front of me anymore. He keeps taking his papers out onto the terrace, like I don't know what he's doing. I feel bad because he isn't getting much work done on the computer."

"Not all my work requires a computer, Clifford," Boris said, stepping through the patio doors. He was wearing a tan pith helmet to protect his head from the last rays of the setting sun.

"What were ya doing out there on the terrace?" I needled.

"You know very well what I was doing," he snorted. "I smell burning coals. Could this mean my dinner is ready?" He sounded hopeful. I was right, the porterhouse steak had gotten his attention.

"Not quite," I said, "but martinis are now being served on my terrace. In your case, Clifford there is a choice selection of sodas and juices."

"Am I coming for steak dinner, too?" he asked.

"Of course, you're part of the team," I said, smiling.

First a computer and now steak. You could tell from the look on the kid's face that this day just kept on getting better and better.

"Besides," I snickered, "you're a really good influence on Boris."

A few minutes later we were all comfortably seated on my terrace, sipping libations and eating shrimp. The potatoes were on the grill, baking over red-hot coals, and the steaks were marinating, patiently awaiting their turn. Angus, awake for a change, had planted himself next to the meat, just in case a big piece fell off the table by accident. It was a beautiful fall evening, and the sunset had painted the horizon in shades of pink and gold. Seemed a shame to ruin the atmosphere, but there was no getting around it; we needed to make a decision about Greenberg's offer.

"And so, what would you like to do?" Boris asked when I'd finished telling the story of my lunch at Gold's Deli.

"I think we should take him up on the offer," I said quickly. "Believe me, I understand this isn't a great job. In fact, the very thought of getting in between Greenberg and the Katz family makes my stomach turn. But we've got two dead women and a lot of questions that need answers. This factory is right in the middle of the whole thing. Ruby even mentioned it to Clifford. Who knows, maybe she did see something going on at the National Manufacturing Corporation. To hear Greenberg tell it, he's being robbed blind."

Boris didn't say anything for a minute or two. He was preoccupied with the shrimp, apparently using them to compensate for the cigarettes he wasn't smoking.

"And what do *you* think we should do?" he continued, turning to Clifford as he sucked cocktail sauce off his thumb.

"Me?" Clifford looked surprised. "You're asking me what you should do?"

"I'm asking for your opinion," Boris said seriously.

The kid sat back in his chair and considered the question.

"I agree with Mr. Donovan," he said finally. "I don't see how you're gonna find the man that killed Momma unless you get out to Brooklyn. And here's a ready-made job, and you can make some money, too. Why not get in there and see what's really going on in that place? Like J. J. said, maybe Momma did see something."

While Clifford was speaking, I put the steaks on the grill. Angus looked a bit disappointed, but stayed with me. As long as the meat was in sight, there was hope for him.

"Okay, Boris, it's your turn," I said, stepping back from the smoking grill.

"Very well," he replied evenly. "I think this is the craziest mess you have gotten us into yet. What looked like a relatively harmless inquiry has lead to a murder scene, interviews with a deranged old wizard, and now the prospect of signing on to help a vulgar, corrupt businessman cheat his partner. The entire affair is tawdry and foul-smelling and I wouldn't be associated with it at any price."

We sat in silence as Boris reached for his cigarettes and then stopped.

"Now, having said all that," he continued, eyeing his cigarettes anxiously, "we have our friends Clifford and Janet Fein to think about. Not to mention this Mr. Tito, who represents a real threat to the boy. I'm forced against my better judgement to agree that we have to do something, and this may as well be it."

There wasn't a whole lot to add. I asked Clifford to set the table in the dining room. When he left, Boris made a grab for his cigarettes. As I flipped the steaks, I heard the match strike and then a satisfied sigh as he took his first puff.

. . .

And so we took the job. Five-thirty Monday morning the alarm clock rattled me out of a deep, peaceful sleep. I fought off the desire to burrow deeper into my nice warm cocoon and sat up. I used the control panel on the nightstand to turn on the stereo and activate speakers located throughout the apartment. Next, I ran the shower, which gave me plenty of time to walk to the kitchen and put on the water for coffee. There was even time to dawdle a bit on the return trip. It takes quite a while for the hot water to make it all the way to the seventeenth floor.

The shower was nice and warm. Too nice. Leaning against the wall, I nearly fell asleep. I probably would have, too, only I ran out of hot water. One minute I was dreaming of hot tubs and buxom women, and the next I was getting hosed down with ice water like some overeager stud. Drying off quickly, I struggled into a pair of blue jeans and a work shirt. I grabbed my socks and heavy work boots and headed for the coffee.

Moving through the living room, I heard an odd noise that seemed to be coming from the kitchen. I was still half-asleep, but it sounded like someone moaning. I stopped for a moment to listen. The music on the radio had changed, too—they were playing a requiem. It was eerie. The dawn was glowing on the horizon, casting shadows in the room, and the aroma of ciga-rettes and the coffee I hadn't finished making floated in the air. There was another smell, too, a pungent scent that I couldn't immediately place. I moved quietly toward the doorway, hoping I wouldn't find anything too strange in my kitchen.

I stopped again. The cigarette smoke was a dead giveaway. I wasn't in the mood for any more surprises, not after my frigid shower, so I decided to discourage future broadcasts of the death-march music. Backing up a couple of steps to make some room, I charged into the kitchen screaming like some crazed Bashi-bazouk.

My mistake was approaching the doorway from the blind side of the couch. Unbeknownst to me, there was a large object lying

102

directly in my path. As I started my war cry, the big black object tried to rise. I tripped and went sailing into the kitchen, a confusion of arms and legs, socks and boots. I slid across the nicely waxed floor and banged my head against the stove.

When I was able to focus again, I saw Boris perched on a tiny stool at my kitchen counter. He was wearing a fur hat with earflaps and looked like a big, weary old bear. The smirk on his lips was his only acknowledgment of my ignoble entrance. The moving obstacle I'd stumbled over was Angus, of course, which explained the odor. They'd just come from their daily predawn walk along Riverside Drive. Taking note of the deep lines in his brow, I guessed Boris was reenacting some great Russian tragedy in his mind. I didn't bother to ask; sometimes it's better to ignore him.

"Good morning, Boris."

I was annoyed about the fall, but relieved to be in one piece. I stood up and patted Angus, who'd come over to apologize and make friends. There was no response from Boris, just more humming.

"How's my coffee today?"

"Donovan, you will be late," he said finally, without opening his eyes.

"Don't get me started, Boris," I muttered, shutting off the music. "By the way, if you can break yourself from that trance, I'd appreciate a cup of my coffee."

He opened his eyes and heaved a tremendous sigh, as if I'd asked him to do something strenuous. I noticed a large stack of printouts on the countertop.

"What's all that stuff?" I asked. I was hopping around the room on one foot trying to lace my boots without sitting down. It wasn't working. I sat on the floor next to Angus, who smelled like a wet wool sweater. Boris doesn't notice these things because he's always got one of those Turkish cigarettes dangling under his nose. "Hey Boris, why don't you give this dog a bath?" I asked, still annoyed about my botched entrance.

"That *stuff,* as you call it, is background information on the

103

employees at your new place of business," he said peevishly. He poured me some coffee and refilled his own mug.

Boris had been busy.

"Is that so? Well, I'm in kind of a hurry here. Why don't you just tell me what you've found?"

"Well, in the first place," he began, choosing his words carefully, "this factory to which you've indentured yourself seems to be a magnet for the least desirable workers the City of New York has to offer."

That didn't sound too good.

"Let me see." He pursed his lips thoughtfully. "As of last week's payroll, the company had two hundred and thirty-one employees, counting both the day and night shifts. I divided these people into groups that I am labelling *skilled* and *unskilled.* I was able to locate material on almost all the members of the skilled group," he said. "I think it would be best for you to meet this cast of nefarious characters before we discuss them; they make very interesting reading."

There was a thick cloud of smoke forming around his large, pale face, making it seem like I was being addressed by the wise and powerful Oz himself.

"There are a total of one hundred and eighty-two general helpers or laborers in the unskilled category," he continued. "My search for information on this group was much less successful, though I managed to locate computer files for one hundred and thirty-seven of these *in-di-vid-uals.*"

He practically spit that last word out. His expression changed from disinterest to concern as he waved the smoke away and prepared to continue.

"In that group of one hundred thirty-seven men and women, there are ninety-three people with criminal records." He paused for effect. "Their crimes include everything from possession of marijuana to narcotics, armed robbery, and manslaughter. I place special emphasis on the high incidence of drug convictions. Since this information is limited to the accomplishments of these individuals since their arrival in the United States, I'm forced to admit the numbers may understate the potential danger. I'm still trying to gather some foreign data, but it is proving more difficult than expected."

He stopped and his face went blank as he considered this annoying fact. There were holes in his data. I didn't have time to sit with him while he analyzed the situation.

"Not now, Boris," I said, coaxing him. "I'm late for work, remember?"

"J. J. Donovan, you are always late." He had just stated one of the absolute truths about my life. It had driven my wife nuts. "You're right, however," he conceded, checking his watch. "I'll be brief. There are five men, currently employed by the corporation, who hold convictions for manslaughter. I've separated their records from the rest and placed them on top of that pile of *stuff*." He motioned toward the printouts. "It would be wise to keep these men in front of you."

"What else?" I asked, trying to sound businesslike.

"Well, naturally, all these references to alcohol and drug abuse would suggest supply-and-distribution networks," he continued. "Again, I caution you to proceed with care. There is also the question of residency status. Given the ethnic diversity of the group, I would guess that some of these people owe their continued presence in this country to the sort of creatures who forge work papers. This suggests a number of possibilities, though frankly, I don't see how the death of Ms. Brice or the other victim could be connected to any of these activities.

"Finally, it seems clear to me that no one with an alternative would chose to work for the National Manufacturing Corporation. Consequently, I consider no one above suspicion. There is a great deal of primal malevolence emanating from this factory. These aren't the sophisticated types you're used to handling. There are no starched collars in this group. Understand this— you must be on your guard at all times. I see no virtue in this thing, James. I know we want to help Janet Fein and the child, but there must be some other way."

"I haven't heard you offer any suggestions," I pointed out.

He issued a sigh of resignation. It was 6.35 A.M.

"If you're going, I suggest you leave immediately," he snapped, checking his watch and doing the calculations in his head.

"By the way, old chap, what are your plans for the day?" I asked, buttering a bagel to eat en route.

"Ah, I'm glad you asked," he said, perking up. "I have arranged for Clifford to take a tour of the high-field functional magnetic resonance imaging system at the medical center. And then, in the afternoon, we are going to the planetarium for an illustrated lecture on the stars, followed by a light show."

I put the bagel down on the counter. "Magnetic resonance imaging system?" I was flabbergasted. "Boris, the kid's only ten years old."

"And your point is?" He looked surprised.

"My point is, maybe he'd like to go to Central Park and fly a kite or something. Why don't you let the kid decide, instead of thinking up these crazy field trips?"

He opened his eyes wider and smirked like the cat who'd eaten the canary. "I did ask," he said, raising an eyebrow. "Functional MRI was at the very top of Clifford's list."

"You're kidding."

"Hardly. Young Master Brice has a particular interest in magnets. He was very excited to learn that they are being used to create images of physiological events."

Boris looked so self-satisfied I wanted to scream. Instead, I picked up my bagel and headed for the front door.

ELEVEN

...

Salsa music rattled the windows on the ground floor of the building as I left the elevator and headed across the lobby. Naturally,
the noise was coming from my car, which was parked at the
curb, idling nervously like a racehorse anxious to get out of the
gate. The passenger door was open and Manny Santos was
lounging in the front seat, sipping a beer.

"Yo, Santos, a bit early for a party, isn't it?" I shouted above
the music. He turned it down as I slid behind the wheel.

"*Early?* It's late, my man," he moaned. "I been up all night
playin' cards."

"Well?" I didn't really have time for this.

"Well, what?" he asked, nodding slightly.

"How'd you do?"

"Got drunk, lost fifty dollas, and ended up gettin' your car
instead of gettin' laid." He struggled to his feet and bent down,
sticking his head into the car. "Don't forget, my wife's sista is
comin' and she gonna clean for you. You promised."

"Look, Santos, I'm running late," I said, quite certain I'd
made no promises. "We'll talk about it later."

Manny stood up to consider this proposition. He was wearing
a heavy winter parka with a fur-trimmed hood and large pockets
bulging with back-up cans of beer. His bright yellow shorts
clashed nicely with the coat and touched his kneecaps. On his
feet, Manny wore black silk socks and dress shoes. There he

was, swaying unsteadily on the curb, enjoying life. I hated to ruin his morning.

"Don't forget, you've got Angus today," I reminded him.

Angus has adapted to the nocturnal habits of his master and stays in most of the day, but he still needs a stroll in the early afternoon. When I'm available, Angus and I take this little constitutional together. But when I'm busy, the job falls to Santos. Since all five feet, two inches of Manny Santos weigh less than one hundred and fifteen pounds, I figure he gives up about twenty pounds to Angus, who's big enough to put his paws on my shoulders and look me in the eyes. God help Manny Santos, I thought, if a poodle decides to wag her tail in our boy's direction. I was trying not to laugh.

"What's so funny, gringo?" Manny asked, looking hurt. "You don't like my shorts?"

"No, man, it's not that, they're perfect." I was really laughing hard now. "I was just wondering how you're gonna handle Angus with no sleep and a load on?"

He hesitated a moment as the full weight of the situation dawned on him. Then his face lit up and he flashed me that gold-toothed smile. "Yo Don-o-van, I think maybe today I'll put a fuckin' saddle on that bull and *ride* him to the park."

I pulled away from the curb still chuckling. Nobody could put a saddle or anything else on Angus if he didn't want it.

The dashboard clock was blinking 7:50 A.M. by the time I saw the sign for the Pennsylvania Avenue exit. The day shift started at eight o'clock; I was cutting it close. I raced up the exit ramp, ran the light on Flatlands Avenue, then gunned the car for about five blocks. But when I pulled alongside the landfill site, I slowed down to the speed limit.

This was the same landfill where the crazy old wizard claimed he'd seen a black car rocking to the sounds of a working woman earning her tip. Greenberg had warned me that the cops operated a speed trap on this desperate little stretch of road every morning. New York at its best: It was one of the most violent neighborhoods in the city, a precinct averaging more than three homicides a week, and they were giving out speeding tickets for doing thirty-five in a thirty.

I turned left onto Berriman and parked my car on the sidewalk, next to the trailers in the shipping bay. I ducked into the building just as the buzzer on the timeclock went off, signalling three minutes till the shift's start. It was my first day, so I reported to Greenberg's office.

"Nice of you to get in here early," he said sarcastically. "It makes such a good impression."

"I wasn't sure about the traffic, Stanley," I said, trying to pacify him. "You don't have to worry, I'll be in bright and early tomorrow."

He looked worried as he led me down the hallway. We stopped in front of a door labeled BOARD ROOM. I could hear loud voices coming from inside. "Fuck you, old man, the prick's late."

Greenberg smiled unhappily and opened the door. It was a dirty, windowless room in which lots of decrepit, mismatched furniture competed for space. Morty and Alvin Katz were sitting on opposite sides of a old, broken conference table, impatiently awaiting my arrival.

Stanley introduced me to the others and we all sat down at the table like friends. He briefly described my background and the role I would play at National Manufacturing, then gave a short pep talk extolling the virtues of teamwork. Morty just sat there sucking on his cigar, listening. When Stanley finished his say, Alvin decided it was his turn to enlighten us. He thought it would help to set the record straight, since we were all together.

Alvin Katz was a large, mean-looking fat man with bad skin. I guessed that he was about forty-two years old. Before starting his speech, Alvin sat up a bit straighter in the chair, folded his hands on the table, and allowed a full thirty seconds of silence to pass for dramatic effect. Then he began to speak, his voice growing louder with each sentence, building toward a crescendo.

"I don't care who you are or what you know," he began, his pockmarked face framed by an enormous pair of rose-tinted aviator glasses. "This is *my* plant and I run it *my* way. I take no prisoners. I don't give a shit what you or any of those turds in the plant think about me. I don't like or trust anybody, and that includes these two."

He pointed his thumb at Stanley and his father.

"I don't know what good Stan thinks you can do," he sneered, returning his focus to me, "because every single mother in the place is an ignoramus. So your fancy business-school shit won't work here. Understand? The best you can do is to force as much product out the door as possible and keep those suckers from stealing us blind."

He motioned vaguely toward the plant.

"And," he continued, his features more animated and his voice much louder, "I don't want to see your ass in front of a computer or sitting behind a desk pushing a pencil. If you're going to be of any use around here, which I doubt, it's out on the floor in the plant. He hired you—" Alvin pointed an accusing finger at Greenberg. "—so I guess I'm stuck with you for now. But, let me make myself perfectly clear—you are to do *what* I tell you, *when* I tell you. Otherwise you're history. Do you understand me?"

I didn't immediately answer.

"I said, *Do you understand me?*" he shouted.

That was enough from Junior. I got out of my seat, walked over to his chair, and locked him into it by grasping both armrests. Then I leaned down, putting my face a few inches from his. All two hundred and forty pounds of Alvin Katz kept perfectly still. You could see tiny droplets of sweat forming on his brow.

"Now you get this straight, *Alvin*," I whispered, squeezing as much sarcasm into the name as it would hold. "You *ever* talk to me like that again and I might not be able to control myself, like I'm doing now. I was hired by Mr. Greenberg to do a job in the plant, and that's what I plan to do. From what I've been told, you can use the help. I'll give you the respect your position deserves, and you'll do the same for me. That way, you and I won't have any problems. Now, have *you* got it?"

I had been talking really softly, and when I spit out that last question, he flinched. From the loss of color in his face and the sickly grin that formed on his lips it was obvious Alvin had gotten the message. I let go of the chair and went back to my seat. There were a few moments of static silence before Alvin finally spoke up.

"Well, well . . . Mr. J. J. Donovan, I think you'll do just fine," he said, chuckling nervously. "I was just, ah, testing you. I wanted to see if you had any balls, 'cause—and I'm dead serious about this—if you couldn't handle a little heat from me, you'd never last out in the plant."

He looked to the others for support, or maybe verification. Alvin was backpedaling—the guy switched personalities as easily as I change a shirt. This new version was trying really hard to start things over on a better note. I didn't buy it for a second. My little scene wouldn't be forgotten; he'd simply learned that bullying me didn't work.

"Ya know, Jay," he said, suddenly very friendly, "now that I think about it, I'm looking forward to having someone like you out in the plant. Truth is, I been wearin' too many hats. I need a good man out there so I can concentrate on straightening out the problems in here. Between you and me, the people in the office, they don't know what the fuck they're doin', and expenses have gone way up. With you handling the plant, I'll be able to clean things up."

He finished with a big grin and looked over at Greenberg, whose expression told me he was hearing this for the first time. Stanley didn't say anything as Alvin sat back, still smiling. The play for control of the office was Alvin's price for agreeing to work with me. It was interesting, watching him manipulate the situation. The guy could move from intense fury to polite calm in seconds, and he was smart.

At this point, Morty finally spoke up. As president of the

company, he thought it would be a good idea for him to introduce me to the men and then give me a tour of the factory. Like a true salesman, he'd kept his head down when the bullets were flying, but now that things seemed resolved, he was available to smooth over the rough edges.

Morty Katz was a tall, thin, stoop-shouldered man of about seventy years. He was completely bald and clean-shaven, though he did have an impressive pair of bushy white eyebrows. His taste ran to expensive, well-cut suits and handmade leather shoes. But his signature was a large Partagas cigar. A conversation with Morty Katz could become confusing because it usually had very little substance. He would string together a long series of dirty one-liners, pausing only for a punch line. He always ended with a question: "So, what can ya do?"

At first glance, the guy didn't seem too bad. He was more of a caricature than a person, and there was something appealing in his easygoing style. I found myself drawn to him, and almost made the mistake of labeling him a victim of circumstances. Fortunately, the spell didn't last too long.

We headed into the factory and Morty had Carlos Rodriquez, the plant foreman, call the men together. When we had a group of sixty or seventy men loosely assembled around us, Katz got up on a box and began his little routine.

"Okay, listen up, people," he began innocently. "This big white man standing next to me is the new plant manager." There was some laughter. Morty smiled; his audience loved him. "His name is Mr. Donovan. When he says something, you are expected to jump. No questions. You do what he says as if I was telling you. Anybody who can't handle it can take a fuckin' walk."

There was a little murmuring as this information was translated into several languages and dialects and passed to those in the back of the crowd. The faces that turned to me had searching eyes as they tried to decide whether this new guy would make their lives more or less difficult. I stood perfectly still and returned the gazes.

"And just in case there is someone here who wants to know why we needed a plant manager," he continued, warming to the subject, "let me give it to you in plain English. You people are a bunch of fuck-ups! Me? I'm a patient man and I try to understand that people make mistakes. But you have been screwing up so much that my partner, Mr. Greenberg, had to go out and hire somebody to keep an eye on you, which is costing us money. I think you all know how Mr. Greenberg feels about his money. So I suggest you pick up the pace and stop dicking around out here."

I was a little surprised to hear Morty use his partner as the fall guy. Then again, a lot of these men had been his people before Greenberg and Alvin showed up on the scene. Maybe he didn't want any of the credit for Stanley's management style. The men seemed to straighten up at the mention of Greenberg's name, and more than a few uncomfortable glances were cast in the direction of the office. I decided to reconsider my opinion of Morty Katz. That quiet, hands-off persona might just belong to a real pro.

"Hey, Clarence! Clarence Roberts, come here, babe." Morty now launched into the entertainment portion of his stand-up routine. This was his version of reaching out. "Hey Clarence, you big turkey, get over here," he coaxed, smiling broadly.

A large jet-black man of about fifty made his way up from the back of the group. He wore very baggy, very dirty blue jeans and a tattered Yankees T-shirt. There was something clownlike about Clarence Roberts. He had multicolored splotches of powdered paint on his dark skin, and he walked with an uneven shuffling gait that made him seem uncoordinated. At first, I thought he was handicapped in some way. Turned out he was. As he got closer, I could smell the booze. Clarence Roberts, manager of the paint line, was pickled.

"Clarence, you hear what I just said?" Morty asked, taking Clarence by the arm.

"Yeah, I did, an I come wan you say."

"You *deed*?" Morty said, mimicking him. "I mean, Did you hear what I said about Mr. Donovan? Not, Did you hear me when I called you?" More laughter.

"Yeah, sure, I heard just fine."

Clarence was the perfect straight man for Morty's act.

"Well, suppose you just repeat it, so everybody can hear."

Clarence grew wide-eyed when he realized he'd been told to address the group. It obviously terrified him and he tugged at his clothes nervously, trying to straighten himself up for the task. There was a lot of snickering and some cat-calling in Spanish as the others enjoyed Clarence's discomfort.

"Well, you said this the new bossmon and don't nobody mess wit him." He pointed at me and everybody started laughing.

"That's my Clarence." Katz chuckled, slapping him on the back.

The whole act took about five minutes. Morty asked me if there was anything I wanted to say. A speech wasn't going to make any difference. Half the eyes I looked into were glassy, and I estimated that the attention span of my audience had already been exceeded by about four minutes. Besides, the last person they wanted to hear from was Greenberg's new enforcer. I said I'd pass.

"Okay then, get back to work, you *pendjeos*," Morty said, a smile wrapping around his cigar. "And try not to fuck up too much stuff this afternoon."

The group broke up quickly and the men headed back to work.

I spent that first day wandering around the plant as unobtrusively as possible, meeting the men and watching them work. It was a real education. Any reservations I had about charging Greenberg for the consulting report vanished.

The National Manufacturing Corporation made glass-and-metal display cases. The biggest-selling design was a countertop unit popular in department stores. It included built-in fluorescent lighting to illuminate the products arranged on the shelves below, and came in a total of twelve different styles, which were available in a choice of six colors.

No matter how you do the math, it adds up to a lot of parts. To run efficiently, that type of manufacturing operation requires constant communication, strong supervision, systematic scheduling of production, good parts counts, inventory management, and effective quality control. National Manufacturing was hopelessly inadequate on every level.

It didn't take long to analyze the situation. Greenberg and his partner had two choices—reduce business to a manageable level amid the chaos, or make a major investment in machinery and personnel and modernize the plant. Their current approach to industrial management dated back to the pharaohs and started with the crack of a whip. Unfortunately for them, whipping doesn't help if the operating procedures don't work.

There were seventy-five work stations in the plant, and we had ninety-seven men on the day shift working at these job stations. Since most of the men couldn't read, write, or count, there was no reliable method to keep track of production. Practically no one, I quickly realized, knew how many parts were being manufactured. And the inaccurate parts counts took on a whole new meaning when all the piecework manufacturing was considered finished and final assembly began. It was only then, when the many parts were moved to the paint line, that a fairly accurate count could be taken, and then it was too late.

To further complicate the situation, only Alvin Katz knew the shipping schedule. Sometime during the day, he would tell the plant how many finished units were to be shipped, and on which truck. The plant foreman had no way to predict what would be needed, so he guessed. If he guessed wrong, and there weren't enough finished units ready for delivery, Alvin would scream and rail at the supervisors, and then put the day shift on overtime and work them until the quota was met. It was just bad business. An analysis of operations would save Greenberg a lot more than the twenty-five grand he'd paid me.

By the end of the day, I was wondering if I'd made a big

mistake. I'd been in some pretty nasty situations before, but this setup was a nightmare. As I drove home, replaying the day in my head, I happened to glance over at the computer profiles sitting on the passenger seat. I hadn't read them yet, but Boris had painted a pretty clear picture. The workers in the factory were not stand-up citizens, not by a long shot. They stole and lied and cheated as a matter of course.

But I'd gotten a little glimpse of their world, and it had a different set of rules. These men sweated forty or fifty hours a week for an average net pay of about one hundred and seventy dollars. They had to support families in New York City on that money. What it bought them was never enough. Their over-crowded apartments were located in neighborhoods where stray bullets were more common than mosquitoes, and they had to defend their homes from thieves and addicts with baseball bats and knives. They relaxed with booze, drugs, and cigarettes; fought with and beat their wives; and sometimes loved their children to a fault. They were capable of doing anything they thought would ease the strain.

My guess was that most of these men gave back in kind what they received. To get them to respect the rules, they needed to be shown some respect in turn. But at the National Manufacturing Corporation there were no rewards for diligence or honesty. The harassment was constant and universal. It made no sense—like trying to tame bobcats with a cattle prod. As I drove along the highway, it occurred to me that the sadist with the cattle prod better remember not to turn his back on those cats.

TWELVE

...

"No me rompes las pelottas!"

Carlos Rodriquez, the plant foreman, was shaking a greasy finger at one of the supervisors. He'd just told the man not to break his balls. There was more, but my Spanish isn't good enough to follow along when things get heated.

"Yo, Carlos, good morning," I interrupted.

It was my second week on the job and a routine was beginning to emerge. Boris and Clifford Brice spent their days together—working on their computers, reading books, visiting museums. I spent my days in a purgatory called the National Manufacturing Corporation.

Carlos turned off the anger when he saw me and turned on a big grin.

"Good morning, J. J. Donovan. Buenos dias," he said with a slight bow.

The bow was a private joke. Carlos would go into this bowing routine whenever Stanley, Morty, or Alvin showed up in the plant. He was a proud man and the feigned servitude was his way of thumbing his nose at them. Carlos was the glue that held everything together at National Manufacturing, but the owners paid him only a fraction of his worth. The guy was being used. They knew it and he knew it.

Carlos and I got along just fine. From the beginning, I made it clear to him that my primary function as plant manager was to make his life easier. This meant keeping Alvin off his back and handling the maintenance and administrative headaches that constantly interrupted his busy schedule. Each morning, Carlos gave me a quick rundown of the current production problems and then we set about a walking review of the morning's work assignments, starting with the brake press area.

The brake presses were supervised by Angel Sanchez. Angel, a squirrel of a man with a pencil-thin mustache and bad teeth, claimed to be an ordained minister of the Baptist church. Since he was also a compulsive liar, it was hard to know what to believe. He was responsible for setting up and overseeing nineteen hydraulic presses, several drilling machines, and about twenty-five men.

During the Saturday shift, one of his men had punched 3,500 small metal brackets upside-down before anyone noticed the error. When I arrived, Carlos was trying to discuss the error with him, but it was frustrating. Angel denied even knowing the job had been running. This was pretty incredible, since Angel did the setup. After many denials and accusations, he finally conceded that the parts would have to be replaced. To remake the parts, he needed additional sheet metal. I made a note to check the inventory.

The next stop was spot welding. Angel Sanchez looked good compared to the guy supervising spot welders. His name was Willie Perez. Willie was a Greenberg recruit, which meant that he liked riding men with discipline problems and following them to the bathroom to make sure they didn't dawdle. Willie was a very capable welder, but he couldn't manage people. He couldn't even fill out the paperwork. Carlos wasted a lot of time in this part of the plant, double-checking Willie and correcting his mistakes. The spot-welding area had more than thirty-five machine stations, including several multi-head welding lines used to construct wire shelves and frames. Spot-welding tasks were more complicated than press work. An operator might be required to apply as many as twelve different spot welds to each display part as he fastened metal clips to stanchions or wires to the frames. The supervisor was unreliable and the probability of making errors was higher, so it was important to take a little extra time reviewing the day's work.

After about forty minutes, we moved over to mig welding. The major weight-bearing welds were made in this area, and the frames of the display units began to take shape here. It was my favorite part of the plant. The welders wore heavy leather aprons and gloves stretching to their shoulders. The high-intensity arc of the welding machines filled the area with blue-white light and often spit out showers of sparks. Mig welders wore deeply tinted glasses or visors to prevent temporary blindness, making them look like industrial gladiators.

This area was run by a fat, middle-aged character from El Salvador who was known to all as Señor Pedro. Pedro was a warm, highly emotional man who could be charming, friendly, and when angered, a force to be reckoned with. He doubled as the plant Shylock. Breaktime, lunchtime, just about anytime, there was bound to be a crowd around Señor Pedro. On paydays, as the men lined up to satisfy their chits, you could hear him saying: "I thank you, my wife thanks you, and my children thank you, too." Sometimes in English, sometimes in Spanish, always with a smile.

In a factory like National, the Shylock was an essential figure, on equal footing with the shop steward. Because wages were so low and needs so great, many of the men lived a week or two ahead, borrowing against all or part of future paychecks. Señor Pedro was the bank. Good old Stanley Greenberg loved having him on site. If a guy who owed the Shylock screwed up and got fired, Pedro was out his money—the collateral was the borrower's job. All Greenberg had to do was hint that a man's job was on the line and Pedro would pay him a visit.

We didn't spend much time with Señor Pedro that morning. He had sixteen welding tables, but only half were in use because they were short of parts. The problem was being remedied, but the necessary stock had to go through spot welding first and wouldn't be ready till after lunch. The balance of Pedro's men had been reassigned. Those who had work were doing it. There were no other problems.

The wire cutting and bending area was located in a small connected building on the other side of the plant. Normally we'd have gone there next, but they were running the same jobs as the day before and it seemed like a waste of time. Besides, Carlos had gone over before the shift started to borrow a chain cutter and everything had been fine. He thought our time would be better spent in shipping and assembly. It turned out to be a good decision because the guy whose job it was to keep product moving out the shipping doors was waiting for us when we tried to leave mig welding.

"Hey, *man,* what the fuck is going on here today, huh? I mean, you want me to lose ma fuckin' mind or what? I don't need this shit, man . . . not today . . . not yestaday . . . not tomorra . . ." His voice just drifted off as he continued muttering to himself.

The voice belonged to Raphael Gomez, aka the Ratman. Raphael stood about five feet, six inches tall in his construction boots, which was deceptive because he wasn't a small man. He sported a goatee and kept his hair long and braided. More often than not, he wore purple sunglasses. His job was tough and he did it well. He was another reason the company managed to get by. The shipping and assembly area was his private domain. It was also the final stop in the flawed production cycle, the point at which all the mistakes finally became apparent.

Raphael handled stress the same way he'd handled it while serving as a Marine sniper in Vietnam. He found his equilibrium by constantly fine-tuning his head with marijuana and by sucking on lollipops. He spoke in quiet tones, his accent mixing street jive and Spanish, like somebody you'd expect to meet in a jazz nightclub. He didn't need to raise his voice; when he spoke, his people listened.

The Ratman was an important guy at National Manufacturing. He'd been with Morty for twenty-one years, longer than anyone else, and he was the shop steward. The employees respected him, and for the most part, Stanley and Alvin left him alone. He also had a reputation for acting a little crazy.

The Ratman got his nickname because of his hobby, which was killing rats. There were a lot of rodents in the building, and each morning when the shift arrived, there would be a few stuck in the garbage barrels scattered around the plant. During the night the rats would climb in looking for food and, if the barrel was less than half full, they couldn't get back out. The Ratman would unwrap a fresh lollipop, take out his well-worn Louisville Slugger, and delight his crew by beating the trapped animals to death.

The Vietnam War had left Raphael with a head full of nasty memories, and his reward had been more than twenty years of hard labor at National Manufacturing. The aftertaste was bitter. Killing the rats and the other nonsense he pulled was all showboat, like a little boy trying to hide his fear of the dark by talking really loud. He'd tell me little bits and pieces of his experience, as if telling me proved that the past didn't haunt him. The stories, all gruesome, were meant to shock.

"I'd get my boy, Donovan," he told me one afternoon, "get this little red dot from my infrared site dancin' on his chest. Then I would pull the trigger and watch the fun. Boy's dead and he don't even know it." He looked up at me, grinning. "They'd get this surprised look and start to reach down to touch the spot where I hit 'em, but before their hands could get to it they'd slump down dead. I loved that, man. It made me feel strong, like I could blow a man down and he'd never even know what happened."

He finished with a broad smile, but there was nothing behind it. Later, I saw him staring off, lost in thought. He could tell that story all he wanted, but he couldn't get it out of his head. I had to keep reminding myself that he was like a rubber band stretched to the limit.

The Ratman had other problems this morning. His area was full of parts he couldn't use because they were speckled with

121

little black dots. Sometime on Saturday, the white-powder booth had become contaminated with black paint. The night shift didn't catch the problem; they painted for six hours without noticing the spots. Now Raphael had hundreds of parts he couldn't use. Behind him, I could see the men hanging the rejected pieces on the conveyor for the trip back to the paint room. It would take time to clean the powder booth, and more time to repaint the pieces.

To keep his men busy, Ratman wanted them to work on a large, fairly complicated subassembly used in the display case they were preparing for shipment. The parts for this section had been coated before the contamination and were clean. By using the down time to do preassemble work, he'd cut his loss in half. But when they started doing the subassembly he discovered that purchasing had gotten the wrong bolts for the job and there was nothing in-house to use as a substitute.

Ratman was busy explaining all this to Carlos, Stu Sawyer, the designer, and me when the ten o'clock buzzer sounded the morning break. He stopped midsentence, turned on his heel, and headed for the coffee wagon parked outside the shipping bay. This was a union shop, and he was shop steward. Break time was his, not ours. As far as Raphael was concerned the problem could wait fifteen minutes.

Carlos and Stewart went into the office to discuss a new job, so I went over to the production desk and called purchasing. Bobby Seldane, an obnoxious, hyperactive little man who'd come from another Greenberg company, answered the phone. Seldane's main function was harassing the vendors into lower prices and quicker delivery dates. He chain-smoked Camel straights and drank too much coffee. This was just his type of problem.

"Seldane," he answered, all business.

"Bobby, this is Donovan in the plant. Somebody screwed up on the bolts for the J. C. Penney display and we're gonna be shut down unless you can get this thing corrected. If that happens, Alvin will be looking for blood." I added the bit about Alvin because I knew Bobby was terrified of him.

"Now hold on one minute, Donovan. Before we go talking about screwing up, we should know the facts. There are all kinds of mistakes being made in this shop, but they don't necessarily originate in purchasing. Why do I always get the first call? I mean, the mistake could have come from design. Have ya talked to Stu Sawyer? Ya know, we only order what we're told to order."

He was talking really fast and I could hear papers shuffling in the background as he sorted through his files looking for the item in question.

"Whoa, Bobby, hold on a second." I was afraid he'd get distracted trying to pin the mistake on somebody else. "Right now it doesn't matter who made the mistake. The real problems will start when I can't put any product together. You understand me? That's the kind of situation we're facing."

He stopped shuffling his papers. I heard his Zippo make a neat *click-clack* as he lit another cigarette. He took a deep drag and then sighed, exhaling the smoke.

"What do you need? How soon do you need it?"

'I gave him the specs for the bolts and hung up. It was a sure bet that we'd have our hardware within the hour. At the very least, Bobby Seldane would die trying. I headed outside to get a cup of coffee.

As the buzzer sounded ending the break, Alvin Katz made his first appearance of the day. He stormed into the plant, barreled over to the control desk, and grabbed the microphone for the P.A. system.

"Donovan, Sanchez, Gomez—to the desk. *Now!*"

I had taken my coffee into the small annex connected to the main building. This space was about eight thousand square feet; it housed wire bending and cutting and the raw materials inventory. I was checking on sheet metal for the brackets Angel's crew had messed up when this summons came over the loudspeaker. By the time I made my way across the plant, the others were already at the desk.

Alvin had a bill of lading in his hand and he was pacing up and down like Captain Bly. Ratman and Carlos were just standing there looking nervous. When he saw me, Alvin stopped pacing and folded his arms across his chest. His expression contorted into a queer grimace that seemed to lock for a moment or two, like a facial tic, and then relaxed back into his normal scowl.

"I want you to see for yourself what these morons have done now," he ranted, waving the document in front of me.

The bill of lading detailed the number and type of displays that had been loaded and shipped on one of the trucks during Saturday's night shift. It listed twelve A units and thirteen B units. The address and shipping information was correct, and the document had been initialed by the night foreman in accordance with company policy. As far as I could see, everything was in order.

"What's wrong with this, Alvin?" I asked, looking up.

"What's wrong with it?" His face turned deep red and his eyes bulged. "I'll tell you what's wrong with it. I instructed these idiots to ship thirteen A units and twelve B units! That's what wrong with it!"

The two types of units were like right and left hand gloves; they worked as a pair.

"Was this a partial order?" I asked, trying to get the facts straight.

My question seemed to intensify Alvin's anger. "What difference does that make? I gave instructions and they weren't followed!"

"Well, if this is a partial shipment," I began calmly, "we can fix the balancing problem when we complete the order. Otherwise, they can use the extra B units as they stand alone."

"It is not a question of partial shipments, Donovan, it's a question of following orders. Since you think the problem is so easy to correct, perhaps I should hold you responsible for these mistakes from now on. That way you can see to it that they don't happen at all," he wheezed, rage overwhelming him.

Alvin thrust the bill of lading at me, turned abruptly, and marched back into the office. Carlos and Raphael were shaking with laughter. Looking around the plant I could see quite a few faces sporting broad smiles. I was gaining quite a reputation for facing down *el grande loco*—the big crazy.

"Great, laugh all you want, but now he's gonna use this to get at me, and you both know it," I said. The words were hardly out of my mouth before the desk phone rang.

"Donovan, is that you?" It was Alvin, his breathing very labored.

"Alvin, about this shipping problem . . ."

"Shut up and listen to me, Donovan," he hissed. "You just showed me up and I can't have that. You're making me look bad and you're setting yourself up as the father protector to a bunch of lazy, low-life scum."

I didn't say anything. There was no reason to let this nonsense warp itself any further out of proportion. Besides, he was right. I was starting to enjoy pressing his buttons.

"Since you think shipping is no big deal, I've decided to let you handle it in the future. That bill of lading I just gave you was written up by Timmy Brown. When he comes in, fire him. I'll let you find a replacement, but until you do, you're responsible for all shipments. That puts you on the swing shift, pal. Your new hours are ten to ten."

He slammed the receiver down before I could get in a word.

This remarkable overreaction left me wondering what was so special about a single B unit. It just didn't make sense. On the other hand, the change in my shift was actually a blessing. I was too busy working during the day shift to focus on anything except my pretend job, which defeated the whole purpose. The staggered shift would give me a lot more flexibility and I'd be free to check out the neighborhood and meet some of the ladies who'd worked with Ruby. Alvin had actually done me a favor.

I hung up the phone and turned to find that Carlos was still standing there, waiting to hear what Alvin had in store for me.

"Well, what did he say, J. J.?"

Carlos didn't look too good. He'd been around Alvin long enough to know that the punishment could get out of hand.

"Let's see. He changed my hours to a split shift, made me responsible for all shipping documents on both crews, and told me to fire Brown. At least, that's for starters. I'm sure he'll have more to say at lunch."

Carlos started cursing. Brown was a decent man, and the mistake was a minor one. From his point of view the change would just cause trouble. He'd lose my help in the mornings and have to deal with the mistakes a new man would make learning the shipping clerk's job.

"Oh. yeah, I almost forgot," I added seriously. "Alvin also wants me to get him a blow-up doll from Forty-second Street so he can go on a date!"

Carlos broke into a broad smile and began to reply, but the sound of his voice was drowned out by a loud ripping noise and then a tremendous crash as a rack of metal parts tipped over. We could see sparks and lots of smoke coming from the big multihead welding machine. I dropped my coffee and started running.

THIRTEEN

■ ■ ■

It's hard to recall the details of those first few minutes; the pictures are fragmented and clipped, like outtakes from a movie. There was a great deal of confusion. People were yelling and calling for help. I could hear Willie Perez swearing in Spanish and, over that, the sound of someone crying out in pain. Carlos and I had to force our way through a crowd to get to the scene of the accident. What we found wasn't pretty.

The fuse panel on the multihead welder was smoking and sputtering ominously. Every few seconds it let out an evil hiss as the power surged. There were three men down on the floor, two of them pinned under heavy metal racks and wire baskets that had been stacked behind the spot welder. Somehow the stack had fallen over during the accident. A third worker, the machine operator, still had one hand on the control arm for the circuit box. His hand had melted onto the lever when the full force of the power surge hit him. His body was smoking and the laces on his shoes were torn open. I had never seen a man who'd been electrocuted. First a woman set on fire, and then a man fried from the inside out—these are not the sorts of things you forget.

I grabbed Willie Perez and shook him. He stopped swearing and stared at me, his eyes filling with tears. This was his area. It was his responsibility.

"Willie," I yelled. "Get over to the main box and kill the power. Do you hear me? Shut everything down. *Now!*"

He looked at me, then down at the sparking machine. Suddenly, my words registered and he made a dash for the central power station. I began pushing people back.

"Carlos, get these people out of here."

There was very little room to move. I noticed Alvin Katz standing on the edge of the crowd, his arms folded across his chest, his face locked in that peculiar mocking expression I'd noticed earlier. "Alvin, get nine-one-one on the phone. Tell them we've got three badly injured men and that one has been electrocuted." When he didn't react I screamed, "Alvin, make the bloody call!"

He turned and plodded off toward the office.

The hissing sound died as the power shut off, and Señor Pedro turned a fire extinguisher on the machine. While he tended to the smoldering wires, I moved in to check on the prostrate-machine operator. This time, I recognized the sickening smell of burnt hair and flesh, and choked down the bile in my throat. I felt for a pulse, but the kid was gone. He was no more than eighteen or nineteen years old.

Behind me, two living men were in need of help. One of them, an older guy called Popo, had his right leg pinned beneath one of the heavy racks. The other man, whose name I didn't know, had been buried under the pile of steel parts that had spilled from the metal baskets. He was barely conscious; his eyes were unfocused and the pupils were dilated. I told Angel to stay with him.

The old man stopped screaming and I heard a forklift start up. He just lay there murmuring and rocking from side to side. I took another look at his leg. It was badly mangled and the pool of blood on the floor was growing. I took my coat off and covered him. The sound of the forklift got louder. When I looked up, I was relieved to see that Raphael was behind the wheel. If anyone in the building had experience with this kind of trauma, it would be him. The Ratman jumped down and moved quickly to my side.

"Yo, Donovan, it's cool, man. It'll be all right," he said, and for the first time I realized my hands were shaking.

"What should we do, Raphael?" I asked.

"Okay, man, les take this one step atta time."

He went over to check the kid who'd been electrocuted, then stopped to look at the other injured men before coming back to me. Carlos, Pedro, Angel, and Willie were all standing by, anxiously looking for something to do.

"José is gone, bro, nothin' to do there but covah him up." Someone moved off to cover the dead boy. "That othah dude, Popo, his leg is bad. We gotta get the rack offa him and stop the bleedin' quick. My boy Tony"—he motioned toward the third man—"been knocked upside his head and that can be trouble. Can't tell what else is wrong till I can get a bettah look. I say, don' move him. Let the medics handle it when they get here. But we gotta keep him real still when we're movin' them racks an' baskets."

That wasn't going to be easy. The racks were each six feet long and about four feet tall. They were made of two-inch square welded steel tubing, and were meant to hold heavy pieces of formed metal, like the stanchions used to frame out the display cases. The baskets were much lighter. They had strong metal frames with chain-link sides and were used to hold loose metal parts. Both the racks and the baskets were designed to stack like building blocks, but it was dangerous to stack more than two at a time, and especially dangerous to mix racks and baskets together.

Some idiot had built a mixed pile four levels high just behind the multihead spot welder. It had probably been done temporarily to open up floor space. Evidently, the force of the electric shock had thrown the young operator backward against this stack, causing the parts to start shifting and the column to topple.

The top three racks had fallen over, trapping the workers and creating a huge pile of tangled metal pieces. We put a crew to work clearing the parts, and a second forklift was moved into position. Angel and Willie did their best to cover the fallen men with coats and jackets, then lay pieces of sheet metal on top of the coats for protection in case anything slipped and fell back on them.

The racks were a couple hundred pounds each when empty, but they could have been moved by hand if there'd been any room to maneuver. With space tight and injured people to worry about, this just wasn't feasible. Instead, when all the parts had been cleared away, we tied the sections of rack together with ropes and chains, then hooked them to the blades on the forklifts.

I stationed men wherever possible around the racks and put several more on the floor to keep the bottom from kicking out when we started lifting. Señor Pedro got on his knees and spoke to Popo and Tony in Spanish, reassuring them and explaining what we were about to do. The leg wound was bleeding heavily—we had to hurry. Carlos got behind the wheel of one forklift and Raphael took the other. I stood next to him on the floor.

"Gotta move it, man. Time's runnin' out," he whispered.

I gave the signal and the engines revved, building power. The blades started up slowly. Popo let out one last scream and fainted. The racks shifted and moaned, but rose. Though they swayed a bit, the men surrounding them held firm. I could hear sirens approaching.

"Stop. Hold it there," I shouted, giving the *kill* sign. "Ratman, get under there and see what you can do to stop that bleeding."

I was afraid that we'd already gone too far by ourselves. This stuff was for professionals, and they were on the way. Since there was no space to put the racks back down, we left them hanging from the forklifts. Our part was finished. There was nothing to do but stand around anxiously, listening to the sirens grow louder as the emergency vehicles approached.

Within minutes the building was alive with firemen and paramedics. The EMS people took control of the situation; we just tried to stay out of their way. Fifteen minutes later both men were on the way to the hospital, and the dead boy was headed for the morgue.

It didn't end there. The fire marshal wanted some answers, and a preliminary inspection of the plant had soured his mood. A young man had been killed on the job, and he wanted to know why. The poor bastard had taken enough raw electrical current to fry a moose when he'd only been trying to throw the shut-off switch on a fuse panel. Safety devices were supposed to protect people, not kill them. Greenberg didn't quite see it that way. He felt that if the men were careful they wouldn't get hurt, and he wouldn't have to waste good money on safety gear. Consequently, the welding machines and brake presses lacked protective guards and the men worked without gloves or safety glasses. But substandard OSHA compliance was nothing compared to the building-code violations. Among other things: the fire exits were padlocked, there were no vents for smoke or exhaust fumes, the sprinkler system wasn't operational, and the power grid had been wired by an unlicensed freelance electrician. Stanley had planned to have an engineer inspect the work, but somehow he never got around to it.

These infractions and many more were on display for the marshal to see, and he wasn't happy about any of them. It was going to cost Morty a lot more than a free dinner to clean up this mess. And yet, of all the disasters waiting to happen at National Manufacturing, a fuse-box accident had seemed the least likely. After all, we didn't make the electrical boxes, so we couldn't have screwed that part up. There had to be something wrong with the wiring or the installation.

While Stanley, Morty, and Alvin were busy trying to pacify the fire chief, I pulled on a pair of gloves and moved in for a closer look at the guilty fuse box. I tried to ignore the bits of skin and flesh still sticking to the handle.

A piece of industrial machinery, like a spot welder, runs according to the same basic principles as an electric lamp. It gets plugged into a power source, has an on-off switch, and between the power source and the switch is a fuse. The fuse acts as a safety device. If the wiring overheats or there's a power surge it will blow, breaking the circuit and disconnecting the power. In this case, the circuit box on the multihead spot welder, acting as the fuse, failed to break the power connection when the switch was thrown. Not only did the current continue to flow undisturbed, but the metal-handled switch came into contact with the live current and sent the full value of that power line surging into the operator's body. The chances of something like this happening by accident were remote.

The handle on the outside of the circuit box was connected to a horizontal metal bar located inside the box. This bar was attached to a large copper switch called a three pole, a single throw, or a knife switch. To me, it looked like the kind of device Dr. Frankenstein gets to play with in the monster movies. Anyway, this copper switch also included a 150-amp fuse. When the control handle was pulled up, the bar and switch moved with it, connecting all three poles of the knife switch and turning the power on. Similarly, by pushing down on the control arm, the bar inside would move down, disconnecting the switch and killing the power. At least, that was the theory.

It hadn't worked this time. Looking at the charred guts of the circuit box, I could see why. The bar had come down as expected, but when it did, the switch wasn't attached to it. The nuts, bolts, and washers used to connect the knife switch to the bar had fallen out. When the operator pulled the control arm down, the metal bar, moving by itself, came to rest against a closed electrical circuit. Enough juice went into the handle to light a 33,000-watt lightbulb.

The kid must have noticed that something was wrong with the firing sequence on the multihead welder, or he wouldn't have attempted to shut the system down. I wondered if he'd said anything to Willie or one of the other operators. Now that I thought about it, there should have been two guys working this station— one to operate the welder and one to handle the materials. I hadn't seen the second man.

More than anything, I wondered about those bolts. For all of them to come loose and fall out at the same time was next to impossible. Besides, if the bolts were installed through the top of the metal bar as designed, then they couldn't fall out when it was in the on position, even without hex nuts. For this "accident" to be possible, someone had to put the bolts in upside down and remove or loosen the nuts.

My thoughts were interrupted by the sound of the timeclock buzzer signaling lunch. It was twelve-thirty. An awful lot had happened in two and a half hours. The area around the multihead machine was roped off, but there wasn't much to see anymore. The men were moving outside in small groups, choosing to eat in the street rather than sit inside. I didn't blame them.

"Hey, tough guy!"

I turned to find Alvin Katz standing behind me, his chubby arms folded as usual. He'd obviously been watching me as I inspected the machine. The smile on his face was so inappropriate, it sent a chill through me.

"Time for lunch, Donovan. You must be hungry after your busy morning."

I stared at him, incredulous.

"What's the matter, tough guy? Lost your appetite?" He started chuckling. "Well, too bad. By the way, we're meeting in the showroom today, 'cause Morty and Stan have the fire marshal in the conference room. Your presence is required."

He started walking toward the office and I followed him with my eyes. When he got about sixty feet away he turned and, smiling broadly, winked at me.

One of the few perks National Manufacturing gave the managers and supervisors on the day shift was lunch. Just before noon, Stanley's friends at Gold's Deli would deliver sandwiches or salads and an assortment of pickles, peppers, and olives. There was a catch, however. Since the company bought the food, we were expected to work during the break.

The free sandwiches were served during our lunch meeting.

All the supervisors and certain members of the office staff were included. If he was in town, Greenberg ran these meetings; if not, Alvin took charge. The lunch meeting was supposed to help us avoid problems and mistakes by giving the staff the opportunity to communicate as a group. Unfortunately, these sessions usually turned into name-calling free-for-alls.

This lunch meeting was an unusually somber affair. The excitement of the morning had taken the fight out of everyone, including Alvin. He sat at the head of the table, in Greenberg's place, and calmly gave us a pep talk. It was fascinating to watch his chameleon act, but the performance was wasted. I doubt that anyone in the room heard a word he said. When Alvin was finished, Bill Smith, manager of the purchasing department, piped up.

Bill was a hard-drinking three-pack-a-day man. He'd spent thirty years in the Navy, earned his pension, and come home to Brooklyn. For most of those years, Chief Petty Officer Smith purchased and/or distributed supplies and ordinance. The switch to civilian purchasing manager was easy; after a lifetime in the Navy, he was prepared for anything.

He worked for National Manufacturing because the job was local and it kept him out of trouble. The money didn't matter; a pension supplemented his low salary. Besides, he needed to keep busy because his lifestyle was threatening to kill him. The one thing he didn't need was more time to party. In the ten years since his retirement, Smitty had divorced two wives and married a third. He'd also managed to survive two major heart attacks. His current wife, a nurse, was doing everything imaginable to save him from himself, but it was a losing battle. Smitty was going to dance himself right into the next world.

His chronic hangovers made Bill an unpleasant guy to deal with in the mornings, but by lunch he'd usually regained his sense of humor. As the afternoon wore on and happy hour approached he became a really fun guy. His daily report included current purchasing problems, an updated delivery schedule for various raw materials, and a summary of new orders and requests. At the top of his current list of requests were the bolts Ratman needed.

"You know, Donovan," he began, giving me the eye over the rim of his glasses, "that shmuck Seldane blindsided me on these fuckin' bolts. Try an gimme some warnin' next time. Okay babe? The guy's outta control."

Bill seemed like a pretty decent man, and I sympathized with him. I don't think I could have shared an office with Bobby Seldane.

"By the way," he continued, "if any of you catch Bobby at the coffee machine, stop him. The guy makes ex-presso. Capiche? He don't need no more energy. Okay, do me a fayva?" He looked down at his notes, hesitated a moment, then brought us all back to reality. "What are we gonna do 'bout that mess in the plant?" he asked, referring to the burned welding equipment and the tangled pile of metal parts.

It was a good question. We couldn't just leave all that stuff sitting in the middle of the factory. The plant was already short on space and we had orders to fill. In fact, we had a large order for wire shelves that had to be made on a multihead welder. The business couldn't afford the down time.

We discussed the options and decided to attempt repairs while Smitty got price and delivery on new and used replacements. The twisted parts that had been in the racks were now scrap metal. For purchasing to reorder, someone had to calculate the raw materials needed to remake the ruined parts. Carlos promised to get a list together after lunch.

His business finished, Smith put his pen down, lit another cigarette from the one still burning in the ashtray, and sat back in his chair. As far as Bill was concerned, his contribution to the meeting was over.

"What's the matter, Smitty," I griped, remembering Raphael's production problem, "did you guys forget me?"

"*Four-get chou?* No, Donovan, we din't four-get chou," he

said, laying it on. "If you look, I think you'll find your bolts and whatnot sittin' on the production desk, and with them, I hope you'll also find a new re-spect for purchasing."

I already had. Bobby was annoying, but he was effective.

The next item on the agenda was the design department. This area was managed by a guy named Stuart Sawyer. Stu was a good-looking, energetic man with too much savvy to be stuck at National Manufacturing. He was in his midthirties, had a degree as a design engineer, and had a pretty wife and child. I couldn't figure out why he stayed. A guy with his talent had options.

Stewart worked very closely with Morty Katz on sales. This meant translating Morty's bull into designs that were cheap but attractive to the buyers from the retail stores. In addition to designing all the display cases, Stu supervised the making of samples, worked up price quotes whenever Morty had an inquiry, managed the jig makers, and served as final arbiter on questions of quality control. It was too much for him to handle, and he was always behind schedule. All day long he rushed back and forth across the plant, trying to dodge the phone calls from unhappy customers.

Morty was bidding on a new order. If he closed it, the order would be the largest sale in the company's history. The customer, a big chain of department stores located in the Pacific Northwest, wanted three different-sized display cases, and wanted them to be unique. The initial order was for at least twenty-five hundred of each unit, with more to come as they expanded the business. It was worth over $3.5 million.

The design work and samples for this bid were finished, and Morty was awaiting word from the customer. In the meantime, he wanted Stuart to figure out how to reduce the projected cost of manufacturing the new displays. As long as the customer couldn't tell, Morty didn't care where the savings came from. This was one of his favorite tricks. Sometimes he'd even have Stu substitute a lower-quality steel or a cheaper paint for the materials listed in the customer's specifications, but that was pretty drastic.

136

In this case, Stu was supposed to see if there were any old jigs or assembling forms in storage that could be modified to fit the design of the new order. To make a display case from scratch, you need about twenty-five different jigs. The new order called for one basic design, but in three different sizes. Allowing for duplication of parts, Stu figured he'd need about fifty jigs. That many assembling frames would take a couple of months to make, though, and the materials weren't cheap. If he could modify some of the hundreds of obsolete jigs stored out back in the trailers, it would save a lot of money. The only problem was that no one knew exactly what was in the five storage trailers. The only way to find out was to empty the trailers. Sawyer was a good guy who had a problem; I volunteered. With a small crew, I thought I could get the inventory done that afternoon.

The last order of business brought us back to the cleanup. It was one thing to get prices for replacement parts, but someone had to deal with the physical mess out in the plant. We paged Sammy Mesa to the office. Sammy was a mechanic of extraordinary talent. If it was broken, he could fix it; if the parts were unavailable, he could make them. Sammy handled all maintenance problems at National. With repairmen demanding fifty dollars an hour, a guy like Mesa was worth his weight in gold. The most obvious and significant indication of his status was the fact that Alvin and Stanley never bothered him.

Sammy was a small, clean-shaven, hyperactive Cuban with olive skin and jet-black hair, and his exploits with the fairer sex were legendary. He kept the machinery running and directed all maintenance work from his command center in the basement boiler room. Sammy stayed at National because they let him call his own shots. Alvin had once made the mistake of trying to blame some of his production problems on Sammy. When Mesa didn't come in for a week and the plant ground to a halt, Alvin had to go to Sammy's house and beg him to come back.

Mesa bounded into the showroom shortly after the page was broadcast.

"Ah, you are here!" he declared, as if we'd been lost. "In the conference room, Señor Mort y Señor Stan, they are no so happy." He frowned, imitating Stanley Greenberg.

"Sammy, what—" Alvin started to ask.

Mesa put his index finger to his lips, indicating silence. He had an infuriating habit of correctly anticipating questions and answering them before they could be asked. "The mess is no so bad." He turned to Carlos, who served as translator for most sentences longer than six words, and said in Spanish, "I will need six, maybe seven men this afternoon to help me." Then, in English, "This is all right?" Carlos nodded yes as he translated. "I will move the bad machine to my work area, and tomorrow you will know what we can and cannot do for it," he continued in Spanish. Then, again in English, "This is also okay?" Another nod. "You are getting prices?" he asked Bill Smith. It was his turn to nod. "Bueno." Back to Carlos, in Spanish: "Please ask for a list of replacement parts for this welding machine. I will bring the serial number." Smith nodded a second time when he heard the translation. "Is there anything else? No? Bueno. Very busy. Adios." Sammy bowed quickly and left.

There was nothing left to do except select the work crews, and that was Carlos's job. For once the noon conference ended without fighting and with most of the food still sitting on the table. Only Alvin had shown signs of an appetite. There was the usual noise as folding metal chairs were closed and the group broke up and headed back to the plant. I was about to do the same when Stanley Greenberg called me into his office.

I closed the door and sat down heavily in the chair in front of his desk. Stanley was nervously playing with a letter opener. He looked a little pale.

"You got anything for me, Donovan?" he asked.

I just shook my head. I wasn't in the mood for a debriefing.

"Well, this thing today, this is bad. I could have big trouble on my hands from this thing. Right now I'm just tryin' to get that fuckin' lawyer, Powers, on the phone." He shook his head. Stanley was really spooked.

"Look, Stan, I've got my own problems just trying to keep

up with the work. Alvin's riding my butt and I've got five trailers to inventory this afternoon. So, if there's something in particular on your mind, say it. Otherwise, let's have this conversation some other time."

He hesitated for just a moment, as if he wanted to tell me something else but couldn't find the words. I could see the indecision in his face, but it passed. Apparently Stan wasn't ready to fill me in. "I heard about Alvin's little scene with the bill of lading," he said, relaxing a little. "But there's nothin' I can do about it. All I can say is the sooner you nail that fuck, the sooner you're outta here."

"I know that, Stanley," I assured him. "And you can believe me when I tell you there's nothing I want more than to get out of here."

"Yeah, well, this shit today . . ." He hesitated again. ". . . this is real trouble for me. I'm lookin' at thousands of dollars in fines from that fire marshal prick, not to mention a possible lawsuit from the family of the guy who got zapped. You take a hard look at that accident, 'cause maybe it wasn't."

He stood up, which meant the meeting was over. When I opened the door to leave, I discovered Alvin leaning up against the wall in the hallway.

"Complaining to the boss, J. J.?" he asked, smiling.

I went over to the coffee table and poured myself a fresh cup from the office pot, loading it with sugar for an extra jolt. Then I walked back to Alvin.

"Tell you what, Bubba," I said, getting close enough to whisper. "When I've got something to complain about, you'll be the first to know. That's a promise."

I stared into his puffy eyes for a moment, then walked back into the plant.

FOURTEEN

...

When I reached the production desk, I found my inventory crew waiting for me. Carlos had chosen three nervous young men who stood together in a tight semicircle, sharing a cigarette. They were wearing overcoats and looked uncomfortable, like guilty children outside the principal's office.

"Habla usted ingles?" I asked. "Do you speak English?"

It was a group question. In response, I got two blank stares and one nod yes. For some reason these guys were scared.

"Okay. What are your names?" I asked the kid who knew how to nod his head in English.

"*Me llamo* Juan," He pointed to himself, then, starting on his left, "Tino. . . . Jesus."

"Good, that's good. Bueno. So, Juan, what's the problem here? How come you guys look so sick? Enfermo? It's nice outside."

"Please, mister . . . soon is the hollyday. . . . Please, for the family . . ."

I didn't know what he was talking about. Most men would have jumped at the chance to get outside in the fresh air. In fact, after the morning we'd had, it would have been considered a reward.

"Juan, we are going outside to work in the trailers," I said as slowly and clearly as possible. "What is wrong? Que?"

"We are not fire?" he asked.

"Look, we're working in the yard this afternoon. No one is being fired. Okay? Tell the others."

They'd been told to put their coats on and wait at the production desk. When I came marching out of the office, they'd assumed the worst.

"Now, I want you," I said, pointing to each of them, "to get brooms, a floor jack, and some pallets. Okay? I will be outside by the trailers with a forklift. Entiendo? Do you understand me, Juan? Meet me there. And tell them if they work very hard, I will buy the coffee."

He nodded his head several times. There was a brief exchange in Spanish and the long faces disappeared. My crew split up in search of equipment and I went to get a forklift.

There were five storage trailers sitting behind the building on the Berriman Street side. It was an ugly patch of dirt filled with shattered bottles, bricks, and rubble. In addition to the trailers, it was home to a large Dumpster and an even larger container for the scrap metal. The old, rusted shipping rigs had been parked one beside the other, with the loading doors facing the street.

Our job was to inventory the contents of the trailers, and the quickest, easiest way to do that was to empty them, count and label the material, and then put it all back. I unlocked all five trailers. The first two were loaded with leftover parts and hardware from completed orders, and the last three were crammed so full of old assembling jigs that some of the frames spilled into the street when we opened the doors. We started by sorting the jigs into piles. My part was simple. I kept a list of the inventory as we went along and helped the guys figure out which jigs went in which piles. It was a bright fall afternoon, and the crisp, refreshing air helped to clear my head.

We'd been at it for about two hours when I noticed the porter, Joe Gagan, working over by the Dumpster. He was a short, solid old Irishman with watery eyes and a red, puffy face. Until Stanley decided to try to force him into early retirement, Gagan was the company's shipping clerk, and had been for more than fifteen years. According to Carlos, Joe was about as good as they come. His fall from grace coincided with Alvin's decision to assume control of shipping and receiving.

When I looked up again, Joe was waving me over as if he wanted to show me something in the Dumpster. I hesitated, because he had a habit of cornering me and launching into long, winded, boozy stories. I wasn't in the mood for one of his tales, but went over anyway because I felt sorry for the guy.

"What's the matter, Joey?" I began, annoyed by the interruption. His eyes were darting every which way and he was acting peculiar.

"I need ta speak with ya, Mr. Donovan," he pleaded, "but it needs ta be in private. Things ain't what they seem ta be here, if ya know what I mean."

"No, Joseph, I don't know what you mean. It sounds to me like the booze is talking for you." He smelled of rye whiskey.

"Despite appearances ta the contrary, it ain't the booze doin' the talkin', Mr. Donovan, just as you ain't what you claim to be, neither." He returned my stare without blinking. There was a spark in those bloodshot eyes. "I been watchin' and I seen you're a fair man, and maybe innerested in seein' the bastards take a fall. If you air, I believe I kin be of some assistance."

This revelation took me down a full two pegs. Here I was killing myself to fill the part of plant manager, and a drunk old rummy had seen right through my disguise.

"Nothing is ever what it appears to be, old man," I said irritably. "If you've got a problem, I'm willing to listen, but don't let your imagination get the better of you."

"Good for you, lad. Don't trust nobody. Good for you." Gagan was rubbing his hands together in delight. He lowered his voice to a whisper. "Meet me up on the balcony in the paint room at the break, and be careful. I'm bringin' a pal wit me and I don't mind telling you that we're, all of us, takin' a terrible risk."

He looked around again and then reached into his back pocket, pulled out a pint flask of Four Roses, and took a long drink.

"Now," he said, wiping his mouth, "start chewin' me out for

bein' a no good so-and-so. And make it look right, 'cause they're always watchin'."

This was a little too dramatic for my taste, but when he pulled out the flask, he didn't leave me much choice. I shouted and cussed at him and even jabbed him a few times with my index finger to reinforce the effect for anyone watching from a distance. He turned abruptly and walked away from me in a huff. As a final exclamation, he spit a big wad of chewing tobacco over his shoulder that missed me by inches. For some reason that really set me off, and I kicked over the garbage barrel he'd left on the sidewalk.

When I turned back to the trailers, my crew was standing there like statues, staring in disbelief. None of them had seen me lose my temper before, and the performance had definitely gotten their attention. Staying in character, I walked over and barked at them for being a lazy bunch of good-for-nothings and for not minding their own business. Then I grabbed my clipboard and stalked off to sit on a parked car and sulk. I needed time to think.

It was possible Gagan was just looking for an excuse to blow off steam. I didn't want to get into that. If word got out that I was willing to listen, the whole plant would end up crying on my shoulder. On the other hand, he hadn't sounded like a man angling for a sympathetic ear. He was worried, and that wasn't like him. Besides, he was offering to help me, and that was something I couldn't afford to ignore. Joe Gagan had been around for a long time, and as shipping clerk he'd been part of the management team. If there were any secrets in that factory, it was a good bet he'd be aware of them.

Still, I wondered why Gagan had chosen to stay on at National after his demotion. Garbage duty was at the bottom of the ladder. With his seniority, he could have just retired and saved himself the humiliation. An hour earlier, I would have said he was a pathetic old drunk who'd lost his pride. Now I wasn't so sure.

The buzzer sounded for the afternoon break, but my crew didn't move. At first I thought they were afraid to leave without permission. Then I remembered the coffee. I'd promised to buy, and they were waiting to see if I'd come through. I called Juan over, handed him a ten-dollar bill and told them they could spend it all. Alvin would have been disappointed—Juan didn't look a bit like a savage beast. He was wearing the expression of a kid who'd just been handed the keys to a candy store.

I watched them run down the block and turn the corner; free anything was exciting for those guys. I waited two more minutes, to be sure I was alone, then made my way down the street, through the side door, and into the paint room.

It was a cavernous area with nearly four thousand square feet of floor space and a ceiling two stories high. There was always a thin coat of powder on the exposed surfaces, like a light dusting of snow, so that you left footprints when you walked through the room. Inside toward the front stood two powder-coating booths, the conveyor line snaked through them on its way to and from the baking and drying ovens.

The ovens were the largest objects in the room, almost as tall as the ceiling. To get to the filters and the thermostat, you had to climb a metal ladder set in the wall, then follow a catwalk behind the superstructure of the baking ovens to a small balcony. It was a very secluded perch. I knew about it because that was where you went to look for Clarence Roberts, the paint-room manager, when he turned up missing during the day.

By the time I got onto the catwalk, Gagan was already crouched down in the corner of the loft talking to someone. He was speaking Spanish, which surprised me. As I made my way along the steel-grated walkway I tried to be quiet, doing my best to avoid the empty beer cans that littered the deck. Apparently Clarence didn't go thirsty while he was loafing. The break only lasted for fifteen minutes and it had taken me nearly seven minutes to get to the meeting place, so there wasn't much time left. Joe and his friend stood up when they saw me, and we huddled together by the railing on the far end of the balcony.

"This is Raul Brito," Gagan said, pointing at the scared boy by his side. "José Comacho, the kid what got burned this mornin', was his cousin. Ain't that right, Raul?"

Raul nodded.

"Now, I give him my word that nothin' will happen to him for talkin' to you, and that's the truth, isn't it, Mr. Donovan?" Joe was talking quickly. He kept looking over his shoulder as if he expected somebody to jump at us from the shadows. The smell of whiskey on his breath had me wondering if the guy was getting a little paranoid, but I'd come this far, so I gave the kid my word.

"Good, real good." He wet his lips. "Okay, son, you tell Mr. Donovan what you told me, and don't be afraid."

Raul blinked his eyes a few times to chase away the fear and then started whispering softly in a pidgin English. There wasn't much time, and I was having trouble following what Brito was saying. I turned to Gagan. "Translate for me, you old scoundrel," I commanded.

It was his turn to look surprised. He whispered something to Raul and the boy started to speak very quickly in Spanish.

"He says his cousin, José, was working on the night shift, loadin' trucks. One night José saw some bad guys and they scared him pretty good. Next day he went to see yer pal Alvin Katz. He told Katz the story, and Alvin made him promise not to tell anyone else. That's how José got the job weldin'—it was a reward for keepin' quiet."

It was hard to contain myself, but I didn't want to frighten the boy, so I took my time and spoke softly.

"Raul," I asked gently, "what did your cousin José see that made him so scared?"

He hesitated a second and his eyes grew very wide.

"Revolvers. Dinero," he whispered. "Guns. Money."

At that moment the warning buzzer went off and I thought the kid was gonna faint. He started shaking, and the fear in his eyes convinced me that this was serious business. It wasn't a simple case of greedy men stealing from each other anymore;

people were dying at the National Manufacturing Corporation. The shift would start again in three minutes.

"Tell Raul that I know he's very scared," I said to Gagan, "but I want him to go back to work this afternoon and try to act normal, like everything's all right."

While Joe was translating, I wrote Manny Santos's name and number on the back of one of my business cards and handed it to Raul.

"Ask him if he has any more family in New York."

The answer brought tears. José had been his only family; they had shared a room like brothers.

"That's tough, but it'll make it easier to look out for him," I said to Gagan. I took a few seconds to collect my thoughts, then continued. "He is not to come back here to work tomorrow, and he is not to go home tonight. When the shift is over, I want him to leave immediately. When he gets to a phone, he is to call that number"—I pointed to the card—"and speak to Manuel Santos. He should tell Manny that Mr. Donovan sent him, and he will be taken care of."

Gagan was translating like a local, and Raul seemed to pull himself together as he listened. It wasn't much, but it was all I could think of on such short notice. Besides, it didn't matter if I was overreacting; he was better off not working in a dump like National. Manny would find him a decent job. I didn't want the kid to have an accident like his cousin.

"Does he understand?" I asked Gagan.

"He understands awright, but whether he'll make the call or just run is anybody's guess."

I took out my wallet and handed Raul a couple of twenty-dollar bills.

"Tell him to use that money to hire a car when he goes to see Manny Santos," I said without taking my eyes off of him. I was hoping Raul would find something reassuring in my face. The second buzzer rang, ending the break. I had to hurry. "If he does as I say, everything will be fine."

Raul didn't wait for the translation. Clutching the bills in his

146

fist, he gave me one last look and was gone like a shot. I stood for a moment, watching him scurry down the ladder and out of the room.

"Where's he working?" I asked, turning back to Gagan, who'd broken out the bottle again.

"He's in wire-bending today," he said, passing me the pint. "I'll keep an eye on him, don't worry."

Without thinking, I took a swig and got another surprise; the booze was watered down. Joe winked when he noticed my expression.

"Nothin' worse than watered-down whiskey, right lad? But then, nothing is ever what it seems to be." He flashed another broad smile.

"How'd you figger out about me talkin' the Spanish?"

"Listen, pops, you aren't the only one around here with his eyes and ears open. I heard you whispering when I was coming up the ladder."

"Is that so?" he said, scratching his chin and grinning. "Well, there's still a whole pile we don't know 'bout each other, but I don't see as there's time for a proper chat just now."

He was right. I could hear the men who operated the powder booths talking down below us as they got back to work. It would be a matter of minutes before Clarence showed up with a fresh six-pack and settled in for the rest of the afternoon.

I pulled out another card and handed it to Gagan. I still didn't know where he fit in, but I had to trust someone.

"Call the number on that card tonight. If you don't get me, ask for Boris. Talking to him is a little weird, but you can trust him."

Gagan chuckled. "Well, son, I thank ya fer the vote of confidence, but I'm way ahead of ya." He opened his shirt and pulled out a sheaf of papers thick enough to fill a good-sized notebook. "I think you'll find this innerestin' readin'," he said, handing me the documents. "I spotted ya the first day, lad, and I been waitin' for the chance to pass this stuff along ever since. I'm glad ta be rid of it."

147

He let out a big sigh, wiped his face with a handkerchief, and took another drink from the bottle.

"Don't be talkin' no prettay bullshit 'roun me, mon!"

It was Clarence Roberts down below, giving the painters a hard time. He would be on his way up in a minute. I looked over at Gagan. He'd stopped smiling.

"Is there another way down?" I whispered.

He pointed to the other end of the catwalk, which disappeared into a hole in the far wall. There wasn't time for both of us to get over there and out of sight before Clarence reached the balcony. It didn't make sense for me to try it; I had no idea where it led, and getting lost or stuck would be much harder to explain than being found on the catwalk. I pulled out my shirt and stuffed the papers down the back of my jeans.

"Get going," I ordered, shoving Gagan in the right direction. As he opened his mouth to argue, the Jamaican on the ladder treated us to a prodigious belch.

"Clarence? Is that you?" I yelled, putting an end to the argument.

Gagan took off.

"Who's der?" Clarence sounded like he'd heard a ghost.

I walked out from behind the oven and stood above him. He had stopped halfway up the ladder and was trying to hide a brown paper bag that was the size and shape of a six-pack.

"I've been looking for you, Clarence," I said. "As you know, we had to repaint a lot of parts this morning. I thought perhaps you could help me figure out why that happened."

His lips were moving as he followed my sentences, but he didn't say anything.

"But," I continued, "now that I've had a chance to look for myself, I think I know the reason we do so much repainting. Why don't you come up here and I'll show you?"

He resumed his struggle on the ladder, still trying to hide the bag of beer. When he finally made it onto the catwalk, I motioned him over with my index finger.

"You see all those beers cans?"

"Ya, mon." His tone was cautious.

"Do you know who drank all that beer?"

"Naw, mon!" He was emphatic.

"I think I do, Clarence."

"Ya, mon?" he gulped.

"Yes. And the person who's been doing all this drinking is probably the same person who's making mistakes and contaminating the powder booth."

"Ya, mon," he said softly.

"Well, Clarence, I hate to say this." I paused and stared at him long enough for beads of sweat to form on his brow. "It must be one of your men, one of those painters working down in the powder booth."

I pointed an accusing finger down at the men working on the floor level. Clarence let out an audible sigh of relief. I put a sympathetic hand on his shoulder.

"Now, I know it's not your fault, but these men work for you, so they're your responsibility. I want you to get this place cleaned up. Then, I want you to find out who is drinking beer during the shift." Clarence looked at me, glassy-eyed. "*You got that?*" I shouted.

He snapped to attention. "*Ya, mon.*"

I turned on my heel, mounted the ladder, and climbed down. When I reached the exit to the street, I opened and then closed the door, stepping back into the room. There was an interlude of about a minute before I heard it. From high above me, up on the balcony, came the familiar pop-pop of someone pulling the tab on a can of beer.

Back at the trailers, Alvin Katz was waiting for me. He stood in the middle of the street, his coat on and his arms folded across his chest. He looked very unhappy. That made two of us. Until that moment, I'd considered him nothing more than a miserable excuse for a man. But the picture had changed. He was involved in something really dirty. I hadn't seen the signs because it was

149

going on during the night shift, but it was happening, and Alvin didn't want anyone talking about it. José Comacho made the mistake of confiding in Alvin Katz, and he'd been rewarded with a new job on the multihead welder. It hadn't been a good career move.

I walked over to him as if nothing were wrong.

"Ah, Donovan, nice of you to put in an appearance. By the way, have you promoted one of these creatures without telling me?" he asked sarcastically.

Juan, Tino, and Jesus were looking even more worried then they'd been when I first met up with them.

"No, Alvin, I . . ."

"Or maybe you think we've got so much money we can just give it away?" he continued, cutting me off. "Because when I came out to see how the inventory was going, I found these three"—he indicated my crew—"picnicking in the back of trailer number four."

"Look, Alvin, we worked into the break. They were due an extra five minutes. Okay?"

"Is that so? I understand you're also subsidizing their wages with free coffee and other treats. What's that for? You trying to train them?"

"What I do with my money is none of your concern, Alvin," I said softly. The hair on the back of my neck was starting to rise.

"In that case, why don't you tell me what you were doing in the paint room?" he asked. "That *is* my business. Last I heard, they weren't serving coffee in there."

The smile was gone now.

"You following me around, Alvin? Checking up on me?" I was getting angry. " 'Cause if you are, you're wasting a lot more than the cost of a few cups of coffee. Greenberg brought me in here so you'd have more time for your work. I doubt he'd be happy to learn that you waste it following me around the plant."

"You're not answering my question, Donovan." His smile was back.

"Okay, Alvin, since you insist." I took a breath and released my anger with a sigh. "I've been concerned about the constant repainting of parts. It's a serious problem and it costs a lot of money in time and materials." I paused for a second breath. He was watching me closely. "I decided to take a good look at the paint room, including up on the catwalk and the balcony. What I found were enough empty beer cans to make a killing on scrap aluminum. Old Clarence must be drinking two or three six-packs a shift."

"And so . . . ?" He was really eyeballing me now.

"Isn't it obvious? The man's drunk and he's making mistakes. That's how the powder booths get contaminated!"

Katz hesitated a moment, then started clapping his hands in mock applause.

"Good try, J. J., very good try," he said. "Now, as far as Clarence Roberts is concerned, he's the same drunk he's always been. I doubt he's suddenly become more of a fuck-up. But hey, I give you points for thinking on your feet. In fact, I believe I'm gonna have to take you more seriously from now on." He looked at his watch thoughtfully. "There's an hour and a half till the shift ends. I think you should get back to the production desk and start your paperwork. I'll finish up out here."

"Paperwork?" I asked, a bit confused.

"You haven't forgotten your new responsibilities already, have you?"

"Oh God, shipping!" I cried, trying to sound as unhappy as possible. I didn't want to ruin Alvin's fun.

"I left instructions for you at the desk," he informed me cheerfully. "But I think you should get hopping. The paperwork can be tricky, and we don't want any mistakes, do we?" He began to move towards the trailers, then stopped. "Oh yeah, don't forget to fire Brown. He'll probably start whining about union rules. Ignore him. He gets two days' severance pay and that's all."

He started to walk away again, but stopped a second time and came back.

"It's your show now, Donovan, and for your own sake I hope you don't screw up," he said flatly.

He'd just thrown down his gauntlet and was daring me to pick it up. I didn't bite. The threat was real enough, but the timing wasn't right. I left him out by the trailers and walked back into the factory.

On my way to the production desk, I passed Sammy Mesa's crew. They had just finished their work and were sweeping the floor. The damaged machinery was nowhere in sight. It had been dismantled and removed, leaving a big, empty space in the middle of the plant.

It was as if the multihead welder had never existed. The racks were gone, the twisted metal parts were gone, and so were any traces of human suffering. I had to blink my eyes. It was as if nothing had happened. The only incongruous sight was the block of clean, unfilled floor space, and by the end of the night shift that would be full of parts and subassemblies, and the plant would get back to normal.

I closed my eyes and replayed the scene again in my mind. It would be a long time before I could shake the image of José's smoking body. I didn't need a pile of charred machinery to remind me. But the memory helped to move my focus away from Alvin's mind games and back to the business at hand. I decided to make a little detour and check up on Raul. He had my word that everything would be all right, and I planned to keep it.

As I turned the corner into the wire bending area, a scuffle broke out across the room. I could see two men in street clothes pushing and shoving someone against the wall over in the corner. Then I saw an object that looked like a black broom handle go up in the air and come down. It was followed by a dull, sickening thud. It was a simple noise, all the more frightening because I knew its source. My knees suddenly felt weak.

There was no time to act reasonably or to analyze the situation. The sound of wood connecting with a man's skull had a chilling effect on me. I went after the strangers like a crazy person. By the time I reached them, the baseball bat was being raised for a second blow. I grabbed the guy with the bat by his collar and dragged him backward. He lost his balance and I slammed his head into one of the columns supporting the roof. He crumpled to the floor.

I ran over to check on the person who'd been struck. It was Raul Brito. He was lying on the floor staring up at me. His eyes were vacant and there was a nasty-looking dent in his forehead, but he was still alive. I could tell because his breath came out as a rasping sound, and little bubbles of saliva were forming at the corners of his mouth. I stared down at him. It was probably just for a second or two. In my memory it seems longer because I can still see that kid lying on the floor. That moment of hesitation almost cost me my life.

I heard someone yell my name and turned just as the second guy took a swing at me. The movement changed my body position enough so that he missed hitting me in the head, which was lucky. Unfortunately, he didn't miss me completely and the baseball bat landed on my right shoulder, numbing that whole side of my body. I'm a southpaw, a lefty, which proved to be a blessing, because my right arm was no longer working. I absorbed that first blow without going down and kept on turning to the right. He came in for a second strike. I feigned left as the big black bat came down again, then moved in under the blow and hit the creep at the base of his nose.

I put all of my one hundred and ninety pounds into that punch. There was a cracking sound as his nose broke and I could feel the bone and cartilage move up and in as I followed through. He fell back against the wall and stood there for a second before his knees gave out and he slowly folded.

I spun around quickly to be sure his friend hadn't gotten back up. Apparently he'd tried, because he wasn't where I'd left him. I found him behind me, a bit to the left, stretched out in front of Joe Gagan. I remember seeing Joe leaning on a baseball bat with an angry expression on his face. Next, I remember looking down at the guy in front of Joe and noticing the tattoo on the back of his hand. It was a crudely etched scorpion.

Then the lights went out.

FIFTEEN

...

When my senses returned, I was lying on the couch in Alvin's office. The only illumination in the room came from a small lamp, which made a bright puddle on the surface of his desk. Alvin was sitting in his chair, just on the edge of the pool of light, humming and flicking his tongue in and out like a reptile. I'd have passed it off as a bad dream if my shoulder hadn't been throbbing. When I tried to sit up, an ice bag fell to the floor.

"That's a nasty bruise you've got there, Donovan. Can I give you a lift to the emergency room?"

Alvin leaned forward and I could see the familiar smirk on his clock. The indirect light didn't flatter him; it just exaggerated the pockmarks on his face.

I rubbed my own face with my good hand and tried to blink the cobwebs out of my eyes. This just wasn't my day.

"What happened out there? Is Raul okay?" I asked, ignoring his offer of a ride. My voice sounded hollow.

"So, you knew Brito?" He paused. "Well, I'm sorry to say he wasn't looking too good when they took him away."

Alvin's voice sounded different, almost mechanical. I put the ice bag on my forehead.

"Look, Alvin, do me a favor and fill in the blanks. The last thing I remember, I was looking down at that guy with the tattoo."

His eyebrows arched when I mentioned the skin painting. He

pursed his lips and locked me in a stare. This was not a good situation. Until my head cleared, I had to be careful or my mouth would cause me even more trouble.

"Let's see." Alvin relaxed, leaned back in the chair, and put his hands behind his head. "As far as I can tell, you got yourself into the middle of a spic vendetta or something like it. As you know, I was outside when it all happened, so anything I tell you is secondhand."

He was smiling again. I guess he thought a little tap from a baseball bat had made me stupid.

"The way I hear it, these two guys had some kind of a personal thing to settle with your friend Brito. Nobody seems to know why they were pissed off, but that doesn't matter. The way these spics think it could be anything. Maybe Brito humped the guy's sister without payin' for it. Who knows?

"Whatever the reason, it was a mistake to mess with those two. They used to work here, you know. Very bad news. I laid them off over the summer and never bothered calling them back. I was happy to be rid of them. Puerto Ricans are bad enough, but Mexicans? Fuhgeddaboutit. And they were brothers, which is even worse.

"The little one is Ramon Veldez. His brother went by the name *Cana Dulce,* which means Sugar Cane. Kinda cute, don't you think? Anyways, they were bad business. Brito should have steered clear or run fast. As it is, they gave him quite a beating before you showed up to play Superman. It looked to me like they used his head for batting practice."

I moved the ice bag back to my shoulder, which was really starting to hurt. In a rare display of civility, Alvin actually got up and brought me a bottle of aspirin and a can of Diet Pepsi. The original Good Samaritan.

"Try a few of these," he suggested, handing me a bottle of Bufferin. "Should I continue or have you had enough for now?"

My mouth was busy with the soda, so I just nodded my head for him to keep talking. He went back to his seat.

"What happened next is pretty straightforward, though you'd

never know it the way the men are talking. There are at least a dozen versions of your machismo circulating in the plant. You could take your pick, but I think Carlos is probably the best source. Don't you? I'll give you his play-by-play.

"He says you dove into the fight like a madman and grabbed the little guy, Ramon, by the neck and hammered his head into a steel column. Then his brother, the Sugar Man, whacked you in the shoulder with a baseball bat. Somehow you stayed on your feet, turned, and with one fatal swing of your mighty fist killed Mr. Cana Dulce. Which should be a lesson to anyone approaching you with a baseball bat. After that, you took a couple of steps toward Brito, but collapsed before you reached him. The bottom line? You are now a fucking legend!" He was really enjoying himself.

I sat back heavily and stared at him for a full minute. The thought of killing a man didn't exactly thrill me.

"You're kidding, right?" I asked finally. "I mean, I didn't kill the guy, I just laid him out. I remember hitting him . . . but, come on."

"Oh, you killed him all right." Alvin smiled broadly.

I stared at him, speechless. I remembered smacking the guy. The sound of the bone breaking and the feel of it moving with the punch came back to me. All at once my stomach lurched and I dove for the wastebasket. There wasn't much besides aspirin and soda for me to throw up, but I knelt there for a while anyway.

Alvin didn't say a thing. You could hear the squeak of his chair as he rocked back and forth. Waiting. I remember wondering if he was doing that snake thing with his tongue. It was suddenly cold and I wished I had my jacket, but it wasn't there. After a few more minutes balanced over the wastebasket, I reached for the can of soda and used the last few sips to rinse my mouth. Then I sat back down on the couch and let my body go numb. The room was too small. I needed to get out.

"I know you've had a rough day, J. J., but I think you're overdoing it a bit, don't you?" Alvin's tone was peevish. "I mean, the guy was a turd. You did everybody a favor by killing him. Come on, you should feel good."

I swallowed back the bile that was rising again and kept my piece. If I was going to make it through the rest of the day, I had to tune Alvin out. I took a deep breath.

"Let's forget that for now," I said. "How did I get in here? Where are the cops? The ambulance crew? Don't tell me you all just went back to work and left the bodies out there on the floor?"

"That's better," he said, smiling broadly. "Your sense of humor is returning."

"Skip the crap, Alvin, I'm not in the mood."

"Let's see." He pretended he hadn't heard me. "The EMS people have already been and gone. They took Brito and Ramon Veldez to a hospital. Sugar Cane Veldez got a free lift to the morgue. I'm surprised that you don't remember—you seemed pretty sure of yourself when they were here. The medic wanted you to ride to the emergency room for a checkup, but you refused. In fact, you were a real pain in the ass."

I had no memory of the time between fainting and waking up on the couch. I moved the ice bag a little farther up my shoulder toward my neck, which was getting very stiff.

"I didn't push it," Alvin cooed, waving a hand in the air. "They checked you out and said you probably had a broken collarbone. Are you sure you don't remember this?"

I shook my head. No, I didn't remember.

"Well, the medical guy strongly suggested an X ray, but you weren't interested. Since you didn't have a head injury and you were acting like such a prick, they stopped arguing. There were other men who wanted and needed medical care, so the ambulance left without you. Until just a few minutes ago you were prowling around out in the plant. Then you decided to faint again. I had the men bring you in here.

"By the way, that's two fainting spells, just in case you're counting."

Alvin actually sounded giddy, like this was a game and all

the excitement had been exhilarating. Under the circumstances, it was a bizarre reaction, even for him.

"The EMS technician said that the first time you fainted was probably from pain," he continued happily. "I sympathize with you, I hate pain. He also predicted that you'd pass out again if you didn't stop trying to act so manly. If and when you fainted a second time, he said to keep you quiet and to ice the shoulder. He didn't seem to think it was serious."

That was easy for him to say. It was my shoulder.

"What about the cops?" I asked.

"The police are still here. They're in with Stanley and my father right now. Seems they want to have a talk with you, too. Hey, they've got to—you killed a man."

He was rubbing it in good.

"May I have another soda?"

My mouth was dry and I needed to replace the aspirin I'd zorked into the wastebasket. The pain radiating across the upper right side of my back was starting to make my eyes water.

Alvin had a small Frigidaire full of soda and other goodies under his desk. To maintain his girth he needed to ingest junk food at frequent and regular intervals. He took out a Diet Pepsi and threw it to me. That was a good test. I managed to catch it, which meant some of my motor functions were returning. While I was opening the can, he reached into his desk drawer, pulled out a prescription bottle, and threw that to me, too. The label indicated Tylenol with codeine.

"What're you doing with this stuff?" I asked casually.

I opened the bottle and pretended to pop a couple, then drank some more soda. It was hard for doctors I trusted to get me to take prescription drugs. Alvin Katz didn't stand a chance. I threw the container back to him.

"I've got bad joints," he answered, smiling. "When they get stiff, I need something for the pain. Those aren't very strong pills, but they're better than aspirin. If you need more, they're in my bottom drawer."

He leaned down to put the pills away. When his head came back up he was pinching his nose and his mouth was screwed up, like he'd just tasted something sour.

"I've got to get that vomit outta here or I'm gonna start throwing up," he said, pointing to the waste bin. "You need anything else?"

What I needed was solid food, like bread or crackers. Alvin took the garbage can with him and promised to look for something edible. While he was out of the room, I tiptoed over to his private pharmacy, looking for the aspirin. When I pulled his desk drawer open, I was astounded. Alvin could have opened a mini-mart for prescription drugs. I found the Bufferin and knocked back three or four, then started copying down the labels on the other bottles. I began to feel a little vague again, so I stopped writing and went back to the couch. I didn't want to faint a third time. My ego couldn't have handled that.

I needed food, secure surroundings, and some time to rest and heal. Closing my eyes, I tried to summon a little Zen magic, like mind over matter. It didn't work. When I reopened my eyes, I was still in Alvin's office and my shoulder still hurt. It occurred to me that what I really needed was a bit of *Celtic* magic, like about six fingers of Jameson Irish whiskey.

A few minutes later, the door opened and Alvin came back into the room with Stanley Greenberg in tow. For the first time since I'd met him, Greenberg actually looked his age. Maybe even older. Judging from appearances, things weren't going his way, either. Alvin handed me a couple of buttered bagels wrapped in paper towels. Patsy, my girlfriend out in reception, was taking care of me. I started to eat and felt better almost immediately.

"You okay, Donovan?" Stanley asked without looking at me.

"I'll live, Stan. Maybe I should ask how you're doing. You look like you're the one got hit with a baseball bat." I went back to my bagel.

"I'll tell you how I am," he yelled, turning on me suddenly. "I'm a fuckin' mess and my business has turned into a disaster area. I spent the morning explaining an electrocution to Smokey the Bear and now I got cops all over the fuckin' joint askin' about the guy *you* snuffed. As if that's not enough, it looks like the kid that got smacked in the head ain't gonna make it, either. How the fuck do you think I feel?"

Unbelievable. Stanley Greenberg expected me to feel sorry for him. The man didn't care about any of the people who'd been hurt, including me. He was pissed off because he was being inconvenienced and was worried about his money.

"You say Raul Brito isn't going to make it?" I asked, changing the subject.

"Was that his name?" Stanley looked over at Alvin, who nodded. "Yeah, Brito. That's right. Well, it don't look good for the kid. But the cops say if he croaks they'll charge that other piece of shit, Veldez, as an accessory to murder."

I let this news settle for a few seconds before continuing, "Look, Stan, you'll excuse me if I don't get too excited about the legal ramifications of this thing, but I've had it. Alvin says the cops want to talk to me before I leave. Is that true?" He nodded. "Then let's get it over with so I can go home."

I won't bore you with the details of my conversation with the plainclothes guy and the two uniforms from the seven-five. They didn't seem to mind that I'd killed a man. In fact, they treated me like I was something special. I guess in their precinct it was unusual for a gringo like me to come out of a scrape in one piece. Anyway, things were moving along on a very cordial basis till they suggested that I take a ride to the station house. I had no intention of going any place but home. That proved to be a big problem.

We talked about it for a while, but the guy handling the investigation didn't want to make a decision. Since I was politely refusing to go with him, he called home for somebody with more rank. After about twenty minutes, a small, compact Mediterranean detective with sad eyes and a rumpled suit paid us a visit.

161

It was Lieutenant Negro, the cop who'd watched my partner faint in the alley across the street. Fortunately, Negro didn't seem to recognize me. From his lousy posture to the dour expression on his face, the guy's whole demeanor said he didn't want any problems and wasn't interested in making waves.

When Negro had heard all the facts and read over the statements from the witnesses, he seemed convinced that mine was a case of self-defense. He even tried to get the district attorney's office on the phone, but the assistant D.A.s were all busy frying bigger fish than J. J. Donovan. That was bad luck for me, because Lieutenant Negro didn't want to be responsible for letting me go home, either. We were back at square one.

For someone who works full-time helping other people untangle problems created by the legal system, this stalemate was becoming an embarrassment. To avoid a policy dispute with the D.A. and to make his paperwork easier, Lieutenant Negro, master criminologist, wanted me to voluntarily ride to the seventy-fifth precinct station and allow them to fingerprint, photograph, and book me on a Class-A misdemeanor. After the formality of booking, my broken shoulder and I would then be asked to join a bunch of really friendly guys in a holding cell to await arraignment before a judge. The arraignment would come the following morning, so it meant a night in jail. I knew the routine. This situation was going from bad to worse. He suggested a misdemeanor or nonfelony charge of third-degree assault, assuring me that it would be dropped later when the district attorney read the case file. I politely rejected the offer. The nightmare had gone on long enough. I had tried being nice, but nice had been completely ineffective.

I asked for a private conversation with the Negro in Stanley's office. When the door was closed and the Lieutenant was seated, I picked up the phone and placed a call. I needed someone important enough to vouch for my character so Negro could protect his butt. My good friend and lawyer Eliot Warner was just the ticket. Mr. Warner is a Brooklyn boy who built one of the most successful law firms in the city. You wouldn't know him if you passed him on the street, but in the back rooms and smoke-field offices where the high and mighty make important decisions for the City of New York, everybody knows his name.

Eliot answered on the first ring.

"Eliot, it's me," I croaked weakly.

"What's the matter, J. J.? You don't sound so good."

I explained my situation, answered a few simple questions, and then handed the telephone to the lieutenant. He took the receiver and almost immediately came to attention. There was a lot of yes-sir-no-sir stuff. I don't know, some people are swayed by titles and uniforms and that kind of thing. In Lieutenant Negro's case, he sounded genuinely impressed. Whatever. After all the time I'd taken to make my point, turns out, all it took to get through to him was a little suction. So much for this business about liberty and justice for all.

Lieutenant Negro finished his chat and replaced the receiver with a kind of reverence. Before he hung up, I heard him promise to be cooperative and discreet—my two favorite traits in a ranking police officer. I suddenly became Mr. Donovan, a guy you should treat like a citizen. It was a moment worth savoring, even if it had taken a phone call to remind the nice policeman about my civil rights.

"How do ya know that guy?" Negro asked seriously.

"He's my lawyer," I said simply.

"Well, you got one helluva lawyer, Buddy. Everybody on the force knows Mr. Warner. He's been a real friend, if you know what I mean."

I didn't, but I knew Eliot, so I had an idea. From my point of view, things now began to move in a much more satisfactory direction. We went back into the conference room and Negro had a few quiet words with his uniformed bookends, after which it was announced that I would not be charged. Alvin seemed a little disappointed, but it couldn't be helped. You can't please all the people all the time.

Looking a bit worse for the wear, the Lieutenant explained that they would take my statement and refer the matter to the

163

District Attorney's office in the morning. I dictated a precise account of the events as I knew them, and Greenberg's secretary typed it up. When she was done, I signed the document and they let me go.

"Hey, Donovan, wait a minute!"

It was Greenberg. He caught up with me just as I was coming out of the men's room.

"What is it now, Stanley?" I wanted to get away.

"Hey, babe, relax, everything's cool." He had regained some of his guile. "Look, I know this has been rough on you, so stay home tomorra, awright? If you need more time, you let me know."

He grabbed my right hand and was about to shake it. I clamped down on his wrist with my good left hand and gave it a squeeze. He let out a little gasp.

"My shoulder, Stan, my shoulder," I whispered.

"Oh yeah, right. Sorry, kid. You take care of yourself and we'll talk tomorra, okay?" He backed away.

There was a note pressed into the palm of the hand he'd tried to shake. I stuffed Greenberg's message into the pocket of my jeans, then checked the seat of my pants to make sure that Gagan's bundle of papers was still in place. It was there all right, though probably a little worse for the wear by now. That reminded me—Alvin hadn't mentioned a thing about Joe Gagan. I wondered how come the cops weren't giving *him* the third degree.

I let it pass; the only thing on my mind was getting away from the National Manufacturing Corporation as quickly as possible. Someone had been kind enough to bring my coat in from the plant, and after a short struggle, I managed to get my good arm into the sleeve and pulled the rest up over my shoulder. It was after seven, so I didn't expect any of the men from the day shift to see me, but I wanted the night crew to get a good look just in case the rumor mill had exaggerated my injury. The more convinced these guys were that I was invincible, the better I thought my chances of surviving would be.

When I came through the door leading into the factory, I found Carlos, Señor Pedro, and Sammy Mesa waiting for me. It was a nice gesture; I hadn't expected it. As it turned out, it was a good thing they'd waited. Although I wanted to be brave, the walk across that plant and out to my car seemed a lot farther than I remembered it from the morning.

Before I could say anything, a big yellow forklift came whipping around the corner. Ratman was at the wheel, and he pulled up just like my own personal taxi.

"Hop on, brotha," he said, " 'cause you ain't walkin' tonight."

SIXTEEN

. . .

It was after nine o'clock when I pulled into the parking garage on Ninety-eighth Street. My stomach had been growling for the last few miles, so I walked down to Broadway and placed a big order at Mr. Wong's Noodle Shop. While they cooked the food, I sat at the bar drinking beer and pitied myself for being unlucky enough to get hit with a baseball bat.

As I hobbled back to my building I started feeling a little better. The beer had helped, but it was mostly the change of scenery; it felt good to be on familiar turf.

In the lobby, Manny Santos and a few of the boys were playing dominoes as usual and listening to the late racing results from Florida. Manny was sitting with his chair tipped back against the wall, sipping a brew. He looked pretty well rested, considering the state he'd been in when I left him. Any other night we would have traded wisecracks, but, all things considered, I wasn't in the mood. Then I noticed the bandages on Manny's knees. He quickly picked up the newspaper and hid behind it. My best guess was that Angus hadn't let him stay in the saddle for very long.

I stepped into the elevator, which just happened to be on the ground floor for once, and started the long trip up. The lift is slow, and labors so much that it wouldn't surprise me to learn that Manny has six or seven of his cousins in the basement hauling it up by hand. Fortunately, the graffiti is plentiful and clever, which helps pass the time during the ride.

It lurched to a stop at the fourth floor and there was Old Will Manners with four or five of his ugly, misbegotten dogs. I told him the elevator was going upstairs, hoping that would discourage him. But he wasn't fazed; Will thought the dogs would enjoy the ride. So he shuffled in and the puppies followed. There was a lot of sniffing and even some growling as we all got settled, but the doors finally closed. It was touch and go for a while; at one point my bag of takeout food nearly set off a feeding frenzy. At the seventeenth floor, I shook off the young male who'd mounted my leg and staggered to my front door.

My shoulder was throbbing badly again, and when I checked the damage in the bathroom mirror I got a shock. The upper right side of my back, shoulder, and arm were mottled in shades of red, purple, and blue. The center of my shoulder, where the bat had made full contact, was a swollen, sinister-looking, dark mass which had leaked blood, gluing the undershirt to my shoulder. I was going to need some help, but Boris was out of the question. After the fainting incident in Brooklyn, there was no telling how he'd react.

I cranked up the shower and peeled off the rest of my clothes, retrieving the papers Joe Gagan had given me. They'd been hidden in my jeans for hours. I put the wrinkled documents on the counter, then sat on the toilet and waited for the hot water to travel seventeen floors. When the mirror started fogging, I stepped into the shower and let the steaming hot warmth soak away my aches. This time I didn't linger too long, which proves that I can learn from experience. At the first hint of cooler water, I reached for a towel.

When my hair was combed and my body was reasonably dry, I gingerly arranged a bathrobe on my shoulders and went back to the kitchen for my Chinese dinner and an ice pack. I loaded a plate with a generous sampling from each of my little white containers and popped it into the microwave. Then I fixed myself a very large, very dry Absolut martini with three jumbo Spanish olives. The first sip was for pleasure, the second to help me down a couple more aspirin. When the food was hot, I put all my goodies on a tray and moved to the bedroom.

I settled back against a stack of pillows on the bed, refilled my martini glass from the shaker, flipped on the television set, and started putting a dent in my takeout food. The New York Knicks were playing the Miami Heat. I tuned in just at the beginning of the second half. The Knicks were losing. I needed something to distract me and the battle I witnessed did the trick. The teams hate each other, and turned the game into a contact sport. It went back and forth, with the Knicks slowly cutting the lead till late in the fourth, when the Knicks hit a three-pointer that seemed to set them up for good. I'd just finished the last of my fried rice. The fans cheered, the network went to commercial, and I closed my eyes, satisfied that a victory was in hand.

The next thing I knew, the phone was ringing. I tried to reach for the receiver, but my right arm didn't work. With the television blaring and the phone jangling, I was stumped for a few confusing moments. I fought off the sleep, got my body turned around, and picked up the phone with my good hand.

"Donovan," I said, my voice heavy with sleep.

"*Dar*ling, it is I!"

The voice on the other end was silky smooth and very deep. There was no sense of urgency in the tone, just the trace of an accent.

"Madame Karina?"

I blinked my eyes some more, trying to focus, and searched for the clock. "What time is it?"

"James, you were sleeping and I came into your dreams?" She made the question seem just a little bit naughty, which was an accomplishment for someone her age.

"If you mean you woke me up, you're right," I admitted, sitting up on the edge of the bed.

There was classical music playing in the background. Typical.

It was the middle of the night, and Karina was just getting the band warmed up.

"Dear boy, it is just midnight. I had hoped you could join me for a few minutes."

"I don't know, Karina," I said honestly, "this has been a really bad day."

"All the more reason, *dar*ling, for you to come visit." There was a pause. "And James, darling . . ."

"Yes?" I asked patiently.

". . . don't forget my medicine."

I sat on the edge of the bed for a few minutes trying to decide whether to go back to sleep or venture upstairs. I flexed my shoulder painfully and noticed that my bathrobe was now glued to the skin with dried blood. It was no good denying the reality of the situation. I was going to need some help, and Karina seemed like my best option. If anyone had the healing touch, she was the one.

With some difficulty, I struggled back into my jeans and then managed to locate another bottle of cognac, which I balanced carefully under my good arm, before starting slowly up the stairs to the eighteenth floor. Leaving my loafers by the front door, I shuffled down the hallway under the sympathetic gaze of Karina's many angels. When I reached the study, I turned the doorknob slowly and tried to peek inside, but someone grabbed the handle and literally yanked me into the room, jarring my shoulder. When the pain subsided and I managed to straighten up, I turned to see who was working the door. I got a shock: Standing there in a mismatched suit and tie, his hair plastered down as neatly as if he were on his way to a wake, was old Joe Gagan. I started to say something, but he put a finger to his lips and pointed to the other side of the room.

It was a full house. Boris and Clara were seated at their instruments and Karina was in her favorite armchair, just as they had been on the night of my little incident out on the BQE. But that wasn't all. In addition to Joe Gagan, I was surprised to find my friendly internist, Rich Steinman, sitting on the sofa, sipping a glass of red wine. They were all staring at me, frozen in time, looking worried.

"What's going on here?" I asked, bewildered.

"Isn't it obvious?" Boris said from across the room. "We've been waiting for you."

"What's Joe doing here?" I asked, pointing at Gagan.

"You gave Mr. Gagan your card this afternoon. He was kind enough to come by and report the circumstances of your misadventure," Boris replied.

"Is that so. Well, if you knew I was hurt, why didn't you contact the plant?"

"You know as well as I do that such a call would have jeopardized your cover."

That was the right answer, but for some reason it annoyed me.

"Look, I've had a rough day and I don't feel like playing with you kids tonight," I said finally. "I think I'll just take my bottle and go home."

"You will do nothing of the kind. Clara, take those spirits away from the poor man," Karina snapped, protecting her interests. "His brain has obviously been addled by this injury."

Before I could react, the bottle was out of my hand and Clara was on her way to the kitchen.

"Now, sit down and take off that robe!"

Karina pointed to a footstool in front of her chair. When I started to argue she clapped her hands. It was a command. I obeyed quietly, peeling the robe off my shoulder and letting it fall to the floor.

"Ah, my poor darling, what have they done to you?" Karina said this so softly, I started to feel sorry for myself.

"Richard," she said to Steinman, "you will please have a look at this man's back."

I started to protest again.

"Tut, tut, dear boy, be quiet. Madame Karina will take care of you now."

Richard Steinman just happened to have his black bag with him. He came over and started to inspect the corpus. He didn't ask me to explain how I'd gotten the injury; they'd already heard it all from Gagan. That was probably just as well; Joe's view had been better than mine.

First Steinman checked out my head to see if I really was addled. Then he flashed a penlight in my eyes and told me to look up, down, and every other way. Next, he took my blood pressure and pulse to see if I was still alive. When that stuff was out of the way, he finally paid a little attention to the big bump on my shoulder.

"Can you lift your arm like this?"

"No."

"Can you move it like that?"

"No."

"How about like this?"

"No."

"Hmmm . . . does this hurt?"

"*Yeesss!*" I hollered.

"Good. That's fine. Now let me see your fingers."

I complied reluctantly.

"Okay, now this is going to hurt, but I've got to see if there's any displacement. Do you understand?"

"If you're asking for permission to hurt me, the answer is no, you may not!"

"James, you will please stop interfering with the man and allow him to continue helping you!"

It was another command from Lady Kostopoulis, so I gave in. The pushing and probing brought tears to my eyes, but Richard went right on with his questions.

"Do you know whether or not you fainted today?"

He had to ask, right? In front of everybody, especially the precious young Clara who always looked at me as if I'd jumped right off the pages of Ivanhoe. I gave him the answer.

171

"Hmmm. More than once?" he asked.

"What?" This wasn't fair.

"Did you faint more than once?"

"Look, Rich, is that a pertinent question or are you trying to get back at me for the other night?"

"You listen to me, Donovan," he said. "I plan to get back at you by sending a hefty bill. Now answer the question."

"Twice," I whispered.

"What did you say?"

"*Twice! I* fainted *twice!*"

I probably spoke a bit too loud. When I bothered to look again, everyone was staring at me, including Richard.

"How about drugs? Have you taken any pills to go along with the booze I can smell on your breath?"

The guy was starting to make me really angry. I guess other people noticed because Karina put her hand on my knee and gently prodded.

"Please, James, this is important."

"All right." I sighed. "What was the question?"

"Have you taken any drugs today?"

"No prescription drugs. I ate about a dozen aspirin, drank a couple of beers, and then followed them with two very tasty vodka martinis. For dinner I had Chinese. Add two Diet Pepsis, three cups of coffee, and several bagels and you have a complete list of the stuff I ingested today."

I stopped and went back over the list in my head. There was something I was forgetting. Then I remembered the pills Alvin had tried to pawn off on me.

"By the way, Alvin Katz tried to get me to swallow these."

Reaching into the pocket of my jeans, I took out the codeine pills. Richard took the tablets and went to examine them under Karina's desk lamp.

"Hmmm, what are these supposed to be?" he asked.

"How should I know? You're the doctor." I was getting very cranky.

"I mean, what did this Katz person tell you they were?"

172

"Oh, Tylenol with codeine."

"And you haven't taken any, is that right?"

"That's right!" I said impatiently.

"Are you in a lot of pain?"

"Yes."

"Good."

I'd love to know what doctors mean when they say "good" like that. Was he glad I was feeling pain? Was the pain itself a good sign? Or maybe it was just "good" I'd been able to give him an answer?

"We're done for now, J. J., you can put your robe on."

Steinman excused himself and left the room. Clara came over and helped me get into the robe. Then I sat down and returned the uncomfortable smiles being sent in my direction. A few minutes later, Rich came back with an ice pack, a large glass of cold water, a snifter of the good stuff, and a loaded hypodermic syringe. There was only one thing on that tray that I wanted and it was in the snifter. Turned out that was the one thing I wasn't going to get. Everything else, however, was for me, including the syringe. When he'd finished assaulting me with the needle, Dr. Steinman pulled up a chair and sat down.

"Now, I want you to listen carefully to everything I'm going to say because I don't plan to argue with you and it's too late to be repeating myself. Okay?"

He hadn't left much room for discussion, so I nodded.

"You have a broken clavicle. It's also possible that you cracked a couple of ribs on the right side. The scapula seems to be intact, despite the nasty appearance of your bruises. In my opinion, you're lucky you weren't hurt worse. I just called St. Luke's and arranged for you to be X rayed and examined by an orthopedist. We've got to be there within the hour, so if you need to converse with your partner before we leave, I suggest you get started now."

"What do I need an X ray for?" I asked belligerently.

"Before we can decide on a method of treatment, it will be necessary to look at the fracture. Understand?"

"Oh." I thought for a moment. "While we're on the subject, what was that shot you just gave me?"

"That was Demerol. It'll get rid of the pain and maybe relax you a bit—you're as stiff as a board. Besides, you're acting like a real jerk and I'm hoping that shot will take some of the fight out of you."

He got to his feet and picked up the brandy snifter I'd been coveting.

"By the way, those pills Mr. Katz gave you were an anti-psychotic medication called Mellaril. Two of them probably wouldn't have caused any harm, but you should not have been given them. I'd also like to know why Katz has that kind of medicine on hand. Now, if you don't don't mind, I'm going to call my service before we head to the hospital."

At that moment, I wasn't interested in Alvin Katz. I was worried about going to the hospital. I started to make a fuss, but Rich cut me off.

"I told you not to give me a hard time, Donovan, so lose the attitude. You're in no condition to argue with anyone. Your body has had a lot to deal with today. For Christ's sake, man, you've already fainted twice, so stop screwing around. You're with people you can trust. Let us do what's right for you and stop causing trouble."

I kept quiet, though it was particularly unfair of him to mention that fainting business again in front of Clara. Her cheeks were flushed, which meant she'd noticed my embarrassment. I suddenly felt like running over to the piano and laying my head in the young girl's lap. That was a sure signal that it was time for me to leave. I got to my feet slowly.

"Look, everybody, I'm sorry about this scene, but I'm just not myself tonight," I mumbled. "I hope you ladies will forgive me."

Madame Karina left me standing in silence while she took a sip of cognac from the crystal glass Clara had provided. When the drink was safely back on the tray, she let out a sigh and turned to me.

"My darling boy, there is no reason for you to apologize. This

174

is just your ego speaking. I am deeply impressed by your strength and courage. I doubt that even my Victor would have been so brave."

That was high praise indeed. I was awake enough to realize that the crafty old bird was feeding my vanity at the same time she was telling me to ignore it, but I didn't care. The flattery made me feel good.

"Now, I want you to do as Richard tells you or I will be extremely cross with you. Is that understood?"

I nodded like a kid.

"Fine. Tomorrow morning, after you've had your sleep, I will send Mr. McCabe down with a good breakfast. You will need food to rebuild your strength."

"Thank you, Karina Mariya," I said, getting familiar as the Demerol went to work.

"Dear heart, I will come to you tomorrow and we will talk then. Besides, it has been too long since my last visit and I miss my big friend, Angoose. I look forward to it. Now go. I will see you tomorrow."

With a wave of her hand, we'd been dismissed. Boris and Joe Gagan filed out. I was just turning to follow them when Madame Karina called me back.

"Ah, James," she purred, lifting her crystal glass. "For now, I will keep the medicine here. Yes?" She smiled innocently, but I could see a twinkle in her eye.

SEVENTEEN

■ ■ ■

Dr. Steinman wanted to make a stop at his place on the eighth floor, so we left him at the elevator and walked down one flight to seventeen. Joe Gagan insisted on taking my arm and helping me. Boris took up the rear. When we reached our floor, Boris disappeared into his apartment, taking Gagan with him. I went to my bedroom to lie down. The shot of Demerol was making me feel very relaxed. I didn't fight it.

Just as I was starting to doze, something coarse and damp grazed my cheek. I opened my eyes and found Angus staring back at me. He was trying to console me with wet kisses and doggie breath. I thanked the shaggy black pony by scratching his ears. He responded by drooling contentedly on the bedspread.

A few minutes later, Boris came bustling into the room. I got up reluctantly and he helped me get my arms into the sleeves of a heavy cotton shirt. When the buttons were all fastened, I went back to the bed and concentrated on staying awake. Boris paced up and down the room like a nervous parent.

"Would you mind sitting down?" I asked politely. "You're making me jumpy."

He looked surprised, as if he hadn't expected me to be able to speak. Knowing Boris, his own right shoulder was probably starting to ache. He lowered his bulk into the big chair near the door to my terrace.

"I am sorry," he said, "it's just that I can't think of what to do right now. So much has happened and yet, thus far, I've really been just an observer."

"So, observe." I sighed. "Tell me what's going on, what does it all mean?"

As predicted, the Demerol had taken the fight out of me. Boris sat quietly rubbing his chin for a minute or two.

"I suppose it would be good to review the facts," he suggested.

"Fire away," I murmured sleepily.

"Well, let's see," he began seriously. "Ruby Brice, a prostitute who is trying to swindle money from a customer, tells her son that she has witnessed something illegal at a business called the National Manufacturing Corporation. She announces plans to try and profit from this secret knowledge. Not long after this announcement, she is found brutally murdered. A suspect is arrested near the crime scene, but our Ms. Fein considers his guilt questionable. She asks us to meet the dead woman's son, and to help him by causing the police to reopen the investigation. From Clifford Brice we learn about Uncle Tito, the man his mother was planning to defraud. Mr. Tito has a strong motive, and there is an eyewitness account linking him to the scene of the crime. Admittedly, the eyewitness is a schizophrenic old homeless man who thinks he's a wizard, but he was there and cannot be completely ignored. Do you agree so far?"

I nodded my head weakly.

"Right. Then after our initial meeting with Clifford, this Uncle Tito makes an appearance at Mrs. Washington's foster home, and Clifford goes into hiding. The incident at the foster home clearly puts the focus on Tito as the prime suspect. However, about the time of the trouble at Mrs. Washington's home, another body is discovered. This victim, an unidentified woman, is found dead and smoldering in an alleyway directly across the street from the National Manufacturing Corporation, the same business at which Ruby Brice claimed to have seen something illegal and profitable. It should be remembered that Ms. Brice's mutilated body was also found in a lot not too far from National Manufacturing.

The spotlight dims on Uncle Tito and brightens on this decrepit manufacturing business. Then, with no clear idea how to follow up on this sketchy information, you decided to apply for a job at the factory, assuming it would place you *in the middle of things*. Still with me?"

"Are you trying to be sarcastic?" I asked, perking up.

"Absolutely not," he sputtered innocently. "I'm merely retelling the facts."

"Yeah, right. Watch it, buster," I warned.

"Well, anyway, your job application leads to a meeting with Mr. Stanley Greenberg, the owner of National Manufacturing. Subsequently, and with some reservations, we agreed to help Greenberg prove that his partner, Morty Katz, and the partner's son, Alvin, are embezzling funds from the company. We didn't much care whether Greenberg got his wish, but hoped that by working in the factory you would be in a better position to unravel the mystery of Ruby Brice's death. And now, less than two weeks after you started working in the plant, two more people have died and five have been injured, including yourself. A lot has happened, but has it made us any wiser?"

"I don't know," I said, sitting up a bit straighter. "What do you make of it all?"

"It is hard to say," he admitted, shaking his head. "Ruby Brice claimed to have seen something and was killed. José Comacho claimed to have seen something and was killed. He told his cousin, who told you, and you were both attacked and could have been killed. Obviously, there is something very bad going on at the National Manufacturing Corporation, but there are still far too many unanswered questions. For God's sake, there's a dead woman we can't even identify, let alone place in the context of these other incidents. This much is clear: your intuition was correct. We're right smack in the middle of it, what ever *it* is."

It was Boris's turn to sigh.

"Hey, before I forget, if you look on my dresser you'll find the note from Stanley Greenberg and that list of Alvin's pills I started writing in the office."

Boris lifted himself out of the chair and went to see for himself. He patiently opened each of the crumpled pieces of paper and tried to smooth the wrinkles out while I finished dressing. I ran a comb through my hair, put on a pair of socks, and slipped into my loafers.

"This is obviously your writing," Boris said, looking at the short inventory of perscription drugs I'd scribbled. "Which means this scrawl must be the note from Greenberg."

He held up a small slip of paper for me, and I read: *Must spek with you off cite. important new info. will call. vry important. S. G.*

It was from Greenberg all right. I wondered what little gem of information he'd been holding back. Boris was studying the other notes, the ones I'd written.

"And you say this is only a partial list of the vials you found?" he asked.

I nodded again. Boris was scowling. I watched him as he studied the list for a minute or two longer. All of a sudden he seemed to come to life.

"Where are the papers Mr. Gagan left with you this afternoon?"

I looked up at him and blinked my eyes.

"J. J., the papers Gagan gave you? You haven't lost them, I hope?"

He seemed genuinely concerned. I pointed toward the bathroom. They were on the vanity counter, where they'd been since I got into the shower. Boris came back a moment later, his nose already buried in the new information.

Right on cue, Dr. Steinman breezed back into the room; smiling, efficient, ready for the next patient.

"Can you wait one more minute, Richard?" I asked.

"No, we can't," he snorted.

"Oh, good," I said, taking Boris aside.

"By the way, about Joe Gagan, is he the real thing?" I whispered.

"Mr. Gagan," he said confidently, "is nothing if not the real thing. We'll talk more when you get back from the hospital."

179

Boris smiled reassuringly, then turned his attention back to Gagan's papers. It was good to see him focusing in on the project. It made it easier for me to concentrate on worrying about myself. And I do mean worry.

I don't like hospitals, especially if my health is the subject of the visit. When I have time to mull over the medical possibilities, I sometimes get a bit worked up. In this case, the symptoms of my anxiety didn't start to appear until we were already in the cab heading uptown. It was one-thirty in the morning.

"Can I have a cup of coffee?" I asked nervously.

"Later, J. J., when we get back," Richard said. "Just relax, this shouldn't take very long."

That phrase is a certain prelude to discomfort. To prove the point, our driver managed to find every pothole on Amsterdam Avenue. The pain from each new jolt brought me a little closer to panic. Rich looked over at me like I was a lunatic. I ignored him.

Our cab turned right at 113th Street and pulled into the St. Luke's emergency room entrance. A male nurse's aide came out to meet us pushing a wheel chair.

"Dr. Steinman, how are you tonight?" he asked.

"What are you asking him for? I'm the patient!" The words were out of my mouth before I could stifle them.

"My friend is a little nervous, Peter. It makes him act like an asshole," Richard said calmly. "Please ignore the lip and accept my apology."

"No problem, Doc. Where to?"

"We're going to X ray."

With my venom so expertly neutralized, I sat back and kept quiet. Peter deftly maneuvered me through the emergency room and deposited me under a big sign which read X RAY. When I turned to offer thanks and my own apology, he was gone.

I'd been left in the middle of the hall because that was the only unoccupied space in the corridor. There were patients and their families everywhere I looked. It must have been the overflow from the emergency room, because it was pretty messy. Lacerations, broken bones, burns, puncture wounds, drug overdoses, bullet wounds, pregnant women, very old people, and quite a few people who just looked sick. It didn't help to close my eyes. The soundtrack was more disturbing than actually watching the patients who were lined up under the neon lights. People were screaming and weeping and yelling and talking all at once. Adding a surreal quality to the scene was the public address operator, who made continuous unintelligible announcements in a dispassionate, synthesized monotone.

The people around me were predominantly black and Hispanic, though I did notice one white guy sitting on a folding chair with an ice pack on his nose. He was wearing a Columbia University fencing jacket. It looked as if he'd gotten into an altercation without his épée. Near him, propped up on a stretcher, was a pregnant Indian woman of approximately the same age. She wore a sari and had a bindi painted in the middle of her forehead. These two very different people were wearing identical expressions of apprehension.

The hospital was full of policemen, too. I wondered why they weren't out stopping crimes. A few minutes later, I got the answer. A man with a chest wound and a web of IV lines running into his arms decided to roll off his stretcher and make a run for the exit. He didn't get far because his left wrist was handcuffed to the gurney, but he tried. As he dragged the stretcher down the hallway, he screamed obscenities at the top of his lungs. It took three cops and an orderly to restrain the man long enough to inject a sedative into him.

In the midst of all the commotion, a very large, clean-shaven black man wearing blue surgical scrubs and a white lab coat sauntered up to me. Behind him, partially obscured by the bulk of the stranger, stood Rich Steinman, my former friend. Rich was smiling.

"Mr. Donovan, right?" the big guy asked.

It's weird, but none of the stuff I'd seen while waiting in the hall had the slightest effect on me. In fact, it had helped to distract me. However, as soon as the big guy said my name and my brain registered that he'd come for me, my palms started sweating again.

"Cat got your tongue, Mr. Donovan?" he asked.

I smiled meekly.

"Well, that's okay. My name is Hiram J. Parker. The name Hiram was a gift from my mother. It would be unwise to make jokes about it. I am a doctor specializing in orthopedic surgery, and you are now my patient. Do we understand each other?"

I just kept nodding.

"Good. A nice young lady named Maria is going to take some pictures of your shoulder for me." He leaned down, inches from my face. "She is a very nice person. You will cooperate with her. Is that clear?"

More nodding.

"Fine. I'll see you when the film is ready," he said and lumbered off down the hall.

Steinman was trying unsuccessfully to stifle a laugh. He winked at me, then turned and raced after Dr. Hiram J. Parker. Talk about payback.

It seemed advisable to behave myself in the X-ray department, so I was a model patient and did everything Maria asked without complaining. When the pictures were developed and checked, she wheeled me around until we found an elevator, then took it to the orthopedic clinic on the second floor. I thanked Maria politely, and she left me to fend for myself.

The clinic was a big, gymlike space. Scattered around the room were weights and pulleys, parallel bars, climbing stairs, and a lot of padded tables with paper sheets. The floor was spattered with the plaster used to make casts, and there were crutches of all sizes hanging from pegs in the walls.

While I was taking in the sights, Rich Steinman arrived, still looking very pleased with himself. I had to suppress an urge to exact some revenge.

"What do you think of the place?" he asked.

"What should I think, Richard? It's not exactly a dinner theater."

"Boy, I can't wait for the old J. J. to return," he said mournfully. "By the way, call Boris. He claims it's important."

Dr. Steinman seemed unaware of the danger he was in, poor soul. Here I was plotting my revenge, and he went right on talking as if everything was normal between us.

"I don't know how he did it," Richard continued, "but Boris managed to locate my beeper number. Can you believe it? That means he'll be able to find me whenever he feels like chatting." He thought for a moment and started to frown, remembering the hours Boris likes to keep. "I'd better have the number changed tomorrow!" he thought out loud.

There was a phone on the counter.

"How do I get an outside line?" I asked.

"Push one, nine, and then your number."

"Thanks, pal," I said sweetly and punched in the numbers. "By the way, you have a Columbia University faculty appointment, right?"

He nodded yes.

"Then I wouldn't bother changing beepers. Boris has access to the computer system. He'll just look up the new number and you'll be right back where you started." I smiled for the first time in hours.

Boris answered the phone on the second ring.

"What's up, Doctor?" I asked.

"Are you all right?"

He sounded anxious, as if his own health depended on the diagnosis.

"Don't know yet, but the sooner I get out of this place the better I'll feel. What's so important?"

"I was wondering if you could give me some guidelines for analyzing shipping documents, bills of lading, invoices from vendors, that sort of thing."

"The papers Gagan gave me, right?"

"Correct."

"Let's see." I thought for a moment. "Do they cover dates before and after Alvin Katz started working for the company?"

"Affirmative."

"With the vendors, I would start by comparing apples to apples. See if the company has changed suppliers and, if so, for which types of materials. Also, check to see if there have been wholesale price increases. That kind of stuff."

I could hear his keyboard clicking as he typed my suggestions directly into the computer.

"Shipping documents are a little different. It's hard to say without seeing the papers myself," I said, thinking out loud. "But to get started, try logging all the information into the computer by category. You know what I mean: date, customer name, city and state of destination, description of load. When you've done that, try to define patterns, like distribution radius and average distance traveled. We're interested in any deviations from the normal shipping pattern. When that's all done, we can run more imaginative queries."

"Looking for what?"

"Double billing, overcharging for partial loads."

"How would that work?"

"If a trucker carries stuff for two different companies on the same trailer and charges them each full fare, he'd be double dipping."

"Hmm," Boris ruminated. "Does this company share time on a computer system, or do they have a stand alone?"

"They have exactly three work stations networked through a small file server. Why?"

"Just wondering," he said. "By the way, I have a few ideas, and I'm going to proceed with them. Nothing terribly complicated, but I'm going to spend some of that retainer you secured from Mr. Greenberg. I'll fill you in later."

Before I could ask a question the line went dead.

"Why, Mr. Donovan, you're up and about. Does this mean we're feeling better?"

184

The big guy was standing behind me. He had my X rays under his arm. I took a deep breath and prepared to hold my ground.

"Listen up, Doc," I said with feeling, "you and Steinman have had enough fun for one evening. Okay? Not long ago, I saw a dead woman burning on a cross. And then today, around mid-morning, I watched a kid get electrocuted. At teatime, a man with a big black bat tried to kill me. Since then, I've fainted a couple of times and been grilled as a homicide suspect. All in all, I think I deserve a break. What do you say?"

Hiram Parker studied my face for a moment, then softened his expression. "Understood, Mr. Donovan," he said finally.

"Just call me Donovan. Everyone else does."

I stuck out a mitt, we shook hands, and the relationship seemed to improve.

"Now, about your injuries . . . ," he began, getting serious.

"Injuries? As in more than one?" My newfound confidence was deserting me.

"Yes. There's a comminuted fracture at the junction of the middle and outer third of your clavicle. You also have a hairline fracture of the fourth rib on the right side. The good news is that the scapula is not broken."

"Would you mind giving it to me in English?"

"You have a broken collarbone and a cracked rib," he said.

It sounded better the other way.

"Why don't you tell me exactly what happened today? It might help me during the examination."

Next thing I knew, I was sitting on one of those padded tables with my shirt off. I gave Dr. Parker an abbreviated version of my misadventures, which covered all the salient points and seemed to relieve my nerves. Parker used the time to give me a physical exam similar to the poke-and-prod routine Richard had followed back in Madame Karina's study.

After I'd been pinched and probed to his satisfaction, Parker went over to a stainless-steel cabinet and rooted around inside. When he turned back to me his hands were full.

"Whoa, Doc, what's all that stuff?" The bond we'd formed moments earlier was beginning to develop cracks.

"This is just padding and a four-inch ace bandage. It's used to make something called a figure-eight splint. I am going to put a splint on you, and except when you're bathing, you are going to wear it for the next eight weeks. Is that understood?"

"Oh no, I'm not!" I said firmly, starting to get off the table.

Hiram Parker's face broke into one of the biggest smiles I've ever seen. As I reached for my shirt, he began walking toward me.

"Don't worry," he said. "This shouldn't take very long."

EIGHTEEN

■ ■ ■

"Richard tells me that after a good sleep you'll be up and about."

"Oh, he does, does he?" I snarled.

It was déjà vu all over again, only this time I'd skipped the part where I get to sleep and then wake up. Instead of sleeping, I'd gone to St. Luke's Hospital, where an ill-tempered witch doctor named Hiram had tortured me with a four-inch ace bandage. Now, at four o'clock in the morning, Boris and I were sitting in my kitchen again. He was drinking coffee. Angus, the sensible one, was snoring loudly.

Boris had been droning on and on about data-sorting techniques, and was, as always, chain-smoking. I got up and turned on the fan in the hood over my stove. By morning, Boris would have all the information contained in Joe Gagan's papers typed into the computer, sorted, and ready for analysis. I was so tired I could barely keep my eyes open.

"Whoa, Boris," I interrupted, "you're killing me with this stuff. I'm sure that your analysis will be thorough. Okay? Now, before I fall asleep, I'd like to know what else you and Gagan talked about."

He looked hurt, but answered, "We spent a good deal of time discussing the personnel data I collected. Perhaps you remember the reports I printed the day you began working at National Manufacturing?"

"Unfortunately, they're in my car, Boris."

He gave me a look of professional disapproval. "Well, no matter." He sighed. "Mr. Gagan was very helpful. He was able to reduce my original list of questionable characters to a much smaller, though no less potent, group of suspects. When that was done, we added the Veldez brothers and a few other former employees to the roster. Mr. Alvin Katz has a curious habit of hiring and firing the same people over and over. It's like a revolving door."

His face lost expression as his mind wandered into some obscure corridor. I watched the ash from his cigarette break free and tumble down the front of his black turtleneck sweater. If I let Boris go mental on me, I'd be sound asleep in my chair before he snapped out of it.

"You said something about spending our retainer?"

I spoke loudly enough to rouse Angus, who lifted his big head off the floor and appealed for a little consideration. He was trying to sleep.

Boris stirred. "What's that you say?"

"You mentioned something about spending money?"

"Oh, that." He sneered, annoyed at being interrupted over an issue as trivial as cash. "I called your friend Ron Blakely at his home and arranged to use a few of his people."

"My *acquaintance* Ron Blakely," I corrected him. "I'm surprised you were able to find him. I didn't think the King of Swing got home before sunrise."

Ron Blakely is a retired New York City transit cop who runs an outfit called Blakely Security Associates. He built the agency with hard work and savvy, and the company still deserves its good reputation. We use them for surveillance work or when we need an extra pair of legs. It can be expensive, but his people are smart and reliable.

Unfortunately, success has turned Ronnie into a superficial creep. As far as I know, he doesn't even review the agency's casework anymore. He gets his kicks at trendy clubs, flirting with the latest flashes-in-the-pan. Ron earns his spot at the bar by arranging well-cut, muscular bodyguards for the socialite pinheads who like to be seen out and about. As if pimping steroid babies for entertainers makes you somebody. It's pretty sad. Ronnie already had the kind of respect most people dream about. He doesn't understand that the people he's pursuing are just the figment of a camera's flattering lens.

"A few people?" I asked. "How many are a few?"

"Let's see." He rubbed his chin. "I put a three-shift team on Alvin Katz and another on his father. Then I sent one solo off with Alvin's prescription inventory and a second to investigate the Veldez brothers."

My mental calculator started clicking—two twenty-four-hour surveillance teams, plus the solos, would total eight shifts per twenty-four hours. That was more than sixty man hours a day! At the rates Blakely charged, we could end up buying the guy a new Mercedes.

"Boris, that's not dipping into the kitty. It's more like a swan dive."

"We'll go over the details in the morning," he said with a yawn. "I think you should go to bed. You look exhausted."

It was okay to bore me to tears with statistics, but when money was the subject he didn't have the time. I had some questions, but my mind was beginning to wander. Until my body got some rest, it was pointless to waste words. I closed my eyes.

"Are you awake?" Boris asked a minute later.

I nodded, but I really wasn't.

"J. J., do you understand me?"

Instead of answering, I stood up and went in search of my big, soft bed.

Eight and a half hours after my head touched the pillow, I opened my eyes. It was past noon. The sun was shining brightly through the terrace doors, the air smelled of bacon cooking in the kitchen, and there were flowers in a vase on my dresser. There was also a worried little boy sitting quietly at the foot of the bed.

"Good morning," I said cheerfully.

189

" 'Morning, J. J.," he replied without looking up.

"What's the matter, Cliff? Last time I saw you, you were glued to that new computer and smiling from ear to ear."

"Last time I saw you, all your parts were workin'," he said sadly.

I tried to sit up, but the pain shot back into my shoulder. Clifford moved over to help.

"I want you and Dr. Koulomzin to stop," he said quickly. "My momma's already dead. There's no point in anybody else dying. It would be something I couldn't live with. I mean losin' my partners, because, well, there isn't nobody else, except Ms. Fein."

He was trying so hard to be a man. I reached out with my left arm and pulled him in close to me.

"Now you listen up, Clifford Brice," I said seriously. "J. J. Donovan never gives up, and neither do his partners. What happened to your mother isn't right and we're gonna set it straight. Besides, I've got a thick hide. It'll take more than a baseball bat to stop me."

I pulled him in even closer.

"You're a brave little man, Cliff," I whispered. "But you're still a kid. It's all right to be scared once in a while. Just remember, Boris and I will be there for you. And that's a promise. Okay?"

He nodded yes as he tried to hide his tears.

"Right. Now, I've got another job for you," I said, leaning back.

He looked up eagerly.

"My partner is busy spending all our money on some high-priced detective agency. I want you to keep track of it. You know, make a spreadsheet or something. Do you think you could handle that kind of a job?"

"No problem at all," he shouted happily.

"Hey, before I forget, is it really true that you *wanted* to see the MRI up at the medical center?"

He came back and leaned on the bed, resting his chin on his hands.

"Actually, J. J., my initial interest was in magnetism. You know, like the attraction for iron observed in lodestone." He sounded like he was just warming to the subject. "But man, this new stuff—you know, like recording physical responses to stimuli—is this cool or what?"

"Oh, well, yeah, I guess it is," I stammered, feeling like a mental midget. "So listen, why don't you get next door and ask Boris for the names and shifts of all the Blakely operatives? That way you can get started on that spreadsheet we talked about. I'll come over in a little while and take a look."

He raced to the door and was gone before I finished speaking. I had to blink twice to clear my head. Physical responses to stimuli. What ten-year-old knows about that stuff? For that matter, what thirty-nine-year-old knows about that stuff? A minute later, Mrs. Martha McCabe marched in carrying a loaded breakfast tray.

"James Joseph Donovan, you should be thanking your maker! The Lord takes care of idiots and fools or we'd be saying prayers over your body instead of feeding your face."

I tried to sit up again, with the same result as before. Martha put the tray down and came rushing over to the bed.

"You know, James, as I've often said, it's a good thing for all of us that you weren't born twins. There isn't enough patience in the whole wide world for two of you! Now, stop that fussing and let me help you up. Don't you have enough sense to realize that you can't put any strain on your arms and shoulders? For mercy's sake, you big dope, they're connected to your broken collarbone! Young Clifford would know that."

"Speaking of Clifford," I said, "do you know about functional MRI?"

"What are you talkin' about?" she shouted. "Don't tell me yer brains is scrambled, that's all we'd need!"

"Relax, Martha, it was just a question." I smiled happily.

She kept right on muttering and fussing. When the pillows were all properly fluffed and the bed covers were folded back, she brought over the breakfast tray. It was a thing of beauty. Eggs overeasy, home-fried potatoes, a couple of Belgian waffles, bacon, and a steaming pot of fresh-brewed tea. I was so happy I tried to kiss her. She gave me a smack on the ear.

"We'll have none of that nonsense," she snapped. "Which reminds me, have you bothered to inform Mrs. Donovan about the trouble you're in, or does the poor child have to learn it from the papers?"

"Mrs. McCabe, my dear mother doesn't read the New York papers."

"You know as well as I do," she said seriously, "that I'm referring to Kathleen Byrne Donovan. The woman whose heart you've broken."

"Martha, I don't think this is serious enough to bother Kate. Besides, it wasn't the sort of incident she'd see in a newspaper." I was busy with my food and waved the possibility away with the confident air of a man about to stub a toe.

"Is that so, Mr. Know-it-All? Then perhaps you'd like to explain this to me."

Martha produced the morning edition of the *Daily News*. She turned to page three and handed it over with a flourish. There was a picture of the factory and a headline that read: SHOCKING TRAGEDY IN EAST NEW YORK! This was followed by a feature-length article. Halfway down the page, under a bullet headline— LIGHTNING STRIKES TWICE—was an old picture of myself and the following paragraph:

> In an unrelated incident, Mr. James J. Donovan, a business consultant, was attacked late yesterday afternoon while attempting to stop a robbery at the same location. In the ensuing struggle, one man was killed and several others were seriously injured. Although details were not immediately available, Mr. Donovan

was said to be in critical but stable condition at a local hospital. The dead man was identified as . . .

Reached at his home in Long Island, Mr. Stanley Greenberg, owner of National Manufacturing Corporation, said that while the accidental electrocution and the robbery attempt were unrelated, they illustrate the sort of problems facing business owners in the borough. He cited unskilled, uncooperative workers as the cause of industrial accidents and emphasized the constant threat from street criminals.

I was still scanning the article when Boris came bouncing into the room. He looked refreshed and excited. The man had been awake for more than thirty hours, and he looked better than I do after a full night's sleep.

"Ah, so you've seen the *News*," he said, nodding toward the paper. "Fortunately, the *Times* buried the story in the Metro Section, and the *Post* went to print before they got it."

Boris was smiling, obviously happy despite the publicity. That was a surprise—I would have expected him to be outraged. Before the morning got any more bewildering, I decided to follow Martha's advice and make that call. The old girl was still standing by the bed, enjoying my confusion.

"Martha, would you hand me the telephone?" I asked contritely.

She placed the instrument on the bed, then folded her arms and stood frowning down at me.

I punched in the numbers with my good hand and waited. The phone rang twice.

"Vanguard Publications, good morning."

"Hello, I'd like to speak with Kate Byrne, please."

"May I ask who's calling Ms. Byrne?"

"Yes, this is James Donovan."

"Please hold, Mr. Donovan."

The earpiece filled with canned music, so I decided to eat

some more of my breakfast. I was about to bite down on a forkful of potatoes when a second voice came on the line.

"Mr. Donovan?"

"Hi, Doris. Is Kate in?"

"Are you all right, Mr. Donovan?" Doris sounded breathless and rather excited. She'd seen the story.

"I'm fine, Doris. Is Kate there?"

"No sir, she's not. Ms. Byrne is in Chicago."

"Well, if she calls, would you tell her that I'm fine, and not to believe anything she reads in the newspapers?"

"Oh, she'll be calling in, Mr. Donovan. She always does."

"Well, when she calls, will you give her my message?"

"Oh, sure. I'm glad to hear you're okay, Mr. Donovan."

"Thank you, Doris."

With Doris Stanger this kind of dialogue could go on indefinitely. I had to get her off the line or end up cross-eyed.

"Well, thanks again, Doris. I'll talk to you soon."

I almost got away with it.

"Oh, wait! Mr. Donovan? Are you still there?"

"Yes, Doris, I'm here."

"Thank God! I was supposed to give you a message. I mean, before Ms. Byrne left, she asked me to call you."

"And . . . ?"

"And what?"

"What was the message, Doris?"

"Oh, right. You're supposed to be at her place tomorrow night, ten o'clock sharp. I'm to remind you that it's your turn to dress for dinner. But she gave me that message yesterday, before your accident. I don't imagine she'd expect you to leave the hospital on her account. I just don't know what to say."

I'd forgotten about my birthday date, the one Kate had mentioned in the telegram. There had also been something about a present.

"Look, Doris, I'm fine. I'm not in the hospital, okay? When Ms. Byrne calls in, please tell her that I'll definitely see her tomorrow evening. Okay? Have you got that?"

"I've got it, Mister Donovan, but I'm not even sure . . ."

"That's all right, kid," I said with the confidence of movie star, "just give her the message."

I hung up before Doris could think of anything else she'd forgotten to tell me.

"Humph! If you ask me, it's a strange way for two people who care about each other to behave. Leaving messages with secretaries! The poor child will be worried sick." Martha couldn't resist sticking in her two cents.

"No one asked you, Martha," I pointed out. "Besides, in case you've forgotten, I'm the one who was attacked. How about showing a little concern?"

"You're a big, healthy man, with a head as hard and stubborn as an old rock. I see no need to be worrying about you."

"Now, wait just one minute," I said. "I was attacked with a baseball bat!"

"And a lot of good it did you!"

She turned and marched out of the room. Boris, who'd been watching this exchange, emitted an audible sigh of relief. With Martha gone, he was free to pollute my bedroom with cigarette smoke. Just as he was opening his package of Balkan Sobranie cigarettes, she stuck her head back through the doorway.

"I'll be coming for that tray in twenty minutes, *Mr.* Donovan. I want you dressed by then. The best thing for you is to be up and about." She looked over at Boris. "Make sure the human chimney sitting there in the corner opens a door if he plans to smoke," she commanded.

Boris instinctively shoved the cigarettes back into his pocket and we waited patiently for the sound of the front door shutting before either of us attempted to speak.

"Okay, Boris, why do you look so self-satisfied?"

His eyes started dancing and, forgetting about pesky old Martha McCabe, he went digging for his cigarettes. I poured another cup of the tea and resumed my breakfast.

"The good news is," he began casually, trying to mask his excitement, "I believe we now have the evidence necessary to implicate Alvin Katz in a conspiracy to commit fraud. Under the terms of our agreement with Stanley Greenberg that should be worth sixty-two thousand, five hundred dollars."

I dropped my fork on the plate with a loud clang.

"What was in those papers?" I demanded.

"Your Mr. Gagan gave us photocopies of unexpurgated monthly shipping-and-receiving summaries, covering a period of about five years. There's only a sampling, but I'm confident that a full audit will bear out the conclusions they suggest."

"Five years," I murmured, thinking out loud, "with Alvin Katz arriving somewhere in the middle of that time span?"

"Precisely." Boris lit a cigarette, then continued. "As you suggested, I organized the data by vendor and type of material supplied, then sorted the shipments chronologically. The results were quite informative. Approximately three months after Alvin Katz started working as General Manager, the National Manufacturing Corporation dropped six of its biggest suppliers. During the previous fiscal year, those six companies had combined to supply National with materials worth one-point-nine million."

"Which industries did the changes affect?"

"Two steel service centers, a custom roll former, the powdered-paint vendor, a hardware company, and a supplier of stamped metals parts. Do you want the names and addresses?"

"Not right now. The point is, those are the big money vendors. Their industries are very competitive and price-sensitive. Sometimes it makes sense to shake them up by letting the competition drive down the cost. If I was going to make a change, I'd start with the group of suppliers you just listed. Changing suppliers isn't a crime, Boris. We've got to show evidence that Alvin profited by the change."

"Be patient, James, I'll get to that."

He began sorting through the stack of papers in his lap. After a minute or two, he found what he was looking for and brought it over to me. I'd licked the breakfast dishes clean, so he put them in the hall and shut the door. I swung my feet out of bed and sat upright. My body was very stiff and sore, but it was working.

"Do you need help?" Boris asked, looking concerned.

"No, I'll be okay. Please get back to your explanation. You've left me dangling."

He smiled like a smart kid who's been given an excuse to show off and handed me a piece of paper with a chart printed on it. There was a list of about twenty-five items labeled "goods supplied" running down the left side of the page. For the first two years, when the original vendors were still getting all the business, the annual percentage change for goods supplied varied irregularly. In fact, the prices for many parts actually decreased. I attributed the lower prices to volume discounts as National's sales rose. However, in year three the irregular pattern magically disappeared and prices increased uniformly by almost six percent. That didn't make sense; raw materials should have been plentiful and relatively cheap. Then, in year four, every single item on the list went up exactly ten percent. I stopped looking for trends.

"This isn't very subtle, is it?" I asked, looking up from the chart. "But why only six percent the first year?"

"Actually, the increase was ten percent from the start of the arrangement with the new vendors," he said, smiling. "You see, year three was several months old when Alvin Katz began to tinker, and it took him a while to put the plan into effect. A ten percent increase that became effective five months into the fiscal year would have only a six-percent effect on the annualized cost figures."

"So how come Greenberg hasn't picked this up? It's too simple a scam to get past Stanley."

"Well, obviously these aren't the numbers being plugged into the central file server, which is connected to the office work stations. These other figures, the real numbers, are probably kept in a second set of files on a computer diskette. In other words, there are two sets of books."

"And so," I said, thinking out loud again, "since the change is a straight ten percent across the board, all the vendor has to do is overstate the number of pieces he ships by that amount when he generates the invoice. *Voila!* He gets his increase, but there's no change in unit price. If the extra pieces are missed at National, Alvin can blame the difference on production mistakes. Since he controls shipping and receiving, there's no one to check his word on the amount of goods received. And with Katz approving the payments, the system couldn't fail."

Boris wore a knowing smile. "That's basically it," he said happily. "Though, if the vendors were merely translating the price increases into nonexistent parts, the corresponding increase in scrap expenses would be too dramatic to explain, even at National Manufacturing. It's more likely that some combination of modest price increases and overstated shipments is being used."

It was a tidy little operation. A 10 percent increase in the cost of goods supplied by the six vendors came to nearly two hundred thousand dollars. If Alvin split the money with the vendors, he was pulling down one hundred thousand dollars. The suppliers were probably paying him in cash and running the expenses through cash accounts, like their travel and entertainment or petty-cash funds. That way, they could also get a tax break on the scam.

Knowing what Alvin was doing wasn't the same as proving it. I hated to stick a pin in the bubble, but that was still a problem.

"Nice work, partner, but where's the proof?"

"What are you talking about?" Boris sputtered. "An audit will verify everything I've said."

"Actually, it won't, Boris. First of all, we'd need the real books. Besides, I doubt there's physical evidence to corroborate that the suppliers played with their invoices, and it's too late in the game to go back now and try to verify parts counts. Then there's the question of money. Can we show it leaving the vendors and ending up in Alvin Katz's pocket? I doubt it. Unless you left something out, I say we still have some digging to do before we can nail him."

Boris looked wounded.

"What about the material Gagan give us? I consider that very powerful evidence." He was grasping for something solid.

"No good in court. Gagan's papers are photocopies, and they're stolen. He could have fabricated the whole thing. If we had the second set of books on a diskette and could somehow tie it to Alvin or one of the suppliers, then we'd be in better shape. But that isn't the case. Don't get me wrong, we can use this stuff, but it's not enough by itself."

There was a sudden banging on my bedroom door. It was so loud and unexpected, we both jumped.

"Time's up, you two! And don't think putting these dishes in the hall is gonna stop me from coming in there!"

Martha McCabe was back, and determined. Boris stubbed out his cigarette, rose from the chair, and headed for the door.

"Very well," he said rather sadly. "I'll handle Martha while you get dressed."

Our conversation had drained some of the enthusiasm out of the big guy. I couldn't think of anything clever to say, so I kept quiet. He opened the door and Martha nearly fell into his arms.

"Well, it's about time," she huffed.

The top of her head was visible as she tried to peer around his bulk. Martha was determined to see for herself whether I'd managed to get dressed.

"This way, Mrs. McCabe," Boris said, pushing her gently back into the hall. "Please, allow me to carry that tray for you."

"What? Did you think I was planning to carry this heavy tray all the way to the kitchen when I had you standing next to me? If that's what you had in mind, you can just think again, bucko!"

Poor Boris. As he was pulling the door shut, I could hear him innocently trying to explain himself. He just didn't understand that Martha was pulling his leg.

NINETEEN

...

Twenty minutes later, I slowly made my way down the front hall to the kitchen. Martha was gone, but the room was sparkling clean and there wasn't a dirty dish in sight. Boris was at the counter, hunched over his charts and papers, murmuring to himself.

"By the way," he said seriously, looking up from the papers, "I was able to learn the status of young Mr. Brito's health. And I am very pleased to report that his condition has improved. He is now expected to recover from his injuries. There will be a lengthy and difficult convalescence, but the boy will live."

With those last four words, my whole body seemed to relax.

"The neurosurgeon I spoke with also made it very clear that a second blow to Mr. Brito's head would have been fatal. You may have killed a man, James, but in doing so you saved another's life."

I sat down at the counter and took a deep breath.

"Thanks," I admitted finally. "I needed that."

Boris nodded his head knowingly. "Now, about this issue of proof," he said, getting back to business. "I am forced to agree with the conclusions you reached this morning. At this point in time, we cannot create a legal case against Alvin Katz. Without the sort of evidence needed to support a criminal charge, he would never voluntarily resign. Since that is our objective, we have more work to do." The corners of his mouth twisted into a smirk. "However, the solution may be fairly simple. Let us assume for the moment that we know what Katz is doing, and how. That leaves only the burden of proof, which in this case would be satisfied by simple verification. I find it hard to believe that Alvin Katz could operate his deception without support from someone in the office. If that is true, it follows that he would have to reward his helper or helpers. By sharing in the rewards, his accomplices must share in the guilt. Greed is a common but unstable basis for an alliance. If one person were to speak out, the whole operation would unravel."

Not bad—a fast, sure way to verify our suspicions and put a lever under Alvin. The successful candidate or candidates would work in the office and have access to the purchasing records. It was a short list.

Bill Smith was a definite. Nothing could happen in the purchasing department without him knowing about it, and Bill was too cagey to let this con get past him. I figured Smitty for a big cut. He didn't need the money, which meant he could demand plenty. Bobby Seldane was a maybe. He came across like a true company man. A Greenberg loyalist. Yet, he was really scared of Alvin, and that made me wonder. It was a hard call, but a smart, nervous guy like him, always double-checking the numbers to cover his own butt, probably wouldn't have missed Alvin's scam either.

A third possibility was Stanley's accountant, Barry Speck. Barry had waited a long time before voicing his concerns about the company's financial health. Since Speck did Greenberg's taxes, I had to assume that he was intelligent, creative, and thoroughly corrupt. It would take a tremendous leap of faith to believe that Barry didn't have any idea what was going on.

It was a small company, and those were the only employees who could have raised questions about deliveries or the bills Alvin was approving for payment. Even if Katz had to lay out a third of his take to cover the cost of his "helpers," there would still be plenty of money left for himself.

"How do you think we should proceed?" Boris asked.

"That all depends," I said. "Any luck getting the financials we talked about?"

Boris had been trying to gather financial data on Stanley, Morty, and Alvin. Despite what you see in the movies, it is not that easy to invade someone's privacy. The procedure is complicated, and you usually have to collect bits and pieces of information from a number of different, often unrelated, sources.

"I'm still waiting," he said unhappily. "But you must remember that this is sensitive, personal information. As you know, I'm unable to access this information directly, and my associates must tread softly. If we take our time and make the search seem routine, there's usually no problem. Putting a rush on the inquiry can lead to very serious consequences, and none of us wants trouble. Besides, I pay for this help by trading favors. At the moment, I'm a bit overextended."

"I'm sorry, Boris, but the financials are critical," I said unsympathetically. "We have to start tracing the cash flow or we're never going to unravel this mess."

He looked uncomfortable, but we needed answers and we needed them soon. There was Stanley's advance to draw on, and when that ran out, I was prepared to supplement from our private operating funds.

"Would it help if we sweetened the payback for your contacts?" I suggested casually.

"What?" Boris exploded. "Are you implying that these people could be influenced with money? Do you have any idea what level of expertise we're talking about?" He was incredulous.

"I don't know about their expertise," I said evenly, "but I am suggesting that money might create an incentive. If it eases your conscience to call it by a different name, go right ahead. We could show our gratitude by offering them some new software or perhaps a select piece of electronic hardware."

Boris had twisted his face into a knot, but he didn't immediately reject my suggestion. He understands human nature as well as the next man.

"How grateful do you think we could be?" he asked after a dignified pause.

"All together, I think we could be somewhere between five and ten thousand dollars' worth of grateful, depending upon how complete and detailed the information is," I said, without sounding too smug. "But I want to add Bobby Seldane, Bill Smith, and the designer, Stu Sawyer."

"Sawyer? Why Sawyer?" he asked, as if he'd missed an important point. "This is the first time you've shown an interest in Sawyer."

"I'd like to know if Morty Katz has him tied up in some way. The guy just doesn't fit in at National and I'd like to know why he stays on. It's only a feeler, but we might as well get our money's worth."

Boris grimaced at the mention of money.

"By the way, what did you get from the shipping documents?" I asked.

"Nothing." He sighed.

"What do you mean, nothing? They had to tell us something about Alvin's trucking operation."

"Excuse me, poor choice of words," Boris explained. "I meant to say—nothing *unusual.* Alvin's trucking firm invoices the National Manufacturing Corporation at the end of each month. All activity for the month is summarized on that one bill. Mr. Gagan provided us with photocopies of five monthly shipping statements. Attached to those monthly statements were copies of the appropriate shipping documents for each delivery, listed on the bill.

"Following your advice, I processed this data so that it could be cross-referenced by customer name, destination, load size, and type of material. Unfortunately, it doesn't tell us anything unusual because all the points of reference checked out. The customers were genuine, and the type and number of displays shipped were consistent with sales for the period. There were no side trips to out-of-the-way locations, no split loads, and no bills for empty trailers returning home. In short, nothing out of the ordinary."

I was disappointed, but it made sense. Alvin didn't need a second set of books or duplicate invoices for the trucking company. That was his baby. There were no greedy partners to keep in line. The file copies of shipping invoices we already had were probably the only records of the trucking expense. To uncover systematic over charging, we'd need input from an independent source, like a truck driver's log or his expense reports. Without that, we'd have to drop the trucking angle and hope we could make do with the purchasing swindle.

I didn't want to give an inch. Whatever José Comacho stumbled into was connected to the shipping area and the trucks. His ill-fated discovery eventually led to a visit from the Veldez brothers, with their bats and scorpion tattoos.

"Maybe Joe Gagan knows one of the drivers," I said, thinking out loud. "Hey, speaking of Gagan, where is he?"

"Mr. Gagan is at work today as usual." Boris was obviously annoyed. "I did my best to dissuade him, but the man insisted that all would be well. When we finished talking last night, I woke Santos and introduced them. Shortly thereafter, Gagan left."

Something was nagging at me. "I'm curious—did Joe tell you how he managed to get hold of all those documents?"

"I asked that question, but he demurred. Said it would take too long to explain."

"Well, I think it would be worth the time now."

I was thinking about the computer diskette with the second set of purchasing records. A copy of that file would be a very handy piece of evidence. In fact, now that I thought about it, there were a number of things I wanted to discuss with Joe Gagan. Before I could act on that thought, the house phone rang.

"Yo, Donovan." It was Santos.

"What's up, Manny? I'm a little indisposed at the moment."

"You what? Look, bro, you bedda get down here."

204

"Why, what's wrong?"

"Yo, man, a butthole named Green-bug is down here and we thinkin' about kickin' his ass!"

Good ol' Stanley, making friends wherever he went.

TWENTY

...

"Hey, babe, do you haveta smoke all the fuckin' time? I mean, come on, Doc, you're like a fuckin' chimney!"

Stanley Greenberg was wearing a path in my carpet as he paced up and down in front of the couch. He was not in a good mood. Bobby Seldane and Bill Smith, looking like a couple of shirts someone washed by hand and put through a wringer, were seated before him, heads bowed. Boris was over in my grandfather's big leather club chair. There were empty cups and saucers on the coffee table, and overflowing ashtrays sat in front of Boris and the lads from purchasing. We'd been at it for a couple of hours.

"Relax Stan, I'll open the terrace door again," I said, rising.

"Forget about the door, you'd need an industrial fan to clear the air in here. With those two yutzes"—he pointed a crooked finger at Bobby and Smitty—"and the Russian, it's like ya gotta fuckin' smoke machine goin'!"

I slid the door open anyway, then collected the coffee cups and went into the kitchen for fresh java. Three hours with Stanley Greenberg felt like a full day's work. When the cups were full, I put a drop of Irish whiskey into each of them. Stanley's whining was pretty tough on the nerves. Of course, Greenberg didn't drink coffee. I had to make *him* herbal tea. Thinking about the special tea annoyed me. I added a second dollop of whiskey to each of the coffee cups.

Boris and I had gone to the lobby to collect Stanley Greenberg. During the long elevator ride back to the seventeenth floor, Greenberg was his usual charming self.

"Look at this place, Donovan, it's a shithole!" he remarked, not explaining whether he referred to the entire building or just the elevator cab. Boris stared at him like a botanist who has just discovered a new plant.

When we got to my floor, I took Greenberg on a tour of the apartment while Boris went off to speak with his computer. I showed Stanley the kitchen, study, bedroom, and living room, then topped it off with a stroll out on the terrace. He was impressed.

"Not bad, kid, you had me fooled. What's the deal? I mean, the fuckin' building looks like a welfare hotel and the lobby's fulla drug dealers. You tryin' to make a statement here?"

"I like the view, Stan."

Greenberg looked skeptical.

"And the rent's really low," I added.

Greenberg nodded his head. Low rent he could understand.

When we were comfortably seated in the living room, I gave him a comprehensive report, featuring Alvin Katz and his clever purchasing scam. It hadn't taken Stanley long to grasp the situation. He'd picked up the phone and summoned Messrs. Smith and Seldane for a command performance.

"If Bobby Seldane is involved in this thing," he fumed, "I'll castrate the little prick."

I guess the boys sensed his mood because they made good time, arriving within the hour. The drive had given them an opportunity to consider their options. It didn't take a genius to figure out that they didn't have many. By the time they reached my place, self-preservation had become their primary goal. They were prepared to do whatever it took to cover their butts. As it turned out, they had plenty to tell.

Greenberg insisted upon grilling them long after we'd exhausted their supply of information. He wanted his pound of flesh. I put the spiked coffee cups and Stanley's tea onto a tray and called Smitty in to carry it for me. I was feeling a little better, but I couldn't lift anything heavy.

"Ah, shut up!" Greenberg snapped as I came back into the room.

"Is everything settled?" I asked hopefully.

"Yeah, what the fuck." Stanley seemed resigned.

Smith and Seldane had confirmed our suspicions about Alvin Katz and the purchasing scam. They'd both been in on it from the beginning, so they were able to supply details. I'd been wrong to suspect Stanley's accountant, Barry Speck. Barry wasn't part of the swindle; he was just incompetent.

As it turned out, though, our other projections were pretty accurate. According to Smitty, who'd done most of the talking because Seldane was scared stiff, the participants in this minor conspiracy were collecting around $230,000 a year from the National Manufacturing Corporation. Of that total, a cut of some sixty thousand stayed with the vendors. The rest, nearly $170,000, was kicked back in cash to Katz and the boys. Alvin gave each of the boys a 15 percent share, which worked out to a little more than twenty-five grand apiece. That left almost $120,000 for Alvin.

"What can I tell you?" Smitty said. "It was real easy money. All we hadda do was process the paperwork and keep quiet. Besides, the guy was firing people right and left. If it hadn't been us it woulda been the guys who replaced us."

The time to keep quiet had passed. As a sign of their renewed sense of esprit de corps, both men agreed to dictate statements outlining Alvin's methods and name all the participants in the scheme. They'd also promised to return the money they'd been paid. For this, Stanley reluctantly promised not to press charges. To create the appearance of formality, I made arrangements for a fellow resident, who happens to be a notary public, to put her official seal on the documents when they were ready.

Boris took the handwritten statements and went back to his apartment to feed them into the computer. On his way past Greenberg, he released a tremendous cloud of smoke.

"Very funny, Russian, very fuckin' funny. I'm gonna send you the dry-cleaning bill 'cause I'm gonna have to get disinfected, you smug bastid!"

"Stanley, why don't you take your tea and go outside on the terrace for a little while?" I suggested diplomatically.

"Oh sure, in this fuckin' cold. You want me to catch my death out there?"

I started to speak, but he raised his hand dramatically, stopping me.

"Never mind, I'm going. The fresh air will do me good. Besides, I'm tired of lookin' at garbage," he growled, pointing a crooked finger at Bill Smith and Bobby Seldane.

As Stanley moved onto the terrace, I watched Bobby let out a sigh of relief. Smitty just yawned and stretched out like he was tired of the whole business.

"It's about time that bag a wind finally shaddup," he said.

"Look, Smitty, the guy's no saint, but you've had your hand in his pocket. I'd say he's got a right to be sore," I said.

"Excuse me, the illustrious plant manager finally speaks up. For Chrissake, Donovan, gimme a break here. Besides, what's it to you?"

"I'm just doing a job, Smitty."

"Meaning you're no plant manager, right?"

I nodded my head.

"Hey, not bad. You had me goin', you prick. But come on, Donovan. You could do better than this guy."

"It's complicated, Smitty. Really complicated."

"It is?" he said, mocking me. "Suppose I uncomplicate it for you. Okay, swabby?"

He held up his index finger.

"Numba one, Greenberg steals from everybody he knows. He steals from the govament, he stole the fuckin' company away from Morty, and he robs the men in the plant every goddamn day. You been in that building, how would you describe the conditions? Hey, he's stealing their health, babe. If this was the Navy, we'd a fragged the bastid."

He held up two fingers.

"Numba two, even though he made it sound like a big deal, the guy was never gonna prosecute nobody 'cause he's tryin' ta sell the friggin' business and he don't need trouble. You got that, pal? Are you listenin'?"

"It's more than the company, Smitty. I'm trying to help somebody. It's someone you've never even heard of."

Bill Smith sat up, reached for his coffee cup, and smiled in my direction when he tasted the whiskey. We sipped our drinks in silence and watched Greenberg nervously pacing up and down on the terrace. After a few minutes Bill's face lit up with a grin and he reached for a cigarette.

"This should keep the old fart out on the terrace a little longer," he said. "You never know, maybe he will catch his death." There was a second pause while Smitty puffed away. Finally he turned to me. "Listen up, Donovan. I happen to think you're okay. I mean, shit, you took one helluva shot for that Brito kid. So I'm gonna give you a break. I'm not sure what good it'll do, but here it is. If you think Alvin's little purchasing con is the end of the line, you're gettin' soft. Alvin's a fuckin' loony. He's allowed to roam free 'cause he provides a nice distraction. His old man's the one. He's got somethin' goin' on the front end, the sales end. I dunno what it is, but it's bigger than this shit. Like they say, you got much bigger fish to fry, my friend."

The doorbell rang, interrupting us.

"Why hello, Alma," I said, opening the front door. "I didn't hear the elevator. How are you this evening?"

"I took the stairs," she whispered, as if we were involved in a conspiracy.

It was our resident notary public, Alma Polhemus, one of the infamous Polhemus twins. Alma is a slight, elderly woman with dyed blond hair that she keeps in a French braid. Alma was wearing a Laura Ashley dress designed for a junior miss, complete with patent-leather shoes. I don't know who does her makeup, but she always ends up looking like Gloria Swanson in

210

Sunset Boulevard. As I started to close the door, someone out in the corridor sneezed daintily. It was Mildred. You rarely find one Polhemus sister without the other.

"Hello, Mildred," I said, sticking my head back into the hall.

"Oh, Mr. James, *please* don't pay me any mind. I'll just wait out here till Ally's finished her work."

She turned to face the wall, as if studying it would keep her busy till Alma was done. As usual, their outfits were identical.

"Why, Mildred, you come right on in here. You know I'm always delighted to see you."

She didn't hesitate a second. In fact, I think she was seated next to Alma at the dining table before I finished my sentence. The girls were in. I couldn't think of anything else to do, so I introduced everyone, including Stanley Greenberg, who'd come in from the terrace.

"Yo, Donovan," Stanley said, pulling me aside, "what's with the freak show?"

"Alma Polhemus is a notary public, Stan. She's going to witness the statements. The other woman is her twin sister. They're inseparable. Deal with it, all right?"

He raised his eyebrows and made a face.

Boris came back in carrying a stack of printouts. He bowed politely to the girls and returned to his favorite red leather chair. When he was comfortably seated, he passed out copies of the statements he'd prepared for signatures. As we scanned the documents, he turned his attention to a stack of printouts in his lap.

The signing went smoothly, although there were some loud sighs and deep breaths taken as the Polhemus girls scanned the papers. And we did have a rather tense few minutes while Alma tried unsuccessfully to assemble her notary seal. I finally took it away from her and put the thing together myself. When the papers were duly witnessed and notarized, Greenberg instructed Bobby Seldane and Bill Smith to go home and call in sick to work the next day. After that, they were supposed to sit tight and await further instructions.

The Polhemus sisters decided it would be *interesting* to escort

211

the unfortunate gentlemen to the lobby. As they waited for the elevator, the girls focused most of their attention on the sulking figure of Bobby Seldane.

"Oh my Lord, but you have been a very naughty boy," Alma was saying when the lift arrived.

"Oh yes, yes, very naughty," Mildred echoed.

As the door slid shut, I heard Smitty: "For Chrissakes, would you broads can it?"

Both sisters let out squeals of outraged excitement. I'm willing to bet that was the longest elevator ride those two guys ever took.

Back in the apartment, it was time for a serious chat. If Bill Smith knew that the company was for sale, how come Greenberg hadn't mentioned it to us? I didn't get into the sale with Smitty because I didn't want to look stupid, but Stanley wasn't going to be so lucky. He was holding back on us and it made me mad.

"It's put-up time, Stanley," I said, marching back into the living room. "We want to know what you're really up to and why you've been keeping us in the dark."

He hesitated for a minute or two, deciding whether or not to argue with me. We didn't have to wait long—even Stanley realized it was time to come clean.

"I want to make one thing clear," he began nervously. "I did not keep anything from you guys that you needed to know. At least, I didn't think I was keeping anything from you. My business affairs are my own. So I don't want any hard feelings over that kinda shit. Okay?"

He didn't get a response.

"Okay, okay, look, I've had an offer for the company on my desk the last two, three weeks. A guy named Mahoney. You'd like him, Donovan, he's one of your people."

I bit my tongue.

"Anyways, I know him 'cause he's been brokering work for us the last coupla years. A very well-connected guy who really knows the industry. He wants to start manufacturing his own

212

displays. For your information, his offer was very sweet, and he's good for it."

When a big corporation or chain of stores needs to buy displays, they usually hire a broker to manage the project from design right through the installation. The broker functions the way a general contractor does on a construction project. If Mahoney was a broker, it made good sense for him to integrate backward into manufacturing. He had all the right contacts to do very well for himself.

"What makes you so sure he's good for the money?" I asked.

"Because I met with his banker and he said so."

A smug Stanley Greenberg was especially hard to stomach.

I noticed that Boris was showing a sudden interest in the conversation. I watched as he started sorting through the stack of printouts in his lap. It looked as if he'd made a connection.

"Excuse me, Mr. Greenberg," Boris said, marking his place with a chubby finger, "would you mind answering a few questions for me?"

"Sure. Why not?"

"What is the full name of your Mr. Mahoney?"

"Everybody calls him Danny, so I guess it's Daniel."

"What is the name of his company?"

"Quality Display Case, QDC."

"And the name of his bank?"

"Chemical."

"Which branch would that be?"

"Linden Boulevard, off Stouten."

"I don't suppose you remember the name of the loan officer you met?"

"Sure. I'm good on names. It was Frank Simeon."

"I see. Well, thank you."

That was it. Boris went back to his printouts. He reached for his dented silver case, slowly extracted a gold-tipped Sobranie, and lit it without taking his eyes off of the papers he was studying. Stanley and I looked at each other, expecting something more, but nothing came. I waited a minute longer, then moved on.

"So, you didn't want a public fight with Alvin Katz because of the impending sale to Mahoney," I said, getting back to my earlier line of questioning. "But you wanted to collect enough dirt on Morty and Alvin so you wouldn't have to share the proceeds with them. Right?"

"Hey, what would you do?"

"We'd better not get into that, Stanley," I said.

"There you go acting holy again. Hey, Donovan, it must be tough carrying that fuckin' cross around all day."

I didn't get a chance to respond. Stanley wasn't through.

"Let me tell you somethin', Mr. Graduate School Smartass, Mahoney offered me two million dollars cash for a business I only put two hundred and fifty thousand into to begin with. After paying down the debt, I was looking at a one-point-two-million-dollar gift. Beat that!"

He paused to search our faces, expecting admiration. I think we disappointed him. "Fuck you both," he snarled.

"I wonder which came first, Stanley. Did you start to worry about the books before or after you got Mahoney's offer?"

"As a matter of fact, the offer came in after I realized I was gettin' screwed. If those two bastids had played straight they'd be in on the deal. Not now. When I figured out they were fuckin' me, I decided to take them outta the loop. Hey, what goes around, comes around."

"Why didn't you just buy them out?" I asked.

"Buy them out!" He was incredulous. "Are you fuckin' nuts? They've been robbin' me blind. As far as I'm concerned, that's all they're gonna get."

I'd had a suspicion early on that Stanley was up to something like this. But after spending time in the plant, I'd given up on the idea. I couldn't imagine anyone wanting to buy the National Manufacturing Corporation.

"Actually," Boris interjected, "thus far, we can only account for a fraction of the money you claim was stolen. Have you considered the fact that mismanagement may have eaten up sev-

214

eral hundred thousand? If that were the case, the amount stolen would be a much smaller sum, an amount similar to the one we've already tied to Alvin Katz."

"Don't give me none a that socialist crap, you commie fuck. This has nothin' to do with management. I know the cocksuckers are stealing from me and you're supposed to find out how they're doin' it."

Boris was momentarily stunned. When he recovered, he moved to the edge of his seat and stared across the coffee table at Greenberg.

"For your information, Mr. Greenberg, I am neither a commie nor a fuck. I am a naturalized American citizen of Russian descent. My education entitles me to be addressed as *doctor*. In the future, you will refer to me as Dr. Koulomzin or not at all."

He sat back again, folded his hands on his stomach, and closed his eyes. Unless something remarkable happened to change his mind, Boris had removed himself from the discussion.

"What the fuck's the matter with him?" Greenberg asked, turning to me.

"Let's just say that you have no future as a diplomat, Stanley."

"For Christ's sake, what the fuck is everybody so sensitive about? What are you guys, a couple of Boy Scouts?"

"Do me a favor and tone it down, okay, Stan?"

"Fine, fine, I apologize," he said halfheartedly.

I was anxious to move on. "Boris has raised a legitimate point about the money. We've pinned everything but the kitchen sink on Alvin, but most of the loss you're claiming is still unaccounted for, and we're running out of places to look. On the other hand, since you've always managed the way you do, it shouldn't suddenly cost you more than it has in the past. So let's assume for now that all the money was stolen. If that's true, the only person in a position to pull off such a big hit is Morty Katz."

"I've been telling you that since day one. What am I payin' you for?" Greenberg asked sarcastically.

I ignored him and continued.

"What I don't understand is why Morty Katz would swindle money from himself. After all, he shares in the profits. What he doesn't steal falls right to the bottom line, risk free. To a lesser degree, the same is true for Alvin. Besides, if Alvin needed money, why didn't Morty just give it to him? What's the motivation for messing with a good thing? It just doesn't make any sense to me."

"Oh, it doesn't make sense to you? I see, very nice. Well, let me explain it to you, hot shot," Stanley jeered. "Morty's got motivation and plenty of it and it ain't comin' from Alvin's action. Overall the cost of goods sold went up eight-point-five percent last year. That translates into six hundred eighty thousand dollars. You got that, genius? After subtracting Alvin's piece, I'm still lookin' for four hundred and eighty thousand. You don't think that's a big enough incentive? When were you born, kid?" He started pacing again.

"No good, Stan. I don't believe Morty wants your money. His whole life is that company. He doesn't like his family, he's got no real friends, no hobbies. What's left? The only thing the guy loves is the National Manufacturing Corporation. His whole shtick comes from the company. He's smart enough to know that if he steals from you he'd eventually get caught. And if he got caught, you'd force him out. There's got to be something else behind it."

Greenberg actually stopped to think for a moment. "Then what about Alvin? Morty had to know what Alvin was pullin'. If the guy's so worried about the business, why would he let that shit go on?"

"I don't know, Stan, but he had to have a reason. Besides, I'm not saying that Morty hasn't been robbing you blind. I'm saying that money wouldn't be his sole motivation. It would be his means to some other end."

"You know what, Donovan, you sound like a fuckin' head shrinker. A lot of fancy words that add up to nothin'."

"That's beautiful Stan," I said, finally losing my patience. "Just when I think I'm getting through to you, you say something really stupid. What were you thinking when you contacted me? What did you expect? Did you think I was going to reorganize your business, audit the books, and tame the Katz family from my lofty post as plant manager? You're the one who should get serious. The whole idea was ridiculous from the start. You don't catch embezzlers by walking around out in a factory. You catch them by analyzing the books.

"But not you. You're so corrupt and greedy you didn't even consider using the obvious legal process to redress your grievances. You had to get even and *profit* by it. So you came up with this stupid idea for a bogus plant manager. To make matters worse, you neglected to tell me that you had a buyer for the company. People were dropping around me like flies and I didn't even know all the facts. Has it occurred to you that selling the business out from under Morty Katz would give him a pretty good motive to disrupt the sale?"

We hadn't considered Morty before because we didn't know about the sale. When the words popped out of my mouth they stopped me short. Stanley decided to outflank me by acting repentant. It was pathetic.

"It's funny you should mention that," a contrite Stanley Greenberg said, "because there's something else I got to tell you."

"What's that, Stan?" I was beat.

"Well, there's been a slight change. Mahoney called me this morning. He read about all the trouble we've had in the plant. It's made him very uncomfortable about the deal. He's taking his offer off the table."

"Am I supposed to feel sorry for you now, Stan, or does it get better?"

"Hey, cut me some slack—I'm trying to be open with you guys, and this is important. Before I came out tonight, I got a call from Morty. He says he feels bad that he got me into this mess."

"So, you two kissed and made up?" I asked.

"Hey, fuck you, Donovan. The creep offered to buy me out."

"He did *what?*"

"Yeah, he offered me half a million bucks to walk. Hey, you know what, it's twice my investment and with all this other trouble, I don't know what's gonna happen. I mean we could be lookin' at civil suits, fines, you name it."

"Are you telling me that you're going to sell the company back to Morty Katz after everything that's happened?" I asked.

Stanley looked embarrassed. But it was pretty obvious he was preparing to do just that—cut his losses and move on.

"I'm not sure," he said, unhappily. "I mean, do I have a choice?"

There was a growling sound as my partner cleared his throat.

"As a matter of fact, Mr. Greenberg," Boris said, without opening his eyes, "I believe that you do."

TWENTY-ONE

...

I stepped out onto the loading dock and filled my lungs with cold fresh air. Behind me the uneven rhythm of the welding and brake-press machinery droned on, muffled by the heavy plastic sheets hanging in front of the doorway. It was Friday evening, and I was back at the National Manufacturing Corporation.

I'd been on my feet since early morning, and it was taking a toll. My upper body was sore and my shoulder throbbed like a bad headache. To complicate matters, it was also my night to meet Kate for dinner, which meant I still had to shower, change my clothes, and get to her place before ten. It had been hard keeping up with the work before I got hurt, but this was just too much.

Thanks to Joe Gagan's paperwork and the statements from Bill Smith and Bobby Seldane, we had a lock on Alvin Katz's purchasing scam; shutting him down would be easy. We also had a pretty good idea what Morty Katz was planning. If Greenberg had been honest from the start there's a chance we'd have figured it out sooner, but that's hindsight. The key we'd been looking for was Daniel P. Mahoney. His name unlocked the puzzle.

Boris had made the discovery the previous night while I was arguing with Stanley. The printouts he'd been studying while we finished up with Smitty and Seldane were the long-awaited financial profiles on Mortimer Katz, Alvin Katz, and Stuart Sawyer. There were also reports on Bobby Seldane and Bill Smith, but we knew where they stood.

Alvin's A+ credit rating was the mark of a solid citizen who liked to pay his bills. He didn't seem to need money. His personal assets included a $300,000 house in Nassau County, which was paid for; two late-model cars; and a ChemPlus account with a balance of $121,435.62. There was also a report on his trucking business. Although his warehouse and offices were in rented space, Alvin owned two used Peterbilt tractors, four new trailers, and a couple of forklifts. They were probably worth an additional $270,000. Alvin liked to convert his cash into assets that didn't draw attention.

Stuart Michael Sawyer was also a solid citizen, but his assets weren't nearly as impressive. He lived in Suffolk County, in a modest house that was mortgaged to the hilt. He had one five-year-old car and a savings account with a balance of $8,289.43. Stu Sawyer wasn't getting rich working at National Manufacturing, so why'd he stay? It nagged at me.

Finally, we came to Morty Katz. His printout was a monument to creative accounting. Other than his stock in National Manufacturing, which was pledged against a business loan, Morty Katz didn't show a single asset in his own name—not his house, not even a checking account. I wasn't too surprised; he'd probably put everything in his wife's name. Morty was cagey. They can't take away what they can't find.

There was one surprise, however, and I'm sure it was an oversight on Morty's part. The profiles listed executive titles and affiliations, like seats on corporate boards. In addition to his position as president of the National Manufacturing Corporation, Morty Katz was listed as chairman of the board of directors of an outfit called MKC, Inc. It didn't require too much guesswork to figure out that MKC stood for Mortimer Katz Company. It was a mistake; he didn't need another title. Morty's almost-blank file must have intrigued Boris's friend, because he'd included a profile of MKC, Inc. Actually, there wasn't very much to report about that little company, either.

MKC consisted of two officers, a small corporate checking account, and all the stock in a wholly owned subsidiary. The chairman and CEO was Mr. Morty Katz. The other officer, the treasurer, turned out to be my pal Stuart Sawyer. I stopped worrying about Stu's motivation for staying at National. The wholly owned subsidiary was an outfit called Quality Display Case. Thanks to Stanley Greenberg, we already knew that the president of QDC was Daniel Mahoney. Now we also knew that he worked for Morty.

A copy of QDC's balance sheet was included with the rest of the documentation. It proved most informative. Quality Display Case had assets in cash and marketable securities in excess of $2.4 million, and the offsetting liabilities were all loans due and payable either to MKC directly or as deferred salary and bonuses to Morty and Stuart. In other words, it was a big piggy bank shaped like Morty Katz, and Stu Sawyer owned a nice chunk of it.

Once I knew for sure that Morty was our man and that his partners both worked in sales, it wasn't hard to come up with an explanation for that pile of cash. Bill Smith was heading me in the right direction when he suggested I take a hard look at the front end of the business. My guess was that Morty built broker's commissions into his big sales and then paid them out to Quality Display Case. The arrangement undoubtedly cost him by way of kickbacks to the corporate buyers, but with a well-known broker like Mahoney fronting the deal, it was a pretty safe investment.

Why was Morty fleecing his own partnership? Well, that wasn't too hard to figure anymore, either. MKC, Inc. and Quality Display Case were formed about a year after Stanley Greenberg muscled his way onto Morty's turf. Either Katz tried to work with Greenberg for the first year and gave up, or else it had just taken a year to put the plan together. It didn't matter. His new partner turned out to be a louse, so Morty started skimming and saving up to buy Greenberg out. The sweetest part of the deal was that he'd be paying Stanley with Stanley's own money.

Enter Mahoney and his offer. Morty Katz read his partner's greed perfectly. Two million dollars was nearly eight times the earnings, and the company was entirely dependent on Morty, a seventy-year-old man, for sales. National Manufacturing wouldn't have been an attractive investment without a guy like Mahoney on the team. Even with him, the offer seemed too good to be true.

The real question was whether or not Morty ever planned to actually spend his two million dollars. The electrocution of José Comacho and the attacks on Raul Brito and me had clearly worked in his favor; it convinced Stanley Greenberg to sell out. When Mahoney pulled his offer to buy, it set Stanley up for the lower offer from Morty.

Either way, we had plans for Mr. Morty Katz and his partners. While I was finishing up my shift at National, Boris was making arrangements for a little skin game of our own design. And it promised to be a whopper.

Back on the shipping dock, I was leaning against the railing and thinking about Ruby Brice and the other woman. I'd come back to the factory in Brooklyn for them, not for Stanley Greenberg. Our work for Stanley was almost done. I had to find out what had cost those two women their lives. My gut told me the answers I needed were in East New York, where they both died. So there I was, but I wasn't alone. A loaded .32-caliber Beretta was sitting quietly in a holster clipped inside my belt.

I decided to wander up the block, hoping for inspiration. It wasn't the kind of street you'd recommend for a stroll, but then I needed help, and time was running out. There was a chance I'd run into one of Ruby's girlfriends working the street, and that was worth the risk. I needed someone to help point me toward the boyfriend, Uncle Tito.

It was a cold, windy fall night and the neighborhood was deserted. I took my time and walked around the entire block, but it didn't do any good; there wasn't anything to see. When I got back to the loading platform, Joe Gagan was sitting on the steps waiting for me. We hadn't seen each other since the little soirée in Madame Karina's apartment two nights earlier. You could smell the booze on him from twenty feet away.

"Don't tell me you watered the Scotch down this time," I said, joining him on the stairs.

"All in the line a duty, son." He smiled.

"How do you figure?"

"Well, these last tree hours, I been sittin' at the bar in a place called Charley's over by the pier. I was doin' the buyin', which made the gentleman sittin' to my left very happy indeed. In fact, we had a most agreeable chat."

Talking to drunk people is like listening to a recording on the wrong speed.

"Now, afore ya pass judgment, James, hear me out."

"I don't know, man, you're a real mess."

"And don't I know it? Didn't I spend a fortune gettin' into this condition?" He smiled again. I just shook my head.

"Anyway, my friend at the bar, name of Brian Fallon, just happens to drive a truck for that darling boy Alvin Katz. As we both know, Alvin doesn't exactly endear himself to the help. So, once my pal Brian unnerstood I was kin'erd spirit, dint he give me an earful?"

I waited as he fumbled with a crumpled pack of nonfiltered cigarettes. He put one into his mouth and lit a match, but that was as far as he got. He couldn't line the match up with the butt. I had to take his hand and hold the flame in front the cigarette for him.

"There's no logbooks, so you can stop looking," he said without removing the lit cigarette from his mouth. "Doesn't mean the bastard didn't double-bill like you said, 'cause he probably did; you just can't prove it. So forget about it, it ain't wort the time! Did I already say that?"

This was going to be a struggle. "Don't worry about that, Joe, just go on."

"Well, did I happen to mention the guns?"

223

That got my attention. "Let's go," I said, trying to drag him to his feet. "I want to dump some coffee into you. This is too important for guessing games."

"Wait one damn minute, Donovan." He shook me off. "Have ya any idea how much whiskey I've soaked up? Why you'd stand a better chance of turnin' water into beer than ya would tryin' to sober me up wit coffee. Jeez, I thought you'd been around, son."

He was probably right. "Okay, forget the coffee. Tell me about the guns."

He leaned against the wall for support. "Well, sir, as you know, we ship to Florida, what is it, a couple, tree times a month? I hear tell that comin' back the trailer is usually carryin' a nice-sized crate or two. And Fallon says they always get picked up at the same place, a roadside joint out in the sticks some- wheres, run by a guy names Jimmy somethin' or other.

"Well, one time my new buddy, Fallon, he was picking up them crates for the trip home and he noticed that Jimmy's got himself a pistol strapped to his waist. 'That's a mighty fine gun you got there,' says Fallon. And this Jimmy, he says, 'Hell, sonny, why don't you jest buy one from your boss,' and slaps old Fallon on the back like it's an inside joke. Well, it was like curiosity and the cat, he opened up one of them crates and she's fulla pistols. Maybe two hunnert in a crate. How's them for some fine apples, Mr. J. J. Donovan?"

Gagan was trying to light a new cigarette using the glowing butt from his last one. I had to steady his hand again. After that, I led him back to the steps and we both sat down. I needed time to sort this news out.

Alvin Katz was bringing guns up from the Florida. And doing what? Selling them on the street in East New York? It was crazy, but possible. After all, anybody with a driver's license could buy firearms in Florida. And, it would be easy as pie for Alvin to have his drivers pick up an unmarked crate or two on their way back north. Alvin didn't even need to dirty his hands with the actual merchandise. That end could be delegated to lowlifes like Cana Dulce Veldez and his brother, Ramon.

"Can we prove any of this, Joe? Did you find out where Fallon delivers the guns?"

I didn't get an answer because Joe was asleep on his feet. I had to shake him awake.

"Right you are and let that be a lesson," he said, coming out of it.

He peered at me, trying to focus.

"What was the question, son?"

"Have you got any proof?"

He shook his head. "No proof, but we got a truck comin' back Mondee."

I hadn't thought about that. "And, the guns, got any idea who Alvin sells them to?"

"Don't know that either, Mr. Donovan, but it seems to me there's quite a few boys on the night shift wearin' that insect tattoo—same brand them Veldez brothers had. Why don't ya ask the Ratman ta help. If he don't already know, he can find out. Anyways, that's what I'd do." He went digging for another cigarette, but dropped the pack instead and then stepped on it by mistake. "For the love a Pete!" he said softly.

"It's time for you to go home, Joseph."

I didn't want to waltz Joe through the plant. In fact, I didn't want anyone to know he'd been there. This man wasn't going to end up with his skull rearranged. Besides, if I wanted to keep my date with the former Mrs. Donovan, I had to leave then anyway. So I gritted my teeth, ignored the pain in my shoulder, and helped Joe into the car. I figured I'd take him to my place and let him sleep it off on the couch. It beat getting shot, clubbed, or electrocuted. At my place, the only thing he had to worry about was Angus, who might try to use him as a pillow. I didn't bother telling the night foreman I was leaving early.

"Joe?"

I slid behind the wheel and started the engine. Gagan had

fallen asleep again. I poked him in the ribs a few times, and he revived briefly.

"Joe, I'm taking you home with me. Is there anybody I should notify?"

Nothing.

"*Joe!*" I yelled.

"Fa cripe's sake, I hear ya, boy. Be off and leave a man alone." He curled up against the passenger door.

"Is there anybody at home waiting for you, somebody who'll worry if you don't show?" I persisted.

"Mr. Donovan, there ain't a soul in this world worryin' about Joseph Gagan 'cept me," he said seriously. "And, now that I think of it, I expect you to behave like a perfect gentlemen."

He let out a belly laugh, then settled back and passed out.

Gagan was wrong about one thing. There was someone else worrying about him. I was trying to figure out how to get a hundred-and-fifty-pound deadweight drunk old Irishman up to my apartment without breaking my collarbone again.

TWENTY-TWO

...

I started driving toward Manhattan, then changed my mind and pulled into a Mobil station along the Belt Parkway. My cell phone was dead again, so I called my partner on a pay phone. Gagan slept on, wheezing and snorting happily.

Boris answered the telephone on the second ring. He was in a splendid mood and cheerfully brought me up to speed on the progress of our little operation. As expected, Stanley Greenberg was performing beautifully; years of experience fleecing the unsuspecting was coming in handy. His job was to line up some of the other players and make sure they understood their parts. We couldn't afford to have anyone fall out of character, not if we wanted to pull this thing off. Apparently, Stanley made Dan Mahoney, over at Quality Display, an offer Mahoney couldn't refuse. Next, he'd gone to work on Morty Katz, softening him up. The trap was set; all we had to do was add the bait.

It was time for a final meeting. That meant bringing Ronnie Blakely and his field operatives in for a tête-à-tête. I asked Boris to arrange the meeting for nine o'clock the following morning at my place. It was also time for a chat with Lieutenant Negro, although we both agreed that Negro's visit should happen after the private cops had come and gone. Saving the best for last, I told Boris about Gagan's night at the bar with Alvin Katz's driver. He got really excited and started firing questions at me, but we were talking on a pay phone and I was out of nickels.

Before I hung up, I explained about the sack of potatoes snoring away in my car, and Boris promised to arrange for some help.

It took about forty-five minutes to drive home, but when I pulled up to the curb in front of our crumbling palace, the troops were ready and waiting. Manny Santos and two of his cousins came out pushing a hand truck. They hauled Joe Gagan out of the car, carefully balanced him on the dolly, then quickly wheeled him through the lobby and loaded him into the elevator for the long ride upstairs. Manny got behind the wheel of my car.

"Whoa, Santos, no good. I've gotta leave again as soon as I shower and change." I probably sounded a little panicked.

"Relax, Don-o-van," he said, popping open a big can of Colt 45 malt liquor. "I gotta run to the discount for some *cerbeza*. By the way, you wanna help out? My boys is gonna be *mocho sed* from carryin' that gringo."

I reached into my pocket for the money clip and I peeled off a twenty. "Be back in fifteen minutes or you're a dead man," I threatened.

"You're welcome," he said, leaving me in a cloud of exhaust smoke.

When I got to the apartment, Joe Gagan was already bundled up on the couch with his shoes off and a blanket over him. Clifford Brice and his pal Angus were standing at one end of the couch watching the rumpled old man. Angus looked up at me, like he wasn't sure if he should bite him, defend him, or just bury the little stranger in the park till we got things sorted out.

"Good boy, Angus," I said, patting him on the head. "You keep an eye on Joe, he's a good friend."

Angus promptly lay down in front of the sofa, prepared to guard and defend.

"What's a matter with this guy?" Clifford asked finally, his eyes wide.

"This is Mr. Gagan, Cliff," I explained. "He's really drunk, but he got that way for a good cause. Thanks to Joe Gagan, I think we can prove that somebody's been running guns out of the National Manufacturing Corporation. It's very possible your mother stumbled into the middle of it. Remember, she told you she saw something bad going down over there."

"Yeah, right," he said, rubbing his little chin.

I started to leave the room, but he called me back.

"J. J., does this mean you found the man that killed my momma?" he asked softly.

"No, kid, it doesn't," I answered honestly. "But maybe we're getting a little closer."

Clifford nodded his head, then sat down on the floor next to Angus. Apparently Cliff had decided to stand guard, too.

I went into the bathroom and got the shower cranked up, then I got out of my work clothes and carefully removed the ace bandage and padding making up the figure eight splint holding my shoulder in place. When that was done, I pulled on my bathrobe and began to search for a clean pressed shirt to wear with my blue Perry Ellis suit.

Boris sauntered in, sucking on a pipe and wearing the self-satisfied expression of a man who knows his worth. I found a clean shirt and laid it out on the bed with a matching tie. Boris followed me into the bathroom and we talked over the noise of my shower.

"Did Mahoney agree to all the terms?" I shouted through a cloud of steam.

"Mr. Mahoney reminds me of a seventeenth-century mercenary soldier," Boris answered, leaning up against the sink. "He willingly gives his allegiance to the group most obviously in control of his destiny."

"I take it that's a yes?" I hollered.

"The appointments you requested have also been made," he continued. "Lieutenant Negro was not very pleased. Seems he's been trying to contact you for several days."

"And why hasn't he been able to reach me?" I asked, sticking my head around the shower curtain.

"I can't be sure," Boris said innocently. "I told the lieutenant I'd have our telephone system checked. Obviously there's some sort of a bug."

"Right, a bug." I turned off the water and grabbed a towel.

Boris drifted into the bedroom, still puffing happily on his pipe.

"Hey, don't go anywhere," I yelled. "I'm gonna need your help putting the splint back on."

I tossed him the bandages. Boris winced. The sight of my purple and blue shoulder made him blanch. I pulled on my trousers and sat down on the bed so he could begin wrapping and tightening.

"Are you all right?"

I took a deep breath, fighting off the pain.

"Yes, Boris," I wheezed, "please, just finish the dressing."

"You've gone awfully red in the face. I don't like the looks of it. We'd better call Richard Steinman." He stopped and reached for the phone.

"Do not call anyone!" I yelled, letting out the air I'd been holding. "I am red in the face because I am extremely uncomfortable. It will pass, but not until you finish putting on the splint. I'm beggin' you, just get on with it."

It took another five minutes to complete the bandaging and ten more for me to finish dressing. During that time, I repeated my conversation with Joe Gagan, word for word. The big news was that a shipment of guns was coming Monday night. That was the same night we were planning to spring our little surprise on Morty Katz. I checked my image in the full-length mirror on the bathroom door, then splashed on something that smelled like the good old days. I still had to get Kate to agree to our plan or we'd be in trouble. Boris watched me, amused because I wouldn't admit that these biweekly engagements were dates. I insisted I was just having dinner with an ex-wife.

"Could you do me one last favor?" I asked on my way out the door.

"I think that could be arranged." He grinned.

"Give Kate a call and tell her I'm on my way. Do not, I repeat, do not tell her about our plans. I'll spring the idea on her during dessert. Ellen promised to serve something chocolate. If that doesn't soften her up, nothing will."

Boris nodded his head and smiled knowingly. If I'd had more time, I might have asked him to explain that smug expression, but I was running late. I rode the elevator down to the lobby and was relieved to see my car outside. Manny, his cousins, and several other members of the Santos entourage were leaning up against it, drinking beer. When they saw me coming the boys started whistling and making lewd noises.

"Ain't you a *bee*-uty," Manny said, puckering his lips. "I think you be what them ladies want."

"You know, Santos, that's not a very nice way to talk to the guy who pays for all your beer," I snapped.

"Oh my, Señor J. J., excuse me," Manny whimpered. The others snickered.

"Okay, that's better."

As I got into the driver's seat, Manny came over and motioned for me to roll down the window.

"What now, Manny? You know I'm in a hurry."

He made a face. "Hey, man, you always late."

"Fine, I'm always late. Come on, what is it?"

He leaned down further, sticking his head into the car, and took a deep breath through his nose. He exhaled enough stale beer breath to render a smaller man unconscious.

"Ahh," he sighed, smiling, "I jus wanna say that you smell preddy, too!"

He backed up out of reach before I could react and accepted hoots of appreciation from his buddies. I was getting pretty tired of being the brunt of Manny's jokes, but there wasn't time to deal with it just then. I pulled away from the curb, mumbling something about revenge.

■ ■ ■

231

Kathleen Mary Byrne, the former Mrs. Donovan, lives in an old, elegantly appointed building on Sutton Terrace on the East Side of Manhattan. It's a fashionable address, if you're into that stuff, and a very convenient location for those who can afford it. She can take a short cab ride to her midtown office, she's close to shops and museums, and near enough to Park and Fifth Avenues for convenient hobnobbing with her well-heeled acquaintances.

My ex-wife is the publisher of a successful fashion magazine. They try for the European look, with serious-looking models advertising cleavage in expensive clothes. You'd recognize the name if I mentioned it. It isn't the largest publication in the United States, but it's big and very profitable. The magazine is the crown jewel in a stable of publishing properties owned by L.P.L. Industries. That makes my Kate somebody to know if you're in the publishing business.

There isn't enough time now to explain what happened to our marriage. We were too young, too self-centered. Who knows? I like to think we just needed some time to figure out what was important in our lives. My path led to work I consider meaningful and fulfilling. Kate's led to a successful career that gives her the security she needs and the respect she deserves. And yet, even after we'd gone our separate ways, there was still something missing. Turns out, that something is each other.

We keep separate apartments and lead professional lives that rarely intersect. But we're very much in love, so we concentrate on that. Two years ago, we bought a cozy little weekend house together. It's up in Connecticut, set on a big lake. It has a beautiful garden and a sprawling yard with lots of trees. In the winter we snuggle up in front of the fireplace sipping hot toddies, and during the summer we have picnics by the lake. It's a private place; we escape to it whenever we can break away from the real world.

■ ■ ■

I checked my watch. I really was late. One of the sore points in our relationship has always been the fact that Kate is punctual and I am not. By the time I raced into the lobby of her building, I was twenty-five minutes behind schedule and the clock was still ticking. The doorman stood by his desk, decked out in a great coat with gold braids and rows of brass buttons.

"You're late, Mr. Donovan. She's called down twice to ask if we was playing dice in the service elevator."

"Ignore the woman, Johnny, she's completely insane."

"That's easy for you to say." John looked glum.

"See if this helps restore your sense of humor," I said, handing out yet another twenty dollar bill like the last of the big spenders. "And while you're at it, you can keep an eye on my car? It's in the service alley." I stepped into the elevator.

"Oh no, not again, Mr. Donovan. Don't you remember what happened the last time? Come on, give a guy a break."

I threw him the keys. "There's another twenty in it if my chariot doesn't get towed," I promised as the elevator doors closed.

The lift was wood-paneled with brass trim. There was even a little upholstered seat in the corner, just in case your legs got tired. The car came to a silent, gentle stop on Kate's floor. I stepped into the hall and stopped in front of the big ornamental mirror to check my tie, then pushed the doorbell.

I could hear the chimes ringing far inside the cavernous apartment. They're so faint, you expect to be kept waiting as someone jogs from one end of the apartment to the other. Not so. The door was opened almost immediately by a maid in classic garb: black dress, white apron. It was a nice touch, but I would have preferred someone under the age of sixty, preferably named Fifi.

"You're late again, Mr. D.," the maid scolded.

"I know, Ellen, I know." I got down on one knee and folded my hands in prayer. "Take me now, Lord, take me now," I begged.

"You'd better stop that," Ellen warned. "You may be about to get your wish."

233

I ignored the warning and got to my feet. "How do I look?" I whispered.

She smiled and glanced over her shoulder to make sure we were alone. "You look nice, Mr. D., you just might pull it off." We winked at each other.

"Ellen? Ellen, is that him?"

Kate was calling from the inner sanctum of the apartment.

"Yes, ma'am. It's himself."

"Well, give the lout a drink. He probably tuckered himself out trying to dream up a credible excuse." There's nothing like a woman who knows you well.

"Pinch on the rocks tonight, or is it a martini?" Ellen knew me pretty well, too.

"Vodka, my darling, and don't forget my olives."

I was talking to the door—Ellen hadn't even waited for an answer. She was already in the kitchen. I left the foyer and strolled into the living room. It was huge by New York City standards and expensively furnished. But it wasn't warm and inviting like our little house in the country or Madame Karina's apartment. Kate didn't care. When she got tired of the decor, she hired someone to change it. She does a lot of entertaining for business and thinks of the apartment as more of a workplace than a home. She saves the personal touches for our place in Connecticut.

I noticed my picture in a silver Christofle frame sitting on a side table near the fireplace. The photo was almost ten years old, and looked it. I made a mental note to get her a more recent image. While I was busy critiquing the decor, Ellen burst back into the room. She was carrying a tray with a shaker, several martini glasses, and a dish of colossal Spanish olives. Instead of stopping to offer me a libation, she marched right on through the living room and out onto the patio.

"Everything's to be served on the terrace tonight, Mr. D., so you might as well get out here and start on a martini while I'm still around to be complimented," she called back over her shoulder.

The sensible decision was to follow her.

Kate's terrace is off the dining room. It's completely enclosed in glass, like a solarium, and offers a remarkable view of the Fifty-ninth Street Bridge and the East River. People who only glimpse the water as they race up and down the East Side Highway don't realize how much boat traffic there is on the river. At night, with the lights ablaze and the ships making slow progress up and down the channel, it makes for a very romantic spot.

"The dinner's ready and so's your chocolate fudge cake. Here you go, son, and bottom's up." Ellen handed me a martini, then tossed one back herself.

I took a sip and closed my eyes savoring it, then sighed with satisfaction. "Ellen, as usual, you have created a magical potion. Bless you."

I blew her a kiss. She waved me off and headed for the door. "I'm going now," she said, loud enough for the neighbors to hear, "and I won't be in till late tomorrow morning, on account of the fact that I'm staying with my sister tonight." She turned and winked at me again.

"By the way, Mr. D., you don't look like you're in critical condition. I guess it's true what they say—you can't believe everything you read in the papers."

Ellen didn't wait for a response. A minute or two later, I heard the front door shut. I walked over to the service table and poured another drink from the pitcher, then sat down and stretched my legs out. The table was beautifully set with Kate's best crystal and china. She'd gone to a lot of trouble.

I didn't want to spoil the evening, but I was going to ask Kate to help us nail Morty Katz, and I wasn't sure how she'd react. The request could have been interpreted as an intrusion into a part of her life I'd agreed to leave alone. All the chocolate mud cake in the world might not get around that problem. I distracted myself by trying to stab an olive with a toothpick.

"Well, what do you think?"

I looked up and Kate was standing before me, the moonlight setting her aglow. She was wearing a black silk sleeveless dress with spaghetti straps. I had to take a breath. Kate is five feet, six inches tall, one hundred twenty pounds, and every curve, every line catches the eye. She doesn't seem to notice or care.

"I think you look beautiful," I whispered.

She turned off the patio lights, then bent over the table and lit the candles. Without a word, she took the martini glass from my hand and walked over to the bar. She produced a cold bottle of Veuve Cliquot Ponsardin and a towel.

"Would you mind doing the honors, Jamie?" she asked.

As I untwisted the wire and worked the cork loose, I watched Kate moving back and forth on the balcony. Her hair is light brown, but when the light hits it just right her natural blond highlights sparkle. She was probably wearing makeup, but not so you would notice. Except for her lips—they were painted a very pale shade of pink to match the roses on the table.

She wore diamond earrings, and around her neck, a diamond pendant shaped like a heart. On the ring finger of her left hand, she wore her engagement ring. They were all gifts from me. Combined with the simple elegance of her dress, the effect was powerful. She came over and gave me a long, tender kiss, then she slowly ran her tongue along my lower lip before pulling back. Right on cue, the cork popped out of the bottle.

"So, how many martinis did you and Ellen drink before she left?" Kate asked softly.

"What are you talking about? You know I don't drink with the help."

She ignored my lie and sat down in my lap, facing me. "I'm mad at you for almost getting yourself killed," she whispered, planting tiny kisses on my neck.

"Hey, come on, it was nothing. I had a little accident."

"The hell you did!" she sat upright, eyes blazing. "You could have been killed. It's not fair."

"What makes you think that's true?" I asked, taking the bait. "You should know better than to believe everything you read."

"I know it's true because Boris told me," she said, still staring at me.

"Boris told you what?" I sputtered. "When did you speak to Boris?" The loudmouth was gonna pay for this one.

"Look, save your breath," she said. "I know everything."

I wondered what she meant by *everything*. "Boris had the decency to explain the situation to me like an adult," she continued.

I began to speak, but she held up a finger.

"You want my help, right? I'll bet you've been sitting there trying to figure out how to ask me."

Boris again. Unfortunately for him, it was going to take a really painful lesson to even this score. I didn't have to say a word; the answer was written on my face.

"Aha, just as I thought," she declared.

Kate stood up, took the champagne bottle out of my hand, went back to the bar, and poured us each a glass. She pushed a switch and the sound of Louis Armstrong's voice singing "What's New?" filled the night air.

"Boris told me about the little boy you're going to help and about the attack on Monday. He says you saved a man's life— is that true?" She handed me a glass of bubbles and started running her fingers through my hair. The mood had changed dramatically. It's no wonder men get confused.

"Did he also tell you that I broke my collarbone and can barely move?" I asked, suddenly worried that she was starting something I couldn't finish.

"He told me everything," she whispered, leaning down so her lips just grazed my ear.

"And?"

"Number one, I've decided to help you with your plan. But on the condition that you take me someplace warm for a vacation when it's over."

She set her glass on the table and stood in front of me for a minute or two looking into my eyes as the breeze from an open glass panel lifted at her hair. Then, she turned and blew the candles out, leaving only the night lights of the city to illuminate the terrace.

"And number two," she said, just loud enough for me to hear, "I'm going to take care of you."

Kate pulled the thin straps of her frock down to her elbows and let go. The dress slipped to the terrace floor. She stood before me—completely, beautifully naked.

"But my shoulder—"

"Don't worry, Jamie. I just told you, I'm going to take care of everything."

As she sank to her knees and started to help me out of my suit, I remember thinking maybe, just this once, I'd let Boris slide.

TWENTY-THREE

...

I left Sutton Terrace very early the next morning. Kate got up long enough to rewrap my shoulder, then went back to sleep. Hours earlier, when we'd finally come up for air and paused to enjoy Ellen's delicious dinner, I discussed the plan with her at length. Kate understood her part; I just hoped everyone else followed the script.

I parked the car in the garage and walked back to my building, enjoying the morning. It was a beautiful, clear October day, and the air was crisp and cold. Despite the early hour, Joe Gagan was up, sitting at the kitchen counter. He looked better than I expected. Angus had his big, black, scruffy head resting in Joe's lap, and the little man was scratching his ears. There was a pot of fresh-brewed coffee on the counter. I didn't smell cigarette smoke, which meant Boris hadn't made an appearance yet.

"Well, well, if it isn't the return of the prodigal," Gagan declared. "And would you mind tellin' me how the blazes I got up here?"

"Believe it or not, Joe, you arrived on a hand truck."

He winced. "Oh, I don't doubt it. Lord knows I was tight as a drum." He licked his lips and his mouth twisted into a sour expression, then he passed the back of his hand across the stubble on his chin. "I don't suppose you'd have a spare toothbrush, some toothpaste, and a blade I could use to scrape this beard off? Maybe even a towel, so's I could wash up a bit. I'm feelin' awful."

I showed Gagan the way to the bathroom and provided the necessary supplies, including a clean shirt and a pair of socks. While Joe showered, I began putting together a breakfast of scrambled eggs and toast. As the eggs hit the skillet, Boris stuck his head into the kitchen, sniffed a few times, then ambled in.

"That was quite a long dinner, old chap," he said, pouring himself a cup of coffee.

"There was quite a lot to discuss," I said coldly. "But I understand you've already spoken to Kate, so I won't bother to report."

He ignored me. "What's that you're cooking? It smells *wonderful*."

The subtle approach. Butter me up, so I'd forget that he spoken to Kate against my wishes. Before I could answer, the doorbell rang.

"Get that for me, will you, Boris? If it's Blakely's people, have them wait in the living room."

I'd called a meeting for nine A.M., so they were right on time.

Gagan's food was ready and sitting on the table, along with a glass of the hallowed Donovan Family Hangover Cure. I took out a fresh skillet, lit a flame under it, and dropped in a chunk of butter. Then I cracked open four more eggs and beat them senseless with a whisk. While the eggs were bubbling, Joe Gagan returned, freshly scrubbed. He looked smaller in my large baggy shirt, but healthier after the shower.

"I fixed you something to eat, Joe," I said, pointing to the table.

"I could eat a horse, Mr. Donovan, and that's no exaggeration," he declared, pulling up a chair.

"Call me J. J. or Donovan, but drop the Mr., okay?"

He just nodded and loaded a fork with eggs.

"I suggest you begin with that tonic," I said before he could take a bite. "It's better to get that stuff into an empty stomach."

He held the fork inches from his mouth and eyed the mixture in the big glass skeptically.

"Might I inquire what's in this potion of yours?" he asked, looking worried.

"Sure thing: one raw egg, hot sauce, celery salt, pepper, sauerkraut juice, a touch of vodka, and half a can of beer."

He smiled weakly.

"Ah, sounds de-*light*ful!"

"Drink up," I encouraged.

Joe tossed it back like a good soldier and, although his face turned scarlet and beads of sweat formed on his brow, he kept it down.

"Not bad, Donovan, not bad at all," he croaked. "You know, I think I'll have another."

"Eat those eggs instead, you'll feel like a new man."

He didn't need to be convinced.

"They're all here," Boris said, peering over my shoulder. "By the way, your friend Mr. Blakely is with them."

That surprised me. I didn't think Ron Blakely got up before noon, especially for a report from a surveillance team.

"Better make another pot of coffee," I suggested.

Boris looked a little hurt, like I'd forgotten him.

"Don't bother acting pathetic. These are for you." I handed him a platter-sized dish, loaded with scrambled eggs and buttered toast.

"Don't worry about the coffee, Doctor," Joe said, jumping up, suddenly very perky. "I'll take care of it. You sit right down and enjoy yer food. Boy, does that tonic do the trick."

Boris looked at me and raised an eyebrow.

"My home remedy," I explained.

"Egad, and you drank it, Mr. Gagan?"

"Sure."

"Believe it or not, he asked for seconds," I said.

Boris pushed his glasses up and peered over at Joe Gagan, apparently surprised to find him upright and mobile.

"Hey, what time did Clifford get to bed?" I asked, realizing the kid hadn't come in with Boris. "When I left last night he and Angus were standing guard over our friend Mr. Gagan."

"He fell asleep on the floor," Boris said between bites. "I carried him up to Karina's around one o'clock. She was rather annoyed that I'd let him stay up so late."

I could just imagine the scene.

"Who are Clifford and Angus?" Joe asked as he got up to make the coffee. "Sounds like I should be thankin' both of 'em for watchin' after me."

"Clifford Brice is the reason I took the job at National Manufacturing," I told him.

Gagan squinted his eyes, concentrating.

"He's the son of a woman named Ruby Brice. Ms. Brice was a prostitute, and she was killed about five weeks ago," I said softly. "Her body was found a couple of blocks from National in an old Dumpster. When the cops wouldn't listen, we decided to help Clifford figure out who killed her. It's a long story, but for his own good, he's staying upstairs with Madame Karina for now."

"Ah, so that's how you come into it," Gagan said, shaking his head. "I remember the killin', nasty business that."

"And this fellow is Angus," I said, patting the smelly pooch on the head. "You'll find a supply of his favorite treats in a large box under the counter."

"Angus! Why, that's a fine name for a pup," Joe declared, thumping the 125-pound puppy on the back and slipping him a piece of buttered toast.

Boris, his mouth full of scrambled eggs, smiled like a proud parent.

I was still wearing my suit from the night before, so I went to the bedroom and changed clothes. When I was comfortably dressed in jeans and a fresh shirt, I went back to the living room.

242

Ronnie Blakely was holding court on my couch, and a stunning redhead I didn't know sat next to him. His other operatives were seated on folding chairs.

When Boris arranged for surveillance, he didn't hold back. We'd had at least one person following both Alvin and Morty Katz twenty-four hours a day for three days. There were also a couple of solo operatives investigating Alvin's medical history and the Veldez brothers.

"Jamie, nice to see you, boy!" Blakely shouted, jumping up.

He knows better than to call me Jamie. "What gets you up so early, Ronnie, discos just close?"

He smiled and ignored the dart. "What's going on down here, Donovan? I've been reading about you in the papers. According to the newsprint, you're supposed to be at death's door. The evidence before me, while not a pretty sight, definitely contradicts the reports. I mean, you don't look great, but you ain't dead." He laughed.

"Broken *collarbone,* not broken neck, Ron." I smiled weakly. "And, what's going down is a private affair. Among other things, we're dealing with a family conspiracy to defraud and embezzle a manufacturing business. Only there's a strange twist—the father and son aren't exactly working together. They're each pulling separate cons at the same business."

"Sounds messy," Blakely remarked, pointing out the obvious. "But if you know the scam, why all this surveillance work? You looking for something else?"

"Actually, we uncovered this cockeyed double scam while we were trying to solve a murder." I sighed. "Ronnie, this thing gets complicated really fast. The count is up to four deaths, three of them murders, and we have a handful of the wounded limping around the periphery. It's not a very big company, but there's lots of bad stuff going down in and around the place. Turns out just about everybody working there has some kind of a private angle. It's unbelievable; they're all trying to screw each other. It's been hard to figure out which lead to follow."

243

"Sounds like I'm hearing excuses for dropping the ball," Blakely said undiplomatically. "I think you better start from the beginning and give me the details."

"Perhaps I should do the honors, Mr. Blakely," Boris interrupted before I could react. He went over to sit in my grandfather's big red leather chair by the patio doors, where he could smoke. "As you know, I tend to keep a distance, emotionally and physically, from the circumstances of our cases. My narrative should be objective and concise."

"It would be a pleasure, Doctor," Blakely said, returning to the couch.

Joe Gagan came into the room with the coffee tray and we introduced him. While the guests helped themselves to coffee, Dr. Koulomzin quickly and efficiently covered all the points. He didn't editorialize, and he didn't divulge our plans. Blakely listened intently, and when he'd heard all the facts, he sat lost in thought for a few minutes.

"Maybe we should hear the field reports," he said, finally.

Boris and I both nodded our heads.

"Jimmy, why don't you start," he suggested.

Jim Bennett was part of the team watching Morty Katz. "The guy's a character, Mr. Blakely," he began. "I mean, he's gotta be seventy, but every night after work, he's boozin' and shmoozin' at this restaurant over on Linden Boulevard. The place is called Angel's. This guy Katz, he's in his second childhood. I ate dinner at the bar last night, so I had a good seat.

"Katz was actin' like Mr. Big—buyin' rounds for the crowd, grabbin' the waitresses, tellin' stupid jokes. He even pulled some babe into the coat room for a tumble. When they come back out, they were both pretty rumpled, if you know what I mean."

He paused to read through his notes.

"It's his money, so I guess it don't matter," Jimmy continued, "but I figure he dropped two, three hundred bucks just at the bar. An' he does that every night. It adds up to a nice piece of change. Other than that and his bein' a pain in the ass, I didn't pick up anything out of the ordinary.

244

"We've had the guy for nearly three full days and the routine was the same each day. A cab picked him up at his house around six-thirty in the morning and took him directly to the business. He stayed at work till five-thirty and the car service drove him to Angel's. Yesterday, he made a side trip to Long Island to visit a company called Quality Display Case. From what Dr. Koulomzin just told us, you already know about them. He was back in Brooklyn in time to make happy hour at the bar.

"As I said, he played very hard at Angel's, but he got home by eleven each night. And when he got home, he stayed home. We only saw the wife once. She was takin' out the garbage Thursday night when his cab pulled up. They exchanged some words in the street, and he smacked her in the face. She started cryin', but Katz just left her out on the sidewalk and went into the house like nothin' had happened. We tried watchin' the house durin' the day, while Katz was at the office, but she never come out. Seems like a pretty tough life for the old girl."

"Okay, Jimmy, thanks," Ronnie said. "You're up next, Zack."

Zackerly Palmer is a soft-spoken, educated man of medium size and average looks. He's so unremarkable people don't pay attention to him, so they never remember him. Zack is the perfect tail; he blends right in. His team watched Alvin Katz.

"You're not going to be happy with this, J. J.," he said, hesitating. "I know how you feel about spending money, and I'm afraid we didn't get much."

Blakely's ever-present smile faded. But there was nothing he could do about it. Zack is one of the best in the business and he speaks his mind.

"Ronnie and I will work the dollars out, Zack," I said reasonably. "Just give your report and we'll see where it leads. Remember, we're just fishing."

"Okay, you got it," he said, moving to the edge of his seat. "Mr. Alvin Katz is an early bird, like his father. He leaves the house shortly after six in the morning and drives to work in a late-model Jeep Cherokee. I won't waste time describing his work day, since you're more familiar with it than I am, but I can confirm that he likes to prowl around the facility. You get the feeling he's stalking someone. Sounds weird, I know, but there was something about him that made the hair on my neck stand up, and that's never a good sign.

"During the time we had him, Katz left the business twice during the day. On Tuesday and again on Friday, he visited a doctor named Coleman. Those visits lasted for one hour. Dr. Coleman is an internist, who likes to dabble in psychiatry. His private practice is located in Great Neck, and he's on the staff at Long island Jewish. Carol has more information on the doctor, so I'll let her tell you about that later.

"Mr. Katz spends his evenings quietly. He lives in Hempstead, New York, in a dull, suburban community. The neighbors think he's swell. His home is a large, well-mainted split-level ranch that sits on a manicured piece of property. There is a two-car garage, which is good because Katz owns two cars, though we only saw him drive the Jeep. He was home by seven-thirty each night and the lights went out at eleven sharp. The only item even remotely out of the ordinary was the night light."

"What about it?" I asked.

"Well, I'm sure that's all it was, a night light, but it flickered a lot, the way a candle would."

"So, what do you make of that?"

"I don't know, I'm probably grasping. It just seemed strange. I mean, who goes to sleep with a candle burning?"

I didn't exactly jump for joy.

"I told you it was nothing," he said.

I looked at my watch. It was ten after ten, and Lieutenant Negro was due at eleven. We had to move along.

"Who's up next?" I asked Ronnie.

"Carol," he said, turning to the woman sitting next to him.

Carol was a very nicely constructed redhead, about twenty-four years old, with legs that didn't quit. I mean extraordinary. And she was wearing a miniskirt that looked like the dot on an exclamation point. A man could get so distracted looking at Carol that maybe he'd say more than he should.

"I had the job of running down a short list of prescriptions drugs that I'm told Alvin Katz had stored in a desk drawer," she began. "When I finally located the prescribing pharmacy, I got lucky. The young man on duty was rather impressionable. I showed him my investigator's license, mentioned insurance fraud, and he jumped at the chance to help. The guy even let me have a peek at Mr. Katz's computer file, which listed all the scripts they'd ever filled for him. And that turned out to be a lot of prescriptions."

Carol's investigator's license wasn't what got the kid's attention.

"Let me tell you, that boy Katz has been eating depth charges," she continued. "I won't say I'm an expert, but I spent most of Tuesday morning at Bellevue interviewing a psycho-pharmacologist. For those you that don't know, that's a doctor who specializes in drugs for head cases. Anyway, the doctor I spoke to was shocked to learn that a patient had been given so many different prescriptions and at such high doses."

She opened her notebook and flipped a few pages.

"Mr. Katz has prescriptions for Mellaril and Lithium, which are used to retard impulsive behavior; Haldol, Trilafon, and Thorazine, powerful antipsychotic medications; and Cogentin, which is sometimes used in combination with the other drugs to smooth out side effects, like nervousness or anxiety. In the hands of a trained physician, these drugs are used either alone or in combination to help normalize the patient, but there are many possible adverse reactions. All kinds of things can go wrong when you dispense these drugs, especially if they're being mixed together. And I'm not talking about something like a hangover. If an amateur was doing the mixing, the results could be very bad.

"I decided to take a look at the witch doctor who's been pre-scribing all this poison. As Zack said, his name is Coleman, John P. Coleman, but he's no specialist. He'll do anything billable, from cardiology to plastic surgery. He's only interested in psy-chiatry because it's a wide-open field and he can exploit it for profit. Dr. Coleman comes up with a diagnosis, puts the patient on medication, then charges for follow-up and maintenance. He's an unethical quack and I plan to make a formal complaint against the bastard when you're through with him."

Apparently there was more to Carol than a great set of pins.

"Anyway, for the second time in a week, I got lucky. His secretary didn't show for work the day I was there, so I didn't have to maneuver past the usual interference. I walked in off the street, with nothing more than a smile to recommend me, and before you know it Dr. Coleman's giving me an unofficial peek at Katz's file. It was enough information to ruin a decent man's life. Believe me, it wasn't a free look, he expected something in return, but I managed to disappoint him. Coleman's a sleaze and somebody should be looking out for the people he's been treating."

"We appreciate your sense of civic duty, Carol, really," Ron interjected, "but what did you learn about Alvin Katz?"

"Cool down, Ronnie, I'm gettin' to that," she snapped, enhancing her image even further. "Our Mr. Katz visits Dr. Coleman two, sometimes three times a week for treatment of paranoia and schizophrenia. The doctor describes Katz as an erratic man who's subject to fits of temper."

"Anybody who works with Alvin could have given that description," I moaned.

"Yeah, but they couldn't bill for it," Carol murmured, glancing through her notes. "This was a shocker: Alvin Katz has been Coleman's patient for more than twenty-five years! Frankly, after all that time on medication, there's no telling what's going on inside the guy's head. My expert says—and I got a second opinion on this—that after so much time on medication patients often develop something called dyskinesia, or abnormal late motion. It manifests itself in lots of ways. The patients get facial ticks or they adopt strange grimaces. A darting or rolling tongue is also a common side effect. Does any of that sound familiar?"

I described Alvin's weird expressions and mentioned the strange rocking-snakeboy scene I'd awakened to in his office.

"Bingo!" Carol said enthusiastically. "That's exactly the kind of thing I meant. This man has been badly mistreated. And it all goes back to a sexual abuse charge brought against him when he was a teenager."

That got everybody's attention.

"There was an incident with another child at a local playground. The kid wasn't hurt, but Katz was charged with attempted sodomy. Alvin was a juvenile and he didn't hurt the other child, at least not physically, so his father was able to work out a deal."

Just like Morty, cutting a deal, as if the victim was a piece of merchandise.

"The judge probably felt that jail time wouldn't help the young man solve his problems," Carol continued. "Instead, Alvin was sent to an inpatient program at the Creedmoor mental health facility on Long Island. He got out three months later, but only on the condition that he continue therapy. His dear old dad picked Dr. Coleman. Alvin's been seeing him ever since.

"If you're looking for a suspect in the Brice murder, I'd say Alvin Katz looks pretty good. The man is erratic, paranoid, and he has a history as a sexual offender. Most of the time, he's so doped up he's probably delusional. Let me put it this way: If he didn't kill Ruby Brice, he's probably guilty of something else."

She sat down, crossed her stunning legs, and took out a cigarette. Boris popped out of his chair and dashed across the room to offer a light. Apparently, Carol has the same effect on geniuses that she has on drugstore clerks and mere mortals like myself.

"I'd love to pin the murder on Alvin," I said, getting back to the case. "It would make for a nice, neat package. But, that wouldn't explain Ruby's friend, Señor Tito. Remember, thanks to Clifford Brice, we know that the guy is real and we know what he looks like. The wizard also gave me a good description of the car he saw that night, and it sounds like the same car Clifford remembers Tito driving. I can't ignore the facts."

Carol looked a little hurt, so I changed the subject.

"By the way, does anybody know what *kitty* means? The wiz-

249

ard mentioned it to me a while back. I'm having it checked to see if we're looking for a personalized license plate, but if that doesn't pan out, I'm stumped."

Heads shook all around the room. Nobody knew anything about *kitty*.

"I don't understand why the black car lets Alvin Katz off the hook," Carol said, sticking to her guns. "Zack said Alvin owns two cars; maybe the second one fits your description."

We all turned to Zack.

"We never saw the second car," he said. "He keeps it in the garage, covered under a tarp."

"Which means, it could easily be the one you're looking for, right?" Carol insisted.

"Carol, Alvin may be a lot of things, but a middle-aged Spanish dude with a salt-and-pepper beard he is not," I insisted. "Besides, there is absolutely nothing connecting him to Ruby Brice. This guy Tito had a relationship with her, and a witness heard Ruby's voice crying out from inside his car the night of the murder. I say we have to find Tito."

That stopped her cold. I felt bad, because her instincts were good. I'd had the same thoughts, but the chain of evidence just didn't lead me to Alvin Katz.

"Well, let's finish this," I said, trying not to sound too disappointed.

John Pressman was the last to speak. It had been his job to do a background check on the Veldez brothers. Boris had already found arrest and conviction records for both men, so we knew plenty about their criminal pedigree. We also knew that they'd done relatively little jail time, which qualified them, or people they knew, as accomplished manipulators of the system.

"I could spend a week on these two," John said, rising. Pressman is a good-looking black man of average height and build. He wears a neatly trimmed mustache on his upper lip and appreciates an audience, particularly when it includes a redheaded beauty with a pair of emerald-green eyes.

"You're well aware that the brothers are hardcore," he said, looking at me, but offering Carol his strong profile. "If the Comacho kid stumbled into the middle of a transaction for guns, it was definitely enough to get him zapped. The real question is: how do these two Veldez *jamokes* fit into the gun-running operation? From what I've been told, they were purely muscle, not a brain between them."

He paused for effect.

"Well, the answer wasn't hard to find. The brothers were part of a gang called the Falcons. Falcons mark themselves with that scorpion tattoo you noticed because their founder and spiritual leader, a creepy dude named Juarez, comes from the city of Durango in Mexico. He's got a thing about scorpions."

"Yes, we know about Durango." I described the note on Ruby's body.

"Do you also know about the Falcons?" John asked, annoyed by the interruption.

"No, no, please go on," I said apologetically.

He paused again before continuing. "So anyway, I checked with several of the local precincts and then did some talking on the street. The Falcons are definitely armed and dangerous. They've been at war with a black gang called the Jakes for a couple of years. The fight's over turf, and the National Manufacturing Corporation is right smack in the middle of the disputed territory."

"How do we find the Falcons?" I inquired.

"That's not hard; the cops are keeping real close tabs on those boys. Besides, I don't think you'll have to find them. It's bad for their public image to let a gringo like you put the hammer to one of their men. They found you once, they'll find you again. I'd say you're a real bad risk to go back to that place—they'll be looking for you."

As that happy thought dangled in the air, Boris dropped his lighter. The sight of Carol sauntering across the room to pick it up for him kind of broke the spell.

"Okay, people," I said, rising, "unless there's anything else, the party's over. My next appointment is due any minute and he'll be wearing a police lieutentant's badge. I don't want him bumping into you folks."

Blakely hesitated for a minute, then decided not to say whatever he had on his mind.

"I'll call you later, J. J.," he said confidentially, "after the badge leaves."

"Badges?" John Pressman shouted. "We don't need no stinkin' badges!"

It was an old joke. No one laughed.

As I shut the door behind the private investigators, I noticed an envelope on the floor in the foyer. The paper was a heavy, expensive stock. I recognized the scent of Madame Karina's perfume when I picked it up. This sort of epistle should only be opened with a letter opener. I went into my office to look for one.

I hadn't seen Karina since the night my shoulder got busted. She'd promised to visit me the next day, then failed to show. With all the other stuff going on, I hadn't given it a second thought. I got quite a surprise.

> *Darling child,*
>
> *Called to Paris, the city of love. Have much to tell you, will report upon my return. Ms. Fein has agreed to house-sit and watch our darling boy, Clifford. Hugs and kisses—Karina.*
>
> *(P.S. Scorpio is the 8th sign of zodiac, Oct. 23–Nov. 21. It is an ambivalent sign, combining images of male sexuality, destruction and the mystical with healing and resurrection. A symbol of life over death? Perhaps!)*

I was staring at the flowery handwriting, wondering what the old girl was up to now, running off to Paris. An idea came to me. It was so simple and obvious, I could have kicked myself. As I stood in the foyer, my mind raced back to something Carol had suggested and my heart began to beat faster. I shoved Madame Karina's note into my pocket and I went to look for the computer profiles.

TWENTY-FOUR

▪ ▪ ▪

Lieutenant Negro showed up at eleven-thirty—late enough to teach me a lesson about who should and who should not be calling meetings. I didn't mind; the extra time gave me a chance to track down the information I needed.

Boris took Clifford Brice, Joe Gagan, and Angus back to his place, where they could all listen to my conversation with the lieutenant over the intercom. They were fortunate to be out of the line of fire—Negro was not in a good mood when he arrived. As he stepped across the threshold, he was wearing the same rumpled suit I remembered, and it looked like he had the same stub of a cigar in the corner of his mouth. Without saying a word, he took a slow, deliberate stroll around the apartment, taking everything in.

"You got a telephone?" he asked finally.

I pointed to the handset on the end table. Negro went over, picked it up, and listened. Then he dialed a number, said something I couldn't hear, and hung up. He folded his arms and stood staring at me. After a moment or two, the phone rang. He reached down, answered it, said thank you, and hung up again. Then he glanced at me.

"I'm a detective, Donovan," he said, softly. "Do you know what I just detected?"

I shook my head.

"I just detected that your telephone is capable of making outgoing calls. I further detected that the unit is capable of receiving incoming calls. Now, I would like you to explain, because, as you know, I'm a reasonable man, why the *fuck* you din't return any a my calls for the last two fuckin' days?"

"Look, I'm sorry, I really am, Lieutenant, it's just that I've been so tired, what with my injury and all, I haven't had a chance to answer my messages."

"Is that right?" he said sarcastically. "So how come the other night at National Manufacturing, you din't mention that we'd met before? It was you in that alley offa Berriman Street. Right? You and a certain pain in the ass named Janet Fein. Your fat dockta friend took a swan dive and all hell broke loose."

"Was that you?" I feigned surprise. "You know, it was quite dark. But now that you mention it, I guess I do remember you."

He gave me a squint-eyed look, then took out his notepad. "Too tired to pick up the phone, bad memory." The volume grew as his blood pressure rose. "Do you take me for a fuckin' idiot? And what about goin' to the factory yesterday, puttin' in a full day and then trippin' the light fandango over on Sutton Terrace all night? Still too tired to pick up the phone?"

He was not a happy man.

"Okay, so you're right, Lieutenant. I'm sorry I didn't return your calls, I was working on something. But you're here now, and I think we can help each other."

He chuckled, but didn't sound happy. "You're gonna help *me*, Donovan? That's a fuckin' joke. The only way you could help me would be to confess to all the cases on my desk, so I can retire a few years early."

"Actually, what I've got to say might close more than a few of those files," I said, sounding a little too cocksure.

"Is that so? You think you're a pretty cute operator, don't you, kiddo?" he asked. "I done some checkin' durin' the last two days and I know a little more about you than I did on Monday. In fact, I know more about you then I ever wanted to know."

He dropped his cigar stub in the ashtray, unwrapped a fresh Corona, and sat down on the couch.

"So you're gonna help me?" he repeated. "This will be a first. You see, I'm just a lowly civil servant, I've got to work with what they give me. But you and your partner, you guys do whatever you feel like. This could be good. Maybe you can help me make a great bust and then, when we're through, I'll get to toss your ass in jail where it probably belongs. How does that sound?"

I ignored the sarcasm. "Why don't you just listen to what I have to say and then you can make up your own mind about whether it's worth your time or not," I suggested.

"So, talk," he said, putting his feet up on the coffee table.

Working backward, I told Negro what I'd been doing in the alley the first night we met, and about my interest in the Brice killing, my job in the factory, and my conversation with Raul Brito on the day he was attacked. I left out our plans for Morty Katz and Stu Sawyer, but you can't have everything. To make up for that omission, I told him about meeting Doc, the old wizard, and about the illusive Uncle Tito. I could see I had his attention, because he put his feet back on the floor and pulled out his notepad.

"Now, that's just for starters," I said, taking a breather. "Before I continue, I need a couple of favors."

"Oh, you do? Well, ain't that nice." The lieutenant's mood hadn't improved much. "By the way, I understand the Brice kid's still missing. I don't suppose you know anything about that situation?"

He was eyeing me carefully. I smiled weakly and shrugged.

"You know, Donovan, I got half a mind to run your ass in," he said finally. "How does that appeal to you?"

"You're blowing hot air, Lieutenant, and we both know it," I replied. "By the way, have you got a first name or were you baptized 'Lieutenant'?"

"Very funny, wise guy. Not that it's any of your business, but my name is Christopher Richard Negro. You can call me Lieutenant Negro or just plain Lieutenant, whichever's easier."

"What about my favors?"

"You don't give up, do you?"

"Well?"

"Why not ask and see what happens," he smirked.

"Fair enough," I said confidently. "The first thing is easy. I need a DMV check on Ruby Brice's boyfriend, Tito. There can't be that many guys named Tito driving brand-new black cars in the metropolitan area. And maybe while you're at it you could check and see if anybody's got a personalized license plate that reads *kitty*."

"Okay, you got it," he said, making a note in his little black book. "What else?"

"This is the hard part," I said, preparing him. "I want you to promise to leave Alvin Katz out of your plans till after Monday night. I've got to finish something and it won't happen if Alvin gets pinched."

"Why should I?" he asked.

"Come on, Chris, just go along with me on this one."

Lieutenant Negro squinted his eyes, trying to see through me. It didn't work. "That's not asking a lot, considering I don't know what he's done," he said finally. "I mean, you say he stole from his old man's business, but nobody's pressing charges. What would I be delaying? Anything else?"

"I'd like to know the identity of the woman we saw burning in the ally."

He looked at me again, his eyes open this time. "Yeah, well, that will have to wait. The forensics lab is still working on the problem. What's that got to do with you, anyway?"

I didn't bother answering. Negro sat on the sofa and chewed his cigar thoughtfully.

"I tell you what, Donovan," he said, leaning across the coffee table. "I'll do these things for you on one condition. Tuesday morning you give me everything, and I mean everything, official or otherwise."

"You've got a deal," I said quickly.

257

"There's another thing, Donovan. Do not fuck with me on this. If you're jerkin' me around, I'll make you regret it for the rest of your fuckin' life. Capiche?"

"Capiche."

A deal was a deal. I told him about the gun-trafficking operation, explaining how the trucking route, with regular trips to Florida and the empty trailers coming back, worked to Alvin's advantage. I explained the connection to the Falcons, and suggested how they probably fit into the picture. Then I tied them all to the killing of José Comacho and the beatings Brito and I suffered. Negro looked like maybe he wished he hadn't made the deal to leave Alvin Katz alone.

"You have been busy, haven't you?" he said, pointing the wet end of his cigar at me.

We talked a while longer and by the time we were done, there was definitely a relationship forming. While Negro was still sitting there, I called Boris on the telephone and relayed the conversation, as if Boris hadn't heard every word. A few minutes later he and Joe Gagan were sitting in my living room. Gagan told Negro about his night in the bar with Brian Fallon. He also told him that a loaded truck was due back from Florida on Monday night. That gave Negro the luxury of two days to come up with a plan of his own.

The lieutenant got up to leave. "Remember, Tuesday morning you're mine," he said, pointing a finger at me.

Before he could get out the front door, though, the telephone rang. Negro stopped in his tracks, removed the unlit cigar from his mouth, and waited.

"The telephone's for you, Lieutenant," Boris said, holding out the receiver.

Negro looked unhappy, but he took the call. The rest of us waited in silence while he listened to a voice on the other end of the line. He asked a few muffled questions, then hung up. He looked tired.

"What's the matter?" I asked.

"Your wizard's dead, J. J.," he said sadly. "A patrol car discovered him early this morning over at the landfill site. The old boy's throat had been slit. As if that ain't bad enough, a pack a stray dogs was fightin' over the body. That's what caught the uniforms attention. It's listed as a robbery/homicide, but I'll change that when I get in. Oh yeah, they found your forty bucks hidden in his shoes."

Negro looked lost. A few seconds later he turned and walked out the door.

TWENTY-FIVE

. . .

I left for the National Manufacturing Corporation at around three
o'clock that afternoon. My appointment with Morty Katz was
for 3:30, but I didn't care if I was late. The death of that old
wizard had changed things again. It was like the killer was taunt-
ing me.

When I got to the factory, the men were working as they did
every Saturday, but they looked confused. Business was not being conducted as usual. I'd come in very late and Bill Smith,
Bobby Seldane, Stanley Greenberg, and Alvin Katz were all ab-
sent. I knew where the first three were, but it wasn't until I got
into the office that I learned Alvin had decided to go to his
business in New Jersey for the day.

Carlos Rodriquez and the Ratman cornered me before I could
get into the office.

"What's up, man?" Raphael demanded.

Carlos's expression echoed the question.

"Nothing," I said lamely.

"Don't give me that bullshit, Donovan," Raphael said. "Be
straight with us."

"Please, J. J.," Carlos asked anxiously, "something's going on.
We're not blind. We have families to feed; it's not right."

We stood facing each other for a moment.

"Okay," I said, caving in. "I'll give you something. I'm outta here, gone, no more plant manager. I never really was a plant manager—I was working as a consultant for Greenberg."

"No shit, is that suppose ta be a news flash?" Raphael asked sarcastically.

"Was it that obvious?" I looked to Carlos for support.

"J. J., my friend," he said, trying to be kind, "my little baby knows more about welding than you do. You're a nice man and a good boss, but you never worked with metal before."

"So what now? You still workin' fa that hump Greenberg?" The Ratman wasn't about to let up.

"Look, all I can tell you right now is that the owners are working out a deal among themselves. When it's done, Morty will own the company. I can't tell you how long he'll get to hold onto the business, but he hopes to be back in charge by tomorrow, and Greenberg hopes to be out. After that, who knows? And no, Raphael, I am not working for Greenberg anymore. I'm working for myself."

I turned and walked away. I was late for my meeting.

Hazel, Morty's secretary, tiptoed into his office to see if I had the necessary clearance for an audience. A moment later, she returned and ushered me in. It was all very polite and business-like. It was a joke.

Morty was sitting in an upholstered leather chair behind a big mahogany desk. He had his feet propped up on the wastebasket and the requisite ten-inch Partagas cigar in place between the thumb and index finger of his right hand. He was smiling happily, like a man who's cornered the market for good luck.

"J. J., how nice to see ya, have a seat." He indicated one of the chairs in front of his desk. "Like a cigar?"

"Look, Morty, let's cut the crap, okay?"

"Whatever you say, it's your meeting." He kept right on smiling.

"As I said on the phone, I'm here to represent Stanley Greenberg. He tells me you've made a serious offer to purchase his interest in the National Manufacturing Corporation. If the offer is genuine, I've been instructed to negotiate on his behalf."

"Hey, Donovan," he swiveled his chair around to face me and leaned his elbows on the desk, "I thought you wanted to cut through the crap. Stop trying to sound like a fuckin' lawyer and say what's on your mind. By the way, from the day you walked through the front door, you've been representing Stan's interests. I've got eyes, kid. I can see."

"Fine, Morty," I conceded. "I'll tell you what's on my mind. I think that you and your son, Alvin, have been behind a conspiracy to defraud Mr. Greenberg. And now, after soaking the business for several years, you're attempting to regain control of the National Manufacturing Corporation by paying Greenberg off with his own money."

He sat there smiling at me, occasionally taking a puff on the big stogie. Morty was in no hurry; he was a professional negotiator. "And what proof can you offer to support these crazy fuckin' lies?" he asked finally.

I told him about the printouts we'd gotten from Joe Gagan, and the signed statements I had from Bill Smith and Bobby Seldane. It would have been very hard to deny that Alvin was running a scam. Morty didn't even try.

"You know," he said, pretending to get serious, "that fuckin' Alvin has always been a problem for me. God forbid he should eva find out, but he ain't even my own. He's just a bastid the old lady give me to remind me that she hates my guts." He smiled again. It was a wicked smirk. "That's why he's the only kid," Morty continued. "I haven't touched that old bitch with my joint since the day she told me."

He was still smiling, but his eyes were ablaze. "But those are my problems," he said evenly. "What I didn't hear you say just now, was how I fit into this whole business of fraud or whatever. I mean, I suppose you got some sort of proof that I was working this thing along with Alvin and the others?"

"Come on, Morty, you had to know what was going on," I said, letting out plenty of line.

He pounced. "Which is a nice way of sayin' you ain't got jack shit!"

I didn't answer him.

"Okay, so now let's get real, Donovan." Morty was warming to the subject, enjoying himself. "That bastid kid of mine has been juicing the business. I know it, you know it. As far as I'm concerned, he should go down for it. If Stanley wants to prosecute the prick, he has my blessing. In fact, between you and me, when I get finished with Stanley and get this place back on its feet, I think I'm gonna have to rethink that accident we had. Maybe my crazy fuckin' kid tampered with that multihead welder?"

This was an interesting direction for Morty to take.

"It's possible, you know," he continued. "The guy's a fuckin' freak of nature. Tried to stick his dick in a little boy's ass when he was sixteen. How do ya like that? Spent time in a nuthouse for it, too. Maybe he finally snapped?"

He was showing me his fallback position, daring me to do something about it.

"You know, Donovan." Morty rubbed his chin, acting like the idea had just come to him. "I gotta believe it would help me outta them fines if I could show that my freaky bastid son hotwired that spic on Monday."

There was a loud crash. It sounded like a stack of cans had been knocked over on the other side of the retaining wall. Morty jumped up and ran into the factory. I followed him as he scurried around the outside perimeter of the office suite and came to the men's locker room. I hadn't noticed it before, but the locker room shared a wall with Morty's office. If you were real quiet, you could probably listen to his conversations.

Morty burst into the locker room and ran right into Clarence Roberts, the paint-room manager. There were two or three large industrial drums lying on the floor and about a hundred beer cans. Except for the beer cans, the drums had apparently been empty, which explained why they'd made such a racket when they fell over. Poor Clarence was trying to clean up, but as usual he was too drunk to be very effective. I glanced at the wall behind the drums and noticed an air vent. Someone had been listening to our talk. If the cans hadn't fallen, we'd never have known.

"What the fuck is goin' on in here, Clarence?" Morty demanded.

"I don't know nothin'," the poor man protested. "I been cleanin' up them beer cans, like the man said."

"I suppose this shit just fell down all by itself?" Morty asked, sneering.

"No way, I come in just when the other mon run out."

"What are you talking about—what other man?"

Clarence stood there blinking his eyes, saying nothing.

"Clarence," I said gently, "what other man?"

"There was another mon come outta the locker," he said defensively.

"Did you know him?" I asked.

"No way. But he was a big guy, with a gray beard. He went out the side door."

By the time I got outside, the street was empty. No cars pulling away, nothing. I walked back to the locker room, shaking my head, wondering if he really could have been that close. Morty was giving Clarence hell.

"And get this place cleaned up, you dumbass," he was yelling as I walked back into the room. "Where the fuck did you run off to?" he asked suspiciously.

"Just wanted to check the street," I said. "Nothing there. Why don't we go back inside and finish our conversation?" A crowd had begun to form; he agreed it was a good idea.

When we got back to his office, Morty was all business, no more cute stuff. The falling cans had spooked him. "I already told Stanley the price tag," he said. "I'll give him five hundred thousand dollars for his stock. He walks, free and clear." He looked at his watch like maybe he had somewhere to go. It was my turn to take the advantage.

"I have a different proposal for you, Morty, and I suggest that you listen up. Whether I can prove it or not, I know you've been working with Alvin from the beginning. It's very clever, not to mention ruthless, to have your son set up to take the fall for you, but that doesn't change my position."

"Is that the way you figured it?" he said, smiling again, quite sure that I'd missed the big one. "Well, aren't you a clever son of a bitch."

"I told you to listen," I said, smiling back. "I won't be repeating myself. Here's the proposal: Stanley sells you his stock in the business for five hundred thousand dollars, as you suggested. Your attorney can prepare the purchase and sale agreement and have it delivered to me, along with a commitment from your bank to finance the five-hundred-thousand purchase price. When I have those two items, I will get the sales document signed by Stanley and notarized. In fact, I'll bring it to you in person."

"So what's different about that?" he asked, growing suspicious.

"The difference is this: you will give me a bonus of two hundred fifty thousand dollars in cash to deliver the aforementioned signed purchase and sale agreement. Call it a transaction fee. We like to think of it as interest on the loans Alvin made to himself."

Morty was staring at me, really boring in. "You're a fuckin' pirate, aren't you, Donovan?" he whispered, seething.

"Given the source, I'll take that as a compliment," I said. "Now, how about giving me an answer?"

"What if I say no?" He was getting cagey again.

"Then we bring in the police, prosecute Alvin, open up the books for an audit, and sue you for letting your lunatic son into the business without making your partner aware of his problems. What's going to happen to the company while all the legal stuff's going on? Let's just say it won't be good for business. Frankly, Morty, I think you should count yourself lucky Stanley wants out. The alternative is a no-win situation, particularly for you."

Morty Katz got this real sad expression on his face, like I was asking him to part with his last nickel. But behind that mask he was laughing at me. He had more than two million stashed away. A quarter of a million was chump change. Besides, he'd still be giving Stanley back Stanley's own money.

"You got me between a rock and a hard place, Donovan," he lied. "I don't want to, but I gotta say yes to your proposal. But it'll take me a couple of days to pull this whole thing together. When do you want to have the exchange?"

"No later than Monday night," I said, giving him one business day.

He turned sideways and leaned back in his cushioned chair. I watched him as he put his feet up on the corner of the desk and relit his cigar. He rubbed his forehead with his free hand and seemed lost in thought for a moment as the cloud of cigar smoke grew. Then I saw the corners of his mouth twist into a smile. He cocked his head in my direction.

"Okay, Donovan, you gotta deal. Now get the fuck outta my office, you prick!"

TWENTY-SIX

...

At nine o'clock on Monday night, October 21, five weeks after I began working at the National Manufacturing Corporation, our plan was put in motion. For this part, I was reduced to a member of the audience. I felt like a nervous stage mother as Boris and Kate went to work.

Despite all the posturing and static, Morty Katz had acted on my offer right away. The next morning, he delivered the purchase and sale agreement and a letter of intent from the bank. He'd taken the bait. Now it was time for us to start reeling him in.

Morty wanted his company back, but he accepted my terms with alacrity in part because he thought he had a hefty new account lined up. This new business represented an entirely different direction for him in the display industry. Instead of making glass cases for department stores, Morty thought he was being offered the chance to make all the magazine racks and stands for the largest distributor of printed material in the world. He couldn't begin to calculate the number of racks they'd want, but the potential was awesome. It meant riches beyond his wildest dreams.

Katz should have been more cautious about those daydreams; they made him careless. After talking to me, he figured we'd stopped looking for suspects; after all, we'd discovered Alvin's purchasing scam. He didn't know that we also knew about MKC,

Inc. and Quality Display Case, and he never suspected that we'd gotten to Dan Mahoney.

The temptation was too great for Morty. When Mahoney first came to him about the new customer, he'd been a little skeptical. It seemed too good to be true. But when he learned that he'd have to grease somebody's palms to get the account, Morty got much more comfortable with the idea. He couldn't believe that anyone would honestly bring him such a great opportunity, but a payoff he understood.

At nine o'clock Monday night, a meeting was held in the conference room at the world headquarters of LPL Industries whose offices took up the top three floors of a building in Midtown, near Rockefeller Center. The reception area, hallway, and conference room were rosewood-paneled and furnished with expensive, art-deco leather furniture. Plush carpeting, original artwork, and understated style exuded the elegance real money can buy. It was perfect.

The guest list for the meeting included Mr. Morty Katz, Mr. Stuart Sawyer, Mr. Daniel Mahoney, Ms. Kathleen Byrne, and Mr. Vladimir Collette. The gathering had been arranged so that an agreement could be formalized among the parties. As a show of good faith, Morty was expecting an initial order for the new magazine racks. Mr. Collette, a buyer for the world's largest distribution company, was expecting a finder's fee in cash.

I was sitting in an office down the hall when the meeting began. Boris had wired the conference room for sound so we could tape the discussion, and had kindly provided me with a speaker so I could eavesdrop—and also provide some security. When the cast arrived, I removed my pistol from the shoulder holster and placed it within reach on the desktop.

"Mr. Collette, Ms. Byrne, so nice to see you again," Dan Mahoney began cheerfully.

He got to open the play and introduce the characters. I thought he did a bang-up job, considering the short notice he'd been given. There wasn't a hint of nervousness or hesitancy in his voice.

"This is Morty Katz," he said, "the president of National Manufacturing, and Stuart Sawyer, his senior design engineer."

"It's a pleasure to meet you both," Kate said, taking charge. "I trust you're familiar with my publication?"

Stu and Morty started cooing about how much they loved her magazine, though I seriously doubt either of them had ever gotten past the model prominently featured on the cover.

"Isn't that nice," Kate said, interrupting them. "Then I'm sure you appreciate how delicately we must treat the subject of this meeting." She sounded nervous, but that was in character.

"There's nothin' to worry about on that score, honey," Morty said. "Let's just take care of business and we'll be outta your hair in no time."

I heard the sound of someone clearing his throat.

"Oh, excuse me," Kate said. "This is Vladimir Collette. Vladimir is the director of purchasing for DelCor, Inc. As you know, his firm is responsible for the placement and display of our magazines and periodicals in the stores. Your business is with Mr. Collette."

It wouldn't have been possible to create this phony scenario without Kate's help. She'd arranged for use of the boardroom and volunteered to sit in on the meeting. Her presence lent a degree of credibility we couldn't possibly have fabricated.

"Excuse me for bein' crass, but I don't quite understand— how do you fit into the picture, honey?" Morty asked. Leave it to Morty Katz to question the one genuine article in the room.

"I have a special arrangement with Mr. Collette, which is none of your business, Mr. Katz," she fired back. "I reluctantly consented to this meeting in order to provide a personal endorsement of the project. I suggest that we sit down and proceed. I am not prepared to give you much of my time."

That shut him up. I could hear the sound of chairs being pulled out and rearranged as the group sat. Things were going pretty well. Morty was on his best behavior; he hadn't cursed even once.

"As Ms. Byrne suggested, it would be most propitious to conclude our business affairs in a timely fashion," Vladimir Collette began, his accent foreign but nondescript. "I suggest we begin by reviewing the design and cost figures I requested."

Morty must have been sitting close to the microphone because I could hear him whispering to Stu Sawyer.

"What the fuck is this *propickus* shit?"

"Never mind, Morty, it's okay," Stu whispered back.

There was the sound of papers being shuffled, followed by a general discussion of Stu Sawyer's design. Kate and Morty were silent. Except for the occasional grunt from Mr. Collette, Sawyer and Mahoney did all the talking. When the design had been explained, Collette asked a few pertinent questions about the manufacturing process, focusing on topics like output and delivery. He implied that Morty would need a new factory to accommodate all the business he'd be getting.

"Don't you worry about delivery, Vlad," Morty said. "I can handle all the fuckin' work you dig up."

There was a moment of uncomfortable silence, during which he was reminded that a lady was present.

"Hey, excuse my French, babe," he added quickly. "It's just a manner of speakin'."

Kate didn't respond, though I sensed that the atmosphere remained rather chilly. The silence didn't last long—Morty couldn't contain himself.

"So now that we made nice, Vladdy, let's talk shop. I'm ready to move if you are."

Mr. Collette cleared his throat again. "As we said earlier, this is a delicate matter, Mr. Katz. It must be handled with some care. I suggest that from this point forward all of our business be transacted through Quality Display Case, with Mr. Mahoney acting as my contact. Agreed?"

"No sweat, my friend. Keep talkin'." Katz was proving that he could be a very agreeable fellow.

I heard the sound of more papers being jostled.

"Well, tonight I am prepared to inaugurate our new arrangement by placing the first order. I admit that it is a small order, relative to the volume of business we do, but I can assure you a satisfactory performance on this job will seal the relationship. Remember, I have superiors to answer to as well."

"Listen, Vlad, I want your business. If that means starting slow, that's fine with me," Morty said, though his voice was a little strained. He wanted it all.

"In that case, please accept this contract purchase order for eleven thousand five hundred of the rack units we just discussed with Mr. Sawyer. At the quoted price of two hundred ninety-five dollars and sixty cents, the total value of this order comes to nearly three-point-four million. I will expect you to begin shipping within ninety days."

I could hear a low wheezing sound as Morty let out a sigh of satisfaction. It didn't matter that he had to retool his whole shop in less than thirty days to come close to Collette's timetable. It didn't matter to him whether he could deliver or not. He wasn't about to let something like the truth get in the way of this deal. Besides, once Collette took the first payoff, Morty would own him.

"This is a beautiful thing you're doin' here, Vlad," Morty gushed, "and I promise you, even if I gotta work my guys twenty-four hours a day, I'll come through for you. I mean that, babe."

Vladimir Collette made no response, and there was yet another uncomfortable silence. I heard people shifting restlessly in their chairs.

"Since no one else seems to be willing to broach the subject," Mr. Collette began finally, "there is the small matter of my fee. At the agreed-upon rate of five percent, my commission on this order comes to one hundred sixty-nine thousand, nine hundred seventy dollars. I was told there would be no problem providing fifty percent of that amount tonight."

I formed a vivid mental picture of Collette smiling amicably at his new partners.

"Could you just give me a minute here, Vlad?" Morty asked. "I gotta have a word with my associate."

"By all means, Mr. Katz, confer." Collette was feeling generous.

Thanks to the positioning of the mike, I could hear the whispered exchange between Morty and Stu.

"What's he lookin' for?" Morty asked.

Stu Sawyer was working his calculator.

"Eighty-four thousand, nine hundred eighty-five," he replied hoarsely.

"How much cash you bring?" Morty snapped back.

"Seventy-five thousand. Not enough."

"Well, isn't that just great. Now what the fuck am I supposed to do? We're short almost ten grand."

"I don't know Morty. I didn't bring a check either."

"You didn't bring a check? Gimme that fuckin' briefcase, you moron. I'll handle this fat kraut."

"I think he's Russian, Morty," Stu corrected him.

"Shaddup, would you?" came the stifled reply.

There was more background noise as the briefcase was lifted onto the conference table. I could hear the *pop-pop* as the locks were snapped open.

"You will have to excuse me, Mr. Collette, but my associate made a slight error when calculating the size of the down payment you'd be needing. I got seventy-five grand wit me at the moment, but I assure you I can make good on the difference."

Collette made a sound in his throat not unlike the growl of an angry dog. "That was not the arrangement," he said menacingly.

There was a pause.

"I'm afraid I find these financial discussions rather distasteful," Kate said in a shaky voice. "You'll excuse me, gentlemen, I can see that my presence is no longer required. Vladimir, I will speak with you tomorrow."

I could hear chairs moving back as the men rose and the sound of the door closing as Kate left the room.

"I have never been so embarrassed in my life," Collette declared. "We have hardly begun this relationship and already you have failed to keep your word. It is an outrage!"

"Now, just a minute, Mr. Collette," Dan Mahoney said, adopting his smoothest tone of voice, "let's all try to be reasonable. An honest mistake has been made. You see, it's really all my fault. I underestimated the size of the order, which led Morty to bring less cash then he'd need. This can easily be corrected."

"He's right, Vlad," Morty chimed in nervously. "Let's not screw the pooch over a little thing like this."

"I suggest a ten-thousand-dollar bonus to be paid when the balance is due," Mahoney continued quickly. "That should take some of the sting out of this embarrassing mistake. In fact, I'll even put up half the money myself."

Vladimir Collette didn't respond immediately. His honor had been bruised. I pictured him in a deep funk, pouting and looking fierce. While the audience waited for Mr. Collette to make a decision, Kate tiptoed into the office and came over to me for a well-deserved hug.

"Is he all right?" she asked, her expression full of concern. "It sounded like the whole thing was about to come apart."

I put a finger to my lips and winked at her.

"I have very grave misgivings about this situation, Mr. Katz," Vladimir said finally. "Nonetheless, I have decided to accept your apology *and* the additional monies as compensation." His voice was heavy, his tone distant. "However, I caution you against repeating this behavior."

I could imagine Collette's eyes narrowing as he delivered this threat.

"Hey, babe, don't sweat it," Morty said cheerfully.

No response.

"Good. Well, now that we've settled things, I think we can adjourn," Mahoney said, taking advantage of the moment. "I'll be speaking to you very soon, Vladimir. And believe me, everything will work out just fine."

The guests got up to leave and Mr. Collette offered to walk

them to the elevators. While we awaited his return, I tried to show Kate what I really thought of her performance. I was about to sweep everything off the top of the desk when we heard the door to the conference room open and close. Next came the *click-clack* as the clasps on the briefcase were snapped shut, and then the voice of Mr. Vladimir Collette came over the speaker loud and clear.

"Act one, curtain," Boris said.

TWENTY-SEVEN

...

At midnight I was back in my apartment. An open briefcase sat on the coffee table. It was supposed to have seventy-five thousand dollars in it. My partner Boris, aka Vlad the Distributor, was busy making sure the money was all there. It was time for act two to begin.

The night shift at the National Manufacturing Corporation ended at eleven-thirty. The foreman needed about half an hour to close out his paperwork and collect the time cards. The place would be empty after that. I'd been instructed to meet Morty Katz in the plant at one-thirty that morning. It wasn't a good time or place, but he'd insisted.

The phone on the end table jangled, startling me. It was Lieutenant Negro checking in. He and about thirty of his brother officers were planning to visit the Falcons at their home on Atlantic Avenue. The visit had been timed to coincide with the delivery of an illegal shipment of firearms. The bust was so well-planned, Negro was bringing a film crew to get it on videotape. His mood had improved a lot.

"Is that you, Donovan?" he asked.

"Yeah, it's me, Chris."

"What's going on, J. J., you all right?" He sounded worried.

"No problem, you just caught me dozing. I'm fine."

"I hope so," he said seriously. "We're all set on my end. Your friend Gagan has been a big help and so has this other guy, the

Ratman. I gotta tell ya though, he's wrapped a little too tight. Been tellin' us stories about the jungle that you wouldn't believe." He paused. "Anyways, I got something for you, but remember we've got a date tomorra mornin'. I got your word, right?"

"Yes, Lieutenant," I sighed.

"Fine. Here it is: I heard from DMV, but it ain't good news. You struck out on both counts. The only Tito to register a new car during the last six months has been in jail since before the Brice woman was killed. Sorry."

"You said I came up empty on both counts—does that mean there's nobody in the State of New York using a personalized license plate that reads 'Kitty'?"

"Oh, there's a Kitty in use," he said. "It belongs to a little old lady up in Essex. There's also a Kitty1, a Kitty2, MyKitty, and so on. There are many variations—I stress the word *many*. This state is fulla cat lovers. In fact, when you come to see me tomorra you can help carry some of the paper to the Dumpster. I got reams."

"Sorry, Chris, busted shoulder, remember?"

"Ain't that convenient." He sighed. I could hear papers rustling. "I got one other little tidbit for you," he said. "We figured out the identity of the Jane Doe you saw burning in the alley."

I sat up.

"Her name was Paula Jones, and she wasn't a hooker. She was a receptionist in a doctor's office. This one makes no sense at all."

"Did she work for a guy named Coleman?" I asked, the hair rising on my neck.

"Wait a minute, how did you know that?" Negro was stunned.

"We'll talk about it tomorrow," I said quickly.

"I got a better idea, let's talk about it right now," he shot back.

"There's no time, Chris," I said seriously. "I promise, I'll explain tomorrow."

There was a moment of silence.

"Donovan, whatever you're up to, try an' be careful. Aw-right?"

I promised I'd try.

As soon as I put the receiver into the cradle the telephone rang again. That startled me more than it had the first time.

"Donovan," I said cautiously.

"J. J., it's Ron Blakely."

"Ah, Ronnie, so nice of you to phone. I presume you're call-ing to discuss the reduction in my bill?"

"Can it, Donovan, I got something for you." Blakely was all business. "I found your Kitty car for you, pal. You still interested in talkin' about my fee?"

I sat up a little straighter. "Go ahead, Ronnie, I'm listening."

"It's a jet-black Jaguar XJ-6, looks like a new one. The license plate says *Kitty*."

"I don't get it. NYPD ran a DMV search for me and they couldn't find it."

"That's because you were lookin' for a New York plate. This baby's registered in Jersey." Ronnie was enjoying himself. "You want to guess where I found it?"

"Alvin Katz's garage?" I asked.

"Yeah, how'd you know?"

I told him about Paula Jones. "Turns out the boy's a Scorpio, too," I continued. "I'm taking odds that he also likes to pretend he's a Spanish dude named Tito. His date of birth was printed on top of the financial profile; I just didn't make the connection." I shook my head.

"What can I tell you, man, it happens." Blakely was being generous.

"Look, Ronnie, I'm late for an appointment, but thanks, okay? I mean it."

"Sure, man. Listen, you watch your back."

"Yeah, yeah. Good night, mother."

■ ■ ■

The plant was dark except for a single lightbulb burning over the side door on the loading platform. It was a very empty street; no trucks or trailers, no hookers or street wizards. Stu Sawyer's car was parked out front, but that made sense since Morty didn't drive.

I parked my car on the sidewalk, switched the engine off, and sat for a while, considering my next move. I checked my gun for the fourth or fifth time, then flipped the safety off and re-holstered the piece nervously. The factory was a creepy place to venture into in the dead of night. I promised myself that it would be my last visit.

After another minute of reflection, I got out of the car and climbed the stairs leading to the side door. It was slightly ajar. This wasn't the kind of security I'd expected for a quarter-of-a-million-dollar exchange, especially not in that neighborhood. Inside the plant, the work lights cast little pools of light just bright enough to illuminate the aisles between the work stations. The rest of the factory was cloaked in shadows. As I stood in the doorway listening, I could hear rats scurrying and the ticking of the time clock. There were bright lights shining in the paint room, and the sound of voices carried over to where I stood. I began moving cautiously.

"Don't argue with me, I want this place retooled within the month. I don't give a shit if your wife divorces you or your fuckin' mothah dies. You will put in the time it takes. Do you understand what I'm saying? Answer me, you little prick."

Morty Katz was giving Stu Sawyer a pep talk.

"I hear you, Morty," Stuart said, but there was an edge to his voice. "Christ, you talk to me like I'm a piece of garbage. After all I've done for you, it's not right."

"What you did, you did for money," Morty replied.

"Just what did you do, Stu?" I asked, interrupting their private chat.

"Well, well, if it isn't Stan's little messenger boy," Morty said, goading me. "How are you tonight, tough guy?"

"I'm serious, Stu," I said, ignoring Morty. "Whatever you did for this miserable old man, was it worth it?"

278

Sawyer didn't answer me.

"Cut the chatter, Donovan," Morty said acidly. "You're just here to pick up and deliver. Don't forget it."

"Fine. Where's the cash?"

"First you show me the papers," he demanded.

I took the signed and notarized document out of my pocket, unfolded it, and showed him the key to his cherished prize. Morty wet his lips hungrily and his eyes sparkled. Without saying a word he picked up a zippered flight bag and put it down on the counter in front of the paint line controls.

"Two hundred fifty thousand in cash," he said. "Now give me the paper."

I handed over the purchase and sale agreement and watched as he beamed down at it. Stu didn't say a word. He was staring at his feet, thinking about my question. Morty started to chuckle.

"You know, Donovan," he began, "I been thinkin' about our conversation on Saturday. Boy, are you a fuckin' loser. You came at me with this bullshit about Alvin, like you're Sherlock fuckin' Holmes. You want to know somethin' sport? You missed the whole fuckin' thing."

He was enjoying himself.

I opened the flight bag and checked the cash; no sense taking home a bag weighted down with paper towels. It was full of money, all right. I closed the bag and put my good arm through the strap. Morty was annoying me, so I decided to give him something to think about.

"Wait a minute, Morty," I began innocently. "You don't think I missed your other companies, do you?"

"What other companies?" he shot back a little too quickly.

"You know, babe—MKC and Quality Display Case."

He stopped laughing and stared at me. "Fuck you, Donovan, there's nothin' you can do. I got my company back and that's all that matters." He waved the purchase and sale agreement under my nose.

"What about Alvin?" I asked.

"What about him?"

"Well, Morty, five people died while you were *arranging* to get your company back. I think your son, Alvin, killed at least three of them. What should we do about that?"

Stu Sawyer looked up when I mentioned the killings.

"What's the big deal?" Morty asked, genuinely perplexed. "I already told you Alvin's gonna take the fall. I can't stand the sight of the creepy bastid anyway. Besides, it might just work out good for me. You know, hang everything on the nut job and settle the fines quietly. It's been in the back of my mind all along."

"Is that so, Daddy?"

We looked up. There was Alvin Katz staring down at us from the catwalk. I glanced over at Morty and Stuart, but no one did or said anything. Alvin didn't look like himself. Tonight he was wearing a flashy gray pinstriped suit with a yellow shirt, purple paisley tie, and matching handkerchief. His hair was slicked back and he had a salt-and-pepper goatee pasted on his chin. Señor Tito had arrived. He sauntered over to the ladder and started down.

As I watched Uncle Tito climb down, my eye caught something else moving higher up, in the shadows near the ceiling. I blinked a few times before I could bring the object into focus. When I did, my heart skipped a beat. There was a small bundle hanging from a hook just above the catwalk. The little package was Clifford Brice. His legs and arms had been tightly wrapped in duct tape and then he'd been hung upside down with some baling wire, like a hunting trophy. There was more tape across his mouth, and his glasses were missing. I could see the terror in eyes as he swayed unsteadily sixty feet from the paint-room floor.

When Alvin got to the bottom of the ladder, he turned to us and smiled. The he reached into the inside pocket of his suit coat and whipped out a shiny silver flask. He unscrewed the top and took a swig.

"Anyone for a drink?" he asked, walking toward us, the little prize hanging from the rafters apparently forgotten.

There was a moment of silence, then Morty let loose.

"What the fuck kind of freak show are you supposed to be?" he shouted undiplomatically.

"*Shut Up, Morty,*" Alvin screamed, spitting the words at him like venom. "I got an earful of your bullshit Saturday. Didn't know about the air vent, did you? I've been listening that way for quite a while. That's how I knew about this little meeting, I heard you talking on the telephone."

Morty kept quiet. Alvin turned to me.

"So, J. J. Donovan, just who do you think I killed?" he asked, smiling.

"I think you did Ruby Brice, Dr. Coleman's receptionist Paula, and that old wizard," I said slowly. "It doesn't take a genius to come up with that."

"Well, you're no genius, shithead. I haven't killed anybody— at least, not yet." Alvin chuckled. "No, sir, all I did was cut a little slice off the cost of manufacturing materials. Compared to slicing up women and old men, that's not even a fucking crime."

He was drilling Stu Sawyer with his eyes.

"What about the guns, Alvin? You just a collector?" I asked.

"Of course not," he said, breaking the trance. "But that was just my way of creating a profitable diversion. As you've heard, my father's has plans for me that aren't very promising. Anything I could do to disrupt them, I figured it was in my own best interest."

I didn't say anything.

"For the record, the business with the baseball bats was just the Falcons' way of handling damage control. The Veldez brothers were following orders. But the murders you mentioned, they were all my pop's idea, even though he got Stuart to do the actual killing for him."

I must have looked stunned.

"Hey, Donovan, don't sweat it. Besides, I'm flattered you didn't try to blame everything on me. I mean, take the Comacho kid—you knew I didn't kill him, right?"

I nodded my head.

"See, that's what I thought. Of course, Morty dreamed up that little barbecue, too. He got restless and wanted to give Stanley some more incentive to sell. Stuart just followed his instructions. Isn't that right, Stu?"

Sawyer didn't look up or say anything, but his hands began to shake.

"You see, Donovan, our stand-up citizen and model husband Mr. Stuart Sawyer got himself into some bad trouble a while back. Seems the little piece of ass he was doing on the side got knocked up, and he couldn't be bringing any brown babies home to his old lady. So he went to my dad for help. Talk about making a pact with the fucking devil."

"That's enough, Alvin," Morty snarled. "We can work this shit out among ourselves."

"*Shaddup!*" Alvin screamed, the veins standing out on his temple. "You've done enough, old man."

Alvin was panting. "You wanna know how Morty helped Stuart?" he asked me. "He got that butcher Coleman to do an abortion, only it didn't turn out too well. The mother died. Bled to death right in front of Stuart, leaving him with this big guilt complex and a lot of legal problems. But Morty got what he wanted, which was the leverage. He needed some poor bastard to do his dirty business for him. And that poor dumb bastard turned out to be Stuart Sawyer."

Alvin started to walk slowly around Sawyer.

"Then I made a big mistake," he said, his eyes blinking rapidly. "I actually told this louse about my Ruby. It was a moment of weakness that I'll always regret, because it gave them a place to start. Isn't that right, Stu?"

Sawyer finally lifted his head. Tears were streaming down his cheeks. He looked at me, his mouth wide open, and shook his head from side to side, imploring me to help him.

"How could you do it, Stuart?" I asked.

"I—I don't know," he stammered. "My girl and her baby were dead. J. J., there was so much blood. I haven't been able to get

282

the pictures out of my head. Then Morty started saying he'd tell the cops if I didn't help him. Don't you see? I couldn't get away from it. There was no place to turn." He was sobbing.

"But my God, Stuart, you tortured them. Sliced them up like pieces of meat."

"No, no," he shouted, covering his ears with his hands. "I killed them first. I promise, I did it very quickly. The other stuff, that I did later, to make it seem like they'd been killed by somebody who was crazy."

"Like me?" Alvin said softly. He put the flask back in his coat pocket, but when his hand came back out it wasn't empty. He was holding a semi-automatic pistol. He walked up to Stu Sawyer and shot him in the face. Twice.

"That's for killing my baby," he muttered. Then he turned to me.

"Talk about crazy. These two lunatics," he said, pointing at his father and the body of Stuart Sawyer, "they were killing people to scare Stanley out of the business. How nuts is that? And it was all designed to set me up. That's why they picked Ruby and Coleman's secretary. Both of them would lead the cops right right back to me. Sawyer even used my car, just in case he was spotted."

I moved my feet slightly. Alvin stepped back and turned the gun on me.

"Let's not get heroic, okay, J. J.?" he suggested sweetly.

"Whatever, you say, Alvin, just take it easy."

He was blinking his eyes and his tongue had started rolling in his mouth.

"If you want me to take it easy, you'll have to put your gun on the floor and kick it across the room for me," he said.

"I don't carry a gun," I lied.

"Not true, pretty boy, I watched you checking it out when you first pulled up to the building. Now, *put it on the floor* and kick it over here before I get angry."

I did as he asked, feeling helpless as my piece slid under the big tubs of water used to wash parts before painting.

"That's a good boy," he smiled. "Now, you got any questions for my dad?"

I looked over at Morty. "Why?" I asked him.

"Why not? It almost worked, too," Morty said defiantly.

"But you had people killed. For what? A business?"

Morty smirked. "They weren't *people*, Donovan," he sneered.

Without another word, Alvin turned to Morty and shot him once in each knee. Morty fell to the floor screaming. When I looked up, the gun was pointing at me again.

"Don't worry, J. J., I have a something special in mind for you. Just be patient."

He turned on Morty, who was crying. "Would you shut up, you worthless fuck!" He silenced the old man with a few hard kicks to the head and neck. "You won't be beatin' on my mother anymore, will ya, Morty?" Alvin started to cackle.

"Let me tie off those wounds, Alvin," I pleaded. "If I don't, he'll bleed to death."

He thought about it for a moment.

"Okay, wrap him up. It's not time to die yet." He was smiling.

There was a box of rags under the counter. I used them to bind Morty's knees. He was in such deep shock, I thought he was dead. But his heart was still beating and his chest moved up and down. While I tended to Morty, Alvin went to work turning switches and dials on the control panel for the paint line. It wasn't long before I smelled gas.

"Alvin, I smell gas," I said softly. "The pilot light for the drying oven must be out. If you're not careful this whole place will go up like a firecracker."

"That's right," he replied, grinning.

This wasn't funny.

"What about the boy?" I asked, pointing up at Clifford.

He seemed surprised that I'd noticed his little stash hanging from the rafters. The muscles in his face tightened and started to jerk wildly.

"What about the boy?" he growled, looking up at the neat

284

bundle. "I'm sending him to be with his momma. We'd have had a little more time together, only you and your fat partner got between us."

He turned back to me.

"You think you're so slick, Donovan, but I've been onto you from the beginning. Get this—I was parked across the street from the foster home the night you and your partner met up with that social worker. The one who worked with Ruby—what's her name—Ms. Fein? I almost got him that night, after you left. When he got away, I decided to keep an eye on your place. It figured he'd show up there sooner or later. By the way, you should never allow a little boy to take the dog for a walk by himself, not in New York City. I don't care how big the doggie is, it just isn't safe."

His smirk was back. Poor Angus, I could only hope he was all right.

"Now it's time for our little contest," Alvin continued, sounding giddy. "So, are you ready?"

He pulled a couple of Morty's big Partagas cigars out of his pocket and jammed one into the prostrate old man's mouth. Morty stared up at him through vacant eyes. Alvin stood back up and came toward me, careful to keep his distance while pointing the gun at my chest.

"Now, here are the rules to the game," he began, producing a fancy gold lighter. "I'm going to give you exactly five minutes to get out of the plant, and then my father and I are going to enjoy one last smoke together on our way to hell."

It was impossible to read his expression. The tic had taken control.

"Alvin, please, let the boy go," I begged.

"I *told* you, he's goin' to his *momma!*" he screamed, the spittle flying.

I didn't say anything else. He checked his watch. "I asked if you're ready," he repeated, panting.

Ready or not, I nodded my head.

"Oh yeah, by the way, this exit's off-limits."

He ran over and shut the paint room door, sealing off the space so I could only get out using the catwalk.

"On your mark, get set—go!"

Luckily, Alvin didn't fire off a shot like a starter. The room was so full of gas, we'd have all gone up in smoke right then and there. I ran to the ladder and started climbing up toward the catwalk. When I reached the top, I slipped and fell down heavily. As I scrambled to get up the shoulder strap got caught on something and broke. The money bag fell to the floor.

At that moment, money was the least of my problems. I picked the bag up and heaved it off the balcony, sending it in the general direction of the washing tanks. Then I reached up and grabbed Clifford Brice by the shoulders and tried to get his feet unhooked. From the other side of the room, I heard a loud splash just as Clifford slipped free and fell heavily into my arms. I pulled the tape off his mouth, but he was too scared to speak. His eyes looked wild.

There was no time to free Cliff's arms or legs. I draped him over my good left shoulder and ducked into the crawl space Joe Gagan had used the day we met Raul Brito. The crawl space led to a wooden catwalk in the attic over Morty's office suite. Behind me, I heard Alvin bellowing like a wounded animal. Apparently he'd noticed that Clifford was missing. I expected him to ignite the lighter right then and there, but for some reason it didn't happen. Maybe he was having some final words with his father. As I ran through the attic in the semidarkness, I kept banging into sharp metal parts hanging on the paint line, cutting my face and arms. There was a hole of light at the far end of the space, and I made for it. The sweat and blood were dripping into my eyes, so that I had to keep blinking to see. If Alvin was keeping to the original game plan, then I had one, maybe two minutes left.

When I got to the end of the attic, I found another ladder. The ladder was bolted into the wall next to one of the large, rolling overhead doors. To get down while carrying Clifford Brice, I had to use both hands, which put tremendous pressure on my broken shoulder. The sharp, searing pain brought tears to my eyes and made me feel faint. At one point I slipped, and Clifford let out a loud yelp as his head bounced off one of the rungs of the metal ladder. It wasn't till I had reached the ground that I realized the overhead door had been chained and padlocked. Alvin's final joke on Donovan.

I panicked, not sure where to run. But before I could decide, I heard the sound of tires squealing and a car crashed through the big barrier, knocking Clifford and me down as it ripped the overhead door off its hinges. I lay on the floor, dazed and disoriented, till someone grabbed me by the shoulders and started to lift. I looked up to see Carlos Rodriquez and the Ratman.

"We heard shots," Raphael said simply.

"No time, no time, Alvin's gonna blow the place," I stammered, breathless.

I remember Carlos sniffing the air, then shouting something in Spanish. The Ratman grabbed Clifford as Carlos helped me up, and we all started to run. We got about halfway across the street before the explosion came. There was a roar, followed by a huge ball of fire. Then the concussion knocked me out.

EPILOGUE

■ ■ ■

The building was completely destroyed in the fire, and so was everyone and everything in it. Carlos, Clifford, Raphael, and I ended up in the hospital with burns, cuts, and headaches. I also managed to bust up my shoulder even better than I had the first time.

Our other casualty, Angus, the half-breed wolfhound, faired a bit better. He'd been fed enough painkillers to numb a rhino, but there was no permanent damage to anything but his reputation as a bodyguard.

Nearly three months passed before I could bring myself to visit the remains of the factory. By then, the embers were ash and the looters had finished with the rubble. It was snowing the day Angus and I went back to take a look at the skeleton of the National Manufacturing Corporation, but snow couldn't soften the picture or the memories. The roof was gone, and so were the doors and windows. The steel superstructure was standing, but it had been charred black and twisted by the fire.

As I walked among the shattered machinery, I was reminded how badly things had functioned at the National Manufacturing Corporation—the business, the equipment, the people. One big collection of broken-down machines. And I'd had the arrogance to think I could fix them.

The purchase and sale agreement I'd delivered to Morty didn't survive the explosion, so everything stayed the way it had been, with Stanley Greenberg controlling 51 percent of the company. That worked for him, because the place was blanketed with insurance. He took a complete loss on the business and collected a bundle.

Stanley Greenberg and Morty's long-suffering widow, Eva Katz, had a frank conversation about Morty's shadow businesses, the two million dollars he'd stolen, and the other shenanigans. Eva was a tough cookie. She convinced Stan that it would be easier and cheaper to split the pot down the middle than to end up in court. Eventually they decided to invest in a new business, which they called S&E Industries. When the paperwork was finalized, Eva Katz moved to Florida, leaving her new partner behind with a big-ten accounting firm looking over his shoulder.

If that wasn't a strange enough turn, S&E Industries subsequently expanded its portfolio to include a display company. The business is called Genuine Display, Inc. and it has an interesting cast of characters on the payroll. Stanley Greenberg is the president and chief executive officer, and Daniel Mahoney is vice president in charge of sales and marketing. Believe it or not, Stanley hired Bill Smith and Bobby Seldane to do the purchasing. The general manager is a stout, friendly guy named Carlos Rodriquez. His plant manager is a short, stocky dude with a penchant for killing rats. They even found somebody with experience to handle the shipping and receiving. He's a red-faced old Irishman named Joe Gagan.

The business plan gave all the key players employment contracts and an ownership interest, which means they share in the profits. I should know, because I wrote it. Stanley only agreed to the plan because I promised to get him written up in the *Harvard Business Review*. Even a guy like Stanley Greenberg thinks about his place in history. I didn't have the heart to tell him they already have a stuffed rat over in the Museum of Natural History.

Actually, Greenberg was really mad at me for losing the quarter of a million dollars I'd gone to pick up. It didn't matter to him that Alvin's gold lighter was all that stood between me and eternity or that I'd chosen to save Clifford Brice instead of protecting the cash. I'd lost his money, and I had to listen to him whine about it for weeks. When it became clear that it wouldn't do any good, he finally dropped the subject. But not before he had a crew sift through the rubble to look for the missing bag.

Despite Stanley's whining and complaining about us not delivering Morty's stock, Boris and I collected the balance of our fee from the escrow account. All told, we netted $117,000 after expenses. I'm not sure if that's a good fee or not. What's it worth to get beaten up with a baseball bat and then blown up in a natural gas explosion? Still, it seemed like a pretty big pile to us, so we gave Hiram Parker, M.D., a donation for the orthopedic department at St. Luke's. I'm hoping for a plaque with my name on it.

There wasn't much we could do for Ruby Brice, Paula Jones, José Comacho, or the wizard. We'd unofficially settled their cases, but that wasn't much consolation. Old Doc was as mysterious in death as he'd been in life—a John Doe without relatives or friends. The best we could do for him was to arrange a proper burial. On the other hand, José and Ruby had families and we could do something for them. In fact, Boris had been working on a plan for Clifford Brice since the day we first visited him.

The plan involved a pair of trust funds: one to pay for the schooling Clifford would need, the other to jumpstart a charitable foundation called the Annie Washington Home for Boys. Mrs. Washington needed to get her kids out of the ghetto and into a decent house in a community where they'd have a chance. We located a home for sale up in Catskill, New York. All we needed was money. To start things off, we put ten thousand bucks from our private account into each of the funds; then I went looking for donors. Stanley Greenberg hadn't changed too much. When I asked him for money he laughed in my face.

"Listen to me, Donovan, you goody two-shoes, that little nigger can make do for himself, just like I did!"

He smirked. It was the same nasty look I'd tolerated back in the factory. This time, though, I didn't see any reason to put up with it. You could say that moment marked the end of my relationship with Mr. Stanley Greenberg. I couldn't help myself—I hauled off and popped him. He had a really surprised expression on his face as he sank to the floor.

In the end, I'd gone back to the factory, even though I'd promised myself I wouldn't. It wasn't a sentimental trip; I had a job to do. I climbed over the rubble and made my way into the paint room. The ovens were charred and twisted beyond recognition, but the washing units were still in place right where I'd left them that Monday night. I worked my way over to the shower booths where metal parts were once hosed down with steaming hot water before moving into the drying oven. It was the gas for the drying ovens that Alvin had used to create the fireball.

The big washtubs under the line weren't in great shape. They were bent and disconnected from the wall in places, but they hadn't been breached—they were all full of water. I climbed up on top of the drainage tubs, took off my coat, rolled up the sleeve on my good left arm, plunged it into the freezing water, and started groping. It took a while, especially in that frigid water, but eventually my hand made contact with something coarse and bulky. I got hold of the broken shoulder strap and managed to drag the waterlogged flight bag to the surface. It wasn't easy; $250,000 weighs a lot when it's wet.

I didn't stick around for any emotional good-byes. I ran to the car and left East New York for good. When I got back to the apartment, Boris took charge of the flight bag while I changed clothes and made hot cider. It took about five hours but the money finally dried out. We used it to pay for Mrs. Washington's new house and to fund those trust accounts I mentioned. And we had enough left over to send Raul Brito home to his family with a fat little nest egg.

She'll never forgive herself for letting Clifford Brice take Angus out for a walk that Monday night, but Janet Fein actually came out of this whole mess all right. There was a closed disciplinary hearing at which Boris, Clifford, Annie Washington, and I all spoke on her behalf. Even Lieutenant Negro put in a good word. Turned out Janet really had earned some brownie points after twenty-three years of service. They made her take a thirty-day paid leave of absence, which she needed anyway, and then she was back on the job; pushing another boulder up the hill.

Speaking of Lieutenant Negro, I never did make that Tuesday morning meeting. And, although I had a very good excuse, he's still acting pissy. If you ask me, the guy's being a little ungrateful—he was given a nice commendation for the Falcons' bust and even got his picture in the newspaper. I guess he's sore because he had to keep quiet about the *accidental* explosion over at National Manufacturing. As I pointed out when he came to visit me in the hospital, I was doing him a favor. There was no point retiring on a sour note.

"It's a good thing for you this shit turned out the way it did," he said.

Which pretty much covers it.

Oh, yeah, I also bought a couple of first class tickets to St. Croix and had them delivered to Ms. Kathleen Byrne, along with the brochure for a nice resort called the Buccaneer. She's supposed to pick a time when she can leave the world of publishing behind for a week or two. I'm not holding my breath.

When the excitement had died down a bit and we'd finished passing out money and setting up trusts, I was summoned to the penthouse. I had broken several appointments with Madame Karina, which is frowned upon. So I grabbed the requisite bottle of cognac and went upstairs prepared to be as contrite as the situation demanded.

It was late on a frigid February afternoon and the thought of sitting by the warm fireplace in the study relieved some of my apprehension. When I entered the room Boris and young Clara were in the middle of the Brahms sonata in E minor for piano and cello. Madame Karina was seated over by the hearth as usual. I went and sat beside her expecting the worst.

"What is this look, dear boy?" she asked. "Karina has no desire to bite you. Come now, chin up!"

She pressed a button on the table and a few minutes later Missus McCabe came bustling into the room.

"What is your pleasure, James?" Madame Karina asked.

"I think I'm due for a pitcher of martinis and a very long nap," I replied.

Old Martha made a face but left us, picking up the bottle of Martel on the way out. Karina and I sat together in silence, listening to the rather somber piece of music till Martha returned carrying a tray with our drinks. Evidently the clanking of the ice cubes interrupted Boris' concentration because he stopped playing.

"Care to join us, old man?" I inquired politely.

"Love to, but I'm afraid I can't," he said mysteriously.

"Can't? Why?" I pried.

"Well, actually, I'm meeting Carol for a drink at the Westend."

"Carol?" I practically shouted. "You don't mean Carol with the perfect set of legs?"

"One and the same person," he admitted, smiling happily.

"And now, James, are you comfortable?" Karina asked.

"I suppose so," I murmured, watching Boris saunter confidently down the hall.

"Good. I can begin."

Weeks earlier, I'd made the mistake of asking her to compile some information on the scorpion symbol. She picked up a pile of notes, jogged them into order, and began to read.

"The Scorpion: This arachnid, with its dangerous venomous sting, has for obvious reasons long been associated symbolically with deadly menace . . ."

The lecture went on for nearly two hours.

". . . according to astral mythology of ancient Greece . . . in the Bible the scorpion, like the serpent, symbolizes . . . in the religion of the Mayas the black god of war Ek-Chuah was portrayed with the tail of a scorpion . . ."

On and on it went. After a while I gave up and just let my mind wander. I'd never expected things to turn out the way they had. Then again, I'd never thought I'd be interested in astrology either. But as Karina droned on, I drank my pitcher of martinis and wondered at the marvel of it all.